# Trovant

## Book 2 in the
## Alaster Trilogy

# A. H. Ostmo

# Trovant: Book 2 in the Alaster Trilogy

ISBN: 979-8-9874011-5-6

Library of Congress Control Number: 2025901985

*To my parents, who are proud of my mistakes because they are proud of theirs (me— I'm their mistake).*

# Contents

# Prologue: Green Microbes

"I love green." Britannica laid on her back and stared at the ceiling as green light reflected from her face.

"Britannica," said the Head Facilitator, "you need to get up once you've been knocked down."

"I'm not knocked down," Britannica kept her gaze to the ceiling with her hands folded on her stomach.

"No?" the Facilitator seemed amused.

"No," Britannica responded, "he is." In a swift move, she flipped onto her stomach, swinging her legs around and knocking her opponent to the ground.

As the broad figure hit the mat in the training ring, Britannica rolled over the opponent and pinned him to the ground.

"You're down!" She shoved her hands over his shoulders.

"Garridon?" the Head Facilitator asked, as if impatient for Britannica's opponent to give his rebuttal move.

"Nope," Garridon looked up at Britannica, who hovered over him and pinned his shoulders to the ground. "I'm pinned."

"Interesting," the Head Facilitator spoke as Britannica rose and helped her opponent, Garridon, from the floor. "In all your training, we've never found an opponent matched to your skill level or a move you couldn't get out of. Yet, you were pinned in this very basic maneuver."

An electronic buzzer sounded.

"What can I say?" Garridon moved past the Head Facilitator and toward the next training exercise. "She took me off guard while talking about green. She distracted me, and it was a clever tactic."

The Head Facilitator grabbed Garridon's arm and pulled the young trainee close. "A word of wisdom. Don't let yourself get distracted." He nodded toward Britannica, who walked away with green light pouring over her brown ponytail that swayed with each step.

Britannica turned, scanning the room until she met eyes with Garridon. "Are you coming?" She raised her voice to speak across the room.

Garridon looked at her, then at the Head Facilitator who still grasped his wrist.

"I am," Garridon said, pulling from the Head Facilitator's grip.

"Great," Britannica turned toward the training machines. "Take the machine next to me so I can beat you at this, too!"

***

"I've been reading the journals," Eddi rubbed one hand over his head while he kept the other on his hip. He looked intently to the corner of the room. He stopped the line of people from progressing to get sustenance.

"And?" Garridon pulled Eddi's arm to move him forward in the line.

"Our lighting systems house bacteria the same way that a living organism is a host to glowing bacteria." Eddi tripped a little as Garridon yanked him forward, but it didn't stop Eddi's focus on the thoughts grinding in his mind.

"And?" Garridon repeated as he straightened his posture.

"And," Eddi lowered his voice almost to a whisper, "don't you think this place feels off?"

"The only thing that is off," a young man cut between Garridon and Eddi, "is you, Edison Fitzgerald." The young man laughed as he squared his shoulders toward Eddi.

"Cut it out, Emmon," Garridon shoved the young man.

"Go on," Emmon taunted, "tell us all what feels off." He put his arms out toward the room as if to make an audience from the people who were in line.

"I don't know," Eddi shrugged. "Everything feels alive. Like it's one organism."

"Hear that?" Emmon shouted to the room. "The facility is alive, everyone."

"Come on," Garridon put his arm around Eddi's shoulders and faced him toward the front of the line, away from the young man who was mocking him. "You don't have to listen to him. Just talk to me."

"Uh—" Eddi was off balance as Garridon turned him forward. "Yeah, okay." He took a step as the line moved to the front of the room, where a person in a green suit was handing out green spheres to eat. "There are just some organisms in the ocean that can produce their own light. But some keep a glowing bacteria alive. Really, it's nothing more than that."

"I'm sure," Garridon rolled his eyes as they neared the front of the line.

Eddi jumped into a firm stance and punched Garridon's shoulder with his lanky arm. "Some sea animals can shoot the glowing substance at predators as a defense mechanism."

"Yeah?" Garridon rubbed his arm and chuckled. "Did shooting glowing stuff work for the prey?" Reaching the front of the line, the person in a green suit waved a machine in front of Garridon's face. The machine beeped, then the person handed Garridon a green sphere.

Eddi didn't answer as he stood before the face-scanning machine. The machine beeped. Eddi received the green sphere and put it in his mouth.

"Well," Eddi chewed the green mush as he spoke, "it was enough for the prey to get away. Did it harm the predators? I can't really tell. The journals were more about using bacteria as a light source than anything else."

"He's just jealous, you know?" Britannica appeared next to Eddi and whispered to him.

Garridon hadn't noticed her come into the room. Had she been in the line the whole time?

"What?" Eddi stepped backward to get away from how close Britannica had stepped toward him.

"Emmon," said Britannica.

Garridon felt like his heart was swelling at the sound of her voice. How could anything sound so precious? He wished he could have the sound of her voice put in a container so he could always have it with him. It would be like the panels that kept organisms alive to illuminate every part of the Trellis facility. Only Britannica's voice felt warmer and more important than light.

"Everyone can see the way Mabel looks at you," Britannica said as they walked toward the room's exit.

Eddi squeezed his hands. The muscles around his mouth strained as he tried to keep from smiling.

"She likes you," Britannica's voice sounded like a song as she leaned toward Eddi.

"Okay, okay," Garridon grabbed Eddi's shoulders and moved him away from Britannica. "Don't encourage him. Mabel gets enough attention as it is. She doesn't need this one creeping around her."

"All I'm saying is, you could give it a shot," Britannica said.

Eddi's shoulders tensed toward his ears, and he couldn't stop himself from smiling.

\*\*\*

The room was dark; almost black. It was covered in wires that made the cramped space hot so that sweat

5

dripped from Garridon's face. An alarm sounded throughout the facility, but it was muted through the door.

"What happened?" Garridon demanded in a whisper as he gripped Eddi's shoulders.

"They were looking through the journals for information about the Alaster ship," Eddi said.

"What is that supposed to mean?" Garridon asked.

"That's not what was important—"

"Of course it's important!" Garridon realized he was pressing his friend against the wall of the tiny room. "Sorry," he released his grip. "Where are Britannica and the Delphinos?"

"They're fine," said Eddi, "I think."

"You think?" Garridon had his nose inches from Eddi's.

Eddi pressed his back against the wall and squeezed his eyes closed.

"Look," Garridon sighed. "I'm..." he wiped sweat from his forehead. "I'm not used to feeling out of control. I'm sorry. I'm scared."

"We're all scared," Eddi opened his eyes and stepped a bit from the wall.

"Where is my wife?" Garridon asked. "And why are the alarms sounding?"

"That's what I was trying to tell you," said Eddi. "The journals indicated that Victoria Menhit is something other than what she says she is. There was a leader who came down from the surface to the Trellis. It was the same person who caused the Black Plague. So this guy came down here and—"

"Please focus, Eddi," Garridon squeezed his eyebrows between his finger and thumb. "What happened?"

"Britannica and Vega left their workstations to go toward Victoria Menhit's quarters."

"Why?" Garridon asked.

"To find out what she really is," said Eddi.

The alarm sounded louder, and the door to the room opened.

Garridon stood in front of Eddi, not knowing who would come through the door.

"I thought you guys might be in here," Britannica came through the door, holding a tablet over her pregnant stomach.

"Britannica," Garridon sighed in relief.

Eddi squeezed into the corner of the tiny room to make space for another person— or person and a half.

"I'm okay." She put her arms over Garridon.

He held her close, putting his forehead to hers. He rubbed her back with her pregnant belly pressing against him. He could almost cry, realizing how afraid he had been about what he had almost lost.

"Nothing happened," she said. "Vega and I tried to open the door to Victoria's quarters and the alarm sounded. No one saw us, but we'll probably go in for questioning when they review the security footage."

# Trovant

Britannica tried to get out of the hug to show Garridon the information on her tablet.

Garridon didn't let go. He shook his head against hers. "I can't lose you."

# Part I

# Chapter 1: Gia— The First Step

My dad grips his defined jaw with eyes fixated at the front of the submarine. Suspended on a platform in a spherical space, the entire wall in front of us illuminates the underwater world outside. Ghostly white sand turns into a rough, black sea floor made of mollusks. A mist flows over the edge of the mollusk field and turns into a pool of fog.

That's the brine.

A tentacle rolls from the brine pool. Our submarine creeps over the sand and toward it. Lights outside the Trellis facility show that we're a few hundred feet from the edge of the mist.

Below our suspended platform in the submarine, voices rumble from the community members who have escaped with us. It's impossible to hear what everyone says, but I catch an occasional gasp or yell when someone points out a sea animal worming through the sand or an eel swimming from the brine pool.

"Eddi," my dad addresses his friend, but he doesn't take his eyes off the scene in front of the submarine. "Is there a way around the brine pool?"

"For a maintenance pod, maybe." Eddi wears a green suit and stretches his arms to motion around the expansive submarine. "But not for this. If we turn around or go to one of the sides, we'll crash back into the Trellis facility. We might damage the exterior of the submersible."

"What are the chances we will get attacked?" My dad's feet are firm on the platform as he squares his stance toward the front screen. He looks like he's ready to fight the ocean outside.

"High," Leal, my best friend, rushes from behind and slams into a seat before a control panel that lines the front of the platform. Wearing a grey suit, he types frantically.

The tip of the squid emerges from the brine pool, strobing between red and white like a broken screen.

Gasps and exclamations reverberate through the submarine. There are countless people throughout the ship, but I'm too scared to look over the high edge of the platform to see what they are doing. Staring outside, I take the seat next to Leal.

"Gia," my dad puts his hand on the back of my chair and leans toward me. "What resources do we have?"

The sea animal rises from the brine, revealing the mantle of a squid that's nearly as tall as our entire submarine. We inch closer to the squid.

"It's warning us," Leal says, still typing. "The red flashing is telling us to turn around."

"We can't turn around, son," Eddi replies.

"Maybe I can slow us down," Leal types even faster. "This submersible is so huge, it's hard to reverse momentum without crashing us back into the Trellis Facility."

"Gia," my dad raises his voice. "Resources."

I sit straight up. I don't have the luxury of not knowing what to do. I scan through my memories like it's a database of all the information I collected about the submarine. It was originally designed to hold 12,000 people, but only 6,000 came down to the Trellis facility to escape from Earth's surface. Behind me, there's a system of ladders and platforms that lead to closed doors. Lyra had made a lab in one of the rooms where she recreated some of the elements of the Trellis facility— things like the lighting, the electric systems, and the food.

"Wires, some metals, bioluminescent bacteria..." I list the resources I can remember on the shelves of Lyra's lab.

"Arcturo," my dad interrupts and speaks to a man who stands on the platform. "Go get the bacteria and have someone find Lyra."

Footsteps pound behind me as Arcturo runs from the platform to follow my dad's orders.

"What do we know about this squid?" my dad asks.

"It looks like a colossal squid..." Leal answers.

"Except that it's too big," Eddi finished Leal's thought.

Our progress toward the squid slows.

"Articles from Earth's surface described the colossal squid as having sharp claws on its arms that could tear through other animals," says Leal.

The submarine is almost at a halt.

"That could potentially tear through the external metal on the submersible," Eddi says. "I don't think we can fight this thing."

"We don't have to fight it," my dad says.

"Then what are we doing?" asks Eddi.

"Distracting it," my dad answers.


"It's down here," Lyra's small figure yanks a piece of the metal wall that is near the floor. "The siphon has an exit outside in case there's too much pressure in the pipeline. I can build the pressure inside, then open the external side of the pipe, and it should be enough force to shoot out and hit the squid. It will just be difficult to aim. Leal will have to position the ship so that—"

"We don't have to hit the squid." My dad grunts as he helps pull the metal away from the wall. "Only hit close enough so that it will attack whatever we shoot out. Is there anything in the pipeline right now?"

"I have the bacteria," Arcturo struggles to carry a large metal vat. Inside, a liquid is glowing blue.

"Yeah," Lyra answers my dad as they get the metal fully from the wall. "Food is in the pipeline. And it's the only food we have left."

"I got it!" Leal trips past Arcturo and lifts tangled tubing and a funnel above his head.

"We'll shoot what's in the pipe toward the squid first," my dad commands as he helps Leal untangle himself from the tubing. "Then use the glowing liquid as a decoy so it will attack that instead of us."

"You can only get to the siphon through there," Lyra points to the small opening in the wall. Inside is a tight labyrinth of pipes and metal. "Someone will need to climb in there and get the bacteria into the pipeline."

"Go up to the control panel and tell Vega to get ready to shoot," my dad commands Lyra.

"Okay," she starts jogging away, "but don't let anyone near the siphon once it's ready to shoot. It's on a pneumatic safety system that has a powerful kickback once the pressure is released."

"Garridon," Arcturo finally reaches us with the container of bioluminescent bacteria. "How are we going to get this in there?"

My dad leans in the small opening near the floor, trying to squeeze his shoulders through the pipes. He's too big. "We'll figure it out." He inches back out.

I take the hose along with Leal and start to put the tubing into the labyrinth of pipes.

"Leal," my dad grips Leal's shoulder and directs his small figure to face the ladder that leads toward the control panel. "Start the ship's momentum toward the squid again. We'll need to be moving over the brine as fast as possible."

"You got it," Leal jogs to the ladder and ascends.

"Pressure is building!" Lyra's voice sounds over an intercom.

"Shoot as soon as we're close enough," my dad yells up in the direction of the control station where Lyra and Vega would be sitting.

"Garridon," Arcturo says to my dad, "we will need to shoot the glowing defense quickly after we offload the food. We need to get this in there now."

Eyeballing the pipes in the wall, the opening looks just big enough for me to fit through. Carefully, I kneel to the floor and poke my head through pipes. My knee was injured as we escaped from the Trellis. I ignore the pain as I look through the metal opening. It seems like my shoulders will fit.

"Just give me a second!" my dad says to Arcturo.

I crawl past the first set of pipes.

The metal space turns downward. Sticking my hands out, I reach in front of me and grip a pipe to pull myself entirely through the opening.

"Gia!" my dad yells when he notices that I'm in the tangle of pipes. "Get back here! We can figure something else out."

I turn my head. The pipes block the entrance so that I can't see my dad or Arcturo anymore. I grab the tubing that's shoved between pipes and I pull it along with me.

Lyra's voice speaks over the intercom again, but it's too quiet to hear over the hissing of the pipes. Sweat beads over my forehead as I search the tight space for something that looks like it might be the siphon Lyra had built.

One of the metallic systems moves forward slowly. There's a bang. Then, a piece connected to the system shoots backward. The force rumbles the area so that I lose my balance. I catch myself on the pipes. That bang must have been the siphon. And that moving piece is the safety mechanism, revealing where I need to put the tubing.

"Gia!" my dad's voice says over the sound of the pipes. "Are you okay?"

"Yeah," gripping the tube, I squeeze my shoulders between two pipes and inch toward the siphon.

"Come back," my dad demands.

"We don't have time," the pipes squeeze my hips as I struggle forward with the tubing in my hand. I see the opening for the siphon.

"Start pouring the bacteria," I say as I get fully free from the pipes and start unscrewing the top of the siphon.

The translucent tubing lights up with a faint blue glow as I put it in the siphon.

There's more yelling outside. Lyra must be commanding something, but the noise and heat from the pipes covers the sounds outside.

The ship jerks back and forth. I slam against the pipes behind and a metal handle jabs into my back.

I grunt and try not to sink into the cramped space.

"We've taken a blow!" I hear Arcturo yell.

"Gia!" my dad shouts through the pipes. "Seal the siphon now and get out!"

I yank the hose from the siphon. Blue liquid pours over pipes and leaks throughout the small area. My elbows are near my ears as I screw the metal top on the siphon with all my strength.

"It's on tight!" I yell.

"Get out!" my dad screams back.

I wriggle in the small area to turn around. I'm not fully turned before the siphon shoots off a second time.

There's a loud bang. I feel a powerful jab against my left side ribs.

"Ah!" I slam into the pipes on my right side.

The hit forces all the air from my lungs.

Wrapping my arm around my ribs, I try to breathe in. I can't get a breath in. Weak, I slink down as I lean on the hot metal.

"Gia!" my dad yells through the pipes.

I try to say something, but I can't get any noise out. I try again to suck air through my nose. It isn't working. Why can't I breathe?

"Gia!" my dad panics. "Are you okay? Say something." I hear clanking and shuffling around the metal.

"Don't!" Arcturo says. "If she's pinned in there, you might shift something to make her more stuck."

"Gia!" my dad pleads.

I put my hand on my head. I just need to focus on getting a breath in. Closing my eyes, I picture where my lungs are and try to tell them to work. Instead, a low hum comes from my throat. It's not a breath in, but it's a noise coming out. That's at least something.

The sweat pours down my neck. My head starts to feel light.

"I see her," a voice sounds close to me.

I open my eyes.

Through a barrier of pipes, I see Leal's blue-green eyes looking back at me.

"Gia?" Leal says as he shoves through the pipes to get close to me.

My eyebrows stitch together as I try harder to get a breath in.

"I think she's okay," Leal yells toward the exit. "She got the wind knocked out of her."

"Can you reach her?" My dad's voice sounds distant.

"Yeah," Leal shimmies through piping to get closer to me. "Gia," he says quieter. "I need you to breathe."

*I'm already trying to breathe*. I could punch him right now if we weren't in such a tight space.

He reaches his hands between the pipes and puts his hand on my cheek. That does somehow help— to feel something outside myself. I take a tiny gasp in.

"Good," he smiles.

*Don't placate me*. I think that, but I still can't speak. He can probably tell what I'm thinking. We've spent enough time together that he can read me better than anyone else.

Leal rolls his eyes at my expression. "Just keep taking tiny breaths until you can take bigger ones."

I shove his hand away from me and take tiny breaths in and out. Soon, they turn into longer, smoother breaths. I feel a sense of relief, even though we're still crammed in a mess of pipes.

"Can you speak yet?" Leal asks.

I cough as I try to speak. "Yeah."

"Is anything else hurt?"

"I don't know," I try to take in the other sensations in my body. I'm hot and I feel trapped. There's sharp pain in my sides.

"Give me an analysis?" Leal asks it like it's a question.

I chuckle slightly. It's something my dad would make me do when someone was hurt— name the injuries the person likely sustained and how long they would take to heal.

The kickback of the siphon's safety mechanism must have hit my side as I turned. My left side was facing the siphon, which is also where most of my pain is. I was hit with enough force to slam me against the pipes, so that gives me some idea of how much damage it could have done. I look back at the metal siphon— the size of the moving piece shows me the surface area that impacted my ribs.

"One or two fractured ribs on the left side," I say in a raspy voice. "And likely some bruises on the right ribs. Four to six weeks of healing time."

"And your knee still hurts?" Leal asks.

"Yeah," I say.

"Can you make it out of here?"

"Yeah." I shift forward to try and squeeze through the pipes. I cough as the metal pushes against my ribs.

Leal grabs my hand to try and help me through.

I yank my hand back.

"Don't do that." I slap his hand.

"Did the siphon also fracture your pride?" Leal starts to back up through the pipes to give me more space.

I don't say anything but chuckle as I shove between the pieces of hot metal. I'm not actually angry with him. We joke around a lot, but I rarely get mad at Leal.

"Someday you're going to need someone's help, Gia Hamiltoni," Leal lectures me as he continues to make his way through the pipes.

"And you won't be there anymore when I do?" I ask as I lean against each pipe, trying to squeeze forward.

"I will be," Leal gives a smirk. "And you'll look back on this moment and feel really bad for slapping my hand."

"I'm sure," I smile.

"It will haunt you," Leal's voice jokes through the pipes, "for the rest of your life." He backs up enough to make it completely out of the pipe labyrinth. I only see the part of his grey suit that covers his feet as he stands outside the small space.

My dad and Arcturo lean down, each reaching an arm in to grab me and pull me out.

My mind flashes back to my dad holding me above the water as the Trellis facility flooded. I did need help. And I hated it. I don't want him touching me.

"She doesn't want help," Leal says. His grey-covered feet pace across my line of vision.

"Come on," Arcturo says as he and my dad grip my arms and pull me through the last bit of pipe.

I cough as the pipes hit my ribs. It's like a sheet of pain blankets my left side as my dad pulls my arm to get me from the small opening.

The two men pull me to my feet and lean me against the wall as I try to control my coughing.

"What were you thinking?" my dad towers over me as I try to get my coughing under control.

"I was thinking—" I choke on my words.

"You weren't thinking," he interrupts. "Did you even realize what could have happened?"

"What could have happened," I straighten up, stepping away from the wall, "is that we could have been attacked by a squid."

"We did take a hit." Lyra stands to the side, rubbing her arm and looking to the ground as she mumbles. "It could have been worse if Gia didn't fill the siphon in time."

"Lyra," Arcturo whispers, "now isn't a good time."

"Everyone is safe," I puff my chest toward my dad. "I don't expect you to understand what it's like to want to protect the people you care about."

He clenches his fists, then turns away from me.

"Garridon," Arcturo puts his hand on my dad's shoulder.

My dad pushes Arcturo's hand as he stomps away.

The metal platform creaks as I step onto it. A murmur of low voices echoes throughout the ship. People at the bottom of the submarine or in the rooms are having conversations, making plans, and making up for lost time. I wonder how many of the conversations are scared and worried about what's next. I grip the metal railing. How many conversations are celebratory to be able to speak freely for the first time? How many are full of grief for the lives we just left behind?

"It's weird to see you so slow," Desman steps behind me with a metal clank. He's hunched over, also using the metal railing to support him as he limps forward. "Vega said to meet at the main platform. Are you getting an early start, too?"

"Early start?" I lean against the railing. We haven't had a quiet moment to speak since we were in Gaines Cyro's quarters. I remember holding the trowel— a small device to insert into the Trellis walls to control the mechanics. The trowel I was holding had code from Alaster. It would shut down Cyro's operations. The screen flickered between Cyro's face, then his predecessors' faces. It had been the same person in control since Trellis' history began.

"To get up the platforms." Desman motions to the ladder at the end of the platform. He wears a skin-tight, green suit. I'm still not used to seeing him in that color. His normal red suit had made him seem authoritative and strong. "I guess we're both trying to make it up these ladders with injuries." The green makes him seem nice.

I remember the feeling of him pulling my hair as I tried to stick the trowel in the control panel. He thought we could save Ara after she was gone. I knew it wasn't possible. When I put the trowel in the control panel, the screen flickered between Cyro's laugh and Alaster's words: *Run*. The ground filled with cold water.

"I just want to get up to the meeting as soon as I can," I say, turning toward the ladder.

"Yeah, okay," Desman says behind me. It seems like he might be shaking his head, but I can't see his expression. "Listen, Gia."

I keep walking toward the ladder.

I remember sitting with him in the holding cells as he said that I did what I wanted instead of what was best for everyone else.

He gently clenches my arm to get my attention. I swing around to face him.

"What?" I cross my arms. The motion creates a burning sensation where the siphon hit my ribs.

"I didn't mean to—"

"Desman," I hold my arms crossed, even though it hurts. "You made it clear what you think of me. We know we can work together, but we don't have to be friends after all of this—"

"Gia," he shakes his head, "I'm trying to apologize. I didn't mean—"

"You did mean," I interrupt and toss my hands up. "You said exactly what you meant: that I'm a selfish Facilitator who only goes with what I want to do."

"I didn't know what was going on," Desman defends. "If you would have told me the plan—"

"Then you would have stopped me earlier," I argue. "You had your own secret plans with Cloplin and—"

"Well, Cloplin is dead, Gia," Desman raises his voice.

I think of the moment as Cloplin wrestled Plangon. He was never my dad— Plangon wasn't— but he was there. My stomach churns as I think of him. Why would I feel sad about losing someone who never actually cared for me? He's the reason Cloplin is gone and he would have killed us too.

I shake my head. "I'm sorry I didn't mean to—"

"You didn't mean; I didn't mean. We argue about nothing. Can we stop trying to hurt each other for once and actually work together?"

Still looking away, I bite my lip and think of all the times Desman and I had to be together. Growing up, we were taught to fight against one another. It was only recently that we had to be on the same team.

I look at his forehead. There's still a gash where I banged his head against the control panel in Cyro's quarters.

When I've spent most of my life fighting someone, how can I learn to trust him? There was so much to unlearn from the Trellis.

"Okay," I look back at him. "I can try."

"So can I." He smiles and reaches his hand out.

I look down at his hand. Cocking my eyebrow, I look back at him.

"It's a gesture," he says, putting his hand out further. "A handshake saying we'll work together."

Slowly, I reach my hand out. We clasp hands and shake them up and down. It's the weirdest moment I've ever had with someone— and that's saying a lot because Leal's my best friend.

"Here," he releases my grip and motions toward the ladder. "I'll help you up."

"No, thank you," I turn to face the ladder.

"Okay," he seems confused as he follows behind me.

"But you can go first," I stop when I get to the ladder and look upward.

"Because you're embarrassed that this is difficult for you?" He smiles as he looks up the ladder.

"Shut up and go."

"You know," he grips the ladder in both hands and takes a slow step upward, "this isn't what working together looks like."

I don't respond as I grasp the ladder in my right hand. I had already ascended one ladder to get to the platform I was on, but he's right, I was slow. It's too painful to pull myself up with my left arm, and my right knee throbs when I put too much weight on it. With my left arm dangling at my side, I reach my right to get a strong enough hold to take a step with my left leg. I pull the right leg behind to get balance, then start over with the next step on the ladder. It works, but it's slow.

Desman is also slow. The metal clanks as our weight shifts over the ladders and platforms. Groaning metal echoes in the wide space of the submarine. Voices still speak all around, but I can't hear what any one person says. It's just a low hum, like a shifting stream of sounds through our underwater vessel.

"I like your shirt, by the way," Desman says as he steps from the ladder and onto a platform. "I don't think I ever said that."

I look down at my shirt. It has kittens flying through the air, shooting lasers from their eyes. Beneath, I wear a green suit. After finding the shirt locked in a box with the journal that Lyra now has, I'm the only one in the community who wears something other than a green, red, or grey suit. I had forgotten I was wearing it.

"I like it, too," I say once I step onto the platform. I turn to follow Desman over the bridge that connects us to the meeting spot.

"How's Pictor?" Desman shouts a bit as we move slowly across the bridge toward the platform that is suspended in the middle of the spherical submarine.

"Dehydrated," Vega turns from the control panel with her arms crossed. She releases her arms and moves toward us. Her tight red suit hugs her swaying hips as she takes each step. Her presence is powerful, not just beautiful. She's the image of who Ara could have grown up to be.

"We need to make a plan fast," Vega says, "and not just for Pictor. We have about 34 hours' worth of oxygen and no sustenance."

"Is there a plan?" Desman looks at me. I couldn't tell if he was curious to hear if I had a plan or if he was blaming me for bringing everyone from the Trellis without one.

"We'll wait for the others before a full briefing," Vega replies.


The murmur of voices seems quiet as I sit next to Desman— both of us sit near the control panel but face the others.

"Can we turn that off?" Leal squeezes his hands in his armpits as he nods toward the entire wall at the front of the submarine that shows the ocean outside.

It's dark, except where the headlights shine. Only a bit ahead of us, the space is illuminated to show pale, grotesque animals worming through the sand or growing like skeletons from the sea floor. White flakes drift in the headlights.

"It's better we keep it on," Vega says. "As much as possible, we need to see what's outside."

"I'll just stand over here," Leal shuffles toward me, then turns his back and leans against the control panel so that he isn't facing the screen to the outside. With his shoulders hunched toward his ears, he covers his head with his hands. "I don't know what's worse. I feel like something is going to get me."

"Nothing will get you," Minji walks from the bridge to join the group. Wearing a grey suit, she keeps her hands glued to her sides as she crosses the circle of people. Her black hair sticks to her back and shoulders so that she looks like a straight object, slicing through the group to stand next to Leal.

Seeing her, Leal releases his hands from his head, but is obviously fighting the urge to hug his arms around himself again. He puts his hand on his shoulder. Then one arm across his chest with the other hand on his cheek. He arranges again to put both hands on the control panel and clench the metal that he leans against.

Minji puts one hand on top of Leal's. He keeps his stare straight forward and his eyes widen. I didn't realize something could make him more tense than seeing the outside.

"Are we ready now?" Lyra grips her forearm like she has to brace herself to speak.

"I think we're all here," Eddi looks around the circle.

With Desman and me sitting in the chairs, the others stand around us— Vega to the left, next to my dad and Lyra. Eddi is across from me by his wife, Mabel. Leal and Minji lean on the control panel to my right.

"Is Jarret coming?" Minji asks.

"He wanted to stay with Pictor," Vega answers. "I told him that Arcturo would be there, but Jarret insisted on staying."

I think of Pictor and his weak voice speaking through the blanket-tent in the Sanctuary. He had been dry heaving as Vega tried to comfort him. Lyra was sobbing against Arcturo's chest as we faced the question none of us wanted to ask: would the delphino family lose someone else?

Like a ghost in the back of my mind, it's like I can hear the screams that filled the workspace when their grandmother's maintenance pod faced the brine pool. Even worse, I can hear the waves bellowing through the Trellis as Ara stood before the wall of rushing water. Her gaze left mine as she faced the waves. The door slammed shut.

"What do we know so far?" my dad asks.

"Alaster is auto-piloting somewhere," Vega replied. "We have about 34 hours of oxygen supply and no sustenance. There's a good chance we can make it to the surface—"

"The surface," Desman puts his hand to his forehead. "This was your plan?" He looks at me. "The surface isn't even habitable."

People in the circle look past Desman and me to the wall behind. I turn to see what they're looking at.

"It is habitable," words are typed across the screen that also shows the dark ocean outside. The words erase. More words type out: "But that's not where we're going."

"I don't believe this," my dad shakes his head as he reads the words. "Vega, what are our options?"

"I can only see two," Vega says. "We can risk going to the surface and face whatever atmosphere is up there. Or we can see where Alaster takes us."

"We don't know how much fuel is left in the ship," my dad says. "So we can't risk going on autopilot for an indefinite period. But there isn't much reason to believe the surface is habitable. Can anyone think of a third option?"

"We could have," a woman's voice yells at the end of the platform. She walks toward us with others behind. I recognize her from the Sanctuary— she was one of the people who kept interrupting Lyra during the meetings. "If you would have asked the people who are here."

"We needed to make decisions," Eddi says to the crowd. "Vega just asked everyone who had information to speak so we can come up with a plan."

"A plan without all of our input," the woman motions as people stream onto the platform. The metal creaks with the weight being added.

"Uhhh," Leal looks around like he is searching for places where the metal might be bending. "Guys, can we talk at the bottom of the submarine?"

"We could have," a man responds with a yell, "but it looks like the meeting has already started up here."

"There are other people on this ship," someone yells as more people crowd onto the platform and shove toward Desman and me at the front.

I stand, backing against the control panel. The metal screeches.

"Everyone," Lyra puts her hands out in front of her like she could convince the crowd not to come further. "Remember this submersible is 300 years old. We don't know how much weight this platform can hold."

I look over the edge of the platform to the drop below. I feel light-headed seeing how far down the bottom is. I grab the control panel with both hands and bend at the knees as I force my gaze away from the edge.

"Look," someone exclaims. All eyes turn to the front.

Looking up, I see words typed across the screen: "We're almost there."

The words erase to write a new phrase: "Everyone off the platform."

As the words erase again, the headlights turn off.

People gasp. The screen shows the pitch-black ocean outside.

Some people panic and rush down the ladders or across the bridge.

"There's no need for pushing," Vega's voice yells at people who shove one another to get off the platform. "We will be fine as long as we don't panic... Lyra?" She looks around for her daughter.

Leal jumps from the control panel and jolts in the direction of the bridge.

"Leal," I grab his wrist to hold him back. "We're the furthest from the bridge. There's no way you'll make it through the crowd."

"I can't stay here," Leal bends over with his head shaking. He seems like he's trying to escape the dark ocean behind him.

"Someone might push you off," I clench his wrist like he's already hanging over the platform edge and he'll fall if I let go.

"It's okay," Minji puts her hand on Leal's shoulder and rubs back and forth. "It will be okay."

Leal's body relaxes. I let go of his wrist.

"Look," Lyra points at the blackness in front of us.

There is something dim in the distance.

The crowd thins out as people scatter from the platform.

As the submarine moves closer, there are bubbles made of dark stone and faint lights streaked across the ocean floor. The lights are cracked through the bubbled stone and are shaped like stagnant lighting bolts of all different colors.

"What is that?" Minji steps toward the front to get a better look.

"The Trovant," Lyra answers.

# Chapter 2: Leal— Crystals

I lift my hand to eye level and hold it in front of my face. It's shaking.

"Leal?" Lyra's voice is somewhere outside the room.

"Yeah?" I grab my shaking hand with my other hand to make it stop. The tremor is my brain's response to tell my adrenal glands to pump hormones that prepare me to fight or run away from whatever danger I face. I wish I could make it stop. Maybe I could invent a mechanism that disrupts neurological communication in a way that—

"Where are you?" Lyra has a tone of concern.

She turns the corner to see me in the small room. I'm sitting on the middle bed in a set of three bunks that line two walls of the room. She stops in the doorway as if deciding whether or not to come in. She carries a tablet in one hand and uses the other to squeeze her arm. After a moment, she comes in and sits in the bunk across from me.

Putting the tablet beside her, she clasps her hands together. "Are you okay?"

"Yes," I say. I sit on both of my hands so she can't see them shake.

She looks at me. I look back at her. I'm not really sure if there's something else I'm supposed to say or if there's a different reason she's here and I need to figure it out. I start looking at the wall. It must be made of very strong material and efficient insulators to withstand the pressure and temperatures outside. I wonder if there's a way to figure out its chemical components and—

"You don't seem okay," Lyra says.

I pull my hands from under myself and tap my fingertips together. Can she tell? I can't even tell. My hands are shaking and I don't know if it's because I faced my doom on that platform or because Minji touched me. Her hand was really soft and a little cold when she placed it on top of mine. And I felt like I should warm her hand, but all I could do was freeze up. When I panicked at the darkness of the ocean, her touch on my shoulder was gentle. But I wished I could be the one comforting her. Is there some sort of bravery serum or a trick that I can learn? I'll have to ask Gia sometime. She never panics at anything.

"Do you know what's going on now?" Lyra asks after I don't say anything. "I've been monitoring the conditions inside the submarine to track our oxygen usage." She picks up the tablet, turns it on, and then hands it to me. "The pressure is changing."

I examine the data on our atmospheric conditions that are plotted on the screen. The oxygen levels are actually going up.

"Weird," I say.

"Do you think Alaster is changing our atmospheric conditions to match where we're about to go?"

That would make sense. I scroll through the information on the tablet. The pressure is going up and the oxygen levels are going up; slowly, but progressively. It would be dangerous if the conditions changed all at once. Maybe that's why we're stuck here. The ship hasn't budged for a while and all Alaster said was that we had to wait before we could go in. We don't exactly know why we're waiting, for how long, or where we're going.

Lyra leans toward me and looks over the tablet. "The oxygen levels and atmospheric pressure have been going up." Her brown hair brushes against my shoulder.

"Yes," I lean back slightly and give the tablet back. Did she want to look at it? Why is she leaning so close to me?

"Do you think we're in here until we're acclimated to the conditions in the Trovant?"

"It would make sense," I clasped both hands in my lap.

It's hard to tell if there's something else we should be talking about, but she isn't leaving.

I gasp.

"What?" Lyra's posture perks up.

"I just realized something."

"What?" she asks again.

"The Trovant has higher atmospheric pressure and oxygen levels."

"That's what we just said," Lyra seems confused.

"What if there are organisms in there?"

"Organisms? Like, humans?"

"Yeah!" I jolt from the bunk to stand. "Like humans!"

Lyra stands slowly. We're standing uncomfortably close because of the bunks on either side.

I look down at Lyra, even though we're standing super close. "What would happen if an organism lived with higher oxygen levels and higher atmospheric pressure?"

"They would..." she trails off and thinks about it. "...be bigger— definitely— likely have longer lifespans, and have much higher muscle mass."

"Exactly!"

"So there might be giant people out there?"

"What?" I look back and forth as I scan the information in my head. "No. Well... yes, of course they would be. But also— the squid!"

"What about the squid?"

I put both hands on Lyra's shoulders. "That's why the squid is so big!" I shake Lyra's shoulders. "We figured it out! Since Earth's surface hasn't been inhabited by humans, there have been major changes in atmospheric conditions. The external environment has possibly reverted to a prehistoric time period that can support a much higher biomass and enable gigantism."

"Great," Lyra smiles. "That's really exciting."

"Yes," I say. "And, it probably was a colossal squid or a relative of the colossal squid, just under different conditions. Wow, that was bugging me for ages. That makes so much sense."

"Well," Lyra laughs. "I'm glad we could sort that out."

"Wait!" I exclaim.

"What?"

"If the squid is way bigger than its ancestors, what else out there is much bigger than we would expect it to be?"

"Well, humans," Lyra says. I think she's going back to the original thing she was trying to say.

"Yes," I say. "Definitely more humans are out there if the journal is correct. But what about, like, more sea animals? I hope nothing else got super huge."

"Yeah—" Lyra starts saying things in agreement, but I can't really decipher what she's talking about. I just think of the darkness outside. The fact that the ocean reaches farther than I could imagine and contains creatures that I don't even know about. And the ones that I do know about could be ten times bigger than what was recorded by scientists on the surface 300 years ago. My stomach starts to hurt.

"You okay?" Lyra asks.

"I feel dizzy," I say.

"It could be the changes in atmospheric conditions," says Lyra.

A familiar, smooth voice speaks from outside the doorway: "You should sit down, Honey." Mom appears in the doorway and leans with her head tilted to the side. "Hi, son."

"Mama," I smile and open my arms wide.

We walk toward one another and she pulls me into a hug. She doesn't let go. I don't mind. My arms don't reach all the way around Mom; the feeling is like a warm place I've missed.

There's a yell outside the door. Someone is exclaiming news to everyone in the submersible.

Mom releases her grip and we rush from the small room to see what the person is saying. There is more yelling as we step onto the metal platform and look below. People run away from the submarine's entrance, crowding up the metal platforms and bottlenecking on the ladders.

The metal screeches. The platform probably wasn't designed to hold that many people at once, especially not after centuries of sitting under the sea. An involuntary trill comes from my throat and I back up into the room. I crash into someone and we both topple backward. Crammed between the bunks on either side of the wall, I squirm with the person next to me and push myself back up. Oh yeah — it's Lyra; Lyra was behind me.

"Leal!" someone's voice is faintly above the others outside. "Leal!" It sounds like Gia.

I stand up and offer my hand to help Lyra off the ground. She's very light as I help her to her feet.

"In here!" Mom still stands on the platform outside the room.

"Leal!" Gia exclaims as she appears in the doorway.

"Get off of there!" I grab Gia's hand and yank her into the room. "Both of you!" I shove past Gia and reach for Mom.

"Honey," Mom says as I grip her forearm. "I think it's okay."

I pull her into the room and the four of us are squished close together in a line between the bunks.

"It's not safe," I say with my face inches from Mom's.

"Okay, son," she laughs.

"It's not funny!" I say.

"I've missed you," she smiles.

"The door is opening," Gia says behind me.

I shimmy around so that I face her. "What door?"

"To the Alaster ship."

"Opening?" I ask.

"Yes," says Gia.

I picture the doorway to the Alaster submersible. When it opened before, it was an entryway into the Sanctuary. There was a large domed space with something like glowing vines across the ceiling. But we weren't anywhere near the Trellis anymore. We're far underwater. I picture the doors opening and water rushing in. That obviously isn't happening or we'd all be drowning. It had to be opening to the Trovant. But what is in the other facility? What is the door opening to exactly? I had read about the Trovant in the journal entries from the scientist who made the facilities. Scanning through the information in my mind, I try to piece together what must be on the other side of the door... There was something about solidified magma with pockets of air.

It's opening now? I haven't fully prepared for everything that could be on the other side. I'm not ready yet.

"Leal?" Gia waves her hand in front of my face. "I said 'yes,' it's opening."

"Opening to what?" I ask.

"We have to find out."


The air is warm at the bottom of the submarine. Though we're not close to the open doorway, I feel like something could rush in and get us at any moment. If there was a giant squid near the Trellis, could this place have oversized bug-monsters that will jump through the doorway and bite someone's head off? Worse yet— what if they have giant birds?

I press my hands on my temples and try to block out the image of birds swooping in, grabbing people with their talons, and flying off to bring us to their nests where their baby birds will—

There's a soft touch on my back.

"Are you okay?" Minji leans into my line of vision with her thumb rubbing my shoulder.

"Yeah," I straighten up and try to put my arms in a natural-seeming position. "I was just... I'm thinking about what could... you know... like... birds."

"Birds," Minji nods slowly.

"Yeah," I say, "birds."

"Everyone, listen up," Vega speaks loudly to get everyone's attention.

People are littered across the platforms, leaning over rails to look down, or standing at the bottom near the open entrance.

I lean toward the open door. It's dark, but there's a red glow.

"There's been some talk about the best way to go about exiting the ship," Vega says.

"I'm not going out there!" someone yells from a platform.

More people start yelling about what we should do or about how they refuse to go outside.

"Everyone, quiet," Garridon speaks loudly this time. "We will form a small scouting party that will gather information in order to figure out the best plan of action."

"Who do we send out there?" someone from the platform asks.

Garridon opens his mouth to speak, but Gia answers.

"Whoever is willing," Gia says.

"Are you going?" a woman on the platform asks.

"Gia," Garridon murmurs to his daughter. "We need to talk about this."

"Yes," Gia answers to the entire crowd.

People start chattering all over the platforms.

"You're injured," Garridon mumbles.

"I'm fine," Gia says to Garridon. She raises her voice to address the crowd. "We'll take supplies we have on the ship. And whoever is willing will go out there to gather information and bring it back here."

"Who else is willing to go?" Vega asks around the crowd.

People look at one another— not answering— maybe deciding what to do.

I look at Minji. She has her hand raised.

"Minj!" I say in surprise.

"What?" she shrugs. "Someone has to."

I lean back to look out the door. I try to picture myself sitting in the submarine while Minji and Gia are both somewhere out there— maybe getting taken by birds.

I raise my hand too.


"Keep these with you," Lyra hands a tablet to each person in the small group near the entrance to the submersible.

The air is hot and it feels thick. It's like I'm breathing through a blanket. According to the charts that Lyra showed me, it's humid. Meaning there's actual water in the air. It's like we're breathing in hot water.

"We'll each have one," Vega holds up a tablet. "These will send comms back to Lyra. If anyone gets lost, we'll be able to track you through the tablet. Do not lose this."

Around the group stand Gia, Minji, Garridon, Vega, Desman, and some people from the community who I don't really know. I recognize some of them from security footage back at the Trellis, but I don't know them personally. Statistically, there were more Cultivators in the Trellis than any other group, meaning that any random sample of the Trellis community should have a majority of people in green suits. But the majority of the strangers here wear grey suits. Vega, Lyra, and some guy are the only people in red and there are only a few people in green. Then there's Gia, who wears a T-shirt over her suit that isn't the correct color anyway.

"The supplies are limited," says Garridon. "There's only enough for two people to hold an incapacitator gun. Whoever has the least physical training should hold one."

A few people around the group hold their hands up like they are requesting one.

"The rest of the supplies," Garridon continues as he hands two of the people an incapacitator gun, "are divided as equally as possible between us. The objective is to gather information about the outside. This includes all details regarding life forms, sustenance availability, environmental conditions, and all possible threats. Leal and Minji," Garridon motions towards us, "will be inputting information into charts that will notify Lyra."

Lyra gives a quick wave.

"She will be conferring with Arcturo," Garridon continues, "to relay all information we gather from the outside. We do not know what's out there. We might be up against new animals, hostile people, and dangerous environments. We will not deviate from the standard protocols. Are there any questions?"

"What if someone gets seriously hurt?" a woman asks.

"We'll follow protocol 540-A from training manual 17," answers Garridon.

"Um," the man wearing red raises his hand. "What is that?"

Garridon sighs and rubs his eyebrow with his thumb. He looks over to Gia. It seems like the expression I always give Gia when I don't know how to respond to someone.

She shrugs.

"Who can tell me protocol 540-A from training manual 17?" Garridon asks.

Like a machine that was given a command, Gia starts answering: "If the in—"

"Someone else," Garridon interrupts. "Who here knows the protocols?"

"If the injured person is well enough…" Minji starts to answer. Her voice is beautiful. "One person will leave the party to escort the injured person to a safe location."

"Good," says Garridon. "Someone other than Minji — what's 540-B?"

I know the answer. I start speaking, but try not to keep looking at Minji as I address Garridon. "If the injured person isn't well enough to move without medical assistance, use training from 232- A through L to utilize surrounding resources for splints, casts, crutches, and so on until the injured person is mobilized. Then refer to 540-A."

"And 540-C?" Garridon asks around the group.

"If the injured person can't move at all," Vega answers this time, "and it is not a crisis situation, one person will stay behind with the injured person until a full team can come to aid."

"Great," says Garridon. "We could go on, but there isn't enough time to go over every single manual. If something happens, follow people who are familiar with protocol. Anything else?"

No one answers.

"Now that you've heard the briefing," says Garridon, "would anyone like to stay behind?"

Some people fidget, but no one answers.

"Let's go." Garridon turns toward the open doorway.

I feel my pulse in my neck as I turn toward the dim exit. I had been loathing the very idea of this moment.

Minji's shoulder is close to mine as we move forward. With her so close to me, will my nervous energy somehow radiate from my arm and she'll be able to tell how afraid I am? It's like how exposed wires work— energy might jump between them if they get too close...

unless there's some sort of insulator. It's irrational; I put my hand over my shoulder like I'm trying to block any emotions jumping over to her. At the same time, I like being so close to her. If her energy is somehow jumping over to me, she makes me feel calm inside. Maybe even a little braver.

Gia steps next to her father. They both look bold and strong, like they were engineered specifically for these sorts of situations.

I convince my feet to make each step toward the exit. The air gets warmer the closer we are to the door. I feel a touch on my left hand. Minji's pointer finger touches mine. She still moves toward the exit as she wraps her pointer finger around mine.

I don't know if she is trying to comfort me or wanting to be comforted, but I can barely keep my vision as I try to hold in all the emotions. Something in me is screaming to turn around, but my mind is fighting to move forward so I can be with Minji and Gia outside. But something feels safe and whole from Minji's touch. Now I really can't block my anxious energy from jumping over to her because she's touching me. There is no insulator.

I want to stop everything so I can sit and think through it all before making decisions. But I keep taking steps forward.

My internal debate is interrupted as Gia steps completely outside the submersible.

"Whoa." She looks around in the faintly illuminated space.

I take the last step from the metal platform and feel my feet on the ground. The floor is dark and hard. Releasing Minji's finger, I bend down to touch the ground. It's rough. Standing again, I run my fingertips over the wall. It's also rough and it's hot. I rub my fingertips together. They're wet. The wall is either collecting or secreting a liquid.

The space is shaped like a corridor in the Trellis that goes one way or the other. To make space for others, Garridon starts moving down the pathway to the right. I don't know how he decides which way to go, but he keeps moving in that direction.

The space is glowing with a faint red light. It's different than the light from the bacteria in the Trellis or the vines in the Sanctuary. Squinting, I lean toward the wall. The streaks of light seem like veins of crystals I have seen in pictures. I try to look deep into one of the veins. It's mesmerizing, like looking into a dancing mist that emits a captivating color.

"Leal," Gia looks around as more of the group steps from the ship, "what is this?"

We start following Garridon down the tunnel.

"The Trovant?" I try to answer her question, but I'm also not sure what she wants to know.

"No," she says. "What does it seem like it's made of?"

I look at the rough walls and the streaks of color. The wall looks like it's made from boulders. "It looks like rock." The journals had described a facility made of stone — but I didn't know it was entirely literal.

"I think so too," Gia touches the wall as she follows her father through the tunnel. "It's hot."

"Don't touch anything," says Garridon, "and stay close."

"Look!" Minji points to a part of the tunnel.

Protruding from the wall is a piece, about the size of my head, that is glowing red. It's rough, like a rock, but it's translucent. Heat radiates from the spot as I get close to see inside the translucent rock. The light beneath the rough surface moves. It's like a red ocean shifts behind the glassy-rock. It gives off more heat than any other part of the wall. Is there an energy source behind there?

Silently, the group moves through the tunnel. More and more, the walls are speckled with misshapen openings of the glowing red crystal. It looks like red stars are scattered over the walls to illuminate our path. It's almost magical.

We are so quiet that I can hear dripping. A drop of liquid hits my face. I look up. Beads of water collect on the ceiling above until the water drop is too heavy and drips to the ground... At least I hope it's water. The environment is hot and the liquid must interact with the rock. It could be turned into a highly acidic or basic liquid. If that were the case, I would feel it burning my skin.

I wipe my face where the water hit me. Then I smell my fingers to see if the liquid has a particular smell. It does have a smell. But I can't really identify it. Nor do I know what something acidic smells like. When I was younger, my dad showed me liquids that had high sulfur content. So I know what sulfur smells like. Our water in the Trellis was usually mixed into our sustenance packets, so I didn't interact much with plain water.

What if this liquid dripping from the ceiling is poisonous? I wipe my face again, trying to rub off any remaining liquid. But I'm sweating from the heat. I can't tell what is sweat and what is the liquid. Another drop lands in my hair.

I rub my hand in my hair and try to get it off.

"Everything okay?" Minji asks in a quiet voice.

"Yeah," I try to smile. "Everything's good." I glue my hands to my side. No one else is rubbing off the drops of water. Neither will I. If this is a poisonous liquid, we'll all be poisoned together.

There's an opening ahead in the tunnel. It's not much brighter, but it looks more expansive. Gia and Garridon reach the end of the tunnel first to journey out before anyone else. Garridon puts his hand out to signal for us to stay behind. Other people are in front of me as we wait at the edge of the tunnel, so I can't see much of what's out there.

Drips patter as we wait. There is soft thumping from Garridon and Gia's footsteps. Minji has the tablet close to her face. Quick tapping sounds come from her fingers as she types. The rocky corridor whispers a hushed tone, but the tapping and dripping carry a muted beat through the space. The glowing, glassy-rocks flare with the tune. I've never heard a song or seen a video that fashioned such an atmosphere. It's almost a privilege that I get to experience this. I will consider it a privilege as long as we don't see any birds or giant bugs.

"Okay," Garridon's voice echoes through the dripping and tapping.

The group funnels from the area and I can finally see outside the corridor.

"What the?" A man in a green suit looks down and lifts one of his feet.

The ground beneath is squishy.

"What is this?" someone else looks up and spins slowly to take in the size of the space.

It's bigger than any place I have ever seen. The walls, made of rock, tower high like indoor cliffs. Instead of the red light, there are massive cracks of white that give light to the area. Just ahead of us are plants. Real, living plants. How do the plants grow? I look at the white lights streaming through cracks in the rocky expanse. Are the lights electrical? Do they mimic the light spectrum from the sun like the lights that grew our algae in the Trellis?

Squatting to the ground, I place my fingers on the floor. It's not squishy enough that we're sinking, but it's soft and slightly damp. It must be mud... or dirt— I don't know the line between dirt and mud. I walk to the boundary of plants ahead and touch one. It's a straight leaf that's dark green with white stripes. It feels stiff and sharp, like it might cut me if I run my fingers over it too quickly.

Beyond, the plants get more and more dense with trees appearing in the distance. This place is big enough to fit whole trees! How far does it go? There's shuffling in some of the plants. I step back and look around the expanse. We're out in the open where birds could see us if there are any in here. But, in the plants, animals could be hiding where we can't see them. What lives in here? Is anywhere safe?

"Look out!" Desman yells.

Something about the size of a trowel flies through the air. I jolt toward the plants again. Is it a bird?

It flies toward Gia's head. Using her hand, she swats at it, but it flies around her with a whizzing sound. She takes her tablet and hits it out of the air.

"Gia!" Garridon yells. He pulls the tablet from her hands and examines it. "What are you thinking? This isn't a weapon."

The creature wriggles on the ground in a circle.

"I was using what I had," Gia squats to look at the creature.

Minji also bends down and puts her hand toward it.

"Oh!" I wrap one arm around myself and bite down on my finger. "Don't touch it, Minji! We don't know what it is."

"I'm not touching it," Minji says in an unwavering voice. "I'm measuring it. It's just longer than the length of my hand from my palm to my fingertip." She pulls out her tablet and starts typing on the screen.

It still wriggles around in the mud-dirt. Maybe it's trying to fly again, but it just coats itself in more of the ground as it writhes.

"Do we kill it?" Desman also bends down to get a better look at the creature.

"No!" I take a step toward the others. "We don't know anything about it. What if it's a social animal and its pack comes to take vengeance? We can't take on a swarm of flying things."

"Leal," Minji's voice is monotoned as if she's enveloped in examining something that isn't going to harm her. "Does this look like anything you've seen as you've looked at the footage of Earth's surface?"

I squeeze my hand over my mouth as I lean toward the creature to see what it is. It's black except for its light-colored wings. What if it can fly in my ears? I release my mouth and cover my ears. The shiny black body is in different sections. It has long, wiry legs.

I let go of my ears but still wrap my arms around myself. "Yes," I step away from the creature. "It looks like an ant. A really, really big ant."

"A flying ant?" Gia asks.

I shrug, now squeezing opposite arms with my hands.

"I guess my shirt has flying kittens," says Gia.

"I don't really think cats could fly," I say.

"We don't know that," says Gia. "We don't know anything."

"We know how physics works." I relax my arms. "The aerodynamics wouldn't work at all." The thought experiment of a cat's body being able to manage flight distracts me from the chaotic world outside my mind. A cat flying— it just wouldn't work.

Garridon searches the area and wipes his hand through his sweat-soaked hair. He rubs his thumb on his pinky finger. He looks like he might be stressed. I'm not used to seeing him stressed.

"Gia," says Garridon. "Given the external environment, what is the best move?"

"External environment?" Gia rises from her squatted position. "I've never been here. I wouldn't know more than you." She seems less rigid than she used to be. She would have never spoken so casually with her dad. Normally, she would just answer as effectively and efficiently as she could.

"I've had to cover up for you before," says Garridon. "And erase evidence of you looking at survival information and warfare tactics from Earth's surface. This is more similar to the surface than anything we've seen. What did you learn from the footage?"

Gia examines the area, scanning over the plants and looking in the distance.

"That way," she points far beyond the plants. "We need to get to higher ground. Then we can analyze the surroundings and make better decisions. We'll also need water. The plants are a good sign that it's close. We will be able to see from above if there's an obvious water source."

Minji types away on her tablet. I should have been typing this entire time.

I lift my tablet and turn on the screen. It shows charts with quantitative information as well as tabs that contain descriptions of what Minji has observed so far. She has written about the tunnel, the liquid dripping from the tunnel walls, the color of the light, the different plants she noticed, and the giant ant. She noted the number of times a drip came from the tunnel ceiling in a 30-second time period. She cataloged the approximate width of the light-veins as well as how many streaks there were in different sections of the wall.

I haven't done anything so far.

"Alright," Garridon says. "Let's go."

"Hold up," Vega looks at a tablet and holds one hand up. "We're losing Lyra."

"How?" Garridon asks.

"In front of the entrance," Vega points to the tunnel, "Lyra's messages come through. She's saying that she's losing signal. If I move to the right or left, I don't receive her messages anymore."

"What's causing this?" Garridon looks at me and Minji.

"Something is blocking the signal," Minji answers.

"Would this place be designed to block our comms?" Garridon asks. "Is this a trap?"

"Well," I squeeze my palms. I don't like correcting Garridon. But he would be even more mad if I withheld any information. "Since this place is made from some sort of rock, it might just be that our signals can't get through the material."

"Our equipment was designed to operate in the Trellis," Minji does a better job explaining what I was thinking. "Our equipment isn't made to operate in this environment. It doesn't necessarily mean that someone is intentionally sabotaging our communication."

Garridon looks away. Then he turns toward Gia. "What are you thinking?"

Gia still looks beyond the plants as she answers. "Physical communication will still work if we lose virtual systems. The incapacitator guns release a blue light and a loud sound when fired. We can spread out the two as communication beacons while others gather information."

Garridon nods. "Here's what we'll do." He spins slowly as the group forms a circle around him. "One group will stay at the entrance to maintain communication with Lyra and Arcturo. In the first group, we'll need an incapacitator gun, someone relaying information to the submarine, and someone who is familiar with protocols."

"I'll relay information," Vega says.

"And you know protocols," says Garridon. "Scylio —" he points to a man in a green suit. It's one of the people who held an incapacitator gun. "Stay here with Vega. At every 30-minute interval, fire one shot in the air to mark that all is well. If anything goes wrong, fire two shots in the air."

The man nods, then steps closer to Vega.

"The next group," says Garridon, "will be stationed at a median point in the plants. We won't be able to see or hear the incapacitator gun far away, so this group will relay the same shots that Scylio fires. Reti," He looks over to a woman who wears a green suit. She is the other person holding an incapacitator. "You'll stay with the second group. Repeat Scylio's communication at 30-minute intervals and fire two shots if anything goes wrong. If we don't see or hear the shots," he looks between Scylio and Reti, "we'll assume the worst and retreat at once."

The two people in green suits nod.

"The rest of us," Garridon continues, "will divide into the median group and a group that will reach high ground. We'll need someone collecting information in each group. Minji and Leal, one of you will go to high ground and the other will stay in the plants."

I look over to Minji. Both of those sound like bad options. If I have to be separated from Minji, I don't know which would be worse— the open high ground with flying things or the dense plants with hidden creatures.

"Minji will stay in the median," Garridon seems to make the decision for us.

"We need people collecting specimens," Minji said. "Lyra requested we bring back plants or animals to see if anything is viable for food or medicine."

"You two," Garridon points to people around the circle. "Stay with Minji to collect specimens. The rest of us will get to high ground."

Gia steps slightly forward. "It makes more sense for you and me to be in different groups. No one else is trained in—"

"We both head to high ground," says Garridon.

Gia argues back. "That doesn't make any—"

Garridon puts his hand up.

Gia doesn't finish her sentence.

Garridon finishes explaining the plan. "As soon as we collect information about the environment and possible sustenance sources, we will regroup at this entrance. No matter what happens, everyone will move back into this corridor 180 minutes from this point. With information collected, we will reconvene with those inside the ship to decide the best plan of action. Keep sight of the objective. Do not abandon protocols."

I hold a pair of wire cutters in front of me as we push through the plants. Ahead of me, Garridon grips a piece of metal that has a cloth wrapped on the bottom to make a handle. It seems like a big, misshapen knife that he uses to cut through the plants. Desman has a similar tool and slices through foliage near Garridon. We already left the median group to stay behind while we head to high ground. Minji is back there with the others— staying in the plants and collecting information.

With my wire cutters, I snip a leaf that's next to me. It makes a little cut in the leaf, but it doesn't really do much to blaze a trail for us. Maybe I could use my tool to stab something if it tries to attack us. But the tip of the tool isn't very long, so it wouldn't stab very deep. Really, wire cutters aren't good for survival; they're good for cutting wires.

"So," Gia almost whispers as she slows her pace so she isn't near the others in the front. "Minji, huh?"

We had just left the median group behind. It seems like Gia had been waiting for the moment to say something without others overhearing.

"What about her?" My cheek muscles tense up as I try not to smile.

"I saw the finger holding back there," Gia smiles.

"No, no," I shake my head and try not to think about Minji. We're trying to survive. We should probably focus on not dying. "It's not anything."

"Not anything?" Gia chuckles. "You do something awkward every day, but I've never seen you blush like this."

"Since when do you talk about this kind of thing?" I rub my cheek like I can rub off any blushing. "We're supposed to be focusing on our objective."

"Since when do *you* focus on objectives?" Gia asks. "I've watched a riot nearly start on our screens while you pretended to be in Louis Armstrong's band."

"That's an overstatement," I laugh. "There was no riot."

"You wouldn't know!" Gia laughs. "You had your eyes closed while you played your imaginary saxophone."

"Gia!" Garridon yells from the front of the group. "We need you up here."

She moves forward, but looks back and me and raises her eyebrows. Then she turns and joins her dad at the front. Garridon holds a tablet while Desman and another person in a grey suit cut a path.

I lift up my tablet and look at it. I had tried to enter data, but I kept tripping. Even Minji was struggling to type information while we trudged through a tangle of plants. Minji— it's hard not to think of her. She grabbed my forearm one time when she tripped. I helped her back up.

What would come after this? What would happen when we get back to the submersible? Or what if something bad happens and we don't make it back to the ship?

"Wait, stop," Gia halts at the front. She grips Desman's hand to stop him from cutting more of the plants.

"What?" Desman seems annoyed.

"Shh," says Gia. "I hear something."

The whole group freezes. We look around for signs of movement.

"There's nothing there," Desman pulls his hand away from Gia and continues his work.

"Keep alert," Garridon commands the group. "We're almost through."

Gia moves her gaze over the trees above and then examines the plants below. She's searching for something. I didn't hear anything either, but I also wasn't paying as much attention as I should have been. It's true— a riot did almost start one time while I was pretending to be Louis Armstrong's saxophone player.

I hear a step behind me. But I'm the last one in our group. Slowly, I turn.

"Gia," my voice quivers as I try to get her attention.

Towering high above me is a dark animal with long claws and a sharp-toothed snarl. It gives a deep growl. I take a small step backward, but trip over something and topple to the ground.

The animal gives a loud roar and lowers onto all four of its paws.

"Leal!" Gia races to me and tries to pull me to my feet.

"Run!" Desman yells and the people in the group shove through the wall of plants.

"Scatter in different directions!" Gia tugs me to the side as she commands the group that is fleeing in the same direction.

Garridon faces the animal with his giant knife.

"Dad! Run!" Gia yells.

"Go!" Garridon swats his knife in the air as the animal stands back onto two of its legs.

It sometimes stands; sometimes it's on four feet.

"It's a bear!" I say.

"Come on!" Gia still pulls me further into the plants.

"Garridon," I yell as vines tangle around my limbs and plants hang onto my suit. "It looks like a black bear. It might not be aggressive if it doesn't feel threatened. Try backing away slowly."

There isn't a reply.

"Dad?" Gia raises her voice but continues to move through the plants.

There's no answer.

"Dad?" Gia stops. She turns around.

There's nothing except for plants around us. We don't have sight of Garridon.

"Dad!" She wades through the plants back in the direction of the bear.

Just beyond the edge of the plants, Garridon finally comes back in sight. He has his hand out toward Gia, motioning for her to halt. His stare is on something ahead of him.

Gia stops the moment she sees Garridon. Then she leans forward to see what he's looking at.

I tiptoe behind Gia and look over her shoulder. Tripping over a vine, I run into Gia's back and push her forward.

"Sorry," I use her shoulders as leverage to set myself upright.

She turns her head and scowls at me.

"I said 'sorry.'" I put my hands up and back away from her.

She looks back toward Garridon.

Just beyond Gia is Garridon, the animal snarls with its teeth showing. Between Garridon and the bear is another person. The person is lunged toward the bear with a long pole that has fire flaring from the tip. Kneeling, Garridon puts his hands above his head. I lean to the side to see more past Gia. Surrounding them are two others with their flaming poles pointed toward Garridon.

They must be Trovantians.

# Chapter 3: Lyra— Eleven is a Lonely Number

There are 11 steps on the ladder that lead to my lab in the Alaster submersible. The 11 steps make it difficult for me to get to the top platform. I don't mind single-digit prime numbers because their values are low enough that it makes sense that they aren't divisible by anything but themselves. They have community with one another— 1, 2, 3, 5, and 7. They are surrounded by other numbers with similar attributes. But, as the numbers get bigger, the prime numbers seem more out of place; starting with 11. Its neighbors are 10 and 12— they are even numbers, both divisible by two. But 11 is by itself, only divisible by itself. It's an unbalanced, awkward number protruding from the perfect sequence of numbers around it. So I skip it.

It's more difficult with a tablet in my hand, but I'm used to it. Gripping the ladder with my left hand, I hold the tablet with the other and wrap my right arm around the back of the ladder. Ascending the ladder, I count each step I take— 1, 2, 3, 4— I continue until I reach 10. Then I have to put my right arm with my tablet on the platform, lift my leg high over the 11th step, and pull myself all the way onto the platform without touching the last step.

There are people speaking through the submersible as I rise onto the platform. I don't like it. No one used to come in here. It was the place where I could be away from people. They even took apart my lab to get their resources for the outside. At least the lab is empty now and I can be by myself. I push open the metal door, then halt.

There are two people inside— a young man and a young woman. Why are they here? Maybe they needed a private place to talk. But the submarine is full of rooms. Maybe they couldn't find an empty one. I've had my lab for years, maybe I'm selfish for wanting an entire space that no one comes into. But where else can I go? Everywhere is full of people.

"Do you mind?" the young woman sits in my chair and looks up at me.

I'm still frozen in the doorway. Is she saying, 'do I mind' if they're in there? Or is she asking me a question to mean that I should go? I do mind that they are in here, but maybe I don't have the right to mind.

"We're talking," the young man says.

I think they want me to leave. I shift slightly back toward the door. But I do need a space to work and keep in contact with the scouting party. My mom is so much better at confrontation. I think Ara was also better at this sort of thing. I wish I could be like them. I wish I weren't like me.

Similar to the number 11, I'm not like the others around me. I'm not comprised with the same attributes that create a perfect sequence— maybe that's why people skip over me.

"This is my lab." I hold up my tablet. "And I have to work."

"Right," the girl rolls her eyes. "You're one of the important ones."

Important ones? There aren't important ones.

"I'm just," I don't know how to respond. I guess we haven't met before. Most people introduce themselves when they haven't met someone. "I'm Lyra."

"Come on." She rises from the chair and nods to the young man. They both leave the room.

The low hum of machinery replaces their fading footsteps. It's even dimmer with the absence of my bioluminescent bacteria. Putting the tablet on the desk, I examine the system of wires connected to the walls around the room.

The people had moved things when they took out the resources for the scouting party. Some guy had yanked out wires to bring as a weapon or tool. I had to shut down the entire circuit so he didn't electrocute someone. Gia told him to put the wires back. He just bent the wires close to the walls, not really putting them anywhere. How could he put them back in properly? The wires would need to be re-cut, the coverings stripped, and some breakers reopened.

I could do that all now, but my tools are gone. I only had one pair of wire cutters— I gave them to Leal.

It doesn't matter anyway. Those wires were part of a mechanism that maintained proper conditions for the bioluminescent bacteria to survive. But the bacteria are gone. The wire cutters are gone. My tools are gone.

"What did you say to them?" My dad stands in the doorway, but his head is turned toward the people who have just left.

"Not much, really." I rub my cheek. "I just told them my name."

"Did you say anything else?" He steps into the lab.

"I told them this is my lab," I shrug.

"Can you tell why they are upset?"

"Um," I look around. People get upset about all sorts of things. I can't really read their minds.

"Could you tell that they were upset before I said something?" my dad asks when I don't answer.

"Yes," I respond.

"Okay," he says. "That's great. We can keep working on those social skills."

"Who's with Pictor?" I ask. My little brother has been sick. There's no more sustenance left in the submersible. He's dangerously dehydrated.

"Jarret is with him," responds my dad. "I wanted to check on you."

"I'm fine."

My dad steps to the wall and looks at the wiring. He knows I'm not fine.

"Where should we start?" he asks.

"With what?"

"Putting this place back together."

"Dad," there's a sour feeling in my stomach. "There's no point. It's all gone."

"This tablet is here," he pokes the tablet on the desk. "And the wires are present."

"I don't have tools to put them back in place." My throat feels tight. I clench my teeth as I try to keep the emotions from bubbling to the outside. We are trying to survive. As much as possible, I can't waste my emotional energy on my attachment to the lab.

My dad picks up the tablet. He opens the communication portal to Alaster and starts typing. The submersible can talk to us— or I guess it types to us.

"There," my dad holds the tablet toward me. "See?"

Words are typed on the screen: "It's okay to grieve the loss of wonderful things."

I bite my lip and try not to make a sound. I hold the tears in my eyes.

"Lyra," my dad puts his arm around me. "You worked hard in here, making something special. This has been the only place that you could make your own. I'm so sorry it was pulled apart."

Still biting my lip, tears stream down my face. I sniffle, but I still can't say anything. My brother is sick. My sister is dead. Leal is on the outside facing some unknown danger. How could I waste my mental capacity on this room?

"Let's just do what we can," my dad releases me and steps toward the wires. Immediately, he identifies the ones that bother me the most. "We can move these underneath the others so they're out of sight." He tucks the yellow wires away so they're barely visible in the cluster of wires. "What are the ones that go in front? Red?"

I nod.

It freaks my mom out— she and my dad have opposite philosophies about how to deal with me. My mom tries to *desensitize*. She would put the yellow wires in front to show me that there's nothing wrong with yellow.

Logically, I know there isn't anything wrong with yellow, but it does make me uncomfortable. It's a demanding color. In a group of wires, it's the first one people notice. Normally, the color yellow makes people happy. But not me. Yellow is loud and excited. It makes me feel exhausted, like I need a break from being around it.

Red is also demanding but in a different way. A color of passion and intensity, it's the color of shed blood while also being the color associated with love. It feels powerful, but also safe when it's contained. My mom and Ara are both like the color red. And they should be at the front. When it comes to loud, passionate colors, people should like red, but yellow should really take a step back.

I move close to my dad as he fiddles with the wires. The black and white ones can be dispersed throughout the cluster of wires, but the blue ones should be to the side. My dad picks out the red ones and I maneuver the blue ones.

Blue is thoughtful, intellectual, and quiet. Like water, it's needed for everything to function. People need it, but they wouldn't go out of their way to be around it. It's like the hardworking code in our technology that keeps everything running; people don't have to notice it. Blue belongs on the side.

"Is that better?" My dad leans away from the wires once they're all in place.

Not really, the wires still don't function. The circuit has been broken and the wires aren't all connected. But, visually, the wires at least feel a little better.

I nod.

I pick up the tablet and look for any recent updates from the party outside.

"Any news?" asks my dad.

Minji has thoroughly cataloged the physical attributes she observed in the Trovant. She's so fast at documenting information. And Leal is out there with her. Does he notice how good she is at this? I would think that she's like the color blue, but she's not to the side. Maybe she's just a better color blue than me.

"Lyra?" My dad tilts his head and leans toward me.

I keep staring at the screen. If I look up at him, he might somehow perceive all the things going on inside.

"Sweetheart," he wraps his arm around my back and pulls me close. "Come here."

He rubs the back of my head and I hold the tablet pressed between us. His microbial suit absorbs my tears as I push my face into his chest. I feel heavy. I imagined that Ara could be here with us. I try not to imagine what could happen to Pictor. The lab was the only place where reality made sense. Now it's gone.

"You don't have to talk about it if you don't want to." He leans back slightly and looks at me. "But I want to hear about it if ever you feel up to it."

I wipe my tears on my sleeve. "Can we go see Pictor?"

"We're trying to limit contact—" he starts to say the protocols as gently as possible.

"You've been around him," I interrupt. "And I've been around you. So I'm already contaminated."

"You know that's not exactly how it works…" he trails off as he looks down at me. "Okay, come on." He turns toward the door, shaking his head and mumbling: "Vega's gonna' kill me."


Pictor's eyes are closed and his skin is pale. He lies in a small room with a blanket up to his chest.

Jarret sits on the bed across from Pictor, reading something on a tablet.

"Lyra?" Jarret sits up more, leaning like he's trying to see if his eyes are tricking him. "I thought we agreed to —"

"It's alright," my dad comes in behind me. "I said she could come in."

"Hi, Pictor," I step toward his bed.

He doesn't move.

"Pictor?"

His chest slowly moves up and down.

"He's asleep," says Jarret. "He's been asleep since we left the Trellis."

"Dad?" I turn around.

Will Pictor be okay? My brain fills with questions and I want my dad to reassure me. But he can't know more than I do. Again, I try to hold back tears.

We're out of sustenance and Pictor hasn't had liquid long since we left the Sanctuary. He was even dry-heaving hours before we left. But we released the remainder of the sustenance to get past the squid.

We had lost so many people to dehydration before we had protocols in the Sanctuary to keep sick people away from anyone else. And Pictor is small. His body can't fight that long without sustenance.

My dad puts his hand on my shoulder.

I put my hand over my mouth with my fingers quivering.

"He'll be okay," Jarret answers instead of my dad. "He's resilient."

"You can't know that," I don't mean to, but I yell at Jarret.

"Sorry, I—"

"You nothing," I say. "You were out there with Ara. You knew her all your life and you still couldn't stop what happened."

"Sweetheart—" my dad tries to comfort me.

I push his hand from my shoulder and stomp out of the room. There's no chance of helping Pictor without sustenance. Who knows how long the scouting party will take? We just can't wait any longer.

With one hand holding the tablet, I bite my thumbnail as I read what Minji documented about the Trovant. I'm supposed to meet with the Trellis community in 45 minutes in order to relay the information from the scouting party. That will give me enough time to get out there and collect liquid samples without anyone noticing.

I look around. No one is at the bottom of the submersible with me. People stay away from the exit because we don't know what's out there. No one peers from the platforms or peeks outside their doors. They are crammed in the small rooms— talking, worrying, maybe hoping.

The signal from the scouting party is weak. They must be getting further away. If anyone does ask why I'm down here, I could always say that I'm trying to keep the connection with the others.

Pulling my shoulders back, I face the exit. According to Minji's notes, there shouldn't be anything dangerous right outside the door. If there is anything out there, I don't have any weapons or way to defend myself. I'm not combat-trained like Gia; I'm just me.

I put the tablet into a piece of fabric that I had tied into something like a bag around my shoulder. In the bag, there are also some glass containers. One of the containers is empty. The others have small amounts of different colored liquids. These colorful liquid mediums were left with me because no one in the scouting party knew how to use them.

My hands sweat as I get closer to the threshold. The metallic floor gives a low bang with each step I take. Then, my footstep makes a patter. The air feels thick and the walls are dark. I'm outside.

Rummaging through the bag, I pick out the empty container. A drip lands on my head. Holding the container toward the ceiling, I try to collect a drip. I need to test the liquid to see if we can drink it. I can't manage to collect any of the falling drips.

Putting a hand on the rough wall, I try to get a foothold to climb toward the ceiling. Stretching as far as I can, there's the sound of one drop crashing into the glass container. That's not enough to test the liquid. There has to be a better way to do this. Gripping the wall, I scan the ceiling to see where water is collecting the most.

My foot slips and I lose my grip. I crash down. My back slams into the ground. There's no pain, but I feel the shock of something hard hitting my head. Everything goes black.

There's still a dim, red light when I open my eyes again.

"Ow." Rubbing the back of my head, I push up to an upright position. The back of my head stings and my brain throbs with a dull pain.

It's still quiet, other than the occasional drips from the ceiling. No one has come looking for me.

"Oh no." On my hands and knees, I crawl over to the place where containers had dropped from my makeshift bag. They're broken. Shattered glass and colored mediums run over the tunnel floor. "No, no, no." I get as close as possible to the mediums. Maybe I can still make out the different colors and see how the tunnel liquid is interacting with them.

Examining the remnants, I feel a jab in my right hand. Lifting up my right hand, a piece of glass juts from my palm. My hand stings as I reposition myself to a seat, then look at the wall as I grip the glass with my left hand. I clench my teeth, then take in a deep breath. I yank the glass from my palm. A burning sensation blazes my palm as I drop the glass and cradle my hand. Blood drips over the floor.

As one of the drips lands, it sizzles. The enzymes in my blood are interacting with the medium on the ground. That's it!

Clumsily, I rise to stand while gripping my right hand. Clenching my teeth, I push into the cut on my right palm to drip blood in different spots. I can tell where each medium pooled on the ground based on the interaction with my blood.

In one place, the blood changes the medium color slightly. That's the one to check the pH levels. But the drips from the ceiling don't change colors. That means liquid from the tunnel is neutral; it could be water. In another spot, the ceiling liquid turned the medium color slightly grey. Is that because of the lighting in that particular spot? Is it because the ground mixed into the medium right there? Or did the medium actually turn grey? I bend closer to see. If the medium did darken, it would indicate the presence of certain metals inside the tunnel liquid. I can't tell. If there are metals, they must be very trace.

The only thing I can't tell by these tests is the salinity of the liquid— whether it could be freshwater or saltwater. That's what the empty container was for. I have to take a sample to the lab and rebuild the circuits to test for salinity. Now, there's no way to tell. Or, at least, no way except one.

My left hand drips with blood as well as the liquid from the ceiling. Looking at a place on my wrist that only has the liquid, I stick out my tongue. Pulling my hand to my face, I lick the liquid.

It's sour.

I spit on the ground.

Could it be toxic? The sour flavor is still there. I keep spitting until there's no more saliva in my mouth.

Then, I close my mouth and try to make more saliva without swallowing.

"Lyra?" There's a whisper from inside the submersible. "Are you there?"

I spit on the ground.

"Lyra," my dad peers around the entry to the submersible.

I hold my hand close to my stomach and turn slightly to keep him from seeing.

"What are you doing?" my dad whispers, but still sounds upset as he storms through the threshold and over to me. "What happened here?" He looks at the broken glass on the ground. Then, he notices the blood. He grips my forearm and pulls my hand so he can see it.

"Don't touch it!" I yank my arm back.

"Oh, Lyra," his head hangs and he sounds like he was the one who got wounded. "What happened?"

"I fell."

"What are you doing out here?"

"Looking for water."

"Come on," my dad says. "We need to get you cleaned up before the meeting. You know people will be upset you came out here."

I follow my dad back into the submersible.


I sit in the chair near my desk as my dad wraps a piece of fabric around my hand. We don't have anything to clean my hands with— just the cloth. There's dried blood on both of us when he finishes and leans against my desk.

With the back of his hand, he rubs his forehead and sighs. "What were you thinking, Lyra?"

"Pictor needs water," I say as I look up at him.

"You don't always have to do things by yourself. We could have figured something out."

"Like what?" I fight back. How could he figure out where there's water?

"Look," he picks up a tablet and shows me a diagram of part of the submersible. "I asked. It's not that difficult. I asked for help."

"From who?" I take the tablet from his hands. The part of the diagram shows a portion of the mechanical wall along with some internal chambers. It's not a part I have been in because it isn't associated with my lab or the siphon.

"Alaster," he responds.

"If Alaster could do that this whole time, why didn't he stop me from going out there?"

Words type on my screen: "I rarely interpose if people don't want me there."

There's like a burning of emotions in my chest. No — I didn't want him there. I needed to help Pictor and no one could help. And I don't want anyone here now. Not Alaster, not my dad, not even Leal… well, maybe Leal.

I set the tablet on the desk. I need to actually help my brother. There is water. That's most important. I read more on the screen— the systems in the submarine released heat that boiled seawater in an internal shell. The precipitation was collected as freshwater. The submersible needs to be moving to get hot enough to do that. And we just traveled pretty far. It must have collected quite a bit of water while we journeyed away from the Trellis.

"Let's go, then." I rise from my chair without looking at my dad.

Jarret maneuvers Pictor upward and sits behind him on the bed. Pictor looks like a rag draped on Jarret's chest.

"Hey, buddy." Jarret shakes Pictor gently to wake him up.

With his eyes still closed, Pictor mumbles something.

"We have water," I sit on the bed with a container of fresh water. "You have to drink it."

"Here," Jarret takes the water from my hand. "Only one of us should be in physical contact." He puts the water to Pictor's mouth and tips some in. Water streams from the sides of Pictor's mouth. "Pictor—" Jarret sits him up more. "You have to wake up for a minute. Can you hear me?"

"Yeah," Pictor opens his eyes slightly.

This time, Pictor drinks as Jarret gives him some water.

"Gross," Pictor finishes and collapses back onto Jarret.

"Lyra," my dad is behind me, monitoring my tablet. "It's time, we have to go."

"I saw you from outside my door," a woman practically yells at me as we stand on the control center platform. It's Dina. She's always upset about whatever I'm doing. "You left."

"I was trying to maintain connection with the scouting party—"

"How did you cut yourself?" Dina interrupts before I finish my explanation.

Others gather on the platform around us. No one wanted to meet by the submersible exit. We decided that anyone could meet with my dad and me at the control center to hear the information collected by the scouting party. Not everyone wanted to leave their rooms, so a group of about 20 people arrive to hear the update.

"I did it outside," I reply.

"That doesn't answer the question," says Dina. "I asked *how,* not *where.*"

People around the circle cross their arms or stare at me. It makes me uncomfortable.

"Is this really relevant?" my dad asks. "We're here to relay updated information regarding the scouting party."

"It is perfectly relevant," says the woman. "We have no reason to trust someone who is known to lurk around on her own and…"

A beep sounds from my tablet. Dina keeps talking, but I stop listening and pick up my tablet to see what the beep is for.

Minji sent an alert. It didn't come with a message; she just pushed the alert button. Maybe she accidentally hit it.

My mom had sent me a message to explain their plan to split into three groups. In a chart, there are serial numbers for each tablet next to a name I gave each one: *Gia*, *Leal*, *Desman*, and so on. Next to each tablet name is a label that says 'active.' There's one that says 'inactive.'

"What?" I move the tablet closer to make sure I'm reading correctly. Minji's tablet is off.

Another tablet starts typing: *"SOS, there's a…"* The label switches to 'inactive.'

"What's going on?" my dad asks. I don't hear Dina anymore. She must have finished her rant.

"I don't know." I open different tabs on the screen to see potential malfunctions, messages, alerts, and signal strength. Another tablet turns inactive.

"Your mom?" my dad leans close to the tablet. "Is she okay?"

I look for the tablet that's labeled *Vega*. It says 'active.'

"Her tablet is on," I say. I type a message to her: "What's going on?"

She types back: "It's well here. What do you see?"

I begin to type, but my mom sends another message before I can finish.

"Two shots fired from Minji's group. Something's wrong."

My dad reads over my shoulder.

I look up at him. "What do we do?"


"Why does it have to be you?" I clench the tablet as I stand before the exit with my dad.

Other people are on the submersible floor, a bit away from us, or on the platforms. They are still afraid of coming too close to the open door.

"Lyra," my dad places his hand on the side of my head, "no one else is willing."

"I'll go," I try to keep my voice even and not let the others hear. I don't want them to see that I'm sad.

"You know we can't do that." He pulls me into a hug. "Please take care of Pictor and make sure everyone here stays safe. Can you do that?"

I nod in his hug.

"Keep the comms open," he says. "And I'll see you soon." He releases me and exits the submersible.

I look down at my tablet and read the newest label on the chart: *Arcturo*.

I run my finger over the names of my parents. What if they don't come back?

# Chapter 4: Gia— The Jungle

No one speaks, but my ears buzz with noise. Sounds I've never heard— I barely know how to describe them. High-pitched, short calls ring in a constant beat around the trees— chirping, maybe? There's subtle clicking and rattling in different tones. Where are the noises coming from?

I scan the green-covered floor, over giant leaves, and up tree trunks. A worm-like creature scoots across a tree branch. Is it poisonous? A four-limbed creature jumps on the branch, grabs the worm, and shoves it in its mouth. The whole thing happens in a flash. Will the creature jump down and attack us?

Looking forward, I inch closer to the strangers who lead our group. They might be hostile, they might be holding us hostage, but at least they have those fiery sticks that can ward away the animals.

The two people ahead of me are draped in brown fabrics. They are more than a foot taller than my dad. It looks like they are wearing blankets from head to toe. I can't tell how much of their figures are made of blanket and how much might be body mass.

I look behind. There's a person at the back of the group, making sure Leal, my father, and I stay with them. Fabric drapes around the person behind, covering everything except slits for the eyes. The person has light brown eyes.

# Trovant

Sweat runs from my forehead and drips off my nose. I sniff and wipe my nose on my sleeves.

The people in front speak to each other, but I don't understand them.

I trip over something and stumble forward. My dad grabs my arm and tries to steady me. Standing upright, I shove his grip from my arm.

The people in front stop. We've reached the edge of the foliage where there's a wall of rock. The people turn and one speaks to us with a man's voice. His voice inflections sound like he's speaking in sentences, but the words don't make any sense.

"What?" Leal asks.

The man up front responds with a word or a sound that's like hacking from the back of his throat — "*Yackhots.*"

"I don't understand." Leal wipes his forehead. He mumbles to me, "Do you understand?"

I shake my head.

"Yackhots!" The other person sounds impatient and motions in front of the group. The blanketed person gets close to the rock wall, then puts both hands on the wall and steps a foot up.

"Huh?" Leal's face scrunches as the person begins to climb the wall. "How is he even doing that?"

"Yackhots! Yackhots!" The person from behind us prods the flaming stick toward us.

"Okay," Leal puts his hands up and walks to the wall.

My dad and I also step where the man seems to command us. Craning my neck, I look upward as the other person climbs the rock like some sort of animal that can stick to walls.

"Woah," I take an involuntary step back as I see how high up the person is climbing.

The person behind prods the stick toward me.

Leal puts his hand on the wall. "How do we even..." he searches for some magic object that might help us levitate up the rock.

"Yackhots!" the person from behind commands.

A man at the front says something with an exaggerated hand motion. He seems to be arguing with the other person. He points between us and the wall, making glottal noises that apparently form words. The two begin to argue like alien giants who carry our fate between their flaming weapons.

Finally, they stop arguing and one yells something toward the top of the rock wall.

Something falls from the sky.

"Whoa!" Leal covers his head and squats down to brace himself from being hit.

A rope slams against the rock. One of the cloaked men laughs at Leal's reaction and grabs the rope.

"Traluque!" the man tugs the rope, then holds it toward my dad. I can't see the man's face, but it sounds like he's smiling. Maybe Leal amuses him.

My dad accepts the rope from the man. He looks at the wall, then wraps the rope in his fists and puts one foot on the wall; ready to climb.

"Nah, nah, nah." The man shakes his hand and takes the rope from my dad. He lifts the bottom of the rope where there are knots, then motions like he's putting one arm into a knotted area.

"I think it's like a harness," I say.

The man hands the rope back to my dad, who puts one arm into a loop.

"Chy, chy," the man nods.

My dad puts his other arm in another loop.

"Nah," the man shakes his head again. "Nah, nah." He grabs the rope and helps my dad get properly into the harness.

Two more ropes fall from above and slam against the rock.

Leal winces and covers his head.

The man laughs again and gets the other ropes to help Leal and me get into the harnesses.

The rope wraps around my stomach and over both shoulders.

"Yackhots!" the person in the back— who seems less patient— commands us once our harnesses are adjusted.

"Traluque!" The other man puts his hand on the wall and motions for us to do the same. He lifts himself onto the rock.

The rope tightens and my shoulders rise toward my ears with the tension. The rope digs into my injured ribs. I clench my jaw as pain explodes from the area. Grabbing the wall, I try to hold myself to the rock as the rope pulls me up.

"Ahh!" Leal twists in circles as the rope lifts him from the ground, but he doesn't have a grip on the wall.

Still somehow attached to the wall, the man laughs deep belly laughs as he looks at Leal, who flails at the bottom of his rope. Between laughs and words we can't understand, the man tries to instruct Leal. He reaches one hand toward Leal, saying something, then grabs the wall as if to show Leal what he's supposed to do.

"I can't get forward!" Leal screams as the rope pulls him higher.

I giggle too, almost forgetting that we're being held against our will. Then, I cough as the giggling rubs the rope harder against my ribs. I turn toward the wall and do my best to copy the people who climb the wall. My injured knee throbs as I take steps upward, but I keep going. The wall is hard like metal, but rough like a blanket. It's like my brain needs to adjust to learn how to grip something made out of rock.

Even further up the wall, my dad grunts as he takes clumsy steps and forced handholds to climb.

The pain dissipates a bit as I get in a rhythm of taking one step up, adjusting my hands one by one, stopping to get a steady grip, then taking another step up.

Our guides climb beside us swiftly but take breaks to wait for us. One man seems to be jesting with Leal, laughing his way up the wall.

"Don't look down!" Leal yells at me. "That's the trick."

I look down. Above the trees, seeing the distance to the ground makes me feel dizzy. I look to the side. The rock stretches out far, but in an uneven way that blocks my view of the entire wall. In the distance, it seems like there are ledges inverted into the rock face. Then, there seem to be small, white ledges protruding from the rock. And... things moving along the wall... are there more people? Or are there creatures scaling the rock? Can they get to us?

"Traluque!" the less patient of our guides yells at me as I look at the surroundings. The pole is no longer on fire, but is attached to the person's back. I didn't see how he put out the flame, but he can't prod fire at me.

I don't want to be on this wall any longer than I have to, so I continue climbing.

Sweat coats my hands as I near the top.

My father, ahead of me, puts his hand on the top ledge to pull himself up. A hand grips his forearm and yanks him upward.

He's out of sight.

What awaits us at the top?

I gaze down at Leal. We can't turn back. The only way out is up.

The rope digs deeper into my ribs as my grip weakens on the rock. Still, I go upward.

I lift my hand toward the top ledge, then someone reaches down and grabs my wrist. With a strong grip, the person pulls me the remainder of the way and I stumble onto the ledge. Tumbling forward, I lie flat on the ground.

"You okay?" My dad bends down to check on me.

"Yeah," I push myself up. I loosen the rope around my ribs.

"Okay," Leal's voice pants from below, "last bit."

"Okayee," the man tries to repeat Leal to encourage him in the final part of the climb. "Lost beet." He isn't fully able to pronounce what Leal had said.

"Last bit," Leal says again.

"Chy," says the man, "lost beet."

One of the people dressed in blankets lies on his stomach, reaching his arms over the edge of the rock wall. Then, he shifts to a squat, pulling Leal's arm up. Waddling backward, the person drags Leal onto the ground.

Then, the man who was climbing beside Leal pulls himself up and stands upright on the ledge. "Okayee," the man says as he grips Leal's harness. "Lost beet!" The giant man pulls Leal up by his harness and sets him on his feet. The man hits Leal on the back. "Lost beet!"

Leal smiles. "Lost beet." He pats the man's bicep.

The space around us is a small cove, like we're inset in the rock wall. Along the inside of the cove are four openings. A cloaked man motions for us to follow into one of the openings. It turns into something like a tunnel.

Unlike the tunnel that leads to the submersible, this one has rocks jutting out from the ground, the ceiling, and all sides. It's like a training course where we have to weave around the rocks that protrude from all sides. Between the rock cracks are beams of blue light.

The tunnel leads to a room made of rock. In the room, the rocks on the ground have been carved into what look like seats. There's a tied-up figure sitting in one of the seats.

"Desman!" I exclaim when I recognize him. "Are you okay?"

"Just fine," he grumbles between his teeth as we file into the room. His hands are tied behind his back and someone stands against the wall with a flaming pole.

Our guide says something and motions for us to sit.

I take a seat next to Desman, then start to untie his hands.

The person near the wall points the flaming stick toward me and shouts.

"Okay!" I put my hands up, as if in surrender, then sit still next to Desman.

"Minji!" Leal leaps up as more people are guided into the room.

"Leal!" Minji exclaims and puts her arms around Leal.

The person with a stick lunges toward them, yelling commands we can't understand.

Leal and Minji release each other and take a seat next to my father. The others in Minji's group also take a seat.

The cave is quieter than the area with the plants and animals, but it's still hot. Sweat trickles down my neck as others from our scouting party come into the room. Soon, Vega's group arrives, followed by a number of people who are draped in blankets. Only, this time, the people had removed the blankets from their faces and we can see them. Each person is much taller than me. They have tan skin and dark hair.

"Hello, hello," a man speaks as he enters the room. "Yes, hello. I am sorry for the hospitality." He moves to the front of the room so everyone can see him. "I am Imeel," he puts his hand on his chest, "a language expert to translate with the plant people." He smiles, as if waiting for a specific response.

"Plant people?" Desman asks.

"From the Necreo," says Imeel. "This is where you are from, no?"

Desman shakes his head. "No."

"Ah," the smile fades from Imeel's face. "Where are you from?"

"Trellis," Vega answers.

"Trellis?" Imeel looks around at the people draped in blankets. "*Trellis, cheea*?"

The others shrug, looking around at one another and shaking their heads.

"Well," Imeel says, "we do not know Trellis. So, what do you want?"

"Uhh—" Leal scratches his head and starts to say something, but my dad interrupts.

"We've traveled very far. We have sick and injured people and we need sustenance."

"Sustenance," Imeel repeats. "What is that?"

"Food, water, medical supplies," my dad starts to list the things we need.

"We made an agreement; you should know," Imeel cuts in. "No more exchange between the facilities except for—"

"We don't know of any agreement," my dad stands up. "We've just arrived and we are looking for sustenance."

"Yes," Imeel crosses his arms and looks up and down my dad, as if examining him. He starts speaking to the person next to him in the language we can't understand. The two talk back and forth, then Imeel uncrosses his arms. "You are new here?"

"Yes," my dad answers.

"You have never been to Trovant?"

"No," says my dad.

"And this is all of you?" Imeel asks.

My dad doesn't answer.

"This is all of you?" Imeel asks again.

"Yes," says my dad.

"No," says Imeel. "We have already found another and he is being brought here. You already lie. How many are you?"

"Please," Vega stands. "We have sick children and we need assistance."

"Then you will tell the truth," says Imeel. "There is no need to lie. How many are you?"

"A whole facility," Vega answers. "An entire facility of people who need help."

"I see," Imeel crosses his arms again, then rubs his chin. "It is not up to me. But I will see." Uncrossing his arms, he moves swiftly from the room, giving no indication of what he's going to do.

"Vega," my dad whispers as he takes a seat. "We don't know if we can trust them. What if we lead dangerous people to the submersible?"

"Alaster can close the door again if there's danger," Vega responds as she sits.

"You don't know that," says my dad.

"I know Alaster," Vega responds.

My dad shakes his head, but doesn't say anything.

As moments pass, we hear footsteps coming from the tunnel. Figures appear, and Arcturo is being escorted by people who hold fiery sticks.

"Arcturo!" Vega stands and steps toward her husband. "What are you doing here?"

"Hi, honey," he puts his hand on Vega's back and they both take a seat. "We lost your signal. I came to find you."

Vega hugs Arcturo before they sit. "What about the kids?"

"Pictor needs sustenance," says Arcturo, "but we found water. Lyra is fine— she and Jarret are taking care of Pictor until we're back."

Vega is quiet— maybe contemplating whether to be happy to see her husband or mad at him for leaving the submersible.

"Yes, hello!" Imeel's voice says from outside the room. "Hello again." He walks into the room, followed by an even larger man. "This is Rasul Midian. He is the overseer of Trovant."

The large man, Rasul, waves his broad hand at the group. He says something with a smile that is masked by his thick beard.

"Rasul welcomes you," Imeel translates. "He says that if you are not plant people, you are friends."

Rasul spans his arms out wide and continues to speak.

"You are *alnaasitos*— small people," says Imeel. "You need help, and we are divinely commanded to help *alnaasitos*."

My dad crosses his arms and sits up straighter.

"Tomorrow," Imeel continues to translate as Rasul speaks, "We will celebrate that *alnaasitos* have joined our family. You will bring the rest of your people so we can have a *hisbon*."

Rasul raises his hands and begins to say commands to the people around the room. In turn, they each receive the order, nod, and leave the room.

"For now," Imeel translates again as Rasul addresses us, "we will show you where you will stay."


Our group stands near the edge of a new rock wall. I inch toward the side and look down. It was as I thought before— people climb up and down the sides of the rock wall. Spread across the rock face are small ledges that look like little white pockets.

"Here you will stay," Imeel motions down the side of the rock wall.

Leal looks around. "Right here?"

"Down there," Imeel points down to the small white ledges. "In the place of honor! The place with the best view. Every person with his own private space."

I picture myself lying on one of the tiny ledges, then falling asleep on it, then rolling off the side. I back away from the edge.

"They already told me," Imeel laughs, "that you need ropes like children." He laughs some more. "Do not worry. You will learn. But we can have the ropes ready for you to learn."

People along the wall pull out ropes that are tied into divots that seem specially carved into the rock. Vega steps forward and reaches to accept a rope.

"Nah, nah, nah," Imeel waves his hand vigorously at Vega. He says something that we can't understand, then takes the rope from Vega. "You are a woman, no?"

"Yes?" Vega seems confused.

"This is your wife?" Imeel hands the rope to Arcturo.

"Yes?" Arcturo is also confused.

"Get her under control," Imeel says. Then he stammers in his own language.

"What?" Arcturo looks between Imeel and Vega. "What did we do?"

"Only man," says Imeel, "Women, go with Dayana." Imeel motions to a woman who smiles and waves at us. Then, he picks up a rope and hands it to Leal.

Leal grips the rope in both hands, biting his lip as he looks at Minji.

"Um," Leal grips the rope so that his fingers get pale. "So the females will stay somewhere else?"

"Chy, chy," answers Imeel, "somewhere very safe. Do not worry."

"Can I go with them?" Leal asks.

"Nah," Imeel hits the back of Leal's head. "We give you the best place, do not disrespect. Do not worry, the women will be safe."

Leal shuffles toward the edge and looks over.

I don't think he's worried about '*the women*.'

The stone room is domed, like the Sanctuary was, but it's even bigger. Voices echo throughout the rock space as children dash across, moms yell at their children, and families hold hands to stay together in the crowd. Animals weave around humans— they're loose in the same space as people. A few birds walk around and make screeching noises. The birds go up to my waist as they cluck around the crowd. A goat is tethered to a rope as a man guides the animal. Are there any cats? Looking around, I don't see any. Nothing here seems to have laser vision.

There are openings along the walls where people come in and out. A child climbs the wall and into an opening that's almost to the ceiling. Where could that possibly go?

"Stay together," Dayana, the woman who leads us, yells over the crowd. She speaks English.

Dayana guides us through the chaos and to an opening in the wall. The opening is large enough that I can still stand as I go in, but I feel like I need to hunch so I don't hit my head. The noises die down as we maneuver, single file, through the narrowing rock tunnel.

"Remember this way," Dayana turns her head for a moment to speak. "Right, right, then a left, then right."

I'm not sure what she's talking about until the tunnel comes to a fork and she takes the right. As we go on, she takes another right, then a left.

"Right here," Dayana points to a small opening near the floor. "Your last right is just below this green light." She points to a glowing green streak in the wall.

"How do we turn right here?" Minji asks from behind me.

"Like this," Dayana bends onto her hands and knees, then sticks her head in the opening. Her voice is muted inside the tunnel— "You go in like this." She takes her head out and then her voice is clear— "This is your room."

"Our... oh," Minji trails off as she looks at the small opening.

"Go ahead, then." Dayana motions to the opening. "Time to see your room."

I swallow, clenching my teeth. I don't look at the others as I lower onto my hands and knees and crawl into the tight space. The green streak of light follows into the small space as I move forward. The space is tight and my knee stings as I crawl forward. Soon, the small tunnel turns upward. Do I go up? I turn my head to look past my shoulder, but my cheek hits the wall. I lower my head to look under my armpit. It's still too tight. I look between my legs. I can see Minji coming behind me.

"What is it?" She stops and tries to look past me to see what's ahead.

"It moves upward," I say. "There weren't any other turns, right?"

"Gia," Minji's voice is shaky, "I can't stay in here much longer. Please keep moving."

At the urgency in her voice, I move forward and crawl to the spot where the tunnel turns upward. It gets dimmer as the green streak ends.

"What's up there?" Minji sounds worried as I try to crawl upward.

"I don't know," my voice bounces off the walls that are close to my face. I squeeze my forearms by my face and try to get leverage to move upward. There seems to be an opening just ahead.

"Gia?" Minji tremors. "I have to get out. I have to turn around."

"I think we're almost there," I yell downward as I shimmy up toward the opening. The upward tunnel turns out to be completely vertical and I move my feet beneath myself and try to stand.

"It's okay, honey," Vega's calm voice comforts Minji. "You're almost there."

"I can't, I can't," Minji panics somewhere out of my sight.

Standing, I am able to stick my hand out of the opening. I press against the wall, maneuvering with my hands and feet to inch out of the tunnel and into the open space. Finally, I peek out of the opening, then prop my arms up and pull myself from the tunnel and into a room. The tunnel is on the floor of the room that's like a pocket of space carved into the rock.

"I made it out," I yell into the tunnel. "Minji, give me your hands." I stay on my knees and reach into the tunnel where I see Minji with her eyes squeezed shut, but still moving forward.

Grabbing her forearms, I pull her upward and help her into the room. I do the same as Vega and the others get to the entrance of the tunnel. Last, Dayana effortlessly pulls herself through the opening and stands in the room.

"This is your space," Dayana says, motioning around the room.

Minji holds her stomach, inhaling and exhaling rapidly.

Dayana points to the wall, where there are large shelves carved out of rock. Each shelf is about seven feet long with two or three feet of space between them. "These are your beds."

"I can't," Minji covers her eyes and rocks back and forth.

"Just listen to me," Vega moves close to Minji and speaks in a soothing tone. "Don't focus on anything else, just the sound of my voice." She keeps speaking to Minji. It's like she's an expert at calming people down.

"You each have a bed," Dayana again points to the wall of large shelves, ignoring Minji's panic. "Now, I will get you clothes."

"Clothes?" asks Reti, a woman from our group who wears a green suit. "We're already wearing clothes."

"Those are not clothes," says Dayana. "It is too tight. You look like you have green skin. You are naked."

I look down at my shirt that has an image of kittens with laser vision. I don't want different clothes.

"Some of you will lead us back to your people," Imeel translates for Rasul. The two cloaked men stand in front of our small group.

I shift in my rock-seat and try to pull the fabric that's twisting around my waist. The fabric bunches around my arms. There's so much of it that I feel like I'm being buried in a pile of blankets. How do people move around while wearing this?

"Some of you show us where to go," Imeel says, "and the rest can help prepare the *hisbon*. Who will show us to your people?"

I lift my hand, feeling the weight of the fabric pulling down on my arm.

My father, Arcturo, and some others also have their hands lifted.

"Nah, nah, nah," Imeel shakes his head.

Rasul says something while motioning toward me.

"You cannot come," Imeel says.

"Why not?" I ask.

Imeel stitches his eyebrows together. At first, he doesn't say anything. He and Rasul mumble something to one another. Imeel shakes his head again and says, "It is very difficult to climb in your garments. We need people who can climb."

I look at my new clothing. "I can change into something else."

Rasul raises his voice and speaks in his language.

Imeel puts his hands up and tries to quiet down Rasul. "Who is your husband?"

"My..." I look around... "I don't have one."

"Who is your father?" Imeel asks.

I turn to the side and see my dad. He also seems confused as our eyes meet.

"I am," my dad looks back at Imeel.

"Then you will do better to teach her," Imeel says.

My dad stands up. Normally, he would be intimidating, but not here. He doesn't seem to care that his stature is so much smaller than the two blanketed men in front of him. "There is no person more highly trained than Gia." His fists are clenched.

"Please, sir," Imeel puts his hands on my dad's shoulder. "I do not mean to disrespect your house. Only to uphold important values. I hope there is no misunderstanding. For now, I will pick who goes. You can come with us," Imeel says to my dad. "As well as you, you, and you." He points to Arcturo, Desman, and Scylio, one of the others who had joined our scouting party. "Dayana," he yells to the back of our group where our guide has been standing. "Gather the supplies. Then show our guests where to prepare for the hisbon."

Dayana nods, then scurries away to begin her tasks.

Supplies wrapped in a blanket and tied with a string— I hold this makeshift backpack and walk toward the edge of the rock wall. People from the Trovant and the four men from our group cluster on the ledge and prepare to leave.

"I don't like this," Vega whispers and puts her head on Arcturo's chest.

"I don't like it either," Arcturo rubs his wife's back and kisses the top of her head. "I'll be back soon with the kids."

Vega takes a deep breath and releases Arcturo.

I keep walking toward Desman and pretend like I hadn't been listening to them. "Here." I slam the backpack against his chest. I had been told to give the supplies to Desman.

"Thanks," he doesn't look at me, but puts the pack over his shoulder. He sighs. "There's no reason to be mad at me. I wasn't the one who said you couldn't go."

"Whatever," I turn away from him.

"Gia," he puts his hand out to try and get me to stay, but he doesn't touch me. "Can we please stop fighting?"

"Gia," my dad's voice rises from across the group of people.

I look back at Desman. He really didn't do anything wrong. "Just," I turn away from him, "be safe or something."

"I'll see you later," he says as I walk toward my dad.

My dad leans toward me as I approach. "Keep your eyes out," he speaks in a lower voice, but not a whisper. "Collect as much pertinent information as you can and be on guard at all times."

"Okay," I say.

"I mean it," he says. "Don't even sleep until I'm back."

"I'll be fine," I say.

He slings his pack of supplies over his shoulder. "I know you will."

I think that might be his way of trying to say something like— *"Goodbye, I love you."*

I put my hand on his shoulder. It feels weird. But it's my best attempt to say something like— *"Goodbye, I love you too."*

# Chapter 5: Lyra— Where Blue is Beautiful

I hear tiny inhales and short exhales. It's silent except for Pictor's little signs of life as his small body is slumped over Jarret's large frame as he sweats into Jarret's suit. I look at my own microbial suit. The blood from my palm has almost been absorbed in my microbial suit, but the blanket fabric wrapped over my hand is still stained with blood from my cut. It stings. There's nothing here to clean the cut. Maybe, if I hold it against my suit, the microbes will clean the wound and I'll have less risk of getting an infection that could turn into sepsis.

Sitting on the floor with my back against the wall, I start unraveling the fabric on my hand.

"What are you doing?" Jarret speaks quietly.

The air stings my cut as I get the bandage off, force my fist to open, and I paste my palm to my side with my cut against my microbial suit. I wince from the pain.

"Are you okay?" Jarret speaks quietly again.

"I'm fine." I pick up my tablet with my other hand and look over the names. I count them again. The number of names on my tablet was initially 12, but my dad leaving increased the number of names by 1. I count once again, as if I could change that number if I just counted more times. It was still the same— that unlucky, double-digit prime number.

"13," I sigh.

"What?" Jarret asks.

"Nothing." I put the tablet down and rub my face.

"Lyra," Jarret says, "it's okay to talk about it."

I don't know exactly what he means. What could I possibly have to say to him? We don't even know each other. I dig my thumb into my forearm. Squeezing, I count in my head. 1... 2... 3... I get to 9 before Jarret interrupts.

"Lyra—"

"What?" I jolt my head up and look at him.

"You're obviously anxious or upset or something," he says. "I just want to help."

"You're not helping," I say. "Now I have to start over."

"Start what over?"

"Counting," I say.

He tilts his head. "Counting?"

"Yes, to 21."

"Why?"

"Because it's better than 13."

He doesn't say anything; just rubs his hand over Pictor's back.

"Okay." He leans his head against the wall. "One. Two. Three..."

I put my forehead on my knees. I feel awkward hearing him count.

He continues: "Four... Five.."

Then, I whisper the numbers along with him. It actually is soothing. It's as if each number I whisper can do something— anything— to make my parents come back. "Six. Seven." His voice is deep and strong. My whisper is small, but it still seems powerful as it reaches out to my parents. "Eight. Nine." My mind journeys through the red-lit tunnel and to an unknown place. "Ten. Eleven. Twelve." I imagine I meet my parents in the red tunnel. "Thirteen." They're safe. "Fourteen." They are ready to come back with me. "Fifteen. Sixteen." Leal and Gia are there too. "Seventeen. Eighteen." Leal is happy to see me. He gives me a hug. "Nineteen." He kisses me. "Twenty." I kiss him back.

"...twenty-one," Jarret finishes. "Is that better?"

With my forehead still on my knees, I nod.

An alarm sounds on the tablet— my worst nightmare shatters my daydream.

I yank the tablet from the ground and pull it toward my face. I scan the information and get to the 13th name on the list: *Arcturo*. I read the new alert blinking by his name: *Inactive*.

"What is it?" Jarret sits up.

My chest feels tight.

"Lyra," Jarret moves Pictor and comes toward me.

"Don't—" I put my hand out and try to keep myself from hyperventilating.

"I'm not going to touch you," he crouches next to me. "Should I count to 21 again?"

I shake my head.

"What will help?"

I close my eyes and pretend he's not there. My dad always holds me to calm me down. But he's out there somewhere. "Where is he?" I heave.

"Who?" Jarret asks.

"My dad," I squeeze my eyes closed.

"Lyra," his voice is deep and kind. "I'm not sure where your dad is. He's somewhere outside."

"I don't know what to do," I try not to cry.

"Can I try something?"

"What?" I keep my eyes closed.

"I've just seen how your dad calms you down," Jarret says. "Can I put my hand on your shoulder?"

It was a weird request, but I nod.

I feel Jarret's hand on my shoulder.

Then, he pulls me into a hug. He rubs my head as I breathe into his chest. I feel his ribs move in and out, slowly. My breath starts to sync with his.

"We'll figure this out," he says once I calm down. "They'll be okay."

My eyes shoot open.

I place my bloody palm on Jarret's chest and shove him. He's so big that I'm the one who topples backward as he stays grounded.

"You're always saying that!" I catch my balance and start to stand.

"Saying what?" He stands too and tries to keep me calm.

"That people are going to be okay," I say. "You don't know if my parents will come back. You can't tell me that anything will be okay."

"Lyra," he says, putting his hand toward me. "I'm sorry."

I jerk away from his hand.

"I'm just trying to help," he says.

"Lying isn't helping." I grab the tablet from the ground, then turn and leave.


Standing in front of the exit, my grip on the tablet is sweaty from the humid air. There have been no messages from the scouting party for almost two hours. I can't keep waiting.

Similar to before, I put the tablet in my makeshift bag that I keep over my shoulder. No one will notice I'm gone anyway. I march toward the exit. Jarret would probably stop me, but he's stuck with Pictor. The red glow encapsulates my vision as I arrive at the opening. Drips patter on the rock-floor. Blood and my mediums are still pooled on the ground, now watered down with the drips from the ceiling. The tunnel goes to the right and the left, but I'm not sure which way the scouting party went.

Leaving the Alaster ship, I step near the warm wall and pull the tablet from my bag. I scan through the information from the scouting party. The information describes drips from the wall, the red cracks of light, creatures that seem to be outside the tunnel, and how far away they were at each moment— but I can't tell how far in what direction. I really should have figured out better systems for tracking them before they set out. How is my dad supposed to find them?

Putting the tablet back in the bag, I look right and left down the tunnel. I have a 50/50 chance of picking the correct direction. I start to walk left down the tunnel.

I hold my bag close and try not to trip over rocks jutting from the floor. It's harder to take in the humid air as I get further away from the Alaster ship. How long do I need to go before I get outside the tunnel? The tunnel still goes further than I can see. Warm liquid drips on my head. How long should I go before I try the other direction?

"One," I whisper. "Two..." I count my steps.

I get to 47, then stop and look behind me. I can't see the entrance to the Alaster ship. Maybe I should try the other direction. But, what if I'm near the tunnel exit and I just need to go a little further?

I start counting my steps again. My foot catches on a rock and I stumble forward and grunt. Sounds of my stumbling echo through the tunnel. But there seems to be another sound too.

I try to see around the bending tunnel. "Hello?" I say quietly. "Hello?" I say a little louder.

There's no repose.

Gripping my forearm, I continue forward. Along the right wall, there's an opening. I lean into the opening and see another tunnel, this one is even darker. No one in the scouting party documented another tunnel. Did they just forget to mention it or am I going the wrong way?

There's a small clatter in the connecting tunnel. I lean in to see if I can find the source of the noise.

"Dad?" I whisper. I step into the darker tunnel. Could he be in here too, or is there some creature trying to lure me in?

There's another sound. This time, it's louder. There's definitely something in here. I hesitate. If it's not my dad, what could be in here?

I start to turn, but my heel hits a rock. I lose my balance and crash to the ground, my palm stinging as I try to catch my fall.

"Ahh," I shriek and pull my hand close to my chest.

A spark flashes in front of my face. There are cracks, like the sound of wires shorting out.

"Beetanway Maristimna!" a female voice yells. There's a pole near my face. The tip of the pole crackles with flames.

"What?" I ask as I look past the fire and see cloaked figures.

The figures mumble to one another. One nudges another.

"What are you doing here?" One of the figures asks. Her voice is strong, like Gia's. But she pronounces words differently.

"I'm," I stutter, but not because of fear. I'm too curious to be afraid. Who are these people? How did they get here? Do they live in this tunnel? "I'm looking for my dad."

"Dad, cheea?" one of the people turns to the other and seems to ask a question.

The person with the pole lifts it from my face, setting the base on the ground.

"Who are you?" she asks. "You are from the plant people?"

"Plant people?" I ask. "I'm looking for my parents."

"You are lost?" She doesn't seem hostile.

Another cloaked person starts arguing with words I can't understand. The cloaked people argue with one another, pointing at me and using exaggerated hand gestures. They're all female voices. And they seem close to my age or just barely older. They stop arguing, then all look at me.

The one holding the pole removes her draped hood. She has dark brown hair and strong features. Her stance towers above me. She seems firm, but not threatening.

"My name is Rhen," she says. "This is Mica, Vana, and Ferris."

Vana and Mica remove their hoods so I can see them better. Ferris crosses her arms. Although their features look like young woman, they are muscular and taller than any man I know.

"You're not from here," Rhen says. "We have questions for you. Come with us."

"I have to find my parents," I say.

Rhen moves like a flash and points the pole in my face. "Come with us," she repeats.

I wrap my arms around myself as we progress through the tunnel. It's cold. The lighting turns from red to light blue. Are the lights associated with the temperature somehow? I shiver.

"Almost there," says Rhen.

Just ahead, there's an opening. Is that where my dad and the rest of the scouting party are?

We arrive at the opening and to a huge space that's as tall as the Sanctuary, but much wider. Jagged tunnels lead in different directions from the walls of the space. Above are overhangs of clear crystals that glow faintly and, on the floor, there are clear blue pools of water. Some pools are still, but some lap gently against the rocky edge. One of the pools is gigantic and seems to glow light blue.

Reverberating through the space are sounds like smooth deep whistles, like a breeze is singing. I wrap myself tighter. There seems to be cold air flowing over the clear blue pools, crystal lights, and jagged rocks.

"What's that sound?" I ask as I follow the group into the open space.

"The music?" asks Vana. She seems enchanted with the low hums that sound through the room.

"The alarm," Ferris corrects. She seems less amused.

"An alarm for what?" I ask.

"The *albharee*," says Ferris. She points to the clear pools on the ground. "We dive in the water to collect food. The pools sustain life for many, including the albharee. They are giant monsters; faster and bigger than any others. They have teeth the size of a *Jundarro* and hunt anything in their path."

"I don't know how big a *Jundarro* is," I say.

Rhen sighs and rolls her eyes. She holds her hands apart to show about how big a single tooth would be. I picture a mouth full of teeth that size, chomping down on me and piercing my stomach. It could cut me in half in a single bite.

"When the albharee swims near," says Rhen, "it creates large waves in the water. The waves hit against those." She points to holes carved near or inside the water. "Those are pipes that run upward." She traces a line with her finger and points near the ceiling where there are staggered openings. "The sounds from the waves come out of those pipes. It was designed after an instrument on the surface called an organ. The bigger the waves, the louder the sounds."

As discreetly as possible, I count the openings in the ceiling. There are 21, which is three times seven. 21 is a number where two prime numbers come together to make something. It's like a place where weird numbers can belong.

Rhen continues her explanation: "We can tell how big and how far away something is by the sound coming from the pipes. Right now, it's only smaller fish or creatures that are very far away."

I stare at the holes in the ceiling, feeling a tiny breeze with each hum from the openings. "You can't go in the water when the alarms are louder?"

"We cannot be anywhere near here when it is louder," said Rhen. "That pool over there," she motions to the largest pool in the area, "is large enough that the albharee can fit through."

"It comes on land?" I ask. "So it's some sort of mammal?"

"It is some sort of monster," says Ferris.

"Is this the only place the creature can get on dry land?" I ask.

"No," says Rhen. "There are other places where it can claw its way inside. No one goes to those places."

"Why are you in this place?" I ask.

"This is the only place with the alarm," says Rhen. "People don't come here because of the albharee, but we take the risk since we have warning before it comes."

"So we should get food while we have the chance." Ferris removes her cloak and steps near the edge of a pool. She has fabric tightly bound across her figure.

I walk near her and lean over the pool's edge. The water is clear and bright. Blue crystal veins run down the sides of the pool and illuminate as far as I can see. In the depths, I notice small things swimming in a mess around the edges of the watery cave. A shadow lurks slowly below the smaller creatures. I back away from the edge.

"Not before we talk," Rhen says to Ferris.

Ferris only wears short bottoms and a small wrap of fabric over her chest. Her skin is tan, but not as dark as the fabric she wears. Her muscles are defined.

I look at my arms and legs. I'm as thin and flimsy as a wire compared to her.

"I am starving," says Ferris. "And we need to warm up anyway. You get a fire going and I will get food." Without hearing a response, Ferris picks a clump of rope near the water's edge and jumps in with a splash.

Cold water hits my face.

I wipe it off and spit in case it got in my mouth. This water isn't sour like the water in the tunnel. It's salty. I spit again.

The others look at me.

Maybe that was the wrong thing to do.

The splashes create waves that hit harder against the wave-alarm. Loud hums magnify in the space, followed by gargling sounds as the wave recedes.

"We will make a fire," says Rhen. "Come on." She motions to others who still stare at me.

I put my hand close to the glowing fire. It's so hot. I pull it away. The air is so cold. I put my hand back by the fire. It's like when my machines overheat, but even hotter. And the air is frigid like when the Alaster ship is empty, but now it's even colder. Squatting, I inch toward the fire and the hairs on my arms stand from the cold, but my arms feel scorched if I'm too close to the fire. I don't really know where to be. That's kind of how I feel about being around people. I feel like I need some sort of warmth from being around others, but I can't get too close. I'm uncomfortable whether I'm close to the warmth or far, but at least I'm used to the cold.

The low hums from the wave-alarm play in the rocky cavern as Rhen puts a piece of wood on the fire. At the bottom of the fire, there appears to be burning coal. I could imagine they found coal somewhere in this cave-like environment. But where did the wood come from? Maybe out where the others are. Minji had written that there were plants, but she didn't document entire trees. How big is this place?

The fire gets bigger and the crackling overpowers the sounds of drips. I back up as the flames grow.

There's a splashing noise behind and I turn to see what it looks like for someone to swim in real life.

"New person," Ferris yells toward me once she breaches the water's surface and swims toward the edge of the pool. "Come hold this."

I walk to the pool's edge, looking at Ferris and trying not to look down into the water. She pulls something behind her that looks like a mess of rope, but it's moving. I look closer. In her fist, Ferris grips a net full of fish.

As if by instinct, I jolt away.

"I said to hold this, Ferris commands once she reaches the edge and lifts the net partially out of the water.

I swallow, then lean over and grab the parts of the net in her fist.

"Do not stand there," Ferris says as she releases her grip. "Pull the fish out."

"Pull?" I look at the fish in the net I grip. Does that mean I'm supposed to reach my hand in the net and get each fish out with my hand? If I loosen my grip on the net, all the fish will swim away. What does she mean?

"Ugh," Ferris yanks herself from the pool. Water pours from her body as she maneuvers on the ground. "Useless..." she mumbles, shaking her head and squatting. She shoves me a bit, taking the net from my hands. "Like this." She yanks the net from the water. Fish splash around as she sets the net on the ground with water flowing everywhere. She releases the net and fish slap on the ground.

"Are you going to help me?" Ferris picks up a rock.

My eyes widen. Is she about to do what I think she is?

Lifting the rock high with one hand, she pins a fish to the ground with another.

I try not to react. What if I act grossed out and Ferris gets offended?

With power, Ferris slams the rock on the fish in her grip. Its head is crushed with guts oozing out. It stops moving.

"Well," says Ferris, "you could try the easier way if you wanted. But it is messier."

"Easier?" My fingers are ice cold as I clench my fist and try not to let on that the sounds squishing fish are somehow sitting in the bottom of my stomach. What if she also secretly holds burdens of trying not to be weird around people and my reactions imply that her social interactions were incorrect?

"Like this," Ferris lifts the net from the ground with some fish still floundering inside. Reaching the net over her head, she slams it down with force and crashes the net to the ground. "See?" She hangs the net in front of my face. Some of the fish have stopped moving, but some still flutter in the rope net. "Some die on the first swing, but some take a few slams. Sometimes guts fling out as you try to kill the rest of the bunch." She resets her posture and goes to slam the net of fish a second time. With fish pieces flying, she hits the net on the ground until no fish are left alive.

My posture feels tense as the sounds of fish flapping on the rocky ground have stopped. Fish guts are littered over the jagged rocks and the smell of fish intestines clouds the space. Some pieces are strewn over the otherwise crystalline pool. Something jets to the top of the water.

I leap away as a huge monster breaks the surface of the water. I topple to the ground and try and scoot away from the water. The monster gulps pieces of fish that had landed in the water.

"Is that the albahar... the monster?" I try to sit up straight and pull my reactions back in.

Bellowing laughter replaces the splashes of the monster. Ferris doubles over, dropping the fish net to the ground as she laughs and shakes her head. "Maybe—" Ferris struggles to breathe as she laughs. "Maybe we should have her gut the fish with me too."

"That is enough," Rhen steps toward Ferris, yanking the net from the ground.

Ferris stands upright again, still giggling, and uses her gut-covered fingers to wipe away tears of laughter.

"What was the place called again?" Vana takes a bite of fish after I explain as much as I can about how I got there.

"Trellis," I say as the fire cracks between us. What if I didn't explain it right? They aren't from the Trellis, so maybe I need to use different descriptions to explain the facility. I look around the darkened rock and try to find something as a comparison.

"Like the plant holder?" Vana asks.

"The what?" I ask.

"The thing that holds up plant vines," Vana clarifies.

"I don't..." I look around the circle at Mica, Rhen, and Ferris. "I don't know what that means."

"It is a structure that—" says Vana.

"It does not matter," Farris interrupts. "She does not know what it is."

"Do you…" I feel confused by how Vana used the present tense to describe something that *holds* vines, rather than something from Earth's past that *held* vines. "Do you have vines?"

"See," Ferris says. "She does not know."

Now Ferris thinks I'm dumb. Should I have worded my question differently? Or am I dumb? I don't know much outside the Sanctuary.

"Stop it," says Rhen. "She is not from here." She says something to Ferris in their language.

Ferris grunts but doesn't say anything back.

Mica sucks meat off fish bones. She seems more present in her food than in the conversation.

"Are you from the Trovant, then?" I ask as I rub my arm and try to sit up straight so I look normal. "Why are you all in these caverns with the albharee alarm? What's the story here?" They are hunched over more. I hunch over too so maybe they will think I'm normal.

"We are from the Trovant," says Rhen. "And the story is simple— none of us belong there."

"What do you mean?" I ask.

"We are part of a warrior club," Vana says.

"Sort of," says Rhen. "My mother was a part of the *Kaleed*— an elite fighting group that is as old as the Trovant. The group was started by my mother's ancestor — Rita Reid, an inventor and fighter in the early days of our history."

"I know her," I say. "I mean, I've read about her in journals. She was friends with Symphony Hamiltoni— the person who designed the facilities."

"Yeah," says Rhen, "that is right. And Rita ended up at this facility and founded our group, in secret, because she was forbidden to invent or train in public. Many of her surviving inventions were kept safe with the Kaleed. Here, women could learn her fighting styles and protect what was left of the inventions." She pauses.

"Did something happen?" I ask.

"Yes." Rhen chews on her lip and thinks for a moment. "The Kaleed came forward in the war with the plant people."

"What war?" I ask. I hope I'm not asking too many questions.

"She does not know," Ferris shakes her head.

"There was a war with the other facility," says Rhen. "My mother and her people offered their resources and skills to fight in the war. The overseers did not approve of women fighters but accepted the help anyway. They sent the Kaleed to the front of the war with no weapons. No one survived."

"Except Rhen," says Vana.

"Except me," says Rhen. "Because I could not join the war. I was eleven, and my mother had been teaching me the ways of the Kaleed, but I still had a lot to learn. I came here, where the Kaleed had trained in secret. I trained the way my mother had taught me and kept the last of the hidden inventions of Rita Reid."

"What are the last of the inventions?" I ask.

"These," Rhen lifts her arms with sleeves draping down.

The fabric is dark, but the light from the flames reflects and almost shimmers across the loose sleeves. The stature of the three cloaked women feels like the expansive cavern walls; rugged, but with an air of a beautiful, delicate song.

Rhen says, "They are fireproof, stab-proof—"

"And very warm," Vana hugs her cloak around herself.

Mica doesn't say anything, but rubs her hands over her clothes and then wraps them tighter around herself. Then, she lies down, snuggling her outfit around her like a blanket. The warm glow of the fire dances over her face as she yawns and closes her eyes.

"Are there more?" I ask. "Is this what everyone in the Trovant wears?"

"Only five of these cloaks were made," says Rhen. "Everyone else wears normal fabric."

"Where is everyone else?" I ask.

"The Trovant," says Ferris.

"Then," I say, "where are we?"

"We are..." Rhen looks around the space that is now dark, "Nowhere, I guess."

"We are home," says Vana as she lies down in front of the fire.

"You live apart from everyone else?" I ask. "Why?"

"We do not belong anywhere else," Ferris says as she also lays on the ground and folds her hands over her chest.

Rhen stands and walks away from the fire.

No one says anything. Should I say something? Does Ferris want to talk more or does she want to sit in silence?

Mica's breathing gets deep, close to snoring. Vana's eyes glimmer in the firelight and Ferris stares at the ceiling.

"Here," Rhen wraps something around me when she gets back to the group. "You look cold."

"What is this?" I ask.

"It is the last cloak," says Rhen.

Ferris makes a noise that sounds like a growl. I feel like I've gotten too close to relational fire and I might get burdened. The cloak shrouds me in a burden of trying to accept and be friendly but trying not to overstep and make Ferris mad.

"You came here all on your own," says Rhen. "It seems like you do not belong anywhere either." She lowers to the ground and lies down.

Putting my arms through the sleeves of the oversized cloak, I slip inside. It does feel warm. I lay down, with the fire painting a warm glow and the hum of the waves singing in the air. There are five cloaks and five of us. Five is a prime number, but not a lonely one. This place might be like the number 21 — a space where weird numbers can come together and belong. It's a world where the color blue looks beautiful. I close my eyes and let the song of the waves lull me to sleep.

# Chapter 6: Leal— Moonstone

I grip the white material and try to muster courage to look over the edge. A rope squeezes my sides. My skin is irritated and my ribs feel bruised. I kept the rope tight all night. I couldn't get the idea out of my head that I might roll out of this spot and crash to the ground… or worse.

Putting my hand to the wall, I gaze far across the indoor-cliff and see giant animals fluttering around the wall. I cover my head and crouch in the white pocket that's glued to the rock wall to make my bed.

I'm in an abandoned BIRD'S NEST.

I hold my stomach to stop from being sick, but there's too much fabric around me. I feel like I'm drowning in fabric. Sweating, I start to yank my cloak off. I can't get it off because the ropes are tied too tight.

"What is going on?" I hear a voice in the nest above me.

Littered across the rock face are white pockets of abandoned nests that make up beds for the most honored guests. I wish I was less honored.

"Desman," I whisper to the nest above me. I can't see who's inside, but I recognize his voice. "You guys made it back?"

"Yeah," Desman says, "we made it back while you were asleep. So now I need to sleep."

"Okay." I fold my hands over my chest and lie back down. I try to relax. But, what if the nest breaks away from the wall? What if the strain on the rope is too much and that breaks too? What if those giant birds fly over here because they need to get a snack for their baby birds?

"Desman," I say.

"What?"

"How much longer will you need to sleep?"

"I don't know, Leal, just let me sleep."

"Okay." I rub my thumbs together. I tap my foot against the nest and try not to think about birds swooping in and grabbing me with their talons. I try to remember happy things— like songs by Louis Armstrong. I start to hum. It works! Humming is distracting me.

"Agh!" Desman exclaims. "Leal!"

"Sorry!" I put my hands over my mouth and stop humming.

"Fine," he says. "I'm awake. What do you want?"

"I want to get out of here," I say.

"So go," he says.

"I'm stuck."

"Stuck how? Is your hand caught in a rock or something?"

"No."

"Then, how are you stuck?" he asks.

"I'm too afraid to go over the edge."

"Leal," Desman sounds annoyed. I can picture him shaking his head. "Just a minute."

I hear shuffling and some grunting. Desman's head appears over the edge of the nest above mine. Groaning, he climbs onto the wall and near my bed.

"Don't come in here," I say. "We don't know if it can hold two people."

"I'm not going in," he says. "You're getting out."

"Right." I nod. "Okay. Yes. I'm getting out."

"Start by standing up a bit."

Trembling, I raise and put both hands on the edge of the white pocket. Looking down, the trees are so far that they look like tiny green rocks. I squeeze my eyes closed.

"Don't look down," Desman says. "Just grip the wall and pull yourself out here with me."

"Desman!" I squeal when I open my eyes and see him. "You don't have a rope!"

"I know," he says. "The rope is too hard on my ribs. I can't breathe with it on."

"You're not safe!" By some effort outside of my control, I reach out and grab the wall, pulling myself onto the rock near Desman. "I'll hold you."

"You will not," Desman slaps my hand away.

"Keep both hands on the wall!" I yell. "What are you thinking?"

"You'd better follow me up in case I fall." Desman lifts one arm above and then pulls himself upward. He climbs the wall.

"This isn't a game!" I climb behind him, avoiding other white pockets that are empty or contain sleeping people. "You could fall!"

"So you better stay by me," Desman says as he nears the top.

Reaching the top of the ledge, Desman pulls himself up and out of sight.

When I get there, he helps pull me up and get me to my feet.

"See," Desman pants, "it's not that bad."

"You could have fallen to the ground," I say. "And then what? What would I tell everyone? You really need to wear a rope."

"I really need to get some sleep," Desman says.

"Here," I untie the rope around myself and start to put it on Desman. "At least while you're climbing."

"Alright," Desman accepts the rope and ties it around his chest. "Only while I'm climbing." He crouches down and puts one leg over the rock wall to climb back to his bed.

People pass to and fro over the rock's ledge, going in and out of tunnels. Just behind a hole in part of a tunnel wall, I see Garridon speaking with Gia. Garridon was in the group that went back to the Alaster ship. Isn't he going to get some sleep? He probably doesn't need sleep; he's basically a robot. But Gia didn't seem like she was going to bed last night and she is not a robot. She gets grouchy when she doesn't sleep.

"Gia!" I call out when she departs from Garridon and walks down a tunnel.

She turns around, looking for who called her name.

"I'm here!" I jog toward her.

"Hi, Lea." She does look tired.

"Is something going on?" I ask.

129

"Why would something be going on?" she asks.

"Your dad was whispering something to you," I say. "He couldn't look any sneakier. Are you trying to keep something from me?"

"I don't want to freak you out," she says. "It's probably fine."

"What's going on?"

"No one has seen Lyra," she says. "There were a lot of people on the Alaster ship, so we're hoping she just hasn't been located in the crowd."

"What about her tablet?" I ask. "If she were in the crowd, her tablet would connect with ours now."

"That's the part that doesn't make sense. Her tablet is still inactive. So she either turned it off, broke it, or she's out of range."

"That's not good," I say.

Gia sighs and bites her lip. Looking at the ground, she shakes her head.

"What is it?" I ask.

"I just... I can't stand the idea that Vega and Arcturo could lose another child."

Both of us stay silent for a moment. The grief of losing Ara has seemed like a physical weight that's been pulling down the Delphino family.

"What are you going to do?" I ask.

She looks in the distance, seeming to think about it. Dark circles under her eyes reveal the tiredness that she tries to mask.

"You need to sleep," I say.

"I need to find Lyra," she replies.

"I'm sure the Delphinos will start searching."

"They have to make sure Pictor is okay first," she says. "What if Lyra is trapped somewhere or in danger and running out of time?"

I stare at the ground for a moment. She's right, Lyra could be in danger. The Delphinos need to look after Pictor and Garridon probably has some super secret robot things to do.

"Alright," I say.

"Alright, what?"

"Let's go."

"Leal," she smiles. "I'm going. You don't have to come."

"If you're going on some perilous quest," I say, "you're going to need someone to protect you."

She laughs.

"What?" I laugh too. "Don't look so amused."

"There might be wild animals," she says.

"All the more reason for there to be two of us."

"There might be birds."

"Ugh," I say. "Don't remind me."

"To be fair," a voice sounds from behind me, "there will be birds whether he stays or goes." Jarret appears from behind a rock wall. "I'm coming too."

"Jarret," Gia says, "we really don't need—"

"I'm coming," he says again. "It's my fault she's out there anyway."

"I'm sure there's an explanation for why—" Gia says.

"I don't need a pep talk," interrupts Jarret. "None of us could help Ara." He looks at both of us. "Lyra stormed out the same way Ara used to. We have to find her."

"Okay," Gia says in a kinder voice, "we'll find her."


"Are you sure this is the best idea?" Jarret asks as he hits away a plant that's in his face. He grips an incapacitator gun. We haven't needed it so far, but we brought it in case we run into a bear or something. "I mean, she could be lost in this area with all the plants. Maybe we should ask a Trovant guide to show us around."

"No," Gia says, though she keeps her gaze fixated on the tablet in her hands. It's amazing she doesn't trip on all the roots jutting from the ground and plants grabbing near our feet.

"That doesn't seem like a terrible idea," I say. "A Trovantian guide would know this area better—"

"No," says Gia.

I rub my arm. Why wouldn't we ask for help when they've been so hospitable? They seemed so friendly.

"Maybe we could just—" I try to convince her.

She looks up from her tablet and gazes at me dead in the eyes. She's like an angry bear and I'm stuck in the jungle without an incapacitator gun.

"Yup," I put my hands up like I'm surrendering, "just kidding. We're not asking anyone for help because we don't do that."

"It's not about asking for help," Gia says as she walks to the edge of the dense forest. She pushes through the last of the plants. "If we asked, they wouldn't let me go."

"Why not?" I ask, following her out of the plants.

"Something about my clothes not being right," says Gia. She steps slowly from the mess of plants and into the open space where we can see the connecting tunnel. "I'm supposed to be helping with the hisbon anyway. They would tell me to stay back and prepare food." She halts without walking too far into the open space.

"Prepare food?" I ask. "How?"

Gia shrugs and hands me the tablet.

She takes slow steps backward.

Food in the Trellis was mostly prepared by machines. Something outside would catch sea animals and they would go through a streamlined process that turned sea animals and seaweed into green spheres that made up our sustenance packets. But here in the Trovant, they grow plants. They have animals. Do they kill things with their own hands?

"What are you doing?" Jarret turns and questions Gia's odd behavior.

With her back against the wall of plants, Gia lifts her hands above her head, reaches behind, and yanks someone from the bushes. She flips the person over her head and he crashes to the ground in front of her.

Groaning and gripping his ribs, Desman lies on the dirty ground in the center of everyone else.

"Gia," Desman winces and rolls to his side. "Why did you do that?" Dirt is streaked over the side of his face. The dirt gets into a gash that was already on his forehead.

"Why were you sneaking up on us?" Gia crosses her arms.

"I wasn't." Desman coughs and gets to his knees. "I heard you guys as you were climbing down the wall. I was just trying to catch up with you."

Gia uncrosses her arms and walks to Desman. "Sorry," she mumbles. She puts herself under his arm and helps him get to his feet. "Can you walk?" She tries to guide him toward the red-lit tunnel.

"I'm fine." Desman pulls his arm from around Gia. "I was just winded." Slightly stumbling, he walks to the tunnel.

The sounds of dripping replace buzzing insects and animal calls. The tunnel glows red from the cracks in the rocky walls.

"What exactly is going on with Lyra?" Desman asks.

Gia starts to explain as we follow red streaks through the dripping tunnel.

The journey through the tunnel seems shorter this time. Soon, we arrive at the entrance of the Alaster ship. Liquids are pooled on the floor near the open threshold.

Desman walks toward the entrance, then looks down as his cloak soaks up liquid from the floor.

"What the?" he lifts his cloak and reveals his shoes that are also made of fabric. They are soaked. "What's going on?"

"Interesting," I say.

"Why?" Desman asks. "What is this?"

Gia lifts her cloak and leaps to the Alaster ship to avoid the pooled liquid.

"I guess," I lift up my cloak and try to tiptoe around the liquid. "This fabric doesn't keep anything out."

"She's not in there," Jarret raises his voice toward Gia as she enters the submersible.

"This will go away, right?" Desman asks as he steps into the metal submersible and his shoes make a squishing noise. "Like how our suits clean things up— this fabric will get rid of the water somehow, right?"

"I don't think so," I look at the bottom of his clothes that are soaked from the tunnel outside.

"That looks like blood." Gia points to a splotch that creeps up Desman's clothing.

"It's not blood!" Desman says.

"It looks like it," Gia says.

"Will I get a disease or something?" Desman starts untying the cords on his waist that are supposed to keep the cloak on.

"Lyra isn't in here," Jarret interjects.

"How do you know?" Gia asks.

Desman pulls off his cloak.

"I told you," Jarret says, "she stormed out. She was upset about her parents; she probably went to look for them."

Desman takes off each of his fabric shoes.

"I thought I heard something in here," says Gia. "It's worth checking. She could have come back here."

Desman only wears the bottoms which are supposed to go under the cloaks. With no shirt on, Desman's bare skin shows defined muscles across his chest, shoulders, and arms. His chest and side are painted very faintly with bruises.

There's silence.

None of us have seen much bare skin on another person except for faces and hands.

"What?" Desman scowls.

"Uhh," I rub my head and look away.

Gia's mouth is slightly open as she stares.

I slap her arm to break her trance... she's being weird.

She looks down, then grabs the tablet from my hand. She starts pushing things on the screen.

I lean over and see what she's doing.

She's just opening random tabs.

There's a faint thud from somewhere above. We all look up, trying to see where the noise came from.

"No one should be in here," says Jarret.

"I told you I heard something," says Gia.

"Leal?" A quiet voice calls my name.

I lean toward the platforms to see who's calling.

"Lyra!" Jarret yells up and then bolts for the ladders. He scales a ladder and makes his way toward her. "We were all so worried about you. Where did you go? Are you okay?"

"I'm coming down," Lyra says.

The metal creaks and more people filter onto the platform.

"Who's that?" Jarret asks.

"We'll meet you at the bottom," Lyra says.

After Jarret rejoins our group on the submersible floor, Lyra and four other figures come down the ladders. The figures are large— obviously Trovantians. They are young women who wear dark cloaks that glimmer slightly. Lyra has a cloak too. The fabric seems almost like the doors in the Trellis— some sort of biological material made of plant genes and iron sulfide. Are their cloaks like our microbial suits? Or possibly they're made from the same materials as the doors in the Trellis? No matter what, they don't look the same as the soaked fabric that lies at Desman's feet.

"What happened to you?" Lyra looks at Desman.

Desman is not dressed because Gia had said there was blood on his cloak. He has dirt on his face from when Gia flipped him on the ground. He has a gash from when she slammed his head into Gaines Cyro's control panel. His bruises are from when Garridon beat him down in his workstation... I guess the Hamiltonis are what happened to Desman.

Gia fidgets a bit, but doesn't say anything.

"The important question," says Desman, "is—what happened to *you*?"

"And who are they?" Jarret motions to the young women in cloaks.

"They're…" Lyra looks back at them. "Friends."

"Trovantians?" I ask.

"Yes," says one of the cloaked women, "and we are leaving."

"You could come—" Lyra says.

"These people have been missing you," interrupts the young woman. "You have somewhere to be. This cannot leave the caverns." She points to Lyra's cloak.

With her face to the floor, Lyra removes her outer layer and gives it to the person. Wearing a red microbial suit, Lyra sticks out almost as much as Desman.

The young women brush past us toward the exit.

"Do not worry," one of them smiles and stays back by Lyra. "There will be a hisbon. We will see you soon." She rushes to the others and they exit the ship, turning left in the tunnel.

*Caverns*— I wonder what that means. Where do these tunnels go?


"You," Imeel shouts as we exit the red-lit tunnel. "You are not supposed to be here." He stands where the line of plants ends.

Others appear from the jungle behind him.

"And you," Imeel points at Lyra. "You should not be wearing that."

"She's the one who was missing." Desman emerges from the tunnel. "She just arrived."

"*You...*" Imeel sounds confused as he looks Desman up and down. "...also should not be wearing that."

Women appear from the foliage, some carrying woven baskets or large clay jars. Minji is in the group.

My stomach feels tight. But I'm also excited. I try not to stare at her. All I can manage to do is wave.

Minji smiles and waves back.

The brown fabric covers her small figure and, somehow, she makes the draped clothing look beautiful. Her pale hands gently grip a woven basket and I can't help but remember the touch of her delicate hand on mine. The woven basket reminds me of the lines of code that she weaved in the Trellis system; her fingers swiftly tapping the control panel as she made the security cameras glitch. Her mind could hold such intricate system designs and her imagination could create complex worlds with information. She's intelligent. She's beautiful. She's—

"Leal," Gia shakes my shoulder.

I shake my head and look at Gia.

"Did you hear any of that?" Gia asks.

Hear any of what? I just keep looking at her.

People scatter in different directions.

Minji walks away with the group of women who hold baskets and jars.

"Apparently not," says Gia. "We're going with them." She spins me around to face a group of people walking toward an opening in the distance.

"There's another tunnel?" I ask.

"And water," she follows the group.

How many tunnels are there?

"What are we doing in there?" I ask.

"You're fishing," says Gia. "I'm learning how to clean robes, apparently."

"Fishing?" I imagine myself in front of a screen trying to catch things outside with a remote-controlled machine. Wouldn't they have automatic machines to do that? Why would humans need to operate the machines?

"Come on," Gia motions for me to follow.

I speed toward her and we catch up with the others.

Arriving at the rocky opening, there's a large space with clear pools dotted across the floor. People's conversations echo in the giant space and their voices are carried by the clear water.

Wait a minute—

I halt at the entrance.

Gia turns to look at me. "What?"

"Are we fishing..." I point at the clear blue pools, "...in those?"

"I don't know Lea," she says. "We're just following the others for now." She grabs my forearm and pulls me to a group of people that cluster near Imeel.

Imeel gives commands in his own language. Some people around the group nod. Women holding jars walk away and kneel by a pool, dipping their jars in and scooping out water.

Imeel holds Desman's soaking cloak. "You," he hands it to Gia. "Follow Dayana and she will show you what to do."

Gia grips the fabric, her jaw clenching as she follows Dayana to one of the pools.

"The rest of you," says Imeel, "we will learn how to capture fish."

I raise my hand.

"Uhhh," Imeel stares at me. "Yes?"

"Can I go with Gia?" I ask.

"No." Imeel walks to the water's edge.

The others follow him.

"Come on," Desman puts his hand on my shoulder and guides me toward Imeel.

"Wait," I look around. "Where's Jarret?"

"He went to help Lyra get to her parents," says Desman. He rubs his hand on the top of my head and laughs. "Where exactly have *you* been?"

I try not to frown. I haven't ever seen Desman heckle. I don't like it. I push him away. I don't like being that close to his half-naked body either.

"Ah!" I jump backward, startled at the sight of other men pulling off their robes.

"You too," Imeel motions toward me. "You will need to undress to get in the water."

"Uh-uh," I squeeze my robes close to my body and shake my head.

"Yes, yes," Imeel steps toward me and starts untying the cords around my waist. "You also must help."

Desman squeezes his hand over his mouth and tries to hide a smile.

"It's not funny," I say. The frigid air hits my bare skin as Imeel pulls off my robe.

"I know," Desman puts both hands over his face. "I'm so sorry. It's not funny." He tries to hold in a laugh.

I hunch over, crossing my arms and trying to cover as much of myself as possible from the cold and from the other people.

Men— large, muscular men— tower over the water's edge and look into the blue pool. With a splash, they dive into the water.

"Come see," Imeel guides Desman and me nearer to the water.

Men swim far below where wooden cages are fixed on rocks or in crevices.

"We set the traps earlier," says Imeel. "Now we gather them. Once you watch, you can help set them again."

"Oh, no," I shake my head and step away from the water. "I can't do that."

"Why not?" Imeel asks.

"I don't think we can swim," Desman answers.

I had a million reasons why I wouldn't do that— but that at least was an excuse that Imeel might accept.

"Cannot swim?" Imeel rubs his chin. "Cannot climb either. You alnaasitos are more helpless than I thought. Can you catch birds, at least?"

My eyes widen. I picture myself trying to get a giant bird from a wooden trap. I shake my head vigorously.

"What about insects?" he asks.

I shake my head again.

"Hmmm," Imeel wipes his forehead. "We have some work to do."

There's splashing as a man breaks through the water's surface. One by one, men emerge from the deep, pulling up traps full of swimming creatures.

The traps aren't just full of fish. Some of the swimming-things are long and straight. Some are wiggly. One is a shell with tentacles coming out. I try to imagine preparing that for food... gross.

Water pours over rock as men slam traps to the ground. Creatures flop around in the traps as water flows out.

I squat to get a better look at some of the creatures.

"Watch out!" Imeel pulls me up by my shoulders and yanks me away from the fish.

A snarling animal emerges from behind a rock. It looks like a mix between an earth-fox and an earth-cat. Its coloring is marbled between light colors and the color of the rock. The animal almost matches the lightness underwater, but could also blend in with the material of the cave. Its eyes are light and its tail is fluffy and soft. It would be cute if it weren't hunched over, growling and showing its sharp teeth at me.

"It is a velsyren," says Imeel. "They have a terrible bite."

"It's beautiful," says Desman.

"It is a pest," says Imeel.

The men start throwing rocks at it.

A rock hits the velsyren's face. It squeezes its eyes shut and rubs its nose with its paw, then scampers away.

"It looked scared," says Desman.

"Good," says Imeel. "Hopefully it will not come back."

\*\*\*

"It looks nice," Gia smiles at me as I come from behind the rock. She stands in an open pocket in a tunnel wall. It's like a private room except that it's connected to the public tunnel.

"It feels silly," I lift my arm that has a draping, orange sleeve that shimmers. It's the festive gown that the Trovantians gave me to wear to the hisbon. I look up at Gia, who had also changed into the festive clothes. "Oh, wow, I like yours."

Gia wears a blue cloak over a silky-white gown. Silver necklaces hang delicately on her neck and her hair is pinned with a blue gemstone.

"How did you get a blue cloak?" I ask.

"They just gave it to me," she shrugs.

"I want a blue one," I mumble.

"Leal?" I hear Minji's voice from somewhere behind me.

Staring ahead at Gia, I freeze. I thought about Minji all day, but I still get nervous every time I hear her voice.

"Behind you," Gia points as if to indicate where I should actually be looking.

I turn to face Minji, who is stopped in the doorway. Her black hair flows over a silvery cloak that covers her shimmering, white gown. A clear stone sits on the end of a necklace that adorns her porcelain skin. The stone flashes with iridescent colors like magic. As she steps toward me, the gown and cloak reflect light like she's a silvery creature from another realm.

"You asked if we could meet before the hisbon?" Minji asks.

"I'm going to go," Gia scoots past me.

My eyes follow her. Gia is always so brave. I wish she could do what I was planning to do instead of me having to do it.

"I—" I stutter when Gia exits the room. "I like your necklace."

"Thank you," says Minji. "It's a moonstone." She plays with the gem on her necklace.

That's what Minji feels like— the footage I've seen of the moon. She's like a transcendent force of nature that's dazzling enough to illuminate darkness and strong enough to control tides.

"What did you want to talk about?" she asks.

I swallow. I've practiced this a million times in my head. I just need to say it out loud.

"Will you go to the hisbon with me?" I blurt.

"I think we're all going," says Minji. "So I was already going to go with you."

"No," I try to explain myself. "It's what I've read people did on Earth's surface. Will you go to the hisbon with me— like a *date*?"

Minji smiles. "I want to show you something."

"Does that mean 'yes?'"

"It means I want to show you something," she grabs my hand and pulls me from the small room.


My heart is pounding as Minji guides me to a spacious room. Smaller pools span across the floor and illuminate the space with colors. Light pink and lavender rays beam from the water and dance across the ceiling. Blue hues radiate across rocks and guide us to the water's edge. Drips echo in the cold space. And so do— *footsteps*?

I pause for a moment, listening. I thought I heard someone else, but I don't see anyone. Reflecting in the pool is Minji's graceful hand holding mine. Colors shift over her silvery gown. My orange outfit is disgraceful next to her elegance.

"Earlier, we were preparing food at this water source," says Minji. "These are some of the few pools with fresh water to drink. And Dayana says it's the only place in the entire Trovant where all these colors come together. The entire time we were here, I couldn't stop thinking that I wished you were the one with me to experience it." She looks up at me. It feels like her eyes are deep pools and I can't swim.

"Can I—" I stop for a moment and think if this is actually okay. "Can I kiss you?"

Putting her hand on the orange fold on my chest, she pulls me in and puts her lips on mine.

Beams of color dance across my mind. It wouldn't matter if I never saw the actual moon because I have something more beautiful and transcendent in my arms.

# Chapter 7: Gia— The Hisbon

I can't help but chuckle as I leave Leal behind to speak with Minji. He's been distracted and nervous all day — an uprising could start in front of his face and he wouldn't notice.

This tunnel in the Trovant seems familiar. It glows yellow as people walk by one another. It feels like a transition time in the Trellis. I shouldn't miss it, but part of me wants the familiarity of knowing that I'll go to sleep on my own platform and wake up to go to my own workspace where it will just be Leal and me. We could look at footage of Earth's surface and dream about not being in the Trellis... here I am, outside of the Trellis; missing it. I miss knowing how to do things. I miss being a Facilitator. And I miss my kitten T-shirt.

"You alright?" Desman, about to pass me in the tunnel, steps in front of me so we both stop.

"I'm fine," I try to move past him.

There's a chattering noise from his brown cloak. He isn't wearing the festive clothing, but holds part of his robes in his arms.

"What do you have in there?" I lean to see what he's holding.

"Nothing," he takes a step back.

I move closer and put my hand out to move the fabric.

He grabs my hand to stop me.

"Just," he holds my hand, "come with me."

He pulls me down a connecting tunnel, then another.

"Where are those stupid tiny rooms?" he asks. "How does anyone know how to get anywhere?"

"There," I point to an opening. At the top of the opening is a strange symbol. I don't know what the symbol means, but it seems like all the small rooms have a label that looks like that one.

Desman and I walk to the opening. It's an empty room.

"You can't tell anyone," he says once we're inside.

"Tell anyone what?"

He pulls back the folds of his robes. Fluffy ears peek from his cloak.

"What?" I move the rest of the fabric. "What is that?"

A creature with big, pale eyes looks back at me and tilts its head.

"I named her Arian," says Desman.

"Her?"

"Someone told me that's the word for silver."

"But she's not silver."

"She's a mix," says Desman. "If you put all her colors together, she'd be kind of silvery." He holds her up to me. "I call her Ari for short."

"Like Ara?" I ask.

"What?" Desman lowers the animal, cradling it in his arms and petting it. "No."

"Why do you have *Ari*?" I ask.

"I don't know," Desman says, looking at the animal in his arms. "People were throwing rocks at her. And they were saying she was dangerous, but she was just trying to get food."

"This just seems..."

"Seems what?"

"Unlike you," I say.

"You don't really know me, Gia," Desman says. "I don't even know me, not outside the Trellis. We've had to fight to survive, but this is like a different place; a new life. All I know is that I saw her and I liked her. She's tough and takes care of herself. She's beautiful and secretly has a sensitive spot... she's kind of like..."

"Like Ara?" I ask again.

"You," he says.

Our eyes meet

I don't really know what to say. He just said I don't know him and then described who he thinks I am. But his words touched something in me that feels true and real. Am I annoyed or touched? I don't like feeling multiple things at once.

"Will you help me?" He asks.

"Help you what?"

"Take care of her in secret," he says. "I don't think the Trovantians will be happy I have her."

"Why not put her back where you found her?"

"She was hungry," says Desman, "and all alone." Ari rubs her face on his chest and closes her eyes. "I told you— I like her. I don't know who I am outside the Trellis, but I know I want to keep Ari safe."

"Fine," I sigh. "I'll help you."

The carved doors are massive. People stream from different tunnels and crowd in front of the closed doors that tower above. The huge doors are made of different colored stones cut and placed into intricate patterns. Some of the stones are marbled with reds and oranges while others are blues and greens. Each neatly carved piece of stone is lined with gold. Some of them have shimmery flecks that catch the light and glisten. The longer I look at the door, the more small details I notice. How long did this take to carve and build?

"Do you think she will be okay?" Desman, now wearing black and gold festive robes, grabs my hand and whispers in my ear.

"She'll be fine." I pull slowly from his loose grip. "I gave her the fish and she's sleeping in my bunk. None of the Trovantians seem to go in my sleeping quarters."

The intricately carved doors crack open. They move slowly. It must take a great deal of force to get such massive stone doors to move.

Golden light shines through the opening. The people around me get closer and the crowd moves through the open doorway.

As I walk forward, Desman grabs my hand again, maybe trying not to lose me in the crowd. It reminds me of the time we rushed through the Cultivator's quarters. It was crowded and I sank to my knees in panic. He picked me up. It's such a different atmosphere now— both of us draped with new colors, walking into a golden-lit space.

Rising at least fifty feet, the walls in the room gleam with different colors. Instead of being multiple kinds of stone in a pattern together, these walls are made of one metallic material. The walls have structured patterns that look like carved images I've seen of ancient Aztec architecture. But the walls are golden with other colors shifting as we move. A section looks blue from one angle but shifts to silver as we walk closer. One part looks purple, but changes between gold and pink depending on where we stand.

Desman releases my hand as the crowd thins.

Some Trovantians wear matching grey clothing and stand upright near the wall. Noticing Desman and me in the crowd of much taller people, the Trovantians motion for us to move forward. They guide us to a place in the room where the metallic material forms into a cube that is as tall as my waist. There are carved seats around the cube and the Trovantians motion for us to sit. This must be an assigned table. Cubic tables like this one are scattered across the giant space. At the front of the room, there's a massive staircase. Also shining with gold and shifting colors.

"Here." There's a voice behind and I feel something pushed into my palm.

I look down and see a tablet in my hand.

"Some of the comms should be up now," my dad stands next to me. "Keep the tablet on you at all times. Put it in your pocket and keep it safe."

I look around at my robes. "I don't have a pocket."

"Yeah, you do," he says. "It's right—" he looks at my robes. Then takes a fold of the fabric and moves it around. "Why don't you have pockets?"

"I don't know," I shrug. "Do you both have pockets?"

Desman slips his hands into his black and gold gown and nods. He has pockets. I look at my dad's off-white and gold clothes. He also has pockets.

Minji walks toward our table with her silver clothing — no sign of pockets. Leal is just behind. I lean to see past Minji.

"What are you looking at?" Leal asks when he gets to the table.

"Do you have pockets?" I ask.

He looks down, feeling around his robes. "Oh, cool — I guess I do."

"It doesn't matter," my dad says. "Keep it with you. Keep it hidden."

Beneath my blue robes, my inner layer is wrapped with fabric around my waist. I shove the tablet between the wrapped layer and my gown, then cover it all with my robe… there's so much fabric.

"Do the comms work everywhere?" I ask. "I thought it was blocked by the rock walls."

"Communication is a priority," my dad says. "I set up a few beacons throughout this place that are connected to one another. They work throughout the jungle and most open spaces. But you have to be careful in the tunnels because the connection is inconsistent. We'll have to work on that in the future."

"Am I waiting for something specific?" I ask.

"What do you mean?" asks my dad.

"I'm supposed to keep this on me at all times," I say. "Should I be preparing for something?"

"Just keep it on you," says my dad. He walks away from the table and into the crowd.

"I told you," says Leal, "he's doing super-secret robot things." He sits at the cubic table.

"He's not a robot," I say as I take a seat. The tablet pushes against my ribs as if to remind me that I was injured from the siphon in the Alaster ship. I try to sit up straighter so the device isn't digging into my side.

Minji and Desman also sit down.

"Gaines Cyro was a robot," Leal says. "We never knew."

"Cyro was a screen," I say. "...or something like that."

"Alaster is a robot," says Leal.

"Is he?" I ask. "He also is something on a screen. We can't really tell what he is."

"Could be the same person as Cyro," says Desman.

"It doesn't seem like it," Minji says. "Why would he fight himself to flood the Trellis and give us enough time to escape?"

"I don't know," says Desman. "We can't really know anything."

"We can," says Leal. "The journal has some information about Alaster. And it seems to be right so far about there being multiple facilities."

"The point is," I say, "Alaster and Cyro were both on screens; my dad is not. He's not a robot."

"Still could be," Leal shrugs. "Or a cyborg."

I roll my eyes.

"By the way," Leal puts his hands on the table. "Don't ingest any of this. It seems like this entire place is made of bismuth crystal."

"What's bismuth?" I ask.

"What do you mean ingest?" Desman asks.

"Bismuth is an element," says Leal. "When it's melted down and then solidified, an air pocket is created and metallic designs grow inside— just like this. This whole room might be a pocket inside of bismuth that was melted down at one point. And it's toxic to humans if it's ingested. Could cause lethargy, delirium, seizures—"

"How could we ingest some of this?" Desman interrupts.

"I don't know," says Leal. "Just don't lick anything."

Desman furrows his eyebrows. "I wasn't planning on it."

Leal leans toward me. "If your dad accidentally ingests some bismuth, we can keep an eye on him. If he shows any toxicity symptoms, we can tell if he's human or a robot."

"Leal," I say, "I don't think my dad is going to accidentally lick a table."

"Have you ever seen him ingest *anything*?" Leal asks.

"He's not a robot," I say.

"Okay." Leal sits back slightly. "But I've never seen him eat anything, or sleep, or—"

"Leal!" I try and get him to stop.

"I'm just saying."

"Well, quit saying."

Something moves in my peripheral vision. I lean to the side and someone sets a plate in front of me.

"What is this?" Desman looks at the colorful food on the plate in front of him.

Our thin plates are iridescent with swirling colors and trimmed with gold.

"Plants," Minji picks up a small orange sphere that has been cut in half. "Or... fruit, I mean. My group picked all this earlier and cut it up for tonight. I've tried some of it already, it's really good." She puts the orange fruit in her mouth.

I pick up a small red fruit. It might be some sort of berry, but nothing like what I've seen in pictures. I put it in my mouth. The textures are familiar— it pops in my mouth and then is squishy. But I've never had anything like the flavors. I don't know if I like it.

"That's delicious!" Leal shoves the different kinds of fruit in his mouth and chews them all. "What a good sustenance time." He leans back and rubs his stomach.

"I think there's more," says Minji. "At least, we collected a lot more and they said it was for the hisbon."

"They said the fish was for the hisbon, too," says Desman.

Leal picks up his plate. "What do you think we're supposed to do when we're done?"

Minji shrugs while holding a berry in her thin fingers.

"No one else is getting up." Desman looks at the Trovantians to see what they are doing. "Put your plate down, Leal. No one else is doing that."

The air is warm and filled with chattering voices that bounce around the golden tables. Like the colors that dance across the geometric walls, the conversations are free to move and shift without fear of surveillance. I relax in my seat.

At the top of the staircase, people have instruments. They play a melody that fills the background of the large room while people's conversations fill the foreground.

Arcturo and Vega sit at a table with Pictor and Jarret. Pictor looks pale, but he's sitting up. He must be starting to feel better. He even takes bites of the fruit. Lyra is hunched at a longer table with a few other young women. I recognize some of them— it looks like the people who were with her in the Alaster ship. Who are they? Why is Lyra with them instead of her family? Lyra looks down at the food but doesn't eat anything. She looks sad.

The music stops playing and someone speaks in the Trovantian language. Rasul Midian stands at the top of the decadent staircase and his voice carries throughout the room. People quiet down.

"Friends, Family, and guests," Imeel stands next to Rasul and translates. "Welcome to our hisbon!"

People clap at the end of Rasul's next sentence.

Imeel translates: "This week, we welcome the newest part of our family— the little people!"

They start a pattern of Rasul speaking and Imeel translating.

"Since the beginning, we have been commanded to help those smaller than us; now we have a divine opportunity. The Source— just as it has made our home— has guided these little people to us. We will now share the resources that have been given to us. The men and women will join us to do the work of the Source until the end."

"What's the source?" I whisper.

"What's the end?" whispers Desman.

Leal shrugs.

Minji just looks forward at the speakers.

"From now until the end," says Imeel, "we will be one people. Welcome to our new family."

In unison, the Trovantians say a cheer and then clap.

Looking at one another, we also clap. But I don't fully understand what we're clapping for.

The musicians again take their instruments and start playing.

People in grey clothes move around the room. Some come by our table and take our plates, then put new plates in front of us. There seem to be cooked foods — maybe meat and vegetables. I sniff the food. "I think this is the fish." I pick up a golden utensil that someone wearing grey had set beside my plate. I look around at the Trovantians. They stab their food with the utensils in order to put the food in their mouths. I try stabbing the meat. But it breaks into pieces and falls back onto the plate, making small clanking noises. I use my finger to shove food on the utensil.

"Do you think we'll be here forever?" Leal asks.

"Where else could we go?" Desman asks.

"The surface," Minji answers. "Alaster said that's where we're going."

"Alaster." Desman rolls his eyes and takes a bite of the meat.

I also chew the meat after taking a bite. It's tough. I keep chewing.

"He's brought us this far," says Minji.

"This far?" Desman puts his utensil down. "We lost people we love, our facility is destroyed, and we're some place we've never been."

"It's better than all of us being dead," said Minji. "Which is where we were headed under Cyro's leadership. Now we're supposed to go to the surface. That's our real home."

"We don't have a home," says Desman. "And what happened to you recently? You used to be shy."

"You were always mean," says Minji.

"I'm not—" Desman takes a deep breath. "I'm not trying to be mean. I'm just trying to accept reality."

"Guys," Leal wrings his hands, "don't fight."

"We're not fighting," says Desman, "we're just—" He stops as someone reaches in front of him and sets something down. It's an iridescent shell with gold around the rim. The person pours liquid into the opening of the shell. It seems like this is a cup.

"Lah-ah-kuh," Minji says to a person who puts a shell-cup in front of her.

"What does that mean?" Leal asks.

"It means 'thank you,'" says Minji.

"You're learning Trovantian?" I ask. Someone also puts a shell in front of me and pours a drink.

"Yeah," says Minji, "it's not that hard. You just have to listen to people talking and you can start understanding individual words."

"Wow, cool," Leal says.

"Very cool," Desman says.

I feel like I should also say something. But I also don't have anything else to say except "cool."

Our conversation dies down. In the Trellis, we spoke if we had business to address. We chatted some in the Sanctuary but it was mostly about surviving or what to do next. In the workstation, Leal and I would stare at our screens if we didn't have anything else to say.

Music plays in the background and people still chatter across the room.

"Pictor looks better," I say.

"Yeah, he does," says Desman.

"I'm so relieved," says Minji.

Leal nods and bites off a piece of meat.

We quiet down again.

"So," says Minji, "what did you guys do today after work for the hisbon?"

I think of Ari sleeping in my bunk. They might find out eventually, but it's probably best to keep it as quiet as possible that we're hiding a velsyren.

"Nothing," Desman answers. "What did you guys do?"

"Nothing," says Minji.

Leal and I exchange glances. He rubs his hands together. He's definitely hiding something. He can probably tell I'm hiding something.

The Trellis was a place where we had to keep everything secret from the world, but Leal and I shared everything. Now, we are free to say whatever we want, but Leal and I are keeping things from each other.

We stand in an open space away from the tables. The band relocated to the bottom of the staircase to be on the same level as everyone else. Their music is even more clear.

"Come here, son." Mabel Fitzgerald takes Leal's hand and pulls him into the center of the crowd that starts to form a circle.

Others grab the hand of someone else and begin to sway with their partners to the rhythm of the music.

"May I?" Eddi Fitzgerald lowers his hand to me.

"You may," I accept his hand. "But I don't really know what I'm doing."

"Of course you do," Eddi says as we start to move side to side. "Just sway to the rhythm of the music."

Tall Trovantians move around us. I try to dance, but also try not to run into anyone or get stepped on. They seem to have rehearsed moves. Or does everyone just know how to improvise that well?

The music has a different beat than what Leal used to play in our workstation. It's not like jazz; it has a different pitch than what I'm used to hearing. The musicians play stringed instruments and wind instruments of different sizes and materials, but none of them are what I've seen from footage of Earth's surface. Some instruments seem to be made of wood, while others are made of shells or carved stones.

Still dancing, Eddi guides me toward Leal and Mabel.

"May I have my wife, sir?" Eddi asks Leal.

"Certainly," Leal gives a tiny bow to Eddi. Then Leal walks to the side of the dancing circle.

Desman steps in and grabs my hand.

"You know how to dance?" I ask.

"Of course," Desman holds me close and begins to sway. "It was part of the training for Promoters. We had to know Earth's cultural customs."

Leal comes back into the circle of dancers, now with Minji in his arms.

The room is adorned with bismuth chandeliers that cast a soft glow on the dance floor as we move in tandem with the musician's chords.

"I didn't expect your ribcage to feel so metallic," Desman says.

The tablet beneath my clothes presses between us.

"Well," I chuckle, "if Leal is right about my dad, I am half robot."

"I'm dancing with a robot," says Desman. "That's pretty cool."

"Half robot," I correct.

He smiles, looking down at me.

Maybe Desman is different here. He seems less rigid. The warm colors in the room reflect off his brown eyes. I feel safe, like the time Mabel hugged me as I clenched a blanket. It feels like I've been fighting my whole life, but I finally have a place to rest.

I put my head on his chest and we move back and forth. I've only been this close to him when we've been fighting. I've hardly noticed that he has a particular smell — subtle, but sweet.

Maybe Desman is less rigid here. Maybe I am too.

Soon, a deep, comforting voice joins the musicians. I look to the side and see Mabel Fitzgerald singing beside the band:

"Hear my heartbeat in the Summer breeze,

as it carries through the Southern trees.

Far away or near to me,

souls entwined are meant to be."

Mabel's voice draws each word through the room like an instrument playing a long chord. Eddi stands next to Mabel. His warm voice continues the next verse:

"Resounding footsteps in the empty room,

the home we share is still the shade of you.

Us apart— no it isn't true.

We're just a person who was once in two."

Mabel and Eddi hold hands and sing the next verse together:

"Our journey has us going far and wide,

but that doesn't mean you're not still by my side.

I think of you each moment day and night.

And I smile as I hold your hand so tight."

I don't actually remember the last time I slept. But, as I rest my cheek on Desman's chest, it feels like the most peaceful dream I've ever had.

# Chapter 8: Gia — The Source

Green cracks faintly glow in the room where I'm crammed in the middle bunk that's carved from the rock. The next bunk is inches above my face. Other women in the bunks lie still, sleeping.

The rest of the hisbon comprised of dancing that got progressively more energetic, followed by more food and drink. But I couldn't eat anymore. Desman and I snuck out early so he could take Ari to wherever he sleeps.

Exhausted, I rolled into my bunk to get some sleep. The others slowly crept in throughout the night, except Vega and Lyra. They've moved to some family-living arrangement with Pictor and Arcturo.

I turn to my side. I'm so tired, but I can't sleep. I can't stop thinking about the hisbon; about the dance. Are things changing between Desman and me? Not that long ago, he lost someone he loved and I lost a friend. How could we move forward and act like it didn't happen?

I roll over again and feel the tablet in the folds of my clothes. I'm so tired, I had forgotten how much it was digging into my side. The pressure releases as I pull the tablet out and rub my side.

I want to think about something else. I still have questions like— what *end* was Rasul talking about? What is the other facility and what about us going to the surface? Normally, Leal would be reading things on the tablet and he could report what he finds to me. But he's far away, sleeping on the edge of a cliff. And I'm sleeping inside a rock. The distance between us isn't just metaphorical.

I squint as the light from the screen hits my eyes. I listen, but no one stirs. It seems like everyone is fully asleep. On the tablet, I open a digital version of the journal from Symphony Hamiltoni— the lead scientist on the Trellis project back when Earth's surface was habitable. I don't know exactly where to start reading. I've heard some of the stories, but the journal had always seemed like a random jumble of information.

I start going through the journal entries— things about different experiments that I don't care about. The Trellis had the same shape as a mechanism on Earth's surface, where it got its name. Another facility was modified from the genetics of *nereocystis*— some plant. The Trovant was inspired by growing rocks... that's what I want to know about. I quit skimming and read more intentionally:

*After experimentation (reference experiments 247a-g) at hydrothermal vent fields near the Juan De Fuca Ridge...*

This is the kind of stuff Leal would read and then summarize for me. I skim again and read something about controlling volcanic activity and making a facility that would keep expanding with a growing population. But the atmospheric conditions would be unstable due to hydrothermal activity... with increasing surface area and water pressure, the facility would eventually collapse.

Is that the "end" that Rasul and Imeel were talking about?

Something about all of this doesn't make complete sense to me. I want Leal to read it and explain it... or Lyra; she is good at this kind of thing.

It's not like I'm going to leave my bunk and wake her up, but I am curious about where the Delphino family is being housed. Now seems like a good opportunity to check how well my dad's comms solution works.

I pull up the information that shows tablets belonging to Vega, Arcturo, and Lyra. The signal is weak, but I can see where they are. It's weird, Vega and Arcturo's tablets are next to each other, but Lyra's is somewhere else. Maybe she left her tablet somewhere.

I pull up a map view to see a more specified location.

*What?*

I jolt up to see the screen better, but I bang my head on the rock above me.

"Ow," I whisper and rub my head. I forgot I was in a shelf-like bunk.

Still rubbing my head, I put the tablet close to my face. Lyra's tablet is moving. It's going through the jungle. Did someone steal Lyra's tablet? Or is Lyra leaving? Is she being taken somewhere?

I roll to my side and lower my feet to the floor. I can't sleep anyway, so I might as well make sure she's okay.

The red light from the previous tunnel has faded completely. There are just a few blue crevices that provide barely enough light to see. I followed Lyra's tablet through the red-lit tunnel, past the Alaster ship, and into a labyrinth of a tunnel system. I mapped my journey on the tablet, so I should be able to find my way back… as long as my tablet doesn't run out of charge.

The tunnel system gets narrower and, in some spots, I have to climb over rocks or squeeze through tight spaces to keep going. Maybe I should turn around. But Lyra's tablet has stopped just ahead. It's not far away.

I listen carefully as I get closer to the place where her tablet is. Seeing an opening ahead, I sneak along the edge of the tunnel, slinking behind rocks to see the open space without being revealed. Lyra might be held against her will.

Poking my head up to view past the rocks, I see Lyra. She's sitting on a rock just above a huge pool of water. No one else is around. I nearly stand and see what's going on, but she makes a noise. She's sniffling. Is she crying? Should I go try and comfort her or does she want to be by herself?

She starts humming. Then, I notice that the room seems to be playing music with her. Deep, slow sounds reverberate from the walls and join Lyra's humming. Lyra starts to sing something. She's quiet at first, so I can't hear her words. Her voice is clear, high-pitched, and delicate. I imagine her voice sounds like a star singing in the night. I start hearing the lyrics she sings:

"I felt;
I felt your touch on my arm;
your lips kiss my nose to keep it warm.

I saw;
I saw your silhouette holding mine
in the reflection of a pool that shows our body lines.

But I woke;
I woke to reality
where you were holding her instead of me.
My hands trembling as I reach for you,
shame screaming that I know I knew
that you were never mine.

Now I see your body lines.

I see the water,
it flows over stones that erode away.
And I feel my chest,
it's sore from late dreams as I watch them fade."

Someone strong grips my shoulders, yanking me from behind the rock and slamming me to the ground.

"Seem-ie harun batten-wei!" A young woman in a cloak points a pole lit with fire.

From the ground, I twist to avoid the fire-end and kick the middle of the pole away. I swing my body to grab the person's feet and trip her over the momentum of her own body. She rolls to the ground as I jump to my feet, but she's quick. She kicks at my legs before I'm fully up. She swooshes with the pole of fire and holds it over my face.

"Seem-ie harun batten-wei!" The young woman towers above me with the fire-pole.

I'm about to kick the pole away and I hear a familiar voice.

"Stop!" Lyra's voice carries through the space. "That's my friend."


"So you're secret warriors?" I sit in front of a low-burning fire.

Lyra and the others are around the circle. Two of them are sleeping while Lyra and the other two explain to me what's going on.

"That is one way to put it," says the one who had attacked me with a pole. She told me her name was Rhen.

The other one who is awake is Ferris. I don't remember the names of the other two.

"And you stay here all day?" I ask.

"Mostly at night," Rhen answers. "We have duties in the Trovant. No one pays attention to where we go after that."

"What are your duties?" I ask.

"The past few months," says Rhen. "I have been harvesting food. Ferris processes wheat. Vana has been teaching children and Mica is part of a team of makers— they collect and process plants to turn them into things like baskets and fabric."

"None of you are in security or anything?" I ask.

Ferris scoffs. "Security?" She shakes her head.

"Well, yeah," I say. "If you have combat skills, wouldn't you be useful doing something along those lines?"

"It does not work like that," says Rhen.

"Oh," I say, "do you take a test or something to get your jobs?"

"No," Rhen sounds confused. "Mica's mother was a maker so Mica is a maker. Ferris's whole family has worked in agriculture so that is what she does. Vana's parents died in the war and she started taking care of other kids. My family is also dead. I do whatever the overseers think I should be doing. It is harvest season, so that is what I do right now."

"Interesting," I say. "Are there engineers or people who oversee resource distribution?"

"Sure," said Rhen. "There are roles like that."

"That's sort of what Lyra did," I say. "Is that what she'll do now?"

"Probably not," says Rhen.

"Definitely not," says Ferris.

"Why?" I ask.

Lyra also looks up from the fire. She seems curious.

"Those jobs are usually for men," says Rhen. "Women do not do those things."

This time, Lyra interjects. "Why not?"

"We are better suited to be caretakers," says Ferris. "Or our clothes are not right. We do not have the same analytical capacities because we are more social. We need protection... You can take your pick of excuses."

"I don't understand," says Lyra.

"Neither do we," says Rhen. "But that is why we're here." She looks around the dark room. "It is like I have said, we do not belong out there."

"But you said that people have the same roles as their families," I say.

"Yeah?"

"So the men who are leaders also have wives and daughters," I say. "What do those women do?"

"I do not know," Rhen shrugs.

"Write books about social discrepancies," says Ferris. "Buy more clothes than they need. Complain when the temperature changes."

"The temperature changes?" I ask.

"Of all the things I just said," Ferris stares at me. "That is the thing that surprises you?"

"No," I say. "It all surprises me. It's weird anyone would have more than one garment of clothing. It's weird that people have time to write books. But, during the hisbon, Rasul said something about the *end*. I was trying to figure out what that meant and I read something about atmospheric conditions changing due to hydrothermal activity. So I'm wondering if changes to the temperature —"

Ferris leans over to Rhen. "Atuh-mo-sphere condish cheea?"

"Pienque sen uminidor," Rhen says back.

"Ah," Ferris nods. "E hyder-o..." Ferris looks back at me. "What was the second thing you said?"

"Uhh— temperature changes?" I ask.

"No," says Ferris, "the other thing."

"Hydrothermal activity?" Lyra asks.

"Hyder-o atomy?" Ferris looks at Rhen. "Cheea?"

"Uhhh," Rhen gazes at the ceiling. "I do not know. What is that?" She looks between Lyra and me.

"Like, underwater volcanoes," says Lyra. "Hot magma. Sulfides or minerals released in gases..."

"Hmm," Rhen looks at Ferris again. "*Lel masde*?"

They turn toward Lyra and me.

"The Source?" Rhen asks.

"What is that?" I ask.

"It is where all life comes from," says Rhen. "It is how our facility was made. It is where all nutrients come from. It keeps the lights on and the heat going."

"Alaster made your facility," says Lyra.

"Alaster visited our facility, sure," says Rhen, "in ancient times. But the Source is what made our home. And the Source keeps us going."

Lyra furrows her eyebrows.

"Is the Source here?" I ask. "Can we see it?"

"It is not safe to get close," says Rhen. "And, about what Rasul Midian was saying— yes, there will be an end to everything."

Ferris starts speaking to Rhen in their language.

Rhen responds and they seem to get into an argument.

"You disagree?" I ask Ferris.

Ferris clenches her hands together. She cocks her head to the side and stays silent for a moment.

Rhen raises her eyebrows at Ferris.

"I do not know," says Ferris. "All we can know is what is in those journals."

"You read the journal too?" I ask.

"Yes," says Rhen. "And Lyra brought us to your ship that she says is Alaster. She showed us the journal that she says is the original one. We spoke to the ship— it even knows our language."

"What did the ship say?" I ask.

"The end is near," says Rhen.

My arms tremble as I grip the wall. As silently as I can, I climb up the rock wall and try not to disturb men who sleep in the white beds attached to the rock face. Not wanting to wake anyone, I couldn't yell upward to ask for a rope, so I'm not tied to anything in case I slip. My knee still throbs from when I was injured it in the Trellis. My ribs still sting from when I was hit in the Alaster ship. The rock is slick in my sweaty hands, but I climb upward, trying not to lose my grip. Finally, I reach the top. I climb high enough so I can put my forearm on the ledge. Pulling myself up, I roll onto the ledge and pause, panting as I lie on my back. The lighting is dim across the rocky ceiling. I wonder how the lights change from day to night. In the Trellis, the bioluminescent lights changed colors, but never brightened or darkened to create a night and a day. I remember thinking that, if I could see the night, I would stay out and look at the stars. There aren't exactly stars here, but there is something magical about the facility telling everyone to sleep at the same time... Everyone except me. The last time I actually slept was in the Sanctuary. Well... not including the time I was gassed and woke up in the holding cell.

I roll to my side and stand before walking toward the tunnel which leads to my new sleeping quarters. I don't remember any rocks being on this ledge, so I step confidently toward the entrance, despite the dim light.

"Oof!" I trip over something in the path.

I tumble to the ground.

"Ouch!" A voice whines when I trip.

Pushing myself to sit on the ground, I see the silhouette of curls in the dim light.

"Leal?" I whisper. "Is that you?"

"Gia?" Leal says as he rubs his head. "Why did you do that?"

"Why are you up here?"

"I can't stay asleep down there," Leal says. "I keep having nightmares where I'm falling to my death."

"I thought you were wearing a rope so you don't fall," I say.

"My dreams don't care," Leal says, "I keep dream-falling. What are *you* doing out here?"

"I was just..." I try to think of how to answer. I can't imagine Lyra would want people to know that she has a secret area where she can sneak off. She had stayed back to sleep there. Her family will know that she's not there when they wake up. But, after chatting with Lyra's new friends, maybe it would be best if no one else knew about the place.

"Were you doing secret robot things?" Leal jokes.

"Yeah," I smile. "Except I'm only half robot."

"Oh, right," Leal says.

We're both silent for a moment.

"Listen, Gia," he says, "I don't like keeping secrets."

"Okay?" I'm not sure if he wants me to tell the truth about where I've been or if he's saying he wants to tell me things.

"I kissed Minji."

"Oh," my eyes widen, "okay." That's not what I was expecting.

"Or, she kissed me." Leal rambles. "It doesn't matter which. We kissed each other. I wanted to tell you."

"Alright," I nod. I have no idea what I'm supposed to say. "Good job?"

"Thank you?"

We're silent for a moment, then both start laughing. We must be the most awkward friends that have ever existed.

I cover my mouth, trying not to laugh too loud and wake someone.

"I have something to say, too," I say in a quiet voice. "Desman and I—"

"Are in love?"

"What?" I shake my head. "No, that's not what I was going to say."

"I saw you two dancing," says Leal.

"Would you let me finish?"

"Fine," it seems like he rolls his eyes, though I can't see fully in the dark.

"We're taking care of an animal."

"Like a pet?"

"I guess so. But Desman says the Trovantians don't like the kind of animal it is. So we're trying to keep it a secret."

"Where is it now?"

"With Desman. He made a harness for it out of rope and I think it's sleeping with him on the rock ledge."

"Yeesh," says Leal. "I hope it's tied tight so it doesn't fall."

"I think the harness is good," I say. "Desman really likes her. I don't think he'd do something he felt was dangerous."

"Wow," Leal leans back, propping himself up with his hands. "You guys have a pet."

"Desman has a pet. I only agreed to help."

"That's sweet that you guys have a pet," Leal teases.

"Whatever," I smile and shake my head.

"You sound tired," Leal says.

"I am tired."

"Wow, you really are telling me your secrets. I don't think I've ever heard you admit that you're tired."

"I haven't slept for a while," I start to stand. "I should head to my bunk."

"And I should head right here," Leal lies down.

"You're going to have to figure something out. You can't sleep right there forever."

"Why not?" He yawns. "It's the same thing as sleeping in other places. It's all just rock anyway." He closes his eyes. "Goodnight, Gia."

"Goodnight, Lea," I say as I walk away.

I'm in a dream-like state as I navigate the series of turns that lead to my bunk. My subconscious seems to know the way as I take each turn, avoid rocks on the ground, and follow symbols that mark tunnels. I arrive at the crack of green light that illuminates the space in front of my sleeping quarters.

"What are you doing?" A voice shouts behind me.

I jolt awake. I didn't even notice anyone around. Someone snuck up on me. My dad would be so disappointed.

"I'm just…" I trail off as I turn and see Dayana. I'm too tired to think of an excuse.

"It is not proper to be out at night," Dayana scolds. "It is not safe."

"I'm sorry," I say. "I didn't know." That's only kind of true. No one technically told me that I couldn't leave at night. At the same time, it does seem like something I'm not supposed to do.

"Now you know," says Dayana. "But stay out here," she bends down. "It is time to wake everyone to start the duties." She crawls into the hole that leads to my sleeping quarters.


"Here you are," Dayana has a baby boy on her hip and leans toward me. "Take him."

Reaching out, I put my hands under the baby's arms and lift. He's heavy. I pull him close to my chest and wrap my arms around him. He squirms and pushes away from me. I feel like he's going to squirm out of my grip. How do I hold him tight but not crush him?

"I feel like I'm going to drop him," I say.

"He's not a newborn, honey," Mabel Fitzgerald stands next to me, swaying side to side with a baby in her arms. "You don't need to support his head like that."

"I'll take him," Vega walks toward me and takes the baby from my arms.

"If we're going to work here," says Mabel, "she should probably learn how to hold a baby."

Vega bounces the baby in her arms. "Maybe she could sit down and practice first."

"Maybe I can do something else," I say.

"You did not volunteer for any duties," says Dayana. "This is all that was left."

"I didn't know what the options were," I say.

"Well," says Dayana, "now this is your option."

"Can I switch with someone?" I ask. "Maybe I can go with older kids or work harvesting food."

"We will assess every few weeks," says Dayana. "For now, this is your duty. Anything else?"

She looks around at the three of us, surrounded by infants. No one says anything.

"That is fine," says Dayana. "I need to train others now. If you need anything, one of you can come find me." She turns and exits the room.

Babies crawl across the floor of the warmly lit room. Tables and chairs are carved out of rock in different places. Blankets and toys are littered across the floor. One of the babies starts crying.

"Have a seat," Mabel nods to a place in the wall that's carved into a curved nook with a seat.

I sit down.

"Here," Mabel hands me the baby that she had put to sleep. Then, she picks up the crying baby and pats his back, bouncing up and down and making shushing noises.

The baby I'm holding starts to stir.

"Like this," Vega helps me prop the sleeping baby against my chest.

The baby whines a little, then stills and slumbers.

Somehow, the baby's small exhales make me feel settled. Her limp body sleeping in my arms makes me want to sleep too. I try to keep my eyes open. Mabel's shushing sounds seem like calm waves or a wind blowing in the room. I blink rapidly to keep my eyelids from drooping.

"How long do you think we'll be doing this?" Vega says as Mabel quiets the crying baby.

"Watching babies?" Mabel asks. "Or living in the Trovant? I'm not sure I can tell the answer for either."

"We can't stay here forever," Vega says. Holding the baby boy, she takes a seat in a chair made of rock. "And Alaster says we won't. I just wonder how long we need to plan on being here. Or what to prepare for next."

"You look tired, honey," Mabel tilts her head as she looks at me. "When was the last time you slept?"

"Me?" I blink rapidly again. "I'm not sure."

"You should pace yourself," Mabel says. "I think we have a long journey ahead of us."

# Part II

# Chapter 9: Leal— Gemstone

Arcturo puts a plate on the ground in the center of us. Minji sits next to me on a blanket and we hold plates with different foods. It's fun that we get to have different options to eat. Yellow light glows from the walls and through holes that lead to a walkway. It's busy out there— like a highway for walking people.

I don't know how much time has passed since we arrived in the Trovant. Maybe weeks? It's weird that I used to calculate every week, every work shift, every hour, every minute, every moment. Now I live in a place where people walk around the tunnels at any point in the day. I don't know where they're coming from, where they're going, or what they're supposed to be doing. It's nice.

The Trovantians all have individual lives with family and friends. A person walking out there might be picking up food to take back to a family with many kids. Someone might be purchasing dye to color the woven baskets they sell in the market. Each life carries a miniature story with a gem-lit walkway as a stage, but no audience to know where the story has been or where it will go.

Gia and Desman come through the doorway. Desman cradles a little creature. Desman's current story is that he found a creature that no one liked, but he kept it. When he walks the tunnels of the Trovant, not many know the story of a young man from a very different life than this, who had anger issues, lost his love, and found a pet.

# Trovant

The Trovantians sometimes furrow their brows as they see him walking around with what they consider to be a pest. When Imeel found out about it, he wasn't happy, but he was trying to accommodate us as much as possible. I wonder what it must be like to have lived in this facility with a certain way of life, then a group of people from a different facility showed up. They were forced to incorporate hundreds of Trellis people into their daily tasks. It's been chaotic, and some things have slipped through the cracks. Minji and I have daily roles, but Lyra never got assigned anything, and there are too many people around for the Trovantians to notice.

"So this is the pet?" Minji asks. She sits next to me on the ground.

Arcturo takes a seat next to Vega, who is by Pictor and Jarret. Lyra also sits and looks at her plate that's on the ground. She hasn't been around much, but her parents asked her to spend more time with us. We've been eating meals at our different living quarters.

Yesterday, we went to mine. We had convinced the Trovantians that I should live with my parents instead of the rock wall. They told me I should already have a wife and my own place. But, since I do not, they let me stay with my parents. And this is my favorite part of the day—when we get to come to each other's living quarters and eat food.

"I don't know if I would call her a pet," Desman says as he lowers down to take a seat on the floor. Gia sits next to him.

Little ears perk from his lap and the creature's glimmering eyes peer up at us.

"Her name is Ari," says Desman.

Arcturo and Vega exchange glances.

Vega picks up plates from the center of us and hands them to Gia and Desman.

"This has caused quite a commotion," Vega says.

"Vega," Arcturo whispers his wife's name with his brows furrowed.

"We already have a lot of fights with the Trovantians," says Vega. "Is getting to keep your pet really worth it?"

"She's worth it," Desman says.

Vega looks at the creature and then back at Desman. "We're stirring quite a bit with asking for different roles and—"

"Vega," says Arcturo, "he already answered."

"Don't interrupt me." Vega's gaze slices the air and meets Arcturo.

"Can we talk about this later?" Arcturo asks.

"I can't even talk in here now?" Vega asks.

"That's not what I—"

Vega stands. Without saying anything else, she turns into a tunnel that leads to the sleeping rooms of the living quarters.

"Vega—" Arcturo calls for his wife, then sighs when she leaves.

Minji grabs my hand.

Arcturo stands, looking where Vega had left.

Minji pulls me closer and rubs my arm.

Lyra shoves her plate, then gets to her feet.

"Lyra?" Arcturo says.

It looks like tears are welling in her eyes.

"Honey—" Arcturo's gaze follows his daughter.

"Don't—" Lyra says to Arcturo between clenched teeth. She storms through the doorway that goes to the busy corridor.

"Lyra," Arcturo calls toward the doorway where his daughter left. Then he looks toward the tunnel where his wife left.

Jarret sits with his eyes wide and Pictor takes a bite as he leans on Jarret. Minji clenches my arm. Desman pets Ari and Gia grips her empty plate.

"Sorry, everyone," Arcturo's shoulders droop as he takes a deep breath and walks to the tunnel where Vega had disappeared.

"Should someone go talk to her?" Jarret says as he stares at the place where Lyra had left.

Desman looks at Gia and nods.

"Me?" Gia grips the plate even harder. "Why me?"

"I don't know," says Desman, "you already talk to her sometimes."

"I could talk to her," says Minji.

"Not you," Jarret and Desman say in unison.

"Why?" asks Minji, "I know how to talk to people, too."

"Yeah," I feel defensive. "Why not Minji?" She's definitely better at talking to people than Gia.

"I'll go," Jarret sighs and stands, disrupting Pictor's comfortable spot.

"Hey!" Pictor topples over as Jarret stands.

"Sorry, buddy," Jarret says as he walks toward the exit. "I'll find you later and we can show the other kids how to play Polty-ball."

"Sweet," says Pictor.

Jarret leaves.

It's quiet, except for the sounds of Pictor chewing.

"That was weird," says Desman.

"And unlike the Delphinos," says Minji.

"I get why Vega's mad," says Desman. He looks at Gia as he speaks. "I mean, it's taken weeks of arguing just for you to be able to try a different role. And they won't even consider you to try something that you're already good at."

Gia sets her plate down. She stares at it. She doesn't look angry. She looks sad.

"Gia?" I lean toward her.

She shakes her head. The sadness on her face is gone.

"Gia," I say. "You can say whatever you want now. There aren't security cameras or anything." I look around. At least, I haven't seen any security cameras here. Could there be hidden ones?

"I'm just—" Gia sighs. "I'm not sure I'm actually good at anything anymore."

"What?" I ask.

"Of course you are!" Minji reassures.

"I'm small and weak here," Gia looks up from her plate. "There are no screens. I can't fight anyone. I can't code anything. I can't even properly wash clothes."

"I've always been small and weak," I say. "So I've never been able to fight anyone. And I've only been able to learn a new role because they gave me the chance to learn. Maybe you don't know how to do everything, Gia, but you know how to figure things out."

She stares at her plate again.

"Is Gia here?" Garridon leans in the doorway.

"Speaking of doing things," I motion to the door, but still look at Gia. "You're involved in some super secret robot things that you won't even tell me about." Since being here, Gia and Garridon would mysteriously disappear during the time when we should be working. Mom and Vega have been covering her because they thought whatever Gia was doing was important.

"You need something?" Gia turns toward Garridon.

He comes into the living quarters and starts to sit down. We all scoot to make space for Garridon. Pictor tosses his plate on the ground and stands. He's really come back to life since being here. It's weird to imagine how sick he was based on how he's acting now.

"Bye!" He jogs toward the door. "I mean—" he stops. "Tell my parents I'm going to play. Bye!" He sprints out.

"Should we be in here?" Minji asks. "None of the Delphinos are left."

We all look toward Garridon. He's the only adult. It somehow seems like whatever thing he does would be the right thing.

Sitting on the ground, Garridon's posture is still straight like a piece of metal. His broad shoulders seem awkward as he puts his hands in his lap.

He doesn't say anything.

"Did you come here for something?" Gia asks.

"To see you," says Garridon.

Gia looks confused and she leans away slightly from her dad. "Why?"

"Just," Garridon pauses, "spending time together."

My eyes shift from Garridon to Gia. What is going on? I look to Desman and then Minji. Everyone looks equally confused.

"So you don't have something to tell me or something for me to do?" Gia asks.

"No," Garridon says.

We are all silent for a moment.

Why is Garridon really here? If he truly doesn't have something to tell Gia, why the sudden change in his entire character?

Garridon looks uncomfortable as he sits stiff on the ground.

"Did Arcturo talk to you or something?" Gia asks.

"Yes," says Garridon.

"You don't have to do this," says Gia.

"I want to," says Garridon.

"Desman," Vega's frame emerges from the living quarters.

"Yeah?"

Vega comes near our circle and Arcturo appears behind her. We shuffle to make room for them both to sit next to us in the eating room.

"I shouldn't have been that harsh to you," Vega says when she sits. "This isn't about you or Ari. And I'm sorry to all of you for making the place uncomfortable."

"It's fine," says Desman.

"Where are the kids?" Vega leans toward Arcturo.

"Right," says Arcturo, "Lyra left. I should go talk to her."

"Pictor went to go play," says Minji.

"I can talk to Lyra," says Vega.

"Vega," Arcturo tilts his head and gives some sort of knowing look.

"Fine," says Vega. "Go find her."

Arcturo moves toward the exit.

"Can you check on Pictor, too?" Vega asks.

"Yeah, I will," Arcturo's voice fades as he exits the living quarters.

"Did you four get enough food?" Vega hands a plate to Garridon. "Gia, did you eat anything?"

"I'm okay," Gia says.

"Here you go," Vega piles food onto Gia's plate. "Mabel told me to make sure you eat enough."

Garridon looks at Gia from the corner of his eye. "Is there a reason for this?" Garridon asks.

I take a bite of the food that's on my plate. "It's weird that we all have different eating habits if we don't have scheduled sustenance times."

"That's not what I asked," says Garridon.

"Oh," I say. "Turns out Gia doesn't eat if she's stressed or upset or something."

"You're upset?" Garridon looks at Gia.

"I'm fine," says Gia.

"You need to maintain a certain caloric intake to support your metabolic activity," says Garridon. "Not to mention levels of protein, phytonutrients... is something funny?" Garridon stares around the circle as Minji chuckles and some of us smile.

"It's not funny," says Vega. "It's sweet."

"What is?" Garridon asks.

"The way a robot cares for his young," I say.

"For the last time, Leal, I'm not a robot."

"It's okay, sir," I say. "Your secret is safe with us."

Garridon sighs. "So that wasn't the right way to encourage you to get the required sustenance?"

"It was fine, Dad," Gia gives a reassuring smile and takes a bite of food.

"Are you stressed about starting the new role?" Garridon asks.

"I'm not stressed," Gia says. "Look." She holds up her plate. "I'm eating."

"When do you start?" Vega asks.

"Tomorrow," Gia says. "Should be fun. Leal will technically be my boss."

"Well," I say, "Not really. You will have managers and stuff."

"But you're telling the managers what to do," Gia says.

"Maybe we can talk about something else," I say.

I feel awkward because I shouldn't have the role at all, let alone be Gia's boss. Minji had told me an idea she had and I went to the Trovantians to tell them the idea. I thought it would help her get a better role. Instead, they gave me a new role.

Minji has just been saying how bored she has been with weaving baskets every day. I was trying to help.

"It's okay," Minji says. "You don't need to feel bad that you got a new role."

I rub her hand.

"Well," I look at Gia. "At least we get to work together again."

"At least there's that," Gia stares at her plate.

***

"Ugh," I squeeze my nostrils so the sour smell can't get in. But I can taste the smell.

"Yes, it is bad," says one of the managers. "You see how the plant people are so disgusting?"

Piles of rotting waste are littered across the area. Men and Gia are scattered around the various piles. The other facility is somehow connected to this one and waste from that facility gets dumped down tunnels that lead to this spot.

The piles of waste have been getting higher and the smell getting stronger. Decomposing waste leached into certain parts of the water. This was poisoning the marine animals and killing them or making them toxic for people to eat. The Trovantians had been doing the best they could to seal off the parts of the impacted waterways. They tried burning the waste, but that made toxic air that got trapped in the Trovant and caused people to get sick.

Minji thought of a solution. She said we should seal off certain parts and mix the waste with material that would absorb some harmful materials. The waste could decompose with specialized microbes and we could trap the escaping methane. The methane could be burned as fuel with the resulting carbon dioxide being diverted out of the Trovant and the resulting water collected. She made a thorough plan of how to sort, store, seal, and neutralize the waste. It was such a good idea that they put me in charge of the entire project.

"This is disgusting," Gia mumbles as I step toward her on the pile of waste.

"Tell me about it," I say. "This smell is—"

"No," she says, "I mean, look at this." She shows me her draping sleeves and the bottom of her draping robes. The fabric absorbs liquid and the sour smell that comes with it.

"Yuck," I say.

"They said I can't wear the suits that everyone else wears," says Gia. "I have to wear a draping thing."

"Why?" I ask.

"Why do you think?" Gia puts her hand on her hip. "Maybe I was better off holding babies." She sighs and bends over to sort through the waste. "Organic waste in the brown baskets, right?" she asks as she picks up something that oozes in her hand.

I squeeze my nostrils again and nod.

She tosses the oozing thing into a basket at the bottom of the pile.

"First try!" She yells when the waste makes it into the basket. "Never mind, this is better than holding babies."

I release my breath as I feel something wet on my eyebrow. I wipe my forehead with my sleeve. Whatever Gia had thrown, she flung some of it on my face.

"Ech," I try wiping my forehead again.

Gia stifles a laugh.

"It's not funny," I say.

"I know," Gia chuckles. "I'm sorry I got that on you. But you should see your face right now."

"Mr. Fitzgerald!" someone yells from across piles of waste. "Come see this!"

"Coming!" I yell and waddle my way down the pile. There's squishing with each step. My foot sinks deep into something. It makes a suctioning noise when I yank my foot from the pile of sludge.

I get close to a group of three men huddled around something on the ground. My heart rate rises as I get closer to the men. Is that what I think it is? "Gia!" I yell over the piles of waste.

"What?" she yells back.

"Come over here!" I yell to her. "I think I need your help."

I stop near the men. At our feet is a baby girl— naked, covered in grime, and not moving. Is she alive? I feel like I could throw up. I bend down and put my hand gently on her chest. Is her chest moving or am I just imagining that it is? I pick her up. Is that the right thing to do? I don't know what to do!

"What is it— oh!" Gia says as I turn toward her with the baby in my arms.

"What do we do?" I ask.

"Hold her on her back and let me see her," says Gia as she bends her ear near the baby. "Her heart is beating, but her passageways sound blocked."

I put my ear down to the baby that is limp in my arms.

"Is she going to live?" I panic.

"Here," Gia pulls one of my arms toward her, "Put the baby like this." She sets the baby's stomach and chest across my forearm so the baby's mouth is between my fingers and facing toward the ground. "Hit her back to see if you can get anything dislodged."

I tap the baby's back with my free hand.

"Not like that." Gia gives the baby firm pats on the back. She listens, then squats down so her face is near the baby's face. She puts her mouth over the baby's nose and mouth. Then she sucks and spits out mucus or waste-ooze that comes from the baby.

"Ew," I say.

"Hit her back again," says Gia.

I give firm hits on the baby's back.

The baby coughs a bit and then stops. Gia puts her mouth on the baby again and sucks out more mucus. The baby coughs again, then starts crying.

"There we go," Gia says. "That's better."

I give a sigh of relief as the baby moves and seems more alive. I turn the baby so she is facing my chest. Her screams get more powerful and blare over the piles of waste. I bounce up and down to calm her down.

"It's okay, little baby," I say to her while the crying is loud like an alarm.

The baby screams so hard that her face starts to turn red. It seems like she's having trouble breathing again.

My heart races. What if I can't calm her down? Do babies scream so hard that they stop breathing? Her face gets redder.

"Gia?" I whimper and look at my friend. "What do I do?"

"Here," Gia takes the baby, pulling her close to her chest and rocking while making shushing noises.

It doesn't work. The baby screams just as loud as before. But at least Gia looks like she has a clue what she's doing.

The baby's screams turn into a quieter cry. Then the baby gives sporadic whines.

My heartbeat slows. The baby sounds like she's breathing normally. So now I can too.

"How did you know how to do that?" I ask when I feel calmer.

"Hold a baby?" Gia asks. "I've been hanging out with your mom."

"No," I say. "Make it so she could breathe again."

"Oh," she says. "Training manual 57, protocol 23-c: obstructed airways in an infant. I've never actually done it, but my dad made me practice by sucking contents through a small hole of my sustenance packets."

"Wow," I say. "I always thought your dad was just being harsh, but that was actually helpful."

"Well, yeah," says Gia. "I don't think my dad was making me train for no reason."

"What do we do now?" I pause and look around at the Trovantians. "Is there a way to find her parents?"

"The parents are plant people," says one of the men. "We do not go up there."

"Is there something that happens to babies without parents?" I ask.

The men shrug.

"I think they just get raised by the community," says Gia. "I met someone who said that she was a kid who helped raise other kids who had lost their parents."

"You could have it," one of the men motions to Gia.

"Uhhh," Gia looks down at the baby. "No, thank you. Here you go." She hands the baby back to me.

The baby cries some but doesn't start screaming again.

"Maybe we can just take her to the nursery," I suggest.

"Yeah," says Gia. "But we need to get her cleaned up and make sure her health doesn't get worse. We should ask your mom what to do."

I look at the baby. "That seems like a good idea." I turn to the manager, who is covered in sour-smelling waste. "Can I take this baby to my mom?"

He nods.

"Can Gia come too?"

He nods again.


"Just me and you hanging out again," I say as we walk through the rocky tunnel toward the nursery where Mom works.

"Yeah," says Gia. "In a cave, covered in waste, with a naked baby— just like old times."

I cradle the baby and try not to trip over any rocks. "Well, I've missed you."

Gia smiles.

"You missed me, too?" I ask.

"Yeah," she smiles. "I've missed you, too."

"Will you hold the baby?" I ask. "I'm scared I'm going to trip."

"You're doing fine."

I take careful steps through the rocky corridor, then look down at the baby in my arms. She has darker skin like me and my parents. "She kind of looks like me." Her facial features aren't very defined, so maybe I don't actually know if she looks like me.

"Kind of," Gia says as she gets a closer look at the baby. "But she has dark brown eyes like your mom. Not blue eyes like you and your dad."

My foot hits a rock and I stumble slightly. But I hold tight to the baby and don't trip completely.

"Leal!" Gia yells. "Watch where you're going!"

"See!" I say. "I can't be trusted to walk and carry a baby." I hold the baby toward Gia.

She rolls her eyes and takes the baby as we get near the nursery.

We lean our heads into the room that should be full of babies.

"What is that smell?" Vega stands with only one baby in her arms.

"Oh, right," says Gia. "It's time for the afternoon meal. Mabel is probably at your living quarters."

"What about you?" I ask Vega.

"One of us stays behind in case parents come at different times for the afternoon meal," says Vega. "This one's parents haven't come yet. Are you two going to tell me what's going on with the smell and the baby?"

"We found the baby in a waste pile," says Gia. "We were looking for Mabel to ask what we should do with her. Do you have any ideas?"

"The Trovantians didn't tell you where to take the baby?" Vega asks.

I shake my head.

"Then my idea would also be to ask Mabel," she says.

"Mom?" I shout through the living quarters when Gia and I arrive.

"Leal?" Mom's voice sounds from around the corner. "That you, son? Oh, my... what is going on?" She walks into the main eating space to see me and Gia, covered in waste and holding a baby. "Leal Isaac Fitzgerald, where did that baby come from?"

"We found it in the waste," I say.

"Oh, thank goodness," Mom puts her hand over her heart.

"What?" I ask. "You didn't think she was mine, did you?"

"I don't know what I thought, son. I just saw you and a baby and I panicked."

"It's okay, mama," I reach my arm out to give her a hug.

"Don't touch me with your smelly hands." She puts her finger out to stop me from coming closer to her. "Both of you need washing up. Hand me that baby and I'll clean her up while you both take care of yourselves."

The baby slumbers in Mom's arms as I take a bite of food.

"You'd better eat." Mom stares at Gia.

Gia's clean hair drips onto the plate of food that she hasn't touched.

Dad has also come in for the afternoon meal and he sits on the ground with us. He hasn't spoken much since Mom explained what happened with the baby.

"We could try again and see if the Trovantians have a way to take care of orphans," says Dad after a long silence.

"What should we do if there is no one to take care of her?" Mom asks.

Dad sighs. "You already know what I'm thinking, Mabel."

"I don't," I say. "What are you thinking?"

"Son," Dad turns toward me. "You know we weren't allowed to have multiple kids in the Trellis."

"Right?" I lean back as I try to figure out where his explanation is going.

"But we always wanted to have more," says Mom.

"But now isn't a good time," Dad turns toward Mom. "We're in some new place and we don't even know what's going to happen."

"Leal wasn't a good time either," says Mom. "There could have been an accident and we didn't know who would be in it. It's never a good time. That doesn't mean it isn't a good thing."

"Whoa," I sit up straighter and look at my parents.

Gia also looks up from her plate.

"What are you two saying?" I ask.

Dad rubs his face. "What we're saying, Son, is that *if* there is no better option, we would be willing to take care of this baby."

Mom smiles and rocks the baby.

Dad sighs. Then smiles. "It almost looks like there's no better option."

"We should give her a name," says Mom.

Dad rubs his face again.

"Gia, Leal, what do you think?" Mom asks. "You two found her."

"Can I hold her again?" Gia asks.

Mom reaches the baby over plates of food and hands her to Gia.

The baby stirs but falls back to sleep in Gia's arms. Gia flips her dripping hair away from the baby. "She's precious." Gia stares at the slumbering infant. "It seems like someone threw her away like she was waste. Could we call her something that reminds her that she's like a treasure that we found?"

"I like that idea," says Mom.

"Minji told me a Trovantian word for treasure," I say. "There's a specific word for when someone finds a precious gemstone in a dirty wall." I lean back and look at the ceiling, trying to remember what the word was… "Takara— that was the word."

"That's not a bad name," says Gia.

"That's a great name," says Mom.

"You want to hold her?" Gia asks.

I take the baby in my arms and look down at her— Takara, that's the right name. I look up at Mom. "I have a sister."

Mom smiles.

Dad shakes his head but also smiles.

I look back at Takara, her eyes closed and tiny mouth parted as he breathes softly against me.

I have a sister.

# Chapter 10: Lyra— A Heebo's Heartbeat

The ceiling drips 17 times every 5 minutes. I grip the tablet and stare as the minutes pass. I try to keep my eyes open so I don't miss the moment that the clock changes. If I can stare long enough, I can perceive each pixel shift as the minute changes from a 19 to a 20.

"Lyra," Rhen steps behind me as I lie on the ground.

"What?" I keep my eyes glued to the tablet. I can't miss the moment.

"You have to stop looking at that thing."

"I need to look at it."

"Why?" It's Ferris's voice this time.

"I need to see the numbers change," I say.

Someone yanks the tablet from my grip.

"No!" I sit up and grab for the tablet.

"You want this?" Ferris holds it above my head.

"Give it back!" I stand and reach for the tablet.

Ferris looks at the tablet, then gives it back to me.

I glue my gaze to the screen. It happened. The number already changed to a 20.

"No!" I slink back to the ground. I guess 20 is not that great of a number anyway. I can wait for 21.

"Lyra," says Rhen. "Come on. You have been staring at that thing for too long."

"I need to see it," I say.

"Why?" Ferris demands.

I think of the Alaster ship. It was where I would go when things were overwhelming. But the ship doesn't look like the same place where I was safe to be myself.

I think of Ara. I only knew her in my imagination. I had imagined us talking— her teaching me about the Trellis and what she knew of the surface. She would teach me how to talk to other people. Maybe I could have had friends. And I think of Leal. I feel embarrassed. I had imagined we could be together. That he would like someone like me. Maybe I could have had another place to be myself. But it was only in my imagination. The good things in my life were never real; only in my head. The only things that really happen are death and heartbreak.

That's why I have to stare at the screen. There's a tangible thing that won't hurt me. I know the number will change. I can watch it happen. It's like there's something outside my head that I can control just by being sure my eyes are open to see it.

"Forget it," Ferris says.

I hear her footsteps fade away.

Rhen sighs, then squats by me. "You want to see something?"

"Like what?" I ask, staring at the tablet.

"You and your friend were asking about The Source. You want to see it?"

I break my gaze from the tablet and look at her.

The plants get smaller and more sporadic as we journey over the rough black rock. There's a strong smell of sulfur. The air is hot and dry. I see something move quickly over the black rock. I jolt up in surprise.

"What is that?" I ask.

"A velsyren," says Rhen.

"I thought those were light-colored," I say. "Like Desman's pet."

"They come in many colors," says Rhen. "It depends on which population you see. The ones near the Source blend in with the black rocks. Others blend with the light rock. There is even a kind that has blue and green scales and can swim. They go fishing and blend in with the pools."

"How can there be so many different kinds in this small space?"

Rhen shrugs. "Why are there so many different environments in the Trovant? I do not know how it happens, but it does."

The air gets warmer still as we walk forward. I don't see where we are going. There is no Source in sight.

"Wait," I say. I think of the environments that were on Earth's surface. "Is there snow here?"

"What is snow?" Rhen asks.

"It's like fluffy ice or something that falls from the sky," I say.

"No," she looks confused. "Nothing falls from above except drips of water."

We turn a corner and it feels like a flash of fire hits my face. The heat is almost unbearable.

"We cannot stay long," says Rhen. "The air is not safe for us."

I squint to protect my eyes from the dry heat.

Beyond cracked black rock is a massive crevice. Walking far enough to see over the edge, the crevice is filled with black liquid that's streaked with orange and red, like the bottom is molten rock. Embedded in the walls around us are columns of metal. The metal looks manufactured rather than something that formed naturally. Why would someone manufacture metal lines here?

"Come!" Rhen grabs my shoulder and pulls me behind a boulder.

The boulder blocks us from the open crevice and makes my face feel cooler.

"Do not speak," Rhen whispers. "I hear something."

When Rhen crouches, I hear voices coming from the tunnel that leads to the Source. They're speaking Trovantian. What are the voices saying? I want to know, but I don't want to ask and make Rhen upset. She seems cautious. Are we not supposed to be here?

The heat is not directly against my face, but it starts to feel like it's radiating inside my body. I'm sweating, but it's not cooling me down.

I need to get away from the heat, but the voices still converse and Rhen still crouches.

The strong sulfur smell makes it hard to take in the air. It's so dry.

Rhen puts her hand on my shoulder as if trying to tell me to stay strong.

I cover my mouth and stifle a cough. I breathe in slowly. Then, it feels like I can't breathe at all. Short bursts of dry air come into my lungs. I give a tiny cough, trying to get the dry air out.

The voices behind the boulder still speak.

It feels like the room is moving. By instinct, I start to stand as if my body is fighting to get out of the place. Rhen puts her hands on my shoulders and pulls me back down. Like my body is fighting without my consent, I struggle and try to stand. Rhen's grip on me is strong and she fights to keep me down. Suddenly, I feel weak. I start to sink. Rhen grips both my shoulders as I look up at her. Black creeps around the edges of my vision. All goes dark.


Sounds of chirping, animals calling, and insects buzzing fill the humid air. Something rubs against my side. I think different plants are scratching my arms or gently caressing my legs.

"Lyra?"

It sounds like someone is calling me in a dream.

"Lyra." Someone shakes me.

Rhen hovers over me when I open my eyes. She's surrounded by dense plants.

"Are you okay?" Rhen asks.

I close my eyes and nod, then I roll to my side and try to push myself up. I feel heavy.

"I am so sorry, Lyra," Rhen says as she helps me sit up and rubs dirt and leaves off my back. "What they were speaking about— I had to hear. I could not risk them seeing us."

"What were they saying?"

"It is not good," says Rhen. "We need to tell the others."

My senses awaken. I look up at Rhen.

"Should I be worried?" I ask. "Should we go tell my family?"

"It is the Trovant," says Rhen. "The end is—" she stops.

"The end?"

"Shh!" She puts her hand over my mouth.

All I hear is the background noise of animal calls. I look around, but can't figure out what Rhen is listening for.

She stands slowly.

"Get up," she whispers.

Looking around, I rise to my feet. Then I hear a low growl. I look at a bush where the growling is coming from. I see a black snout and sharp teeth.

"Back up slowly," says Rhen. "Do not turn your back to it and do not run."

My gaze moves from its teeth to its dark eyes. It's a black creature like I've never seen. It seems like a mix between a wolf and a bear. It steps from the bush; even bigger than I thought.

"Back up," Rhen whispers.

I realize that I haven't moved.

The animal towers above my head, but I don't want to move. I'm not frozen from fear, I just don't care. It almost feels like I'm outside watching myself. What difference does it make if this animal takes me now or if there's some imminent end to the Trovant? What difference does it make if I have a long life before I die or if I just give in to this moment?

Rhen tugs my hand as she takes steps back.

I let her pull me backward, but my foot catches on a thick vine and I tumble backward.

The animal roars and shifts toward me.

Something soars through the air and hits the creature on the head. It roars again and looks to where the object came from.

"Rhen!" A voice cries through the jungle.

The creature jolts toward the voice.

"Ferris!" Rhen helps me up and looks around. She picks up a rock and throws it at the animal.

"This way!" Rhen yanks me toward a rocky edge. It might be the edge of a cliff.

The creature runs back toward Rhen. She picks up a stick and turns, just in time to hit the creature in the neck and divert its bite.

Seeing the creature go for Rhen, my heart races. I pick up a rock and throw it as hard as I can. It looks like a small pebble bouncing off the animal. The creature jerks its attention toward me.

"Ajitarus!" Rhen yells something in Trovantian. Apparently meant for me, but I don't know what it means.

I grab a long vine that's on the ground and jolt toward the edge that drops out of site. The creature lunges for me as I shift to the side, hanging on to the vine. The vine hits it in the chest as I topple over the side of the drop. Clinging to the vine, my body weight yanks the vine across the animal's chest and pulls it off the edge with me.

The drop turns out to be a steep incline. I still cling to the vine as my body slams against the side. The creature's heavy body crashes on top of me. The weight pulls me off the vine and down the incline. I squeeze my eyes closed as I hit rocks and plants, tumbling down. I try to cover my head as I feel my body slam against the terrain.

Everything stops. I open my eyes and see dust swirling in the air. Beyond the dust is a heap of black fur. The creature has forced breathing and it looks directly at me. It's not getting up. It must be hurt.

I cough from the dust, then push myself up. There's a small puddle of blood in the dirt. I touch my face, then look at my hand. Blood streams down.

The creature shifts like it's trying to get up, but can't. It looks scared.

"I'm sorry," I say to the animal. I feel something heavy in my stomach. "I didn't mean to hurt you."

"Lyra!" Rhen yells over the side of the cliff.

"I'm okay," I try to yell back but I can't make my voice very loud.

"We are coming down!"

Rhen and Ferris journey down the incline, cautious not to lose their footing. Dust billows in the air as their feet shuffle gingerly through dirt and plants.

I inch toward the creature. It jerks away from me and growls.

"Leave it alone!" Rhen yells from the incline.

I reach my hand toward the animal. "I'm so sorry." Somehow, I see my own pain reflected in its gaze.

It doesn't jerk away this time.

I set my hand down and feel the animal's chest move up and down.

"We have to get you out of here," Rhen says when she gets close to me.

"It's hurt," I say.

"Good," says Ferris.

"I don't want to leave it," I say.

"There is nothing we can do," says Rhen.

I put my ear close to the creature. Nothing sounds wrong so maybe it's just in shock. I lay my head on it to hear its heartbeat. It sounds fast. My head moves up and down with the creature's breathing. I run my hands through its fur. Maybe it attacked us because it was scared. And it's afraid now, just like I am. I close my eyes and listen to the heartbeat. The fear, aggression, loneliness, sadness— it's like every emotion inside me is entwined with the heartbeat that settles as I listen. I think the heartbeat is slowing down, but I'm not counting the beats so it's hard to tell.

The creature moves. I lift my head. It sways clumsily as it places each leg in position and pushes itself up on four massive paws. It looks at me, then takes a step. It looks away and takes another step. Stumbling slightly, it limps away.

Rhen's gaze follows the creature.

"That was one of the strangest things I have seen," says Ferris. "The *heebo* is never kind to people."

"Maybe people aren't kind to it," I say.

"We need to get you home now," says Rhen. She picks me up, like someone picking up a small child, and sets me on my feet.

I sway a little, trying to stay upright.

"Can you walk?" Rhen asks.

"Yeah," I say. "I just need a minute." I don't feel pain, but my balance is off as I stumble forward.

Rhen grabs my arm and helps me move in a straight path.

Ferris comes to my other side and holds my other arm.

I'm not used to having people touching me, except for my dad when he's calming me down. It feels vulnerable.

"Lyra, Honey!" My dad jolts from the ground when we come through the door. He's probably panicked to see dried blood on my face.

I had tried to wipe off the blood before I came in, but it was already dry and mixed with dirt.

"Lyra?" my mom comes around the corner of our new family home.

My dad rushes to me and wraps his arms around me. "What happened?"

My mom rushes over, too. She doesn't say anything, but checks my face and scans the rest of my body for injuries.

"I'm okay," I say. "We have to talk."

"Of course," says my dad. "Anything you need. Let's talk."

"No," I say, "Not here. Not about... this," I lift up my arm as if summarizing all the injuries and dirt on me. "We have to go somewhere else. And bring everyone."

***

The low hum of the albharee alarm flows through the caverns and over the crystal blue pools that glow. The air is cold and my body is stiff. My parents and Jarret sit on rocks that are close to me and others sit on scattered rocks or on the ground. Ferris, Mica, and Vana sit next to Leal and Minji.

My head stings now that the adrenaline has settled and we've cleaned out all my wounds. It feels like my brain is pulsing from having to be in the same room as Leal and Minji. Are they able to tell what I'm feeling? Maybe I should try to act more normal. I try to sit up straighter and keep my tired eyelids from drooping.

Rhen stands as Gia, Garridon, and Desman come through the rocky threshold to join us. Gia's cheeks are red and her eyelids are half-closed. She walks as though each step is heavy.

"This is everyone?" Rhen asks when Garridon stops and stands next to a tall rock.

I look at Leal and try to sound normal. "Are your parents coming?"

"No," says Leal. "My sis— ummm… they have to take care of a sick baby."

What was he going to say about a sis? I want to know more, but I don't want to talk to him. It hurts too much. "I think this is everyone," I say to Rhen.

"What's this about?" Garridon asks.

Gia sits on the ground, slumped on a rock, propping herself up with her hand. Her lips are parted and her eyes look glossed over. Is she going to be okay?

"Leal and I have been measuring atmospheric conditions," Minji says. "And the data seems strange. Do you know anything about that?"

"I overheard something," says Rhen. "From the overseers of the Trovant. It is about the end. When the Source made our facility, it was never expected that humans should be down here permanently. In case the time here was extended, the Source could pour out molten rock outside that would keep expanding the facility to accommodate a growing population. When the Trovant was made, measuring systems were installed to check how solid the growing walls were. As the Trovant is still expanding, the walls are becoming weaker. People were not supposed to be down here this long. So the walls were not intended to last forever. I could not hear everything, but it seems like the walls are weakening and the heads believe the end will come very soon."

"What do we do?" Minji asks. "Is there a way to tell how long the walls will last?"

"I was hoping you could answer that," says Rhen. "Only the overseers have instruments to understand the systems that measure the stability of the walls. But now you all come here with tablets and a talking ship. Maybe you can tell us what we need to know."

"What happens if a wall breaks?" Leal puts his hand on his forehead. "Do you have anything to seal off parts of the Trovant in case there's a crack that leads to the outside?"

Rhen shakes her head.

The low hum from the holes in the ceiling gets louder.

Garridon doesn't seem to notice the alarm. "We should—"

"Shh," Rhen cuts him off. She listens intently, monitoring the volume of the sound.

216

Ferris, Mica, and Vana stare at Rhen, waiting for her verdict.

A wave laps against the side of the pool and the alarm gets louder.

"We need to go," says Rhen.

"Why?" Desman asks.

"Now." Rhen helps others who are sitting on the ground and then turns toward the exit.

We crowd into the narrowing tunnels that lead toward the Alaster ship.

"Where are we going?" Desman asks.

"Your ship," says Rhen. She walks in the direction of the Alaster ship.

"Oh, good," says Gia. "I needed to charge this anyway." She lifts up a tablet and trips slightly over a small rock.

Garridon pulls the tablet from her grip and examines it. "You let it die?"

"It was a long journey just to charge it," Gia says.

"You are more cautious than this," says Garridon.

"She hasn't been well, sir," says Leal.

The ceiling drips and my parents walk in front of me. It's a weird group of people to be walking through a rocky tunnel that's normally empty. I don't like all of them learning about the cavern. It feels like the time that everyone crowded into the Alaster ship. It was supposed to be my space.

"I'm fine," says Gia. "I don't really get sick."

"You sucked mucus waste from someone else's lungs," says Leal. "If there was an exception to you getting sick, this would be it."

"You what?" Garridon looks at Gia.

"Yeah—" says Desman, "what?"

"It's a long story," says Leal.

"What happened?" Garridon ignores Leal and still looks at Gia.

"There was a baby with obstructed airways," says Gia. "I followed protocol."

"And it was totally awesome!" Leal exclaims. "She took the baby and put it on my arm and then—"

"That's enough," Garridon cuts off Leal. He keeps his critical gaze on Gia. It's hard to tell whether he's upset that she did something that made her sick or that he's pleased she followed protocol.

Garridon is very different than my dad. I don't know if he's hard on Gia because he cares about her or if he's just always mad at her. I can't imagine my dad being like that. But if I had a dad like Garridon, maybe I could do things like save suffocating babies. And then maybe Leal would like me.

I look at the ground as we approach the Alaster ship. It's damp from the dripping ceiling, but there's no blood or medium pooled in front of the entrance. Did the rock absorb the liquid? Did it evaporate?

The rocky ground turns to metal as we enter the ship. I close my eyes for a moment. It sounds different with my fabric shoes hitting the floor instead of the bottom of my microbial suit. The air isn't as humid and it smells cleaner. I've missed it here.

Gia places her tablet on the control panel as it charges. There are two chairs, but she turns and leans against the control panel instead of sitting in a chair. Leal and Desman are against the control panel on either side of her. It looks a lot like the time we were trying to figure out where to go when we journeyed through the ocean. Except now we're draped in blankets and we smell bad. The microbial suits used to take care of bacteria that caused body odor. In the Trovant, people buy perfumes or oils to cover up bad smell, but it doesn't really work.

Ferris crosses her arms and stands next to Vana. Mica slumps in one of the chairs. My parents and Garridon stand across from me.

"Tell us everything you know," Rhen says to Minji.

"Only this," Minji taps on the screen of a tablet and then hands it to Rhen. "We know about the fire in the walls and we've been measuring atmospheric conditions throughout the Trovant. Garridon and Gia have set up instruments in every environment that capture any information we could use. And Leal has been studying the journal to glean information about how the Trovant was built."

Rhen looks at the tablet but it doesn't seem like she's taking in the information on the screen. "What do you mean about fire in the walls?" she asks.

"It explains it here," Minji points on the tablet.

Rhen hands the tablet to Minji. "I do not read in English."

"Oh," Minji accepts the tablet. "Of course. Sorry. I thought you would know… the information about the fire in the walls was in the journal."

"We don't normally read that one," says Rhen. "We read the journals written by the early people in the Trovant. They shed light on the old journal you have."

"And the beauty of the writing is preserved in our language," says Vana. "It is poetic and touches the heart."

Ferris rolls her eyes.

"This is the information we've been using," says Minji. "It says that there are two rock layers that comprise the walls of the Trovant. There's an outer wall that is strong enough to withstand the pressure of the ocean. Then there is something like an air pocket and then another layer that forms the walls we see inside. When the Trovant was made, the methane from hydrothermal vents was diverted into the air pocket between the inner and outer walls. The methane was lit on fire and there is a continuous flame as long as methane flows through the walls. That's why most of the Trovant is hot— the fire between the walls creates a natural heating system."

"What about the pools?" Garridon asks Minji. "How are we connected to the outside but also covered by rock?"

"It's hard to say exactly from the journal," says Minji. "It seems like some underwater caverns were formed as a part of the Trovant. The part we are in seems like a trapped air bubble."

"But it's lasted all this time," says Desman. "So it won't pop or something, will it?"

"I can't say what kind of danger we're in," says Minji. "I don't know much. But it wouldn't *pop*. If anything, the rock walls would cave in from the water pressure outside."

Gia's head droops to the side and she stares out into nothing. She doesn't seem like she's following the conversation. It's unlike her.

I look at my mom, who stands silently by my dad. She hasn't said anything, which is also unlike her.

"What do you need to get more intel?" Garridon asks Minji.

"I've been going in circles trying to figure that out," says Minji. "I don't see how to get information about the strength of the outside wall without putting a probe near it. But I don't know how to make instruments that can get the information we need. And I don't know how we'd get to the outer wall without putting a hole in the inner wall, which could risk unleashing a flame that could burn us all."

"A flame?" Rhen asks. "Would a flame make it so you can get to the correct place?"

"Possibly," says Minji. "A flame might mean there's a hole in the inner wall."

"We have a flame," says Ferris.

"An eternal flame," Vana adds. "It burns so long as we care for the soul of our people."

"We have a flame," Ferris repeats herself with her arms crossed. She looks at Vana from the corner of her eye.

"That could be methane leaking from the inner wall," says Minji. "If we get to the flame, maybe we can put a probe in the wall. But all of the instruments we have currently set up to measure environments were already in the Alaster ship. I don't know how to make a new one that can withstand methane and fire."

My parents look at me. Then, everyone looks at me.

"What?" I ask.

"You made all of those instruments," says my dad.

I look around at the people and try to figure out what instruments they are talking about. "I don't think I did."

"All the instruments that were in the Alaster ship," says Minji. "Didn't you make those to measure the different parts of the siphon?"

"Oh, those," I say. "That's what you've been using?"

"Yes," says Minji. "I can't make the instruments. I just programmed yours to measure different variables."

"Lyra," says my dad, "can you make a probe that could go inside a wall without burning up?"

"Sure," I say. "I can make something that will collect information and withstand a harsh environment. But I wouldn't know how to get it inside the wall."

"And it would need to move inside the wall," says my mom. It's the first time she has said something. "We would need to make something that we could control remotely. Lyra, have you made anything like that before?"

"No," I say. I remember reading about robotics at one point and trying to figure out mechanisms that move, but I've never made anything like that.

"My dad can," says Leal. "He worked on all the machines that moved outside the Trellis. Most things had to be controlled remotely."

Gia now leans on Leal's shoulder with her eyes nearly closed. Her nose is red and she breathes through her mouth.

"You plan to put something inside the eternal flame?" Rhen asks.

"It sounds like a good option," says Minji.

"It is not a good option," says Ferris.

"Why not?" Leal asks.

"The flame is sacred," says Vana.

"It is difficult to get to," says Ferris.

"How difficult?" Minji asks. "Gia and Garridon have been getting to some difficult places. I bet they could—"

"Nearly impossible," says Rhen. "You must swim. Down the pools, through an underwater tunnel, and up to an opening where the flame continuously burns. There is very little air and you must swim through a passage that is wide enough for the albharee."

"What is that?" Leal asks.

"A monster," says Ferris.

"Yeesh," Leal scrunches his face.

"Or we could take the information from the overseers," I say.

Everyone looks at me.

"What do you mean?" asks my dad.

"Rhen overheard the information from the overseers," I say. "They are getting the information somehow. We can either get the information from them or tap into their instruments."

"We can work from multiple angles," says Garridon. "The situation is this: there could be a weakness in the walls, but we won't know how bad it is or how to fix it unless we have more intel. The solution is to gather more information. We have two options: put a probe between the Trovant walls or tap into intel from the overseers. Lyra will work on both angles— making a probe for the wall or gathering intel from equipment already in the Trovant. The Fitzgeralds will work on a mechanism that can control a probe remotely. You four," he looks at Rhen, Vana, Ferris, and Mica, "can work with Lyra and the Fitzgeralds to guide the probe to the flame and in the wall. I will scout options to acquire information from the heads along with Gia, who can—" he looks at Gia, who is fully slumped over Leal with her eyes closed.

"Sleep," says my dad. "Gia can sleep, Garridon."

"Right," Garridon rubs his fingers together and looks at my dad. "Gia can sleep."

It's quiet for a moment while we look at Gia, then to the wall behind her where words are typed out: "I can help."

"We're done here," says Garridon.

"Just wait," says my dad. "Let's see what he says."

"I said we're done," Garridon turns and walks toward the bridge that leads to the platforms.

I sit in my old chair and stare at my tablet that has a blank screen.

"You've been in here a while," my dad pops his head into the room.

"I'm charging," I point to my tablet.

"Ah, I see." He steps through the doorway with his hands in his cloak pockets. "You want to talk about what happened to your head?"

"What's with Garridon?" I ignore my dad's question.

"What do you mean?" asks my dad. "Like what happened up there on the platform?"

"Yeah," I say. "And everything else too."

My dad leans against my desk. "He's upset at Alaster about what happened to his wife."

"Oh," I say. I think back to what happened to Gia's mom. I think of the security footage that showed

Britannica wading through freezing water as she shivered with dripping hair. She had inserted a trowel into the wall and stopped the accident. But then she was gone. All Alaster said was 'she's with me.'

"And he's worried something could happen to Gia."

"I could understand that," I say. I think about how I stare at the clock on my tablet because life seems to be full of death. We all do strange things to avoid the pain of loss. "So we're just going to go with what Garridon says?"

"Sort of," says my dad. "I did talk to Alaster. I'm not going to stop Garridon or the others, but Alaster says we're going to the surface before the end."

"Why not just go now?"

"He says he's waiting for the people in the facilities. Apparently, he's the one communicating to the overseers here through their own equipment and he's also communicating to the people in the other facility."

"Are we just supposed to sit here in the meantime?"

"The facilities won't last," says my dad. "So maybe we could tell the people in both facilities to come here with us."

"How can we know that the walls won't break before we can escape?"

My dad bites his bottom lip and thinks. "Maybe we can't. Maybe we should test the walls and see for ourselves when they will break."

"Hmm," I look down at my blank tablet. I've already lost more than I could have expected. I don't see a reason to believe that there won't still be walls caving in or facilities flooding. "Maybe testing the walls would be the safest thing."

"Well," says my dad, "it sounds like the others can't do it without you anyway."

"They would figure it out," I say. I look down and fiddle with the edge of my tablet.

"Why do you assume that?"

"There are a lot of smart and capable people in the group," I say. "Leal and Minji can basically do anything I can do. Garridon is good at organizing people and making plans. Gia is good at pretty much everything—"

"Lyra," my dad interrupts my list and sighs. "I wish you could see how special you are."

I keep my eyes diverted away from him. Maybe someday he will realize that I'm not as special as he thinks.

# Chapter 11: Gia— The War

There are no sounds of animal calls or people chatting in tunnels. My eyes are closed, but I hear a quiet buzz of machinery. It takes all my strength to open my eyelids and see where I am.

Desman is in a bunk across from me, looking at a tablet.

"There's our sleepyhead," Leal crashes down to sit next to me. I have no idea where he came from.

I look around, trying to see if anyone else is here. I'm on a bunk in the Alaster ship. I close my dry mouth and swallow. But my nose is plugged, so I can't keep my mouth closed long.

"Why are we in the submarine?" I ask.

"You are very sick," says Leal. He crosses his arms. He seems proud that he was right about me being sick— how annoying. "We had to stay here because we didn't think you could make it through the jungle and up the rock wall."

"Did my dad carry me down here?" I have memories of falling in and out of sleep during some sort of meeting on the platform.

"Like a baby," says Leal.

"We're just glad you're getting rest," says Desman. He puts the tablet to the side and sits up to talk to me.

"Do I have a task or something I'm supposed to be doing?" I sit up and try to remember what we were talking about on the platform.

"To sleep," says Desman.

"Sleep?" My body aches as I try to stay upright. "That doesn't sound right." I'm not sure if I'm swaying or if the room is swaying.

"By the looks of it," says Leal, "you need a lot of sleep."

"I think I just need to get my blood circulating," I say. "If I move around, I'll probably start to feel better."

Leal puts his finger on my shoulder and gives a little nudge. The swaying in the room gets more intense and it feels like gravity pulls me down with Leal's small push. I start to tip to the side and can't stop from falling. Leal grabs my arm to stop me from crashing into the bunk.

"Case in point," says Leal. Then he lowers me down to the bed.

"Cut it out, Leal," says Desman.

My cheek is pressed up against the bunk, but the room still feels like it's moving.

"Are we moving because it's a submarine?" I ask with my face squished on the bunk. "Are we going somewhere?"

"We're not moving," says Leal. "But we should probably figure out how to get—"

"Are we going to the surface?" I ask. I heard Leal say we're not moving, but it definitely seems like we are. And the surface is where Alaster said we were going.

"We are going to get you some rest," says Desman.

"We should probably get her something to eat and stuff," says Leal. "Maybe she can stay with my parents until she gets better."

"How can she get to your living quarters, Leal?" Desman sounds irritated. "She can't even sit up."

"Maybe Rhen can carry her the whole way," says Leal.

"No one is carrying me," I say with my cheek pressed against the bed.

Leal pats my shoulder. "Sure."

"Has anyone tested this?" Desman asks. "She won't slip out or anything, right?"

I'm on my feet, but I feel heavy. My back is against Desman's shoulder to help me stay upright.

"It should be okay," says Rhen. "Such harnesses are for Trovant babies. This one at least is made for a toddler, so hopefully it will fit her." She ties some fabric in knots and starts to put it around herself.

We stand in front of the rock wall. I try to picture myself climbing up. Maybe I could do it on my own. If I just get moving, I can clear my head and I'll be okay to climb up myself. I lean away from Desman and take a step forward, but I start to dip toward the ground.

"Gia!" Desman pulls me back up. "Don't do that."

He holds my back against his chest with his arms around my waist. I put my hands on his forearms; they're muscular.

We had seen a giant snake on the way here that was wrapped around a tree. Desman's forearms are muscular like the giant snake and they are wrapped around me.

"You have nice snake arms," I say.

"What?" Desman asks.

"She's delirious," says Leal. "We'd better get her back to sleep."

"It is ready," says Rhen.

The three of them guide me to the rock wall and help slip a harness over my head and under my legs. Rhen stands completely and my feet leave the ground. I'm pressed against her back in the harness. She starts to climb the wall with me attached to her back.

I look down and see Leal and Desman look up at me. It feels like I'm floating except that the harness is digging into my skin. I look up to the ceiling and then out at the jungle. I'm usually too focused on the wall to see the view.

"I'm flying, Rhen," I say as she grunts her way up the wall.

She laughs.

I feel like I could fly except that the harness is digging into me. Maybe I can just take it off.

"What are you doing, Gia?" Desman yells. He is also on the rock wall climbing near me and Rhen.

"I'm taking the harness off," I say.

"Don't do that!" Desman yells and climbs to me. He reaches and tries to grab my hands.

I swat at his hand to get him away.

"Guys!" Leal is also on the rock wall. "Please stop!"

"Do not worry," says Rhen. "The harnesses are designed to make sure toddlers cannot get out. It will only loosen from the front."

"Will you take it off?" I ask. "I don't like it."

"I do not like it either," says Rhen. "But we are almost there."

My weight seems like it could crush Rhen as she pulls us both onto the ledge and I lie against her back. She pants and loosens the harness. She lowers me to the floor and I lie down completely on the ground.

I had a surge of energy on the rock wall, but I feel it dissipating as I lie there, listening to Rhen catch her breath.

"Thank you," I say. I'm embarrassed that she had to carry me through the jungle and up the wall.

"It is okay," says Rhen, panting.

"Why are you so nice to us?" I ask with my head heavy against the ground. "Why not just leave us alone?" I think of the other Trovantians I know. They often seem annoyed at how much they have to help people from the Trellis. Why did Rhen keep helping us?

"Let us get you somewhere to rest," Rhen says. "Okay?"

Desman's snake-forearms appear over the ledge and he pulls himself up. Leal comes after him.

"You scared me," Leal says as he bends over with his hands on his knees. He sticks his finger out and wags it back and forth. "Don't play on the rock wall."


Mabel ladles steaming food into a bowl. "She'll have to sit up to eat this."

I lie on the ground in the Fitzgeralds' living quarters. The lights give a warm glow as evening covers the Trovant.

"Rhen, you'll stay to eat something, won't you?" Mabel asks as she bends down and puts a bowl in front of me.

"I will have to go," says Rhen.

"You will have to stay," Mabel puts food in another bowl and places it in Rhen's hands.

"Come on, Gia," Desman puts his hand on my shoulder. "You should eat something."

"Too tired," I say as I stay on the ground.

He pulls my arm until I'm seated upright, slumped in front of the bowl.

Leal comes into the room holding Takara. "Poor little thing."

Her nose drips, her face is red, and her cheeks are wet with tears.

"That *poor little thing* was screaming for hours," says Mabel. "She was up most of the night and still won't go to sleep even though she's exhausted."

"Two stubborn, sick babies," Leal says as he cradles Takara and sits down. He turns to me. "Now, eat your food."

Rhen takes a seat beside me.

"Where does your family stay, Rhen?" Mabel asks as she serves more food.

"I do not have one," says Rhen. "They died in the war."

"Oh, I'm so sorry," says Mabel. "I didn't know." She hands a bowl to Desman. "There was a war? Here in the Trovant?"

"Yes," says Rhen. "In both facilities."

"How did that work?" Leal asks. "I mean, you couldn't have bombs and stuff inside a place like this."

"Bomb?" Rhen asks. "I do not know what this is."

"Like an explosion," Leal says. "That's what war is like from the descriptions in the journal. There was a tank blasting things with bullets and people running from explosions."

"I do not know what these are," says Rhen. "But the war happened in both facilities."

"How did people die?" Leal asks.

"Leal!" Mabel scolds him.

"It is okay," says Rhen. "It is good for you to know what happened. In our facility, we would often lure or smoke people into caverns and block the exit. The people probably suffocated or starved. In their facility, they would often get our people into a branch of the plant and then cut it off, sending it floating into the ocean. That is how the majority died."

"Yikes," says Leal. "That sounds gruesome. So, there's an actual plant, then?"

"Yes," says Rhen.

"What were you fighting about?" Desman asks.

"There were many reasons that built over the years," says Rhen. "We needed them because their facility had more clean air, but our facility could sustain resources, animals, and food. Our overseers would argue that we did a lot of work harvesting our resources and they did nothing to provide air."

"So how did that start a war?" Desman asks.

"My people stopped giving them resources," says Rhen. "So their people started blocking passageways to their facility and our caverns would run out of oxygen. Our people suffocated in their homes."

"Oh," says Leal. "That's not good."

"It was not," says Rhen. "And their people starved. You could imagine both sides would be willing to go to war to get the resources of the other."

"What stopped the war?" Desman asks.

"Rasul Midian," says Rhen. "That is why he leads us now. He brought peace and convinced both sides to stop fighting. We share the resources we need to survive, but no one travels between the facilities anymore."

"Could you travel between facilities if you wanted to?" Leal asks.

"Mrs. Fitzgerald?" Lyra pokes her head through the entryway.

"Come in, Lyra," says Mabel.

Lyra holds her forearm and takes little steps into the living quarters. She has a big gash on her forehead and bruises on her face and hands. Her cloak covers the rest of her skin so I can't tell if there are more bruises. "Is Mr. Fitzgerald here?"

"He's asleep after a long night... and day," Mabel says and looks at Takara. "Why don't you stay here until he's awake? Garridon came by and told us to be expecting you."

"I can come back," Lyra takes a step backward.

"It would be great if you stayed," Mabel prepares a bowl for Lyra.

It seems like all of the parents have been trying to get Lyra to stay around more. All of the parents except mine, of course. They have also been trying to get me to eat more. They must have some secret discussions about us.

I reach for the spoon to take a bite.

Lyra looks uncomfortable but sits next to Rhen.

"So this is her?" Lyra says, looking at the baby in Leal's arms.

Leal nods.

"She's quiet now," says Mabel. "Maybe she just wanted her brother."

"Maybe," Leal rubs his thumb over Takara's cheek.

Lyra seems to force a smile. "What's her name?"

"Takara," says Leal.

"That's nice," says Lyra.

"You could call her Ara as a shortened name," says Rhen. "That is the word for a streak of raw silver."

I don't think we mean to, but we all stare at Lyra.

She silently holds her bowl.

"I was thinking of calling her Tak," says Leal. "Does that mean anything?"

"No," says Rhen.

"Perfect," says Leal. "Let's call her that."

"Why?" asks Rhen. "The name Ara comes from a beautiful story in the journals when a drip of starlight fell from the surface and created ores of silver. When we come across silver, we are to remember the hope of finding our way home to the surface."

"I like Tak," says Leal. He tries not to make eye contact with Lyra.


"Here you go," Mabel leads me to a carved platform of rock.

I sit on the rock and then lie down. There's a pillow made of fabric stuffed with something. I've seen pillows a few times since being here. They are usually stuffed with feathers, fur, or dried plants. The pillow crunches as I lay my head down. This one is stuffed with dried plants.

It's dark in the living quarters. The crystal lights have dimmed. The facility tells everyone at the same time that it's time to go to sleep, like magic.

Mabel puts a blanket over me. I'm sweating, but I'm also cold. I clench the edge of the blanket and squeeze it up to my chin.

"This is like the time we first met," I say.

"We first met when you were a baby," says Mabel. "I can't imagine you'd remember."

"This is like the first time I remember meeting you," I say. "There was a blanket. And you hugged me."

"And I think it scared you," Mabel chuckles. "That wasn't really too long ago. And you seem like such a different person since then."

Leal comes in holding Takara.

"I'm the same person," I snuggle the blanket around myself. "The inside can be on the outside because there are no security cameras."

"Did that make any sense to you?" Mabel asks Leal.

"I think so," he sets his sister on the ground and puts a blanket over her. "No one step on Tak. We don't have a baby bed."

Takara whines when Leal stands and takes a step away from her.

"Is there a such thing as a baby bed here?" I ask.

"I don't know," says Leal. "If there is, we don't have one."

Leal squats next to Takara and then lies down. She stops whining.

"Aren't you going to sleep in your bed?" I ask.

"You're in my bed," says Leal. "But I'm not going to sleep here. I'll just stay here until Tak falls asleep and then go into the eating space."

"Sleep well, you three," Mabel leaves the room.

I stare at the crystal-lit ceiling. I remember sitting in our workstation, wishing that I could see nighttime and stay out all night to watch the stars. There aren't stars here, but the crystals are beautiful.

"Leal?" I say, staring at the crystal cracks in the wall that give dim light.

"Yeah?"

"Do you ever miss the Trellis?"

He thinks for a moment. "I miss Louis Armstrong."

I smile, thinking of him pretending to play the saxophone in front of our control panel.

"I miss being able to see footage of the surface," says Leal. "And having the hope that we were meant to live a different life than the one we were living."

"You don't hope that anymore?" I ask.

"Not in the same way," says Leal. "It feels like we're just trying to catch up with the lifestyle that already exists here. It doesn't feel like there's anything beyond this."

"So you don't think there's a surface?"

"Of course, I still *think* there is a surface," says Leal. "I just don't *feel* like there is one right now."

"That's fair," I say.

"It was nice of your dad to give us that time to be ourselves."

"What do you mean?"

"I mean," says Leal. "He was covering up for us all that time when we were looking at footage of the surface and talking about whatever we wanted. Garridon wasn't present the same way my parents were. But, from a distance, at least he gave us a place to be ourselves. Not everyone in the Trellis got that."

I roll to the side. "I never thought of it that way."

"I guess some robots can be loving parents," says Leal.

I chuckle. "He's not a robot."

"Whenever you're ready to admit you're a cyborg," says Leal, "I'll be here for you."

"And whenever you're ready to stop being annoying," I say, "I'll be right here."

\*\*\*

Takara pulls my hair as I walk into the eating area with her in my arms. The Fitzgeralds seem quiet when I enter and take a seat next to Leal. Takara wiggles in my arms so I put her on the floor.

"You're sure you're feeling better?" Mabel asks.

"Yes," I say. "Thank you for letting me stay here."

"You're always welcome," says Eddi.

"You're sure you're strong enough to climb into your own living quarters?" Leal cuts in. "From what Minji's told me, it sounds pretty hard."

"I'll be fine," I say. I've started feeling better over the past few days. I still sound sick because my nose is plugged, but everything else is working. "I think I'm even fine to start working again tomorrow."

Leal rubs his arm and looks at the floor.

"What?" I ask.

Leal looks at his parents.

"You have to tell her, son," says Mabel. "It's your role now."

"Listen, Gia," says Leal.

I don't like the tone in his voice. It sounds like he's trying to be polite or something.

"You know how you got sick and all?" He wrings his hands. "Well, some of the managers are thinking that maybe it's best if you did a different role."

"What do you mean a different role?" I ask. "Because I got sick one time? Why would that mean I need a different role?"

"They think... well..." Leal wrings his hands even harder. "Maybe your immune system isn't good enough to be around the waste. That's all it is."

"My immune system, specifically?" I lean toward him.

He stares at the floor and shrugs.

"Is it because I'm not a man?" I ask.

He shrugs again.

"Leal!"

Takara starts to whine.

"Okay, fine! Yes." He looks at me. "They said the female immune system is not meant for that kind of work."

"Gia—" Mabel tries to calm me down.

"Do *you* think that?" I ask Leal.

"Of course not!" Leal picks up Takara and rocks her. "You ingested mucus waste to save someone else. Any of them would have gotten sick if they had done the same. But they just couldn't perform protocol-whatever-whatever. I know that. You know that. But they won't listen to me."

I shift back and sit, realizing that he probably did try and stick up for me.

"Look," I say. "I shouldn't yell at you. I know it's not your fault."

"And you better remember that," Mabel gives me an intense stare. "Don't mistreat the people who are on your side."

"I'm sorry," I move to get up. "I should go. Thank you for the hospitality."

"Gia," says Leal. "Don't go."

"I need to figure out what I'm going to do now."

"What you're going to do now," says Mabel, "is sit back down and listen to what Leal has to say to you."

I sit back down. I'm not going to stoke the fire that is Mabel Fitzgerald.

"Okay," I say. "What else do you have to say?"

"It's what we were talking about before you came in here," says Leal. "They're moving us."

"What do you mean moving?" I ask. "Are you getting another new role?"

"No," says Leal. "New living quarters. I guess people with my role live in a different spot."

"Oh," I say. "Like how you moved from the Cultivator Quarters when you became a Facilitator?"

"Yeah, kind of like that," says Leal.

"So it would be nicer, then, right?" I ask. "Since your role has more responsibility?"

"I guess so," says Leal. "But I can't imagine a single living space that's bigger than this."

"I can't either," I say. "Maybe you'll live in the jungle or something."

"Don't say that," Leal squeezes Takara close to him.

"Do you think they have treehouses?" I ask.

"I don't want to think about anything to do with trees."

"This sounds like good news," I say. I try to sound supportive after I just yelled at Leal and was then scolded by his mom.

"You could come with us," says Leal. "I'm told there are a lot of rooms."

"Oh, I don't... think..." I look around at the Fitzgeralds. They are a loving family that eats food together and sticks up for one another. I'm okay being a tag-along at times, but I don't really belong in this sort of family. I belong in the kind of family with a missing mother and suspiciously robotic father. I couldn't possibly live with the Fitzgeralds indefinitely.

"You don't have to answer now," says Leal. "Just think about it."

"Leal," I say, "I'm not sure—"

"Just help us move our things there," says Leal.

"What things?" I ask. "The blankets and pillows that were already here?"

"The food," says Mabel. "We need help moving the food."

I think she's just making an excuse to get me to see the living quarters.


"Are you sure we're going the right way?" I ask.

Leal's family and I walk along a path with high ceilings. Giant columns are carved from rock on one side, with doorways and windows arched across an apparent building made from rock. We keep walking past the massive building that has colorful stones inset into detailed patterns.

I carry a bag of vegetables and fruit as Leal carries a bag of belongings from their living quarters. Eddi carries Takara as Mabel lags behind with another bag of food.

On our other side, we pass a huge building made from white stone. It isn't carved from the rock, but it looks like the stone was taken from somewhere else and built into this part of the cave. The doors and windows on this one are lined with a marbled, green stone that contrasts the bright white.

"I probably should have asked someone to guide us," says Leal. "But it should be around this bend."

As we turn the corner in the tunnel, there's an expansive opening. There's a pathway with rows of glowing pools on either side. The path leads to a sleek, black building with silver trim. A massive door has pieces cut from green, white, and black stones that are arranged in patterns with the entire pattern framed in silver.

"This should be it," says Leal.

It's quiet as we walk up the path. The pools on either side of us are shallow and perfectly round as if they were carved. Each one glows a different color and little creatures swim in them.

"Tak!" Leal turns around. "Look! Fish!"

Eddi lowers Takara by a pool so she can see inside. She reaches for the creatures.

Some look like tiny fish, but some have shells with tentacles coming out. Some have claws, some are squishy, and have legs.

"I don't think those are fish," I say.

"They swim," says Leal. "Close enough."

He turns back up the pathway and I follow him.

Leal grips a silver circle attached to the detailed stone door. "I hope this is it." He pulls back on the silver handle and the door opens. "Hello?" Leal peeks his head through the entrance.

"Are you expecting someone to be here?" I ask.

"What if we showed up at the wrong place?" Leal wanders inside.

I follow behind.

The entire space is made of sleek, black rock that has been carved and smoothed. From the ceiling, dripped crystals form a giant light in the middle of the space. There's a tabletop formed of a swirling blue slab of stone. On the table is a giant shell filled with fruits and a note on top.

"Paper?" I pick up the note that has Trovantian writing.

"That's my name," Leal points to a part of the note.

"Can you read this?" I ask.

"Nope," says Leal. "But Minji and the Trovantians worked together to make us written names in their language. I recognize that word— it's me. So this is the right spot."

Scanning the open space, there are shelves carved from the black rock. On the shelves are iridescent shells trimmed with gold. They look similar to the cups we used at the hisbon.

"What the?" Leal steps toward the shelves and picks up a light-colored disk. It must be a plate. "That's strange. This looks like marble."

"Why is it strange?" I ask.

"There's no indication there is a limestone cave in the Trovant," says Leal.

"There are a lot of different parts of the Trovant," I say. "Maybe marble grows somewhere."

"Marble doesn't grow," Leal puts the plate down. "It forms." He walks to an opening in the carved black rock.

"Same thing," I follow him.

"No," says Leal. "It's not a plant. It doesn't just grow up from the ground."

The black tunnel is speckled with tiny crystal lights from ceiling to floor. They look like they could be stars. I smile as we walk through a tunnel like the night sky.

"The Trovant isn't a plant," I say. "But it grows."

We walk into a room where colorful, woven blankets cover a carved bed. The bed looks cushioned, like the frame is carved from rock but something soft has been laid on top. I place my hand on the colorful blanket and press down. The bed squishes beneath my hand. It's comforting. I turn and crash down onto the bed. A soft cushion envelops me and it feels like I lay on air cloaked in tapestries.

"These are cool," says Leal. He examines off-white drapes that are woven with an intricate pattern. He pulls aside the drapes to reveal a tiny room with colorful garments hanging on hooks. "Woah! Come look at this."

I push myself from the bed and walk toward Leal to peek my head into the tiny room. I see… myself. A clear reflection of me. "Whoa." I touch my hair and watch every strand fall to the fabric on my shoulders. I've only seen myself in security footage, pieces of metal in the Trellis, or reflected on pools in the Trovant. I've never seen such a clear, up-close image of what I look like.

"It's a mirror," says Leal. "Look at my hair." He smiles and plays with his curls. "Who let my hair get like this? It's so tangled."

"Look at my eyebrows," I chuckle and lean toward the mirror. "They're so dark and my eyes are so light."

Leal grabs a shimmering blue garment from a hook behind him. He puts it over his clothes and looks in the mirror. "Finally, I get a blue one."

I yank a silver robe from a hook and slip it on.

"Finally," I say. "Pockets."

"Madam Pockets," Leal faces the mirror and bows to me.

"Mister Blue," I curtsy to him in the mirror.

"I like my new role," Leal laughs.

"Don't let it go to your head," I smile.

"Gia!" I hear a faint voice calling in the living space. It's my dad. "Gia?" He appears in the doorway. "What are you doing? I've been looking for you."

"How did you find me?" I ask.

"I came here for Eddi," says my dad. "Doesn't matter. I'm glad I found you. I talked to Lyra and everything is ready. We need to stay together."

"Everything is ready for what?" I ask.

# Chapter 12: Lyra— An Idea as Perfect as She Is

Hunched over my work table in the Alaster ship, I lean over a magnifying glass that is suspended over the internal parts of the mechanism I'm making. I sniffle in the quiet room that used to buzz from my servers. I delicately grip a tool that can fuse components to a circuit board. Pushing a button, sparks crackle from the tip of my tool; just enough to melt tiny metal prongs that protrude from each component. Slightly blinded by the burst of light, I blink to adjust to the dim lighting. I lean closer to the magnifying glass. The last piece is fused in place. I pick up the circuit board and examine the prongs on the fused component— 4 prongs, what a normal number.

As I pick up a different circuit board with attached wires, my mind runs like a software program that is designed to solve the next problem. How do I make the device fully submersible and able to withstand extreme heat, pressure, and corrosive elements? Aluminum is readily available here but it reacts with hydrogen sulfide in extreme temperatures. Titanium has a high strength per mass; an alloy wouldn't corrode quickly from chemicals coming from hydrothermal vents.

I count the wires hanging off the circuit board. There are 6. I had to use the 5-jex wires, which are yellow. I move the yellow wires to the side. This will be covered.

Still, I will always feel slightly uncomfortable knowing there is yellow inside the machine.

Steel would be stronger but it might corrode from hydrogen sulfide and extreme temperatures. Then again, the device doesn't need to last for years.

I place the circuit board to the side and lean toward the magnifying glass to check the motherboard. Do I focus on protecting it from heat, pressure, or harsh chemicals? The motherboard is complex, sophisticated, and powerful but it's also vulnerable. I need to anticipate the biggest threat and know how to protect it. It won't be underwater long and it shouldn't be near hydrothermal vents. Inside the Trovant wall, the methane gas is being burned and the byproducts would be carbon dioxide and water. So the device won't need to withstand harsh chemicals. It will be in the heat the longest. I need an insulator. And I want the outer layer to be steel.

I lean back and look around the space. Is anything here made from steel?

The shelves are littered with gutted electronics. Wires still spew from the wall, but the yellow ones are tucked away. There's a single glass container with a clear liquid. I pick it up and give it a swirl— that was the last of the bioluminescent bacteria. It's dead now.

The container clinks as I set it down and scan the shelves for something made of steel. I pick up a trowel. It doesn't have anything to connect to anymore. It's weird how the things that were a part of everyday life— like the bacteria or a trowel— are now things I never even think about. In such a short amount of time, my life is completely different than it was. I can't think about whatever my life is now. Steel; I'm thinking about steel.

None of the devices across the room has what I need. I step to one of the walls, bend down, and feel the caps that secure the metal wall pieces in place. What material is the wall made of? I stand and grab my pliers, then go back to the wall and squeeze one of the metal caps in my pliers. The pliers bend and scrape, but the caps aren't scratched. My pliers are made of iron. At least that's a sign that the caps are stronger than iron. Gripping the pliers, I stab the wall and scrape downward with all my strength.

"What is that noise?" Eddi Fitzgerald covers his ears as he walks into the room. In one hand, he holds a small bag and presses it against his ear to block the sound of my scraping.

I rub my finger on a line across the wall formed by my pliers. The wall isn't scraped away, but traces of the pliers rubbed off. Whatever the wall is made of is also stronger than iron.

"Breaking the Alaster ship?" Eddi asks as he steps closer to me while holding the little bag.

"It's already broken," I say. "What do you think these walls are made of?"

"Hmm," Eddi puts his fingers in the bag, then pulls out some nuts and puts them in his mouth. He holds out the bag to offer me some.

Will he be offended if I don't eat any? I don't want any, but maybe I should take some anyway to be nice.

He finishes chewing. "Based on materials in the Trellis, I'd say aluminum." Maybe he doesn't notice that I didn't accept any of the food.

"Was anything in the Trellis made of steel?" I try to focus on metals instead of the fact that I'm spending time with Leal's dad.

"Not internally that I know of," says Eddi. "It was usually aluminum or titanium."

"You mean titanium alloy, right?"

"Well, yeah," Eddi snorts as he chuckles. "That would be silly to have plain titanium."

I smile a little. He seems to have such a simple joy. "Yes, that would be silly."

"What are we working on?" he asks, turning and looking around the room. "Is this it?" He steps into my workspace that has the internal mechanism I was making.

"Yeah," I move next to him.

"Very impressive," Eddi sets his snack down and examines the motherboard. "Really delicate work. We only found out about the Source yesterday. I'm amazed by what you've created in such a short amount of time." It seems like he's thinking out loud rather than talking to me. He adjusts the magnifying glass. "I don't think I could accomplish this with my giant hands." He continues to examine the parts of the mechanism, but he seems to talk to me now. "I've always been more of a nuts and bolts kind of person. And rightly so. It looks like I should leave the computer systems to the professionals. I wish you could have worked with me in Trellis. I could have used this kind of expertise. But, then again, it sounds like the Sanctuary needed you." He looks up from the magnifying glass. "Sorry, Mabel says I ramble sometimes."

"It's fine," I say.

"Don't encourage me," he smiles. "We have a big project and you'll regret telling me that it's fine to ramble."

"I don't mind," I say. The sound of his voice was distracting me from thinking about how life is now. I feel somehow like the motherboard— complex, maybe even powerful, but vulnerable. I need some way to insulate my inner-self from the harsh environment outside.

"So we need an external casing," says Eddi, turning his attention back to our task. "I have an idea about how we can make it swim and how to control it from land."

"And we need an insulator," I say.

"Oh, I know just what to use," says Eddi.

"What?"

"Nothing!" Eddi says. "Nothing is the best insulator."

"Right," I say. "How should we coat the device in nothing?"

"Oh!" Eddi seems excited. "Let's create a vacuum."

I start to think of ways we could have an inner and outer structure and create a vacuum between the two. "What can we use for the external casing?"

"This will be so much fun." Eddi seems to be lost in an idea as he walks toward the exit.

"What are we—" I yell after him, but he's already gone.

"The railing!" he yells from outside the room.

***

"Remember, this is just a trial." Eddi grips a tablet as the melody from the albharee alarm plays softly in the caverns.

Rhen and Ferris stand nearby. I don't know where Mica is. Vana didn't want to be around while we disrupted the sacred eternal fire.

"But it might work," says Rhen. "Time is not on our side. We need to put the device inside the wall."

"We need to make sure it won't fill with water," I say as I hold the device and walk to the edge of the large pool.

"If it does not fill with water," says Rhen, "will you go all the way to the flame and put it in the wall?"

I look at Eddi.

He peers up from the screen. "I don't see why not."

I squat to the clear pool that laps gently on the dark rock. My heart beats fast as I lower the device into the water. We're running out of materials; we can't lose this device.

"The camera is working," Eddi says as he stares at the screen. "Shall I put it under?"

I stand from the pool and nod. The device bobs on the surface of the water.

"I don't know why I'm nervous," Eddi says. "This seems like a monumental occasion." He presses on the screen.

The device sinks. Small ripples appear on the surface of the water as the propeller engages.

"Any signs of water leaking into the processor?" I step over to Eddi and look over his shoulder.

He shakes his head. "All good."

The screen is lit with pale blue light and small fish swimming in and out of view.

"This is kind of cool," I say.

Rhen and Ferris also crowd around the screen.

"I have never seen the water like this," Rhen smiles.

I read information on the side of the video feed. There's no sign of water leaking in. The temperatures are stable. The internal pressure is stable.

"It is working," says Ferris. "So you will guide it to the eternal flame now?"

"I guess so," says Eddi. "Where do I take it?"

I somehow feel relieved that it works and also nervous about getting it to the eternal flame.

"Only Ferris has gone," says Rhen. "It takes bravery and strength to get there."

"Let's hope this little device has both," says Eddi.

"Turn it that way," Ferris instructs Eddi.

The camera view pans slowly in the water as the device changes directions.

Ferris commands as Eddi guides the little device through a maze of underwater caverns. The tunnels are complicated and narrow, like the time I tried to navigate the Trellis to find Ara.

"This is it," says Ferris. "Now, just go upward in this tunnel."

The screen pans as the device turns upward. Light from the surface of the water shifts across the camera view. They were right, there must be an air pocket right there. There's a faint, yellow glow. Could it be the eternal flame?

The camera stops.

"What is happening?" Rhen asks.

I read the screen. The propellers are moving at maximum speed. The device seems like it's jerking back and forth. A tentacle suctions on the camera lens.

"No," I lean toward the screen.

Eddi presses buttons to start and stop the propeller, maneuver back and forth, or do anything to get out of the tangle of tentacles that fill the screen.

"Did you put any weapons on it?" Ferris asks.

"Like what?" Eddi asks.

"We didn't have time," I say. "And we are running out of materials. This was the best we could do." I put both my hands on my cheeks and shake my head. What if we can't get it free?

The propeller stops moving. The screen shakes as the device seems to be slammed into the wall. Video shows the wall slowly passing by as the device sinks.

"Can we get it moving again?" I ask.

"The propeller is broken," says Eddi, still looking at information on the screen.

"Maybe I can retrieve it," says Ferris.

"Wait," Eddi says. His tone seems serious; maybe anxious.

"What is it?" I ask.

"The device is still sending its readings," says Eddi. "See how this water is shifting? It's not a current, but it's big."

"Big like what?" I ask.

Eddi doesn't answer.

"A big rock or something?" I don't know why I ask that. I just don't want to think of any alternatives.

"Rocks don't move," says Eddi.

The device still sinks lower and lower as fish pass by and the water's surface gets further from view. Pillars of rock line the underwater cavern.

The device steadies as it hits the floor. A shadow lurks.

Rhen grips my arm. "We need to leave."

"What is that?" I ask as the shadow gets closer to the camera view.

Something like two fins are the first things I notice. They're stiff, like sharks' fins would be, but sharp claws jut from the end of the fins like daggers. The fins move, then

257

claw into a rock pillar as the creature propels itself toward our device. Jagged teeth charge toward my view as Rhen tugs my arm and Ferris pushes Eddi toward the exit. The albharee alarm sounds.

My legs shake. I lean against the wall of the tunnel that leads to the Alaster ship.

Eddi bends over and puts his hands on his knees, his eyes wide as he stares at nothing.

"That was the albharee?" I ask Rhen.

"Only a baby," she replies.

I put my hand on my head and try to imagine something bigger than that. "Why does it have dagger fins?" I speak more to myself rather than to get answers. Why would a shark species need this adaptation?

"So it can claw through caverns," says Rhen. "It can pull up on land. Which is why we need to be careful."

"Why do its teeth protrude from its mouth like that?" I ask.

Rhen shrugs. "This is how it eats."

"Why do we hang out in there?" I ask.

"Because no one else does," says Ferris.

Occasional patters from dripping water sound in the warm tunnel.

"When the albharee is gone," says Ferris. "I can retrieve the device. We can try again."

I turn my attention to Ferris. Is she serious? She can't go in that water after what we saw.

"It sank to the bottom," says Rhen. "That is even further than you have gone without air."

"We could make another device to retrieve the first one," says Eddi. He straightens up, seeming to get some of his senses back. "The one that sank has hardware we need to measure external conditions. We can't lose that."

"We can't lose anything else," I say. "We can't put any more materials into another device that we might lose."

"What would you suggest?" Eddi asks.

He seems to genuinely want my opinion as if I'm the expert on the situation.

"Work it from the other angle," I say. "There are mechanisms that the Trovant heads are using; we can tap into those."

"But you cannot stay long near the Source," says Rhen. "That is where the heads retrieve information."

"We can think of something," says Eddi. "Any option has to be better than what we just saw." He rubs his chin and thinks. It seems like the terror of seeing the albharee has passed. "By the way, Lyra, it's probably best not to mention this to Leal. He already has nightmares about aggressive squid. It would probably be best not to add clawed sharks that can come on land to his bad dreams."

***

"This doesn't make any sense," I say.

"That is what it looks like," says Rhen. "Look." She pulls a white rock from the folds of her clothes.

Does she always keep a small rock with her?

Rhen crouches near the rough, black ground. She grinds the small rock on the ground.

Eddi crouches and leans toward the spot where Rhen's small rock leaves lines on the ground. She sketches what she saw near the Source.

"That is correct," Ferris confirms. "This is how the metal pieces come from the Source and climb up the walls."

"What doesn't make sense?" Garridon crosses his arms and peers at the sketch. He had joined us after Eddi told him that our mechanism sank. "The metal coming from the Source isn't random. It's clearly manufactured rather than natural metal deposits."

I look around at the space where the jungle meets the barren entrance to the Source. I don't see anywhere that the metal could go from the Source into the rest of the Trovant.

"What are you thinking?" Eddi stands and looks at me.

"None of the metal touches another piece of metal?" I ask Rhen.

"No," she shakes her head.

I look at Garridon.

His arms are crossed and his large frame towers over me.

I look away. I don't want to explain what I'm thinking. If I'm wrong, I don't know what he'll say. I'm not strong enough to withstand Garridon's criticism. I'm not like Gia.

"Lyra," Eddi's warm voice says my name. "You can just add ideas to the conversation. You don't have to have the whole answer."

I look at the wall and not at Garridon or Eddi. "It looks like a circuit."

"Hmm." Eddi rubs his chin. "Where would it connect?"

"That's what doesn't make sense," I say. "None of the metal lines overlap, which makes me think they can't touch. Maybe they become completed circuits somewhere else." I look down at Rhen's sketch. I feel embarrassed saying only half of any idea. "But I don't know where the circuits would be completed." I'm used to waiting until I have the full answer before saying anything out loud.

"Where do the rest of the metal lines go?" Garridon asks Rhen.

"Up," says Rhen.

I try to think back to when I saw the metalwork near the Source. I can't remember there being an option to go upward.

"Can we climb up and see where the metal goes?" Garridon asks.

"You can," says Ferris. "But you would have to be okay if you slipped and fell into a pool of melted stone."

Garridon stares at the entrance to the Source.

"Don't even think about it," Eddi slaps Garridon's shoulder.

"Can you make a device that will fly?" Rhen asks.

"Fly?" Eddi looks at the Source entrance, then at me.

I shrug. He's the one who made our previous device swim. I can't build things that move. I just make... the inside stuff.

"I've never needed to," says Eddi. "I'm not sure I can." He rubs his chin again.

"You think Leal can?" Garridon asks. "He's read all the information he could on the surface. He must have at least seen schematics for a flying machine."

"Maybe," says Eddi. "So we just need to see where the metal goes?"

"Yes," says Garridon. "Maybe that way we can see how the Trovant heads have retrieved the information. I've been trying to get the information from them directly, but they've been apprehensive."

"Do you think we could risk sacrificing a camera?" Eddi asks.

"We can ask Minji," says Garridon. "I'm not sure what inventory is left. We will send Lyra into Minji's sleeping quarters to ask her what equipment is left."

"It's evening," says Eddi. "We will take Lyra to her living quarters so she can sleep."

"Yes," says Garridon as he looks absently in the distance. "We will do that." He turns to me. "What is your role in the Trovant?"

I shrug. "I wasn't there when they divided the roles and I think they forgot about me. I just do what my parents are doing." I look at Rhen and Ferris. They know that I haven't been joining my parents much. I've been in the caverns or in the Alaster ship working on the mechanism.

"Good," says Garridon. "We can use that. Tomorrow, you can briefly join Minji's tasks and ask her about the cameras."

"Great," I look at the ground. Minji is the last person I want to talk to.

Garridon looks into the jungle, reaches into his pocket, and pulls out an incapacitator gun. He had brought it in case we saw any dangerous animals. After examining it, he puts it back in his pocket.

"Come on," Eddi motions toward the jungle. "It's a long way back. Let's get you home before it's too dark."

The lighting from the crystalline cracks begins to dim. Insects chirp and buzz as the air seems to cool slightly with the low lighting.

Ferris and Rhen step off the black rocks and into the foliage.

"I'll see you tomorrow," I say to them. I wish I could follow and sleep in the Caverns. But I know my parents get worried if I don't come back at night.

"Peace be with you this night," says Rhen as she walks in the direction of the Caverns with Ferris. I think that's a Trovantian phrase. Rhen usually says that to me when we part ways at night.

"How is Gia?" Garridon asks as he steps into the jungle.

"Still sick," says Eddi as he swats a plant from his face.

"Does she need..." Garridon also swats a plant as he passes it. "Medical attention or something?"

I'm shorter than both of them and the plants go over my head as I walk by. The path opens up somewhat and I scuffle to stay beside Garridon and Eddi.

"I don't think so," says Eddi. "The illness is wearing her out, but I don't think it's more than a nasty bug. Hasn't Gia ever been sick?"

"I'm..." Garridon hesitates. "I'm not sure. She had to train no matter what."

"Don't be too hard on yourself," Eddi reassures. "We all did what we could to survive."

"When I put her into the bunk on the ship," says Garridon, "that was the first time I held her since she was small. Maybe since Britannica..."

There is silence.

I don't know if I'm supposed to say anything or not say anything. Do they remember I'm here?

"Apologies," Garridon says. "I haven't slept for a while."

"You should get some sleep," says Eddi. "You're only human."

"Not according to your son," Garridon responds.

It seems like Garridon has a faint smile. Did he just make a joke?

"Believe me," Eddi says, "I make robots. If you were one, you'd be a lot easier to deal with."

Garridon laughs.

Garridon can laugh?

It's dark when I get to my parents' living quarters. My eyes are tired, my body is tired, my emotions are tired. I think of how often Gia had to stay awake and wasn't allowed to be tired. Maybe it is good I don't have a dad like Garridon. I walk toward the carved opening that creates a small room with a bed where my parents sleep. I hear sounds of slumbering and lean through the doorway. My dad stirs in his sleep. I turn quickly. Then a small figure pops out of nowhere. I jump as I almost run into Pictor.

"Where've you been?" Pictor asks.

"Go back to sleep," I put my hands on my little brother's shoulder and spin him in the direction of his room.

"Lyra?" I hear my dad's sleepy voice from the other room.

"Go," I whisper to Pictor and we both scurry to the rooms where we have beds to sleep.

I roll onto the carved platform that makes my bed.

"Lyra," my dad steps into my room.

Lying on my side, I stay still and face the wall.

"I know you're awake." He comes fully into the room and sits at the edge of the bed.

I stay frozen. I want to talk to him, but I don't want to accidentally say everything about Leal or Minji or how I've been a failure at getting the information about the Trovant.

He sighs. "I'm sorry for whatever you're going through." He leans over and kisses my head. "Remember that you don't have to go through it alone." He rubs my cheek, then stands to leave.

A tear trickles down my face.

***

"Ah!" I duck as a creature jumps from a market stall. Avoiding the animal, I run into someone's legs.

"Trajique prack!" The person yells at me.

"Sorry," I crane my neck to see the person who walks away.

Sellers quibble behind stalls built from rock and buyers bargain to trade animals, spices, or whatever else they have. I don't understand the system of buying and selling, but I understand that it's loud.

Two kids rush on either side of me and bump my shoulders.

I cover my eyes and take a deep breath in and out. I need to stay focused.

"Oof!" I'm hit in the back by someone's leg.

The person shouts something at me but keeps walking.

"Minji," I say to myself. "I need to find Minji."

Music plays over the sounds of haggling customers.

I can barely hear my own words. "Pass the vendor who sells sea creatures to cook." I repeat the instructions from Eddi. "Then count five stalls down and look on the left where there are stacks of baskets."

I see a man who stands over a display of dead creatures with fins, tentacles, claws, shells, and anything else that comes on marine animals. Bugs the size of my hand buzz around the dead creatures and the vendor swats them with something that looks like a paddle.

"One. Two." I count the stalls I walk past. "Minji!" I shout as I get closer to where she should be. Maybe she will hear me from here. "Three. Four." I see baskets. "Minji?"

Minji's perfect, black hair and deep eyes peek around the corner. My stomach hurts.

"Lyra?"

I can barely hear her over the sounds of the market.

"Lyra," she steps closer and motions for me to follow her somewhere. "Dayana might see you." She guides me to the side and behind one of the merchants. "You could get in trouble."

There's a narrow opening behind the merchant where Minji takes me.

# Trovant

A faint voice says Minji's name and something in Trovantian.

Minji turns and calls in her soft voice: "Yija la-a eela yun." She then faces the opening and steps into a narrow tunnel.

"What was that?" I ask as the noise from the market gets quieter.

"I told them I'm going to the bathroom," Minji says as she speeds through the tunnels.

She walks so fast.

"No," I try to keep up. "I mean, you speak Trovantian?"

"I've learned some," she says.

Why does she have to be so cool?

"This way," she takes an abrupt turn. Her straight hair sways as she swishes into a small cove in the rock tunnel. "Dayana probably won't come down this way."

The sound from the market is almost completely gone.

"I hope this doesn't sound too negative," she says, "but why are you here? You could get in trouble for not having a role all this time."

"I mean," I say, "technically, I think my role is whatever my parents are doing."

"What is that?" she asks.

"My mom is with babies and my dad is harvesting food."

"You aren't doing either of those," says Minji. She fidgets her fingers. "Someone might see you somewhere where you aren't supposed to be."

"I don't think it's like the Trellis," I look at the ground. It seems like she's concerned, but I don't know why. It's none of her business anyway. "People can wander around in the Trovant."

"Okay," she also looks at the ground. "I'm sorry."

"It's fine," I say.

It's quiet. There are very faint sounds from the market, but no noises of people walking in the tunnels near us.

"So—" she says.

"So," I rub my arm. "I'm supposed to ask you about cameras."

"What about the cameras?"

"Do we have any left?" I ask.

"Yes and no," Minji says.

"What does that mean?"

"We still have all the cameras," says Minji, "but we've taken parts out of all of them to power the communication beacons and the atmospheric sensors. What do we need the cameras for?"

"We need one to see into some part of the Trovant. It's near the Source. There are some sort of metal lines from there that might create a circuit."

"What happened to putting a mechanism in the eternal flame?"

I look down again. "Our mechanism sank."

"Oh, I'm sorry," she says. "So we need a camera to see the Source? We could remove the parts from a sensor or communicator then reassemble a camera if it's needed. It just depends on what is more important."

"I don't know which is more important," I say. I don't even know why Garridon sent me to ask her. He's the one who set up the other sensors; he would know what is more important.

"Maybe there's another solution," says Minji. "You said there were metal pieces?"

"Yeah," I say.

"I might have an idea."

Of course, she has an idea. It's probably perfect, just like her.

# Chapter 13: Leal— Boulders

"It's a mirror," I say. I pat the curls on my head that are reflected with more clarity than I've ever seen. "Look at my hair." The mirror shows messy hairs that zig-zag out of the curls and make a ball of poof. "Who let my hair get like this? It's so tangled."

"Look at my eyebrows," Gia laughs and leans closer to the mirror. "They're so dark and my eyes are so light."

In the reflection, I see a glimmer of blue behind Gia.

"Finally," I turn around and see robes hanging from hooks. "I get a blue one."

Gia does the same and slips on a silvery robe.

"Finally," she says. "Pockets."

"Madam Pockets," I bow to her in the mirror.

"Mister Blue," Gia bows back to me.

"I like my new role," I play with the hem of the blue garment.

"Don't let it go to your head." Gia swishes her hands in her pockets.

A noise comes from another room and someone calls Gia's name.

Garridon appears in the doorway. "Gia? What are you doing? I've been looking for you."

"How did you find me?" Gia asks.

"I came here for Eddi," Garridon says. "Doesn't matter. I'm glad I found you. I talked to Lyra and everything is ready. We need to stay together."

"Everything is ready for what?" Gia asks.

"To retrieve the information," says Garridon. "But I'm not sure what the Trovant heads will do once we have it. It's better if we aren't separated, especially when they find out."

Gia stands with her hands in her pockets and her head slightly tilted. She was ill for most of the plans for retrieving the atmospheric conditions. She was also sick when Dad and Lyra's mechanism sank. She hasn't been updated on anything that happened recently.

"Come with me," Garridon seems impatient. "I will explain on the way."


The air is cool and carries a song as water gently laps against the side of the cavern pool. Blue light settles over the expansive area and waterfalls over Minji's hair and shoulders. She stands gracefully in the center of the cavern beside two cloaked Trovantian women.

One of the Trovantians gives us a skeptical glance as we approach. "Why are you wearing festive gowns?" I don't remember her name, but she's one of Lyra's friends.

The other Trovantian is Rhen. I remember her because she carried Gia through the jungle and up the rock wall.

I look down at my blue robe, then shrug. "They were in my living quarters. I liked it."

"And you are wearing man's clothing," the Trovantian says to Gia.

"It has pockets," Gia says as she sticks her hands in her pockets.

"Is everything ready?" Garridon asks as we journey further into the room and to the group in the center of the cavern.

Dad and Lyra look up from a screen that Dad holds. Lyra wears a dark, shimmering cloak. It's the same as the two Trovantians wear.

"Should be good," says Dad.

"So what exactly are we doing now?" Gia asks.

I have the same question. Garridon gave Gia an update about everything I already knew, but he didn't yet explain what this cavern had to do with anything.

"Over there," says Minji. She points to a sleek piece of metal in the corner of the massive space. "I noticed it when we were in here before. I thought it was odd to have a manufactured beam of metal in the wall. I assumed it was what produced the white light that makes all of the plants grow. Lyra mentioned something similar coming from the Source. Maybe it's all connected— the walls, the lights, the Source…"

"I should have noticed this one, too," Lyra mumbles.

"It's okay," Minji rubs Lyra's shoulder.

Lyra steps slightly away from Minji.

Minji takes her hand away from Lyra and tucks her hands in her sleeves.

Garridon looks up at the metal, which goes into an opening. "Rhen climbed through that opening as far as she could and has fixed a sensor inside. The opening became too small for her to continue. But she said she could see some sort of machine through the opening."

"The atmospheric conditions are favorable," Dad cuts in. "One of us will be able to climb the rest of the way through the opening and connect this mechanism," he holds up a small machine. "Once this is connected, the information will go to my tablet and we can access whatever the heads of the Trovant have been reading."

"Who is going up there?" I ask.

"It's a very tight space, son," Dad replies.

That doesn't sound very reassuring.

"I'm going," says Minji.

"What?" My eyes widen. I think of Minji's graceful frame and gentle skin scraping against narrow rocks. What if one collapses on her? "You're afraid of tight spaces." I blurt out the most logical reason I can think of to stop her from going.

"I can close my eyes," Minji says.

"The whole way?" I ask. "How are you going to climb up there?"

"We reassembled a camera," says Minji. "You can guide me from here."

"There's no audio on your tablet," I say. "You'd have to open your eyes to read the screen. I'll go instead."

"You aren't briefed on this equipment," Dad responds. "Minji knows what to look for and how to use the devices we've made."

"Still," Garridon says as he looks at the opening near the metal beam. "Someone should go up with Minji."

"Based on the diameter of the smallest opening," Dad looks at the screen, "I'm not sure you'll fit." Apparently, Dad assumed Garridon was volunteering himself to go with Minji.

"I can go," Gia says.

Garridon clenches his jaw.

Dad looks at the screen again. "You should be able to fit." He looks at Gia, then at Garridon.

Garridon paces.

"Garridon—" Dad says.

"I'm thinking," Garridon interrupts.

"I can go," I say.

Both of them look at me.

"Son," Dad says. "Minji might need someone who…" he trails off.

"Can climb without panicking," Gia says.

"I can—" I grab my shoulder and look at the height of the ceiling where the opening is. I picture myself trying to be brave and guide Minji to the high ceiling and then through tight spaces. I bet I could muster courage if it were for Minji. But then I picture how I was on the platform on the Alaster ship. She was the one who was comforting me. "I'm sure I could do it." My fake confidence might not be that convincing.

"And you would need to swim," Rhen's voice cuts through the low hums reverberating through the cavern.

"Swim?" I panic. "Why would anyone need to swim?"

"The tunnel goes downward," she explains, "then dips under the water, and turns back up to a pocket that meets the metal pieces once again."

"Can the monster get in there?" I ask.

"We do not know," she answers.

I look at Minji and picture her trying to swim away as a monster chases her. I have to try to go with her. But how could I protect her from any of this? I can't swim. I can barely climb. I'm sure I can't fight a monster.

"We can go," the other Trovantian says. "We can guide you until we cannot continue further."


Gia folds her festive cloak and puts it on a boulder. Then Lyra gives Gia a bag made of a blanket.

"This has a tablet and the mechanism inside," says Lyra. "Both should be okay in the water, but not to be submerged for more than 15 minutes."

"I don't think I can be submerged for 15 minutes either," Gia says as she puts the bag around herself.

I wring my hands as I watch one of the Trovantians put a harness on the ground that is meant for Minji.

"Ferris," says Minji, "I feel weird about this."

"Do you think you can climb into that opening?" Ferris points to the ceiling.

Minji looks up and shakes her head slightly.

Rhen looks at the harness and then at Gia.

Gia shakes her head. "I don't need it this time."

"It is only until the first ledge," Ferris says as she puts on the harness and Minji gets in a position to be secured onto her back.

Rhen grabs hold of a rock and takes the first step up the wall.

Gia does the same as Rhen climbs upward.

Garridon steps near Gia. "You are likely to still be weak from being ill," he says. "Make sure to take breaks so you don't overextend your capacity."

"Take breaks?" Gia says as she starts to climb the wall. "You've never said that to me before."

"I'm saying it now," Garridon stands beneath Gia as if he's ready to catch her if she falls from the rock.

Gia climbs to a point where the rock wall curves into a rock ceiling. I can hear her panting as she clings to the ceiling. Her nose is still congested. She pauses, taking in a deep breath through her mouth, and then moves her hand to the edge of the round opening in the ceiling. As she grabs with her other hand, her feet come off the wall. She dangles with her arms gripping the opening and her feet moving in the air.

I squeeze my mouth. Was that intentional? Will she fall?

Garridon stands far below Gia, still ready to catch her.

Gia swings her legs back and forth. Once she has momentum, she forces her legs up to the edge of the opening. She gets a foothold. Then, she sticks the other foot on the wall. With her back pressed against one side of the opening and her legs on the other, she moves her hands up the wall, grabbing above her head. She pulls herself up, then presses her back against the wall and moves one foot at a time. In this way, she inches upward and out of sight.

I look at the tablet that Dad holds. Lyra had fixed a camera to the strap of Gia's bag. The footage on Dad's tablet shows the edge of the ruffled fabric as well as Gia's legs extended to the rock wall.

"Watch out," a voice says through the tablet.

"The camera has a microphone," says Dad. "But we don't have one on our end, so they can't hear us."

A rope cascades through the camera view.

I look up and to the opening as a rope plunges toward the ground. It stops, dangling through the opening.

With Minji strapped to her back, Ferris tugs the rope that is secured somewhere through the opening. Why couldn't Gia have waited until the rope was there and then climbed that?

Gripping the rope, Ferris starts to climb. Minji squeezes both hands over her eyes as the fabric harness dangles her over the rocky ground.

Garridon stands beneath them. I trust Garridon more than myself to catch Minji if she comes out of the harness. But what if Ferris slips from the rope? She would crush Garridon and Minji.

Ferris climbs through the opening with much more ease than Gia. She doesn't need to press her back against the rock to get leverage but does struggle to fit through the opening without crushing Minji.

"They're all in," Dad looks at the screen. "Gia and Rhen have made it to the first ledge."

Lyra steps away from the tablet and looks up through the opening. She tugs at the rope. She seems to be examining the space. Voices sound from the tablet and I turn my attention away from Lyra.

The tablet shows Ferris coming over the ledge with Minji on her back.

"You okay?" Gia's electronic voice asks through the tablet.

"Just get this off," Ferris unstraps the harness that holds Minji.

Gia and Rhen help remove the harness and lower Minji to the ledge.

"Look at that," Gia's finger points to a part of the rock where more of the metal pieces run through the wall. Metal lines are close together, but not touching.

The metal seems embedded in the wall with nothing between it and the rock. I wonder what sort of insulator is used to ensure the frequencies from the metals don't meet until the circuit—

Minji ducks into a tunnel that has rocks jutting out from above and below. The Trovantians crawl, but Minji crouches as she maneuvers over jagged rocks that could cut her delicate skin. Gia's hands sporadically come into view as she hoists herself over rocks and the camera shuffles around on her bag strap.

There's another part of Dad's screen that shows video footage of water. Particles float around and an occasional fish swims by.

"Is this where they are going?" I ask as I point to that footage.

"No," Dad responds. "This is where the mechanism sank. This one is still sending a video feed. We'll keep it on until the battery dies."

"How much battery is left?" I ask.

Dad taps on the tablet and switches the information on the screen, which blocks the feed from Gia's camera. "About 2%."

"Bring the other video back up," I say as Gia's voice comes through the screen but I can't see what they are doing.

They've arrived at the part of the tunnel that meets the water. My heart rate rises. The expansive pool is even bigger than the one in the cavern near me. The monster could definitely fit through that.

I look at the other footage showing where the camera had sunk. Still, particles float across the camera view. There's no sign of anything dangerous.

"Don't let go," Rhen says through the camera. "And hold your breath."

Gia's hands reach around Rhen. The camera is pressed against the dark fabric and the footage goes black.

Sounds swish through the tablet, which is the only indication they are underwater. The sounds keep swishing, but I can't see what's happening. The camera continues to be dark, which means Gia hasn't let go of Rhen's back. That's a good sign she isn't suffocating.

I look at the other footage, which is still peaceful. I squint to ensure nothing is lurking in the distance. I don't see anything.

There's a crack of light from the camera attached to Gia's bag. Is she letting go of Rhen? Is she drowning?

We all lean in toward the tablet.

The footage shows Rhen's cloaked figure swimming upward.

"Why is Gia letting go?" I ask.

"She could be near the top," says Garridon. "It would be faster if both of them swam upward than if Gia were deadweight."

"Gia can swim?" I ask.

"She had been training," Garridon responds. "Before she was ill."

I think of the time before Gia was sick. She worked with the babies during the day. Apparently, she was with Garridon setting up beacons and sensors in the evening. And she was also learning to swim? When did either of the Hamiltonis sleep?

Swirls of bubbles and splashes of water crash over the video footage. Gia's voice breaks in and out of the sounds of slushing water.

Gia and Rhen pull themselves onto a rocky ledge. Ferris emerges from the water with Minji still clasping her back. Gia's hands grip Minji's arms to pull her from the water. Minji crashes onto her hands and knees and coughs as water pours from her hair and clothes.

I grab Dad's shoulder.

"They made it out," he pats my back.

"Phew," I lean on him. "They're out."

Rhen's voice plays through the tablet. "This is where we leave you."

The camera view pans down and stops at a small tunnel. More metal lines stream through the tunnel ceiling.

"I could have fit through there," Garridon says.

"It gets even smaller," Dad replies, still looking at the tablet. "I don't think they should touch the metal. We didn't talk about that." He starts tapping on the screen to write a message.

Minji's voice interrupts. "We should probably avoid touching these if we can."

"Oh." Dad deletes the message he was typing. "Exactly what I was going to say."

"Is it better if I go first or you?" Gia asks.

"If I go first," says Minji, "then you will be blocking the exit."

"So you want me to be in front of you?"

"No," Minji responds. Her figure crouches by the tunnel entrance as she looks in the tunnel, then toward Gia. Her beautiful, dark eyes face the camera. "I can't have the option to turn around. I need you to block the exit."

I wrap my arms around myself. "It should have been me," I whisper.

"They'll be okay," Dad says as he wraps an arm around me.

What have I even been doing? I think back to the amount of time Minji and Gia have been making or setting up sensors and communication beacons. Dad and Lyra made and trialed a mechanism. I had just been working in that waste heap and sometimes taking care of Takara. Now my friends are the only ones who know how to work the devices and I can't do anything to help.

I look up from the tablet and back to the rope. Where did Lyra go?

Minji's voice starts panicking from the tablet.

My focus turns back to the footage. The metal lines disappear into the rocky wall as the tunnel narrows even more.

"I can't," Minji says.

"You've got this," Gia tries to comfort Minji.

Comfort isn't really Gia's strength.

I can't see the opening that Minji needs to squeeze through. In our view, the footage is pressed completely against the tunnel. Rock scrapes against the microphone.

"I'm not sure I can fit," Gia tries to sound calm.

"Don't say that." It's hard to hear Minji.

"Minji," says Gia, "I need you to look ahead. Good. Do you see the opening up there?"

There's a faint sound of Minji's response.

"Now close your eyes," says Gia, "and move toward it."

Gia grunts as she struggles and the rocks grind against the camera. "Good. You're doing great, Minji."

With scraping noises, the camera view finally moves. Gia made it past the point where she had been stuck.

Gia and Minji shimmy through the narrow passage for what feels like eternity. Light peeks through the camera view as Gia emerges from the tight space and into a spherical opening. Minji stands but ducks her head as metal lines from across the spherical space meet in the center, where a machine hangs from the ceiling.

"According to the schematics from the inventor, Rita Reid," Minji trembles, "this is where we could input Eddi's mechanism." She points to a part of the machine that hangs from the low ceiling.

Gia's hands dig through the bag and pull out the mechanism Dad made. She hands it to Minji.

Holding the mechanism, Minji crouches and then unlatches parts of the mechanism.

"What is she doing?" I ask.

"She's removing the waterproof casing," Dad replies. "And then she'll prep the machine to be inserted.

It's not my machine, though, Lyra also made—" He looks around the room. "Where'd she go?"

"She's climbed the rope," Garridon states.

"Why?" asks Dad.

In the video feed, Minji unhinges a piece of the mechanism and pushes some buttons.

"She said she saw something," Garridon answers. "I couldn't stop her. But she can come down with the others. It may be safer if Rhen is there to help her own."

"Are you receiving the signal?" Minji looks at the camera.

Gia pulls the tablet from her bag.

Dad types on the screen: "Yes."

"Eddi says 'yes.'" Gia reads the information to Minji.

"I'm putting it in," Minji says as she rises from the ground and inserts the small mechanism into the machine hanging from the ceiling. A small light on the mechanism blinks yellow. Then, the light turns to a steady green.

"Are we getting information?" I ask.

"Oh no," Dad says.

"What?" I panic.

"It's okay, Leal," Dad says. "The information is just in Trovantian. It's not the worst that could have happened, but I can't read it."

"One of the Trovantians up there can interpret," Garridon says.

Gia moves the camera to her face. "Are you receiving the information?"

"Well," says Dad, "we have all the information that they can get from that machine. It's in Trovantian but they can't do more on their end." Dad types: "Yes."

"Good," says Gia. The camera drops back in place and shows Minji crouched by the tunnel. "Let's get out of here."

Minji closes her eyes, lies on her stomach, and sticks her head in the tunnel. She pulls her head out again and then shakes her head.

"You did it before," says Gia. "This is the last time. Then we'll be out of here."

Tears well in Minji's eyes.

My heart breaks. I want to hug her and kiss her forehead and tell her it will be okay. Maybe I can tell Gia to hug her.

Gia pats her shoulder. "There. There."

Gia is terrible at this.

With a tear rolling down her delicate cheek, Minji squeezes her eyes closed and shimmies into the tight opening.

Again, rocks scrape against the camera's view as Gia makes her way behind Minji.

Minji whimpers and says something, but it's too soft to hear what she says.

"We have to keep going," Gia says. "We can't turn back now."

Minji gives a muffled response.

Gia's hand reaches across the camera's view. With barely any space, she grips the tablet and presses it between herself and the wall so she can see it.

"Leal," she whispers to the camera. "What do I do? I want to get out of here. Can I shove her through the opening?"

"No!" I yell.

"She can't hear you," says Dad.

"Give me that," I yank the tablet from Dad and type a message to Gia.

"Ugh," Gia sighs when she gets the message.

Minji whimpers again.

"Just a second," Gia says. "I need to remember the words."

I type a line on the screen: "Like clouds drifting in endless skies."

Gia sighs again, then shoves the tablet back in the bag and starts to sing: "Like clouds drifting in endless skies. You're the calm in my restless eyes…"

"That's helping," Minji's muffled voice says through the camera.

"… A song that floats through evening's haze," Gia grunts and sings as she squeezes through the rocky space. "Softly sung, yet sets ablaze. I was alone…" Gia pauses. She might be stuck again in the narrowest spot.

Minji says something but I can't make out the words.

"I was alone," Gia sings again as she grunts, "Then your hand found mine in the dark—" There's more light as

Gia seems to approach the end of the narrow passage. "The warmth of a steady flame, a single spark."

Gia comes from the opening and Minji looks at the camera with a faint smile.

I smile back at her.

Dad smirks and looks at me from the corner of his eye.

I try to stop from blushing as I hand the tablet back to Dad.

"Ready to go back?" Rhen towers high above Minji and then crouches.

Minji nods as she stands by the edge of the pool. She puts her arms around Rhen to make the journey back through the water.

"Wait!" Garridon shouts. "Tell them to wait."

Dad types on the screen, saying to wait.

Ferris also crouches and the screen goes dark as Gia presses against Ferris and the camera submerges underwater.

"What is it?" Dad asks. "I don't think they saw the message."

"Listen," says Garridon.

The sound of water sloshes through the tablet.

"The water?" I ask.

"The alarm," says Garridon.

I look around the cavern. The waves of the pool hit stronger against the land. The hum of the albharee alarm raises.

"I need to tell Lyra," Garridon says to Dad. "She should be safe up there but she can't come down." Garridon jogs toward the rope hanging from the opening.

I look back at the tablet to the screen where the camera had sunk to the bottom of the watery cavern. A shadow lurks in the distance.

"What is that?" I say.

"Get out of here!" Garridon shouts to us. "Lyra!" He yells through the opening in the ceiling. "The albharee is coming! Stay put, it can't reach you up there!"

"Let's go," Dad tugs my arm.

"What about Gia and Minji?" I back away from the pool, but don't run for the exit. "They are in the water."

Garridon turns toward us. "Go!" He starts moving away from the opening.

"Uh," Dad looks around the cavern. "What can we do? What can we do?" He sings nervously as he looks around.

The alarm gets louder.

"Maybe we can cross the circuits," I panic. "Yeah, we can climb up to those metal lines and connect them."

"That could cause an explosion," says Dad.

"Yeah," I say. "Maybe enough to cause a cave-in here and block the section where the monster is. That would keep it from getting to the others."

"We might not survive such an explosion."

I look at Dad. I don't see another option.

"Okay," he looks to the tablet. "How do we connect the metals? And how do we lure the albharee here so we don't trap our friends?"

"Where is the albaha— monster?" I look at the tablet. The shadowy figure is gone from the screen.

"I don't know," Dad shakes his head.

"Ahh!" Lyra screams. She dangles on the rope.

The alarm roars.

"Where is it?" I yell.

Garridon turns back toward the opening where Lyra hangs. "Lyra, get back!"

A huge wave erupts from the pool as huge teeth burst from the water. Claws like spears stab into the rock and the albharee thrusts from the pool and toward us.

"Run!" Dad yells as we bolt toward the exit.

The albharee changes direction. Still running toward the exit, I watch as the albharee rushes toward Garridon. Lyra is out of sight.

There's a loud bang. The ground shakes and heat radiates through the air. Fire burst from the opening in the ceiling. A massive chunk of ceiling crashes on the albharee. Its jaw opens and closes as it writhes back and forth beneath the weight of the fallen boulder.

"Keep going, Leal." Dad pulls me to the exit as rocks crash down.

Piece by piece, the boulders pile over the area.

The loud crashes quiet down as smaller rocks roll down the pile.

Dad coughs from the cloud of dust and rubble. But the dust settles quickly from the moisture in the air.

"Dad," I run to the pile of rocks. "Where are they?"

He rushes to my side and starts pulling rocks from the pile. "Go get Arcturo."

"Where?" I look back and forth, trying to still my panic. Where is Minji? Where is Gia? What happened to the others?

"In the harvesting fields," says Dad.

"Minji's not in a field," I say.

"What?" Dad shakes his head. "No, Arcturo is in the fields. Go get him."

"Right," I turn and run toward the red-lit cave that connects to the rest of the Trovant. "I'll get Arcturo."


"Yajora," a Trovantian yells as a large machine is in place, strapped around a huge boulder.

"Everyone, stand back," Arcturo says as he steps away from the area.

Trovantians turn the machine with a long handle and it slowly pulls the boulder from its place. Rocks roll and settle into place as the boulder moves.

Arcturo rushes over and pulls the rocks away. His arm muscles bulge and sweat pours from his forehead as he tosses the rocks out of the way. Jarret and Desman join in.

It had taken hours to get to this point, but I guess the Trovantians already had a machine and protocol ready for cave-in emergencies. Vega joins Arcturo to move the rocks and Pictor remains seated on a boulder where Vega told him to stay.

I step over and pull the rocks that I'm capable of moving. I try not to work next to Desman. He was raging when he got here, saying that no one told him what we were doing and some Trovantian gave him the news that his friends were stuck.

Jarret also seems worried, but his type of worry is less aggressive than Desman. He's been pensive and focused— like Arcturo— working hard and never taking a break. His biceps also flex as he moves a heavy rock. Something about his stature is like Arcturo.

I squat and drag a rock as far to the side as I can. These have been painful hours, seeing how heavy these rocks are and wondering if there's any chance we will find our friends alive.

"What is—" Jarret's gaze follows something in the cavern.

"What?" I ask, looking for whatever he sees.

"I saw something," says Jarret.

I look to the spot where Jarret gazes. My view pans over to where the albharee lies dead. Its teeth are gigantic. Daggers jut from its fins that are larger than a Trovantian. I look away.

"I'll be right back," Jarret leaves to follow whatever he saw.

Desman's voice echoes from the pile of rocks. "We have something!"

People pull rocks from a person lying on his back.

"Garridon?" Arcturo says as he approaches the spot where his friend lies still. Arcturo crouches.

"Is he alive?" Dad steps cautiously over rocks.

Arcturo feels Garridon's neck. "His heart is beating." He shakes Garridon.

Garridon's eyes crack slightly. "Arcturo." His voice is exasperated as he tries to get the name out.

"Hey," Arcturo says. "You're alright now. Stay awake."

Garridon forces words out: "I tried."

"I know," says Arcturo. "Eddi told me. It wasn't your fault. And we're going to get them, okay? Both of our girls."

Garridon's eyes close.

"We need help!" Dad yells. "He needs medical attention!"

"Someone is already coming," Imeel steps over the pile of rocks. "I am afraid this is the end."

"What do you mean?" Arcturo stands. "There are others in there."

"The roof has caved in," says Imeel. "This is as far as we can go without risking further collapse."

"We have to keep going," Arcturo faces the rocks where a big boulder is rooted into the ground.

"You mean?" Vega bends at the knees. "Our daughter is still in there." She looks to where her husband grips a massive boulder that he can't move.

"We would be risking the entire Trovant," says Imeel. "That is not an option."

Arcturo starts grabbing the ropes on the boulder-moving machine. None of us would be strong enough to operate the machine without Trovantians.

"No," Vega falls to her knees, hands gripping the ground. Her wail fills the cavern as her arms tremble to keep her upright. She heaves in and out.

"Mom!" Pictor jumps from the boulder and runs to Vega.

"We'll find her," Arcturo rushes to Vega and holds her. "We'll find her."

Pictor crashes next to his parents and Arcturo envelops his wife and son.

Jarret appears from another part of the cavern. He walks toward us with arms full of dark fabric that shimmers slightly.

He walks over and kneels next to the family. Arcturo pulls back the fabric in Jarret's arms. Lyra's closed eyes are pressed against Jarret's chest as he cradles her still body.

"Please help," Arcturo sobs toward a medical team that already approaches Lyra and Garridon.

I look over to the pile of boulders and rocks that block the way to Minji, Gia, and the two Trovantians. The explosion was far enough away from them that they could have easily escaped the cave-in. They must be out there somewhere.

# Chapter 14: Lyra— Starlight Drips Under the Sea

I should have noticed the metal piece in the caverns. I spent enough time looking at the ceiling and recounting the 21 holes at the top. Minji was only in here once and she noticed the metal— how could I have missed that?

I step over to Eddi, who holds a tablet that plays Gia's camera feed.

With Minji harnessed to her back, Ferris grabs hold of the rope that swings from the opening in the ceiling.

I look at the footage as Gia climbs onto the ledge and more metal lines run through the rock. Something glimmers in the wall. Is there a crystal in the wall? I look closer as the camera view shifts with Gia's movement. It looks like a piece of metal. Could it be silver? The camera moves away. Maybe I'm fantasizing to make myself feel better.

I lean in again as Gia's camera moves across the area and catches the glimmer in the wall. It looks like it could be a piece of raw metal.

I step over to the opening in the ceiling to see if I can get a better look. Ferris climbs through the vertical tunnel. Minji puts her hands out in front of her to stop herself from getting bashed into rocks.

I touch the rope as Ferris and Minji pull onto the ledge. Would I be strong enough to climb this? I've been climbing the rock walls near the jungle and I've always climbed the ladders in the Alaster ship. I grip the robe and pull up. My arm strength isn't enough to hold my body weight. But maybe if I use my feet...

"Stay down here," Garridon's commanding voice says to me once Ferris and Minji disappear over the edge.

"I think I saw something," I say.

"Stay down here," Garridon pauses, "please."

Whoa, I can't imagine Garridon says 'please' very often. I let go of the rope.

Garridon walks back toward Eddi and Leal.

But I need to know what's up there. What if it actually is silver? I grab the rope again and clutch the bottom between my feet.

Garridon turns around. "Lyra, it will be safer if you stay here."

"It will just be a minute," I say as I hop my feet up, gripping the rope with my hands and then moving my feet before pushing myself up. He watches me inch myself up like a worm.

I hear him sigh. I look down as he stands under me, possibly ready to catch me if I fall.

I can't believe I just defied Garridon. I can't believe I'm strong enough to climb a rope.

As I get to the ledge where the others were, they have already gone through the passage toward the machine.

I look around the metal pieces along the wall and to the place where I had seen the glimmer. As I walk toward it, I think of what Rhen said about silver and the origin of the name Ara: a drip of starlight fell from the surface and created ores of silver that symbolize hope of finding our way home. I touch the slightly glimmering surface. I bend down to grab a jagged rock from the ground, then I scrape the cavern wall that holds in the metallic piece. I chip away the rocky wall and more of the shimmering metal is revealed. It is silver.

The jagged rock cuts my hand. I reposition my grip and continue scraping and chipping away near the silver. There's this sense that Ara could be here with me as I hack at the cavern wall and release the silver ore. It's as if I could work hard enough to mine a piece of hope that I can take with me everywhere. Sweat drips over my head as I use all my strength to unveil the silver.

I scrape the wall and think of losing Ara. Maybe we could find our way home together if only I could get this silver out. I chip away and think of Minji. If I can get rid of my rough edges, maybe I could shine like her. I stab the wall and think of Leal. Maybe he could love me back if I could dig out something valuable inside myself.

Tears join the sweat that pours over my cheeks as I get closer to unearthing the piece of silver ore. I drop the jagged rock, then dig my fingers in the gap I carved between the silver and the wall. I pull on the silver. It doesn't move. I pull again. I need to get this. I yank with all my strength.

I crash to the ground as the silver releases from the wall. My back bangs against the ground, just beside the edge. My cracked fingernails and sliced hands bleed as I clasp the sliver. I look at the piece of metal and I cry. I want to hold on to an object of eternal hope, but the silver is still just metal and I'm still myself, lying on the floor with bloody fingernails.

"Ara," I sob. "I need you to tell me what to do."

Gripping the silver, I pull the metal to my chest and curl up, crying as I hope for something, anything, to change. "Alaster," I whisper. "Are you there?"

"Lyra!" Garridon's voice shouts through the opening. "The albharee is coming! Stay put, it can't reach you up there!"

I sit up and wipe my face. Then I look over the edge to see Garridon through the opening.

"Stay there," he says, "okay?"

Looking over the edge, I nod.

I hear Leal and Eddi faintly as they yell over the albharee alarm: "What about Gia and Minji?"

Scrambling to the tunnel, I lean through to try and spot the others. "Hey!" I yell through the tunnel to see if anyone is close enough to respond. If they are on the other side of the water, they won't be able to hear me. "Is anyone there?"

"Maybe we can cross the circuits," Leal's faint shout sounds over the alarm. "Yeah, we can climb up to those metal lines and connect them."

"That could cause an explosion," Eddi responds.

I look up at the metal pieces across the wall where I stand. I'm the only one close enough to connect the circuit lines. I look down at the silver in my bloody hand. If this causes an explosion, it might be enough to rip open the wall, which is filled with methane. Everything nearby would burn up until the methane is blocked off by rubble.

"How do we connect the metals?" Eddi asks. "And how do we lure the albharee here so we don't trap our friends?"

Looking at my fingers, I remember when Ferris flung fish blood over the water's surface and it attracted a smaller monster. If the albharee was close, would it be attracted to the scent of blood?

I rush to the edge. Garridon is out of sight from the opening. Hopefully, he and the others are all far away from the opening. Placing the silver on the ledge, I grab the rope so I can climb closer to the bottom.

"Ahh!" My grip isn't strong and I slip from the ledge. I squeeze the rope and stop myself from falling completely to the bottom.

Dangling, the slip on the rope cut my hands even more and blood drips from my torn skin. Perfect. Resituating on the rope, I grip with my knees and feet so I can get one hand free. I squeeze my hand and drip blood on the ground.

The albharee alarm howls.

I start to pull myself back up the rope.

A huge monster erupts from the massive pool as water crashes on the ground.

"Lyra, get back!" Garridon commands from the other side of the cavern.

I yank myself back up the rope as fast as I can. Pulling myself back over the ledge, I pick up the piece of silver. I turn to the metal lines in the wall. Wrapping the cloak around myself and even covering my hand, I put the silver ore in the fabric that covers my hand.

"Rhen said these were fireproof," I say to myself as I pull the hood over my head.

I orient the silver ore near two of the metal circuit lines that are close to one another. I turn my face and squeeze my eyes closed. I touch the silver ore to the metal lines. My muscles tense. Electricity jolts through my arm. I scream as the force blasts me off my feet and I feel heat all around as I slam into a wall.

There's a dripping noise. I crack open my eyes. My vision is foggy. I try to focus on something. Rocks and boulders are stacked around the space. It's completely dark except for a warm glow coming from a rock. I focus on the glow. It's a single flame, dancing over the cracks in the rock. It continues to glow as I stare at it. Is this an eternal flame?

A giant, black paw steps in front of the light. I force my gaze up to see a massive nose sniffing the air. It's the animal from the jungle— the heebo.

I prop myself up, trying to get oriented so I can escape.

But the room sways as my arms weaken and I crash down, banging my head on the floor.

The heebo opens its mouth. I feel its teeth clench over my cloak as everything fades to black.

\*\*\*

The room is quiet and warm. I don't hear dripping caverns. Instead, there are hushed tones of people speaking gently. I open my eyes.

My dad stands in the corner with his arms crossed, but one hand gripping his chin. He speaks to Jarret, who nods and responds in a quiet voice. Jarret's eyes skim over to me. He does a double-take, then puts his hand on my dad's shoulder.

"Lyra," my dad turns to look at me. He rushes to the rock-hard bed where I lie.

I try to push myself up, but I don't have the strength.

"Don't get up," he sits on the bed and puts his hand on my forehead.

I look around to see where I am. It's my own room in our family home. The last time my dad sat on this bed, he was trying to be there for me. I wanted to talk to him, but I didn't. Maybe things would be different if I had. My throat gets tight as I think of the silver ore, of wishing I had something to hope for, of feeling so alone in all of it.

I start to cry. "Dad."

He bends over and kisses my forehead. "I'm here, honey."

"I'm so sorry," I sob.

"You have nothing to be sorry for—"

"Lyra!" My mom rushes in and kneels at the side of the bed. She puts her hand over my father's that strokes my cheek. She starts to cry and kisses my forehead.

Jarret comes into the room, escorting Pictor, who walks slowly.

"Hi, Lyra," Pictor says with his hands clasped in front of him.

"Hi, Pictor," I say through the tears that are on my cheeks.

"Are you going to die?" Pictor asks.

I laugh and wipe my cheek. "Not today."

My parents chuckle and sniffle as my mom rises and sits next to my dad on the bed.

Jarret leans in the carved opening, maybe considering whether he should join the family.

"Jarret found you," my mom sniffles and motions for him to come in. "He said he followed some animal."

Jarret walks toward my mom. "I'm glad you're okay."

I think of the animal I saw in the caverns— did the heebo save me?

"Wait," I look around. "Where is everyone else?" I remember Garridon commanding me to get back. I don't know how big the explosion was, but I hope it didn't reach him. I couldn't tell how close the albharee was to Leal and Eddi. I'm not sure where everyone else was in the caverns. "Are the others okay?"

"You don't have to worry about that now," my dad says. "We're taking care of it."

"I brought something," Jarret comes into the room. "Mabel cooked it." He holds a bowl with a spoon and clutches a blanket beneath his arm.

"You hungry?" Jarret asks as he sits on the bed.

I shake my head.

"You should probably still eat," he says. "Here," he places the bowl on the floor and grasps the rolled blanket. "Let's prop you up." He helps me sit up some, then puts the rolled blanket under my head.

There's pain when I move, but I can't pinpoint where it's coming from— it's everywhere. And I feel weak. I don't think I'm even strong enough to hold the bowl.

Jarret bends over to pick the bowl back up.

"You're feeding me?" I ask as he grabs the spoon from the bowl.

"Is it weird?"

"Yeah."

He smiles. "I guess it will just have to be weird. Your parents are speaking with the Fitzgeralds and you haven't eaten for who knows how long."

"What are they speaking about?"

"Remember when we first met?" he offers a spoonful of soup that Mabel made.

I take a sip from the spoon. The soup is warm as it hits my stomach. It's comforting. But it's also awkward to have someone else feed me.

"What are they talking about?" I ask again.

"That first day, we were in the tent that you and Pictor shared," Jarret says with a smile.

He obviously isn't going to answer my question. Jarret makes me think back to the Sanctuary. I miss being surrounded by blankets. Sometimes, Pictor and I would stay up playing games or talking. I haven't spent much time with my brother for a while.

"I had just learned what a bowl was," Jarret says with a smile.

"Pictor was laughing at you," I can't help but smile as I think of when Jarret accidentally called it a 'mole.'

He offers me another spoonful of soup.

"It's funny looking back," he says as I eat the soup. "Now it's an everyday object. A bowl now is as common as a trowel was then." The smile dims slightly from his face. "Things are so different now."

"Different in a bad way?" I ask as his demeanor appears more glum.

"Why were you up in that place?" Jarret asks.

"What do you mean?"

"Eddi said you had climbed up to some ledge and you caused the explosion. What were you doing up there?"

"Uh—" I try to hide my fingernails that are cracked and getting infected.

"I'm sorry I have to ask this, Lyra, but I do." He pauses and places the spoon in the bowl. "Were you trying to die?"

I wasn't trying to die, but I wasn't trying very hard to live either. "No."

He picks the spoon back up from the bowl.

"I'm not hungry," I say.

He puts the spoon down again and sighs. "I don't want to see you hurt the way Ara was."

"The way she died?"

"No," he says, "the way she hurt. Every day; surrounded by people who loved her and cared about her. But she never really let anyone love her fully." He looks at me. "Except your grandmother." He looks to the ground and seems lighter, as if picturing a sweet memory.

I think of the time Jarret held me in the Alaster ship, counting to try and calm me down. He feels like someone I've known for a long time.

"Will you tell me about them?"

"What do you want to know?"

"What was my grandmother like?"

"She was crazy," he looks up at the ceiling and smiles. "But she was right."

He starts telling me of a time my grandmother, Norma, nearly caused an uprising because electronic lights were blinking to communicate with her. Which would sound crazy, except that we were interfering with the frequencies to try and communicate. He tells me about the times Ara stuck up for my grandma and how much trouble she got in.

I drift to sleep with stories of my grandmother and sister, like stars dripping light to reach me under the sea. They remind me that I come from a family of strong-willed troublemakers, defiant against anything that tries to keep them from pursuing what is true.

\*\*\*

There are somewhere between 52 and 56 divots across my ceiling. Every time I count, I get a different number. And I can't decide if certain parts are divots or just slightly misshapen parts of the ceiling. There are no holes, but there are crystal-filled cracks that run through the walls and illuminate the space. Falling in and out of sleep, I haven't been able to keep track of when the crystals are dim or bright. Time has felt disorienting— like walking through a wall of steam. It's only been recently that my mind has been clear enough to count the divots in the ceiling.

With my brain powering back up, the ceiling is the only thing keeping me from wondering what happened and if the heebo saved me; wondering if we got the information from the machine; wondering where the others are.

I should start again counting the divots— I hope there are 54.

"How are you feeling?" Eddi steps into the room with a tablet held to his side.

I try to sit up, but I'm lightheaded and I feel heavy. It's like my body is a bag full of rocks. I lie back, with gravity forcing me down.

"You don't look so great," says Eddi. "I should probably let you—" he turns back toward the exit.

"I have the solution!" Pictor barges into the room.

A Trovantian boy follows Pictor. He's probably the same age as Pictor, but he's much taller.

"This is my friend, Roen," says Pictor. "He can read Trovantian."

"What's this about?" I ask.

"Nothing, really," Eddi sounds flustered. "I shouldn't have come in. You really look like you need more rest."

"We need someone to read the Trovantian," says Pictor. "And Roen can."

"O-okay," Eddi stutters. He hands his tablet to Roen. "Can you tell us what this says?"

The Trovantian boy accepts the tablet and looks at the screen. He smells it. Then, he hits it.

"Oh!" Eddi exclaims. "Maybe— don't do that." He takes the tablet back from Roen.

"Pictor," I say. "Does Roen speak English?"

"Well," Pictor looks up at his friend. "I don't think so."

Eddi rubs his forehead.

I smile at the thought of Pictor coming up with his brilliant scheme and not realizing that he and his friend don't speak the same language. "So you need someone who can read Trovantian and tell us what the information says?"

"Yes," says Eddi. "But, given your condition, I'm sure we can find someone else who has connections that can—"

"Like who?" I ask. "Where would you find Trovantians who also want to know what's on that tablet?"

Eddi scrunches his lips to the side of his mouth and thinks.


"Where did you get the chair part?" I ask.

Leal and Eddi stand next to a chair that has a metallic headrest. The chair has a leg in the center with a ball on the end, but it also has four metal pieces coming up from each side. The pieces then fix on the ground so that the thing looks like a four-legged spider.

"From the Alaster ship," says Leal. "I took one from the control panel."

My dad leans in the doorway and looks at the insect-like chair. "I don't know about this."

"Maybe we shouldn't—" Eddi rubs his arms. "Maybe we shouldn't push this."

"It's fine," says Leal, "look." He sits and toggles a controller that's affixed to the chair. Two of the legs take a step forward, then pull the rest of the chair forward. He maneuvers the controller again and two legs take a step back, which pulls the chair back. "Most of the weight moves on the ball at the end of the center leg. But, when there are rocks or trees in the way, the four big legs can lift the center wheel over the obstacle."

Something about the machine looks unstable or dangerous. But it also looks super cool.

"But first," says Leal, "we will have to put things on your arms and legs so you aren't moving your bones if they are broken."

"What things?" I ask.

"All we have is metal," Leal says. "Or rocks."

"We don't have any casts," my mom comes in with straps and pieces of metal. "These might be the best we can do."

"How does it feel?" Eddi asks after my dad helps me get into the chair that's now in our eating space.

"I feel like I'm a pole," I say. My forearms and shins are strapped to pieces of metal and I lean my head against the metal headrest.

"Try moving the chair," Leal says.

"But not too fast," my dad says as he chews his thumbnail.

I place my fingers on the controller, though it's awkward with my makeshift cast. I toggle the controller. Two mechanical legs lift in the air. "Whoa!" Everything feels unstable as the chair moves forward and the other legs follow. "I'm moving, but I'm not actually moving." I smile as the chair walks around without any effort from my legs.

"That is so cool!" Pictor bursts into the eating space where the group crowds around the chair. "I want one."

"This is amazing," I say. I haven't had the strength to sit or stand, let alone walk. "Thank you both."

"No problem," says Leal. "Now off we go!"

"Shouldn't we let her trial it more first?" Eddi asks and then turns to me. "The last thing we want is to push you."

"I will be okay," I say. "And we need this information as soon as we can get it."

"Just," my mom puts her hand on one of the metal-spider-legs. "Go slow, okay? And be careful."

"I'll be coming too," says my dad.


*Jjjt, jjjt, jjjt* — the chair makes a noise with each step as I move through the tall grass with Eddi, my dad, and Leal. It's not normal to hear machines moving through the Trovant, with wires and metal humming and scraping. It seems out of place among the plants and bugs. The path bumps me up and down as the legs take steps and pull me along in the spider-chair.

Soon, there's an area with a wall of grass that's even taller than a Trovantian.

"Mica?" I look back and forth across the wall of plants. This should be the section of the fields where Mica would be collecting grass for making baskets and fabric.

"Lyra?" I hear a trembling voice. Mica peeks her head from the wall of grass. "What is that?" She doesn't come out from the grass.

"It's okay," I say. "It's just a machine. It won't hurt you."

Stepping from the grass, she wrings her hands together with her eyes fixed on my chair.

"Why was it making that sound?" she asks.

"I don't know," I say. "That's just how it sounds. It's okay. Look, I control it with this." I push on the controller and the chair takes a step.

Mica jumps back toward the grass.

"It's okay," I say again. "You can even try the controller."

She shakes her head.

"This is the only way I can get around," I say. "We came to ask for help."

"Maybe you shouldn't have come here," she looks at my chair and then back to where others peek through the tall grass to look at the machine. "At least not with that."

I sit in my chair and look upward at the ladders in the Alaster ship. "This can't climb, can it?" The others had to lower me down the rock wall with ropes, but I don't know how we could get my chair up the ladders.

My dad looks worried.

"Not really," says Leal.

"Only over rocks or fallen trees," says Eddi. "But not up a ladder."

"We can talk down here," says Mica. "I do not like those anyway." She looks at the ladders and platforms. "They are cold and slick."

"Here is the information," Eddi says, handing Mica the tablet. "Can you tell us what it says?"

"Umm," Mica looks over the information on the screen. "I do not know what this is." She points to some symbols. "These are numbers. And this... I know what this is but I do not know the English word."

"Can you describe it?" Eddi asks.

"It is when the uminidor is too much," says Mica.

"What is uminidor?" Leal asks.

"This," Mica motions all around.

Leal looks around. "The Alaster ship?"

"No," Mica says.

"Air?" I ask. The metal against my skin starts to get colder now that we're away from the Trovant.

"Maybe like air," says Mica. "But not the part to breathe in. It is what is all around."

"Temperature?" Eddi asks. "Maybe humidity?"

"I do not know what these are," says Mica.

"Temperature is like hot and cold," says Eddi. "Humidity—" he pauses. "It's like water in the air."

"Water is down below," says Mica. She looks confused. "In the ground. Not in the air."

"What are the numbers?" Leal asks. "Can you type them here?" Leal taps on the screen that Mica holds and he opens a section where she can type English next to the Trovantian.

She looks at the Trovantian symbols and then types a number in English. Slowly, she pushes the English numbers to make a string of numeric information.

"Does this mean anything to any of you?" my dad mumbles to us.

"Hmmm," Leal rubs his chin. "Maybe. I've been trying to learn some of the measurement systems here for my work. There's usually a translator, but I'm getting used to knowing what the numbers indicate. It would just be easier to interpret if I knew what uminidor and the other terms meant."

"This one is thickness," says Mica. She points to some numbers on the screen.

"Thickness of what?" Leal asks.

Mica shrugs.

"Can I see this for a moment?" Leal asks as he takes the tablet. He opens a blank space on the tablet and traces a semicircle with his finger. He puts numbers on one side with arrows pointing down on the semicircle. Then he writes Mica's numbers on the other side of the semi-circle and starts an equation to calculate pressure over surface area. "That can't be right," Leal says as he reads over the numbers. "I must not be understanding these numbers correctly."

"What's not right?" asks my dad.

"If these numbers were the thickness of the outer wall of the Trovant," says Leal, "the pressure of the water would fracture the wall at any moment. Anything could set off such a small fracture. We might have been dead a long time ago. Or just very lucky."

"If this number was something other than wall thickness," Eddi says, "how could we interpret the numbers?"

"We don't have the full picture," says Leal. "I don't know what any of these other terms are. There could be some support beams or something I am not taking into account. Or maybe I don't have any of it right."

"Maybe Rhen would know the English words better," says Mica.

"I've been trying to find them," says Leal. "I just don't know the next thing to try."

"What do you mean next thing?" I ask. "What have you been trying?" The others have been trying to keep information from me so I could rest and not worry.

"Lyra—" my dad says.

"I'm already out here anyway," I say. "You might as well stop keeping things from me."

Leal looks at me, then my dad, then he turns toward the tablet and starts typing on the screen. "Their tablet occasionally makes contact with one of our communication beacons. I'm assuming they don't know when it happens or else they would have sent a message. It at least gave us their location and it showed that the tablet has been moving. Which is a good sign that they are okay."

"And you haven't tried to go find them?" I ask.

"Some of us tried," says my dad. "Desman went the furthest. But we keep running into dead ends in the caves. We don't know how to get to whatever tunnels they may be in."

"Is there a map of the tunnels or anything?" I ask as I turn toward Mica.

"I am not sure." She shakes her head slightly. "I do not use a map."

"Look," Leal says as he taps on the screen. "Here are the locations that their tablet sent to the communication beacons. Can you tell me generally how to get to their last location?"

Mica looks at the tablet intently, then shakes her head. "What is this?" She points to a small image in the corner of the screen.

"Gia's video footage," says Leal. "Some images also made it through when the tablet connected to the beacons." Leal expands the pixelated footage and images.

"I know this," Mica points to a tunnel with an oddly shaped boulder in front of it.

It's amazing she knows where something is based on a blurry photo of a boulder.

"Did they go from this picture to this one and then this one?" Mica asks, pointing to various images of rocks and tunnels.

"Yes," says Leal. "That's the exact route they took. How did you know?"

"This is not good," says Mica.

"Why?" Leal asks.

"They are going to the in-between."

# Chapter 15: Gia— The In-Between

"Anything?" Minji sits near the edge of the water with her arms wrapped around herself.

Rhen swims toward us.

Water splashes as Ferris appears from beneath the water.

When we had been swimming back toward the caverns, the water suddenly turned tumultuous. The tunnel back to the caverns was blocked. Rhen and Ferris turned around to let Minji and me back on the land. Then they tried to find a way through the blockage.

"It is completely blocked," says Rhen, swimming to the edge where Minji and I sit.

"What do you think happened?" Minji asks.

Rhen pulls herself onto the ledge. "Does the tablet say anything?"

"It says 'out of range,'" I read the tablet. My voice echoes over the water. "The communication beacons must not be able to get through the blockage."

Ferris pulls herself onto the land. "There must have been a cave-in."

Water runs over the ledge as the four of us sit in our soaked clothes. It's cold. This part of the Trovant is colder than the living quarters or the jungle. In the Trellis, there wasn't a lot of variation in temperature. I don't like having to think about being too hot or too cold or what clothes I might need if I'm swimming or climbing in different temperatures... or getting stuck in some cold caverns. I miss the microbial suits. And I miss my laser kitten shirt.

"What do we do?" Minji asks.

Sitting, Rhen pulls her knees to her chest and stares at the water.

Ferris sits on a rock and wrings out her long hair.

"We have a few options," says Rhen. "When there is a cave-in, the Trovantians will try to dig if anyone is trapped, unless it would risk the structure of the facility. We could wait here and see if they will unblock the passage."

"How long could that be?" I ask.

"At least a few hours," says Rhen. "Maybe longer. If ever."

"What would be another option?" I ask.

She nods to a tunnel that is across the pool. "We could see what is down there."

Minji squeezes herself tighter. "Is there a third option?"

"We could starve and die," says Ferris, flipping her hair over her shoulder.

"Or," says Rhen, "we could wait for a while. If there is no movement in the blocked passage, one of us can scout the tunnel to see what is in there."

"Why wait?" Ferris stands. "One of us can go now."

"We should stay together for as long as we can," says Rhen. "We do not know these tunnels and we could get lost or eaten."

"Eaten?" Minji's eyes widen. "By what?"

"The heebos sleep in the caves," says Rhen. "The velsyren also but they can't hurt us much."

"There is no use waiting," Ferris says, standing. "And I am cold. I want to move."

Rhen snaps at Ferris: "Jan sobeste seem."

Ferris says something back in Trovantian and motions to Minji and me.

The two start arguing.

"We won't freeze to death," Minji interrupts.

They stop arguing and look at Minji.

"What?" Ferris asks.

"Me and Gia," says Minji. "We won't freeze. I don't mind waiting if it will be safest for all of us."

"You understand?" Ferris asks.

"Not everything," says Minji. "But I understood that."

Rhen raises her eyebrows at Ferris. "Seem liljuste?"

Ferris rolls her eyes and sits back on the rock.


Lying on my back, I stare at the tablet, hoping something will change. The light shines on my face since the crystals in the area have dimmed. If the tablet makes connection with a communication beacon, maybe I can ask someone if we should wait or find a different way out.

"You should keep the screen off," Minji says, also lying and staring at the ceiling. "We might need to save the battery."

I click the screen off and put the tablet by my side.

"So this is how you read your journal?" Rhen asks. She lies on the rocky ground.

Ferris sits with her back against a boulder.

"Yeah," I say. I think of the paper I had seen with Leal's name on it. How do they make paper? "Do you read yours on paper?"

"We usually listen to it," says Rhen.

"Do you have it written down?" Minji asks.

"Yes," says Rhen. "We have the journals written in books. But most people prefer to listen to it spoken or in song."

"Can you say any of the words?" Minji asks.

Staring at the ceiling, Rhen opens her mouth and sings with an earthy voice. Her song echoes over the water: "Ya-jun may-a-wen say-unsay. Seem-ie ack-am la way-on-way."

Her voice quiets and the water stills.

I turn my head towards her. "Can you translate it?"

Ferris leans her head back against the boulder. "Vana would say it is most powerful and beautiful when the words are read out loud in our language. It would not make sense in English."

"And what would you say?" I twist toward Ferris.

She looks at the ground, then shakes her head and looks at the water.

"What does your journal say about the beginning?" Rhen asks. "How does it say we got down here?"

"Do you know of the Black Plague?" Minji asks.

Ferris looks at Rhen. "Swade Almar?"

Rhen shrugs.

"Maybe," says Ferris. "When the evil man, Babu, decided to end all of humanity."

"If it's the same story," says Minji, "his name in our journal is 'Manavjeet.' He believed that humans on the surface needed to be fixed through natural selection. He thought the population had been causing social hierarchies and injustices. His solution was to have a selection event to kill off a portion of the population, just like plagues in Earth's history. But humans couldn't be allowed to decide who lived and who died; nature had to. So he manufactured an event and called it the Black Plague. Alaster could stop the plague once it started, but humans needed to be away from the impact of the first wave so Alaster could absorb the plague. The facilities were built down here to wait for Alaster to bring us back up."

"How did he absorb it?" Rhen asks.

"Um," Minji says, "I'm not sure."

"So why did we stay down here?" Ferris asks.

"Power, I guess," says Minji. "The first Head of the Trellis wanted to keep control, and the people didn't trust that the surface would be safe, so they didn't go back to the Alaster ship to take them up." She pauses for a moment, thinking. "What do your journals say?"

"Something similar," says Rhen. "But our journals were made to fix the corrupted one you have."

"What do you mean?" Minji asks.

"Yours has been edited and changed," says Rhen. "Ours was given from the Source."

I try to picture a pot of magma writing a book. "How?"

"Through our past overseers," says Ferris.

Minji and I are both silent. I don't think either of us wants to argue with Rhen. But we've come to trust what the journal says. What if ours is wrong? What would that mean about Alaster and going to the surface?

"What does yours say about the end?" I ask, thinking of what Rasul Midian and Imeel had said a while ago.

"That the Source will take us to the Earth's surface," says Rhen. "And yours says Alaster will take us?"

"Yeah," I say. I pick up the tablet but keep the screen turned off. Staring at it, I want to read the journal again. The last time I tried, I felt like someone needed to explain the details to me. I want to try again to understand, but I can't waste the battery on the tablet.

I roll to my side in the darkened room. Ferris adjusts herself and lies down. Still lying on her back, Minji closes her eyes.

Quietly, Rhen sings a soothing melody. The song dances over the water and warms the air as I close my eyes.


A cold splash lands on my face. I jolt up.

Rhen stands on the land and watches as Ferris swims in the pool.

"Apologies," says Rhen, "we did not mean to wake you."

Ferris makes her way toward the tunnel across the water.

Minji rubs her eyes and sits up.

Ferris arrives at the tunnel and hoists herself upward. She crawls inside and disappears.

The crystalline cracks are brighter than before and I can see clearly in the space. I'm not used to being asleep while other people make plans. At least, I wasn't used to it until I got sick. I lie back down on the wet ground. I prop my arm beneath my head and try to think of what I should be doing. We need to eat, but I don't know how to get food here. I don't know how to navigate our way out. I don't know how to do anything.

I notice something along the wall of the room. It looks like a large, green pouch made of seaweed. I push myself up. "What is that?"

Rhen leans toward it.

I remember them saying that the other facility was a plant. Are we near the plant? The glowing crystals just

barely give enough light to show the silhouette of
something in the pouch.

"It is an albharee egg," says Rhen.

I take a step back from it as if it could eat me.
"Should we do something?"

"We can leave it," says Rhen. "Do not point it out
to Ferris. She will kill it."

"I mean," Minji rubs her arm. "Is that so bad? It has
adapted to come on land to eat us."

"No," says Rhen. "It comes on land for this." She
points to the egg. "To give life, not to take it. The albharee
only attack us because we hunt them. They protect
themselves."

"Will this one survive?" I look at the egg and
imagine it hatching and falling into the water. Our way
underwater had been blocked. There are other underwater
tunnels, but Rhen says she doesn't know where those
ones go.

Ferris appears again in the tunnel. She stops at the
edge without getting back in the water.

"What is it?" Rhen's voice echoes across the
water.

"There is good news and bad news," says Ferris.

"Do you know where we are?" Rhen asks.

"Yes," says Ferris.

"What is the bad news?"

"That is both the good news and the bad news."

The four of us stand in front of a pile of boulders and rocks. The pile blocks one side of the tunnel but the other side is open. I don't see what the bad news is, except that we had to swim to the tunnel and now stand in soaked cloaks.

"This leads to the Trovant," says Rhen, facing the blocked passage.

I turn to face the open side of the tunnel. "Where does this go?"

Rhen shakes her head and says something in their language.

Ferris turns toward the open passage and says something back.

They start to argue again.

"This doesn't sound good," Minji says as she slowly turns toward the open passage.

"What is it?" I ask.

"The in-between," says Ferris. "It is the only option."

Rhen doesn't say anything back.

"What is that?" I ask.

"It is the place between the two facilities," says Rhen.

"So will we have to go to the other facility?" I ask.

"No," says Rhen. "This blocked passage goes from the jungle to the in-between. But there are other passages that go from the in-between to the market or homes. But we must go in-between first."

"Why is that so bad?" I ask.

"No one goes there since the war," says Rhen.

"Except those who live in-between," says Ferris. "To escape both facilities."

"Well," Minji rubs her arm. "Isn't that what you do? You stay in the caverns to be away from other Trovantians."

"Not like them," says Rhen. She doesn't seem offended by Minji's question. "They escape because they kill or steal."

"Kill people?" Minji slinks back.

"Kill or steal," says Rhen.

"What happens if you're stolen?" I ask.

"You would wish to be killed," says Rhen.

"I would rather face the heebo," says Ferris.


Minji covers her nose as we move through the tunnels. "What is the smell?"

"Shh," says Rhen. She stops and puts her hands on Minji's shoulders. "We're getting close." Rhen unties the ropes holding the fabric around Minji. Then she configures the fabric so that it drapes over Minji's head before wrapping it over her body. "They may assume you are children because you are small. But we can't let anyone see we are not from here. Keep your head down. And don't speak to anyone."

I untie the ropes around my waist and put them around myself like Rhen did for Minji. Rhen and Ferris pull their hoods over their heads and silently journey through the tunnel.

There's a yellow-orange glow as we move deeper into a sour smell of urine and decomposing feces. Soon, raspy voices and out-of-tune instruments broadcast in our dripping tunnel.

What can we expect when we get there? Rhen didn't even brief us on what might be there or what to do if things go wrong. Are there protocols to follow?

Turning the corner, the tunnel ends and we come to the edge of an expansive opening. I step to the edge of the opening where there's a metal barrier. The place is shaped like a cylinder with rows and rows of ledges and tunnels. Each ledge has a metallic barrier keeping people from falling off the edge. There are people treading along the ledges, some with missing limbs and many wearing torn cloaks and large bags. Looking down, the ground level seems to be a circle with a ring of mirky water around it. No one is on the ground level.

The smell now includes a deeper, somewhat metallic stench mixed with body odor and dirt. It's like I can taste the smell. I close my mouth.

"This way," Rhen mumbles, keeping her head down.

Walking alongside the metal barrier, I try to keep my head down without losing Rhen. People's feet walk in and out of my vision as we follow the ledge along the curve of the cylindrical space and to another opening.

"Stay close," Rhen says to me as we walk into the opening that turns into a crowded area.

Cloaked bodies move around one another and the sounds of coarse laughter and off-tune instruments get louder. Chattering people and the raspy-voice singer compete to be heard. Sweat beads on my eyebrows as the dense crowd fills the air with their stench and noise. Still keeping my head down, I follow the dark shimmering tail of Rhen's cloak and I weave through the crowd.

Suddenly, the cloak swishes out of my sight. I walk fast to try and catch up with the cloak. I still don't see it. My heart races. What if I lose Rhen? I don't know where we are or how to get back. I turn my head up, looking for Rhen.

There's a tangle of cloaked people around market stalls and places to get food and drinks. It looks like the marketplace in the Trovant, only dirtier. The people tower above my head, but some are lanky, not the normal muscular build of Trovantians. I spot Rhen's cloak in the crowd. She's stopped, trying to cover her face while also looking for me. Ferris and Minji are next to her. I turn my face to the floor and move to Rhen. When I arrive, Minji is peering up and taking in the sights around.

She turns her face to the ground. "Oh no."

"What?" I ask.

"Someone made eye contact," she says, moving swiftly to follow Rhen and Ferris.

I scuffle behind as I hear a man's voice shout something from behind.

"Move quickly!" Rhen shouts as her pace increases and she shoves through the mess of people.

Others shout around the dingy market. I look up to keep track of the others.

A large woman steps in front of Rhen. Her giant palms move to close around Rhen's shoulders, but Rhen ducks.

Rhen shouts something as she crouches. Ferris runs up Rhen's back, then leaps as Rhen springs up and Ferris flies toward the woman. Ferris's feet kick the woman's face and she crashes to the ground as Ferris rolls to land safely.

Minji screams. Someone squeezes both her wrists above her head and pulls her off the ground as she kicks to get loose.

"Minji!" I yell. "Headbutt!"

Held from the ground, Minji jolts her head back and uses all her force to hit the person in the nose.

"Agh!" The person drops Minji.

Fingers grip around my neck. I elbow the person behind me, which is right at the level of the person's groin. The fingers release from my neck as a man grunts and sinks to the floor.

"Run that way!" Rhen yells as different hands grip her wrists, shoulders, and waist.

I try to run toward her, but someone yanks my hair. Hands clasp both my hands and an arm reaches around my neck. I struggle to get loose but the grip on me is strong.

Punching someone with all her strength, Ferris pushes her stunned victim into people who hold onto Rhen. Pieces of fish, grains, and sauces fling as those holding Rhen crash into a food stand behind them.

Ferris lunges toward people who still hold to Rhen and she jabs one of them in the trachea. Then she squeezes his hair in her fist and knocks his head into the head of the person next to him. One last person hangs on, but Rhen yanks her hand from his grip as Ferris takes the man's bag and wraps it around his neck. Ferris squeezes the grip on his neck.

Rhen commands something and pulls Ferris to move in the direction to escape.

A man steps behind them.

"Rhen! Ferris!" I try and warn them. The arm tightens around my neck.

The man opens his arms wide, with a needle poking from each of his fists. He stabs Rhen and Ferris with a needle.

Both Rhen and Ferris stop, then sway a little. They collapse to the ground.


The man smiles with crooked teeth. Squatting, he shoves his face toward Rhen as she tries to stay awake and upright, with her hands tied behind her back. Now in a small room, the four of us are sitting on the ground, soaked with foul-smelling fluids that cover the floor. Minji coughs from the smell. Rhen sways back and forth, also trying to stay conscious and upright.

The man says something in Trovantian as he stands. There are a few others around the room who chuckle.

"What did he say?" I whisper to Minji.

"The chemist was worth the money," says Minji. "I think." She pauses. "He said a word that means chemical, but the end of the word was what you'd use to denote a profession."

The man turns and shouts something at Minji.

I look at her, seeing if she would translate, but her lips are puckered closed.

The man squats again, speaking to Rhen. His hot breath smells of decay. He pokes her on the forehead to push her. She sways. Hands still tied behind her back, she can't catch herself and she crashes fully to the ground. Splashes of the liquid hit my face.

The others across the room laugh. The man speaks to us, then looks directly at me.

"What is he saying?" I lean toward Minji.

The man nods and motions as if it's okay for Minji to speak.

"He says we are lucky," says Minji. "Captives are for, um— hebion— I don't know what that is."

"Entertainment," Ferris slurs.

"We are lucky that we are muhara," says Minji.

"What is that?" I ask.

"Woman fighters," Rhen mumbles from the ground.

"Why is that lucky?" I ask.

Minji fidgets. "Because we are fighters, we will die soon in glory instead of living the rest of our lives in shame."

There's a young man in the dark room across from us. A piece of metal clasps around his neck and connects to a metal pole that is embedded into the wall. There's a woman sitting in a chair, with metal pieces securing her to the seat. She has one hand missing. There's a person sitting on the floor with a metal mask over his entire face. Other people through the rocky room wear different metal restraints. Minji, Rhen, Ferris, and I have metal pieces around our waists that are then chained to one another.

I look at how the metal pieces are linked together. "We could get out of this."

"They will kill you," says the woman who is restrained in the chair. I guess she speaks English. "It's not too hard to leave this room. But no one has left the in-between."

"We can't just sit here," I say.

"The best chance to live is to win," says the woman.

"Win what?" I ask.

"The Alashab," the woman says.

The young man with the neck restraint says something to Rhen in Trovantian. He leans toward her as much as he can, though his neck is stuck in one place. His chin is scraped from the metal. He must have a hard time keeping still in that restraint.

Rhen is more awake since we were put in this new room. She looks annoyed at the young man but doesn't say anything.

"What did he say?" I ask.

Rhen doesn't answer.

I look at Minji.

"He wants to trade something for information about how to win," says Minji.

"Trade what?" I ask.

Minji shrugs. "I don't know the word he's using."

The young man looks at Ferris and starts talking.

Ferris furrows her eyebrows but doesn't look at him.

As he speaks, it seems like he's trying to make suave gestures from his restraints.

Ferris clenches her jaw. Rhen says something to Ferris as if to calm her down. The man doesn't stop speaking. Then, he makes a kissing face.

"Ah!" Minji and I both shout as Ferris lunges toward the young man and yanks our connected restraints.

"Ferris!" Rhen yells. "Lack-ah seem-ie!"

As Ferris leaps at the young man, she swings her fist back and jabs him in the ribs. Then, she puts her thumb beneath his metal choker, just above his manubrium— in the soft part of his neck. She says something to him as if challenging him to make her press harder on his neck.

There's metallic clanking and screeching as the locked door creaks open and two people hobble into the room. One grips a blade. A woman tears Ferris from the young man and slams her to the ground. The force yanks our connected restraints and I topple to one knee. The other person takes the blade and raises it high, then crashes down on Ferris.

Ferris grunts, but the person shrieks like he is injured.

Rolling over, Ferris grips her side where the blade had hit her, but didn't stab through her cloak.

The assailant holds his bloody palm, where the knife apparently sliced him.

The woman kicks Ferris, then grabs Ferris's wrist and pulls back the cloak. She raises the blade and stabs.

Ferris screams as the blade slices all the way through her forearm. The woman wiggles the blade in Ferris's arm and yanks it out.

Someone in the corner of the room gives a high-pitched cackle and rocks back and forth. Another person claps chaotically. Blood streams from Ferris's forearm.

The two guards leave the room, one gripping the bloody blade and the other holding his bloody hand. The metal door slams shut.

Ferris cradles her arm, repressing screams.

The eerie cackling still sounds and the clapping person chants.

Rhen kneels and speaks to Ferris in Trovantian, trying to help.

I kneel to Ferris. With the amount of blood pouring out, no major arteries were damaged. I lean in to better examine the wound. Laceration of the tissue with damage to the muscle but no damage to major arteries. Twelve-week recovery time… as long as it doesn't get infected.

I look at our cloaks that had been soaked from the foul-smelling floor of the other room. The wound needs to be cleaned. We need to get out of here.

I try to find a clean part of my cloak.

"Maybe it will get infected," says the woman in the chair.

The man with the metal mask nods.

"That is an easy target for the murien," says the woman.

Minji's gaze shoots toward the woman. "What is that?"

"Deadly creatures," says the woman. "We will battle the animals and each other to the death. Maybe she will die fast and the murien will eat her and not be hungry for us."

Ferris winces as I fold the tie of my garment to cover her wound and apply pressure.

"That will be ideal," says the woman. "Last time I was in there, a murien took my hand. But I took its life."

I picture the woman in an open space with a creature to fight. Maybe we can escape when we are released to fight the creatures.

"How long until we fight?" I ask.

"Until the next Alashab," says the woman.

"Which is when?" I ask.

The man wearing the metal mask shrugs.

***

Ferris trembles as she lies on the floor, still connected to us by the waist restraints. We now sit on the ground, thinking of what's ahead. I've been trying to plan our way out, but I don't know what *murien* we will face. Will it be an albharee? That's the most deadly creature I can think of. I don't think I can battle any human to the death. Once we are at the Alashab, we need to find somewhere to hide or run.

Suddenly, there's rumbling over the ceiling. It sounds like crowds are storming across the level above us. I hear faint screams.

"Do you hear that?" I ask.

The cries get louder.

Rhen and Minji hone their attention to the metal door, listening for the screams.

"Can you hear what they say?" I ask.

Minji shakes her head but still listens intently.

The yelling gets louder and the voices more clear. A cry sounds just outside the door. There's clamoring and sounds of footsteps fading away. Did the guards leave?

"What did that scream say?" I ask.

Minji stares at the metal door. "They said— it's coming for us."

"What is?" I ask.

With her lips parted, Minji continues to stare.

"What is it?" I ask again.

Outside the door, the screams are gone.

"Arachna vishar," says Rhen.

"What is that?" I ask.

The metal door clanks.

"Spider demoness," says Rhen.

The door creaks open.

I leap up, but I'm yanked back down by the connected restraints.

A figure lurks near the door.

A curl pokes out from behind the door.

"Leal?" I say.

"Gia!" Leal partly hides behind the door, then jumps into the room when he sees me. "Minji! Are you okay?" He moves through the room and kneels by us.

"What is going on?" Minji asks. "Where is the demon spider?"

"Demon spider?" Leal pulls a tool from his pocket. "That's just Lyra." He presses a button on the tool and sparks fly across our metal restraints. The tool is normally used for fusing wires, but it has higher settings that can weaken the restraints enough to get them off.

A shadow is cast through the doorway.

"Leal," I say. "Turn around."

Leal turns but still kneels next to us.

# Trovant

The man with the crooked teeth steps through the door. He speaks in Trovantian, mostly addressing Rhen.

Then, cloaked people come in, dragging limp bodies behind them. The limp ones are Arcturo and Eddi. The cloaked people drop Arcturo and Eddi on the ground.

Leal puts his hands up and shrinks back.

"What did the man say?" I ask.

"He says they have an agreement," says Rhen.

"What agreement?" I ask.

"All of us can go," says Rhen, "if the spider demoness can beat a murien."

# Chapter 16: Leal— Tooth

We are at the ground level of a massive cylindrical space. There is light emanating from the ceiling. It doesn't look like a crystal or crack, but the whole ceiling is a light that curves upward and out of sight. Is the light made from bioluminescent vines like in the Sanctuary, or is it burning methane like the Trovant? Or maybe it's illuminated from microbes like most of the Trellis.

Minji grabs my hand and looks ahead. A ring of dirty water separates us from a circular platform— almost like a moat. What is in the water that smells so bad?

Chains clank as Arcturo tries to move. He has his hands and his neck in metal restraints with chains that are held by a guard. He's woozy after they injected some sort of sedative. He wouldn't stop fighting the guards when they said Lyra would face some creature.

We all wear some restraints on our wrists, waists, or ankles— though not to the same extent as Arcturo. Ferris curls up on the ground with her forearm wrapped in fabric. Others are chained to her and look around the circular ground or up at the crowd. I look up at the rows of ledges along the cylindrical area. People crowd at metal barriers to see us below. Fights break out across the ledges while people cheer.

Scanning the ledges of people fighting or cheering, I see Mica looking down at us.

"Hey," I say to those around me. "I think I found Mica."

"Is she okay?" asks Dad.

"She looks fine," I say. "Why is she fine? I was so worried when we lost her."

"That is her cousin," Rhen says, looking at a man who stands next to Mica. "She is not an outsider here."

Mica nudges the man and points to us. The man smiles and waves at us.

Gia furrows her eyebrows. "They're acting like they aren't trying to kill us."

"Mica is worried for us," says Rhen. "See how she wrings her hands? At least she will be safer with her cousin than with us."

"How can she be safe with these people?" I ask.

Minji cranes her neck to look at Mica. "It's like tribalism."

"What is that?" Rhen asks.

"It was something on Earth—" Minji trails off.

A squabble near Mica gets heated as a man punches someone in the face. Then, the two grip one another and shove toward the edge. Struggling, one of the men manages to flip the other over the metal barrier. Unable to grab the ledge, the man plunges to the ground.

I squeeze my eyes shut and bury my face in Minji's shoulder. She squeezes me close as I hear a thud.

"Ooo," the crowd muses.

Opening my eyes and turning from Minji, I see the man twitching on the circular platform. Blood pools around his smashed head. His twitching slows, then stops.

"What a great start to the night!" A man wearing a dark blue cloak walks onto the platform, stepping around the pool of blood.

A second man with decaying teeth stands next to him. He says something in Trovantian and the crowd cheers.

"We have a once-in-a-lifetime show," says the man in the blue cloak.

The decaying-teeth man says something after. He must be translating.

"For the first time ever," says the blue-cloaked man, "we have a fighter who has already defeated the king of water-murien."

The crowd cheers.

"Our fighter has killed an albharee."

There's more cheering.

"Today," says the man, "we will see if Arachna Vishar can kill the king of land-murien!"

The crowd erupts with shouts and claps.

The blue-cloak man and crooked-tooth man both move to the edge of the circular platform and across a small bridge to pass over the dirty water. A metal door opens along the wall and they go inside, closing the door behind.

Nearby, another door opens. Metal spider legs reflect the light from the cylindrical space. Lyra emerges from the threshold. Nested by metal that stabs into the ground, Lyra darts over the small bridge to the circular platform. There's clapping and yelling from every direction. Some people boo as she gets to the center of the platform.

I hold my stomach, thinking of what monster Lyra could be facing. "I think I'm going to be sick."

"She is not wearing her cloak," says Rhen. "Where is her cloak?"

"It was getting in the way of her casts," I say. Vega had strapped metal to Lyra to keep her from further injuring herself. I wish I could go back in time and tell Lyra to put the cloak over the casts.

"Leal," Gia whispers. "Pass me the wire fuser."

Reaching into my pocket, I pull out my tool and hand it to Gia.

Thinking the guards are distracted, Gia presses the button to try and break our restraints. The tool sparks. A guard notices.

He yells something, then whacks Gia in the back of the head.

She topples over, pulling Minji, Ferris, and Rhen, who are chained to her.

The guard snatches the metal fuser from Gia— that's the last one we have.

Lyra's metal chair stands in the center of the circle as the crowd cheers. She doesn't look at us.

Arcturo is bent over, still delirious from the sedative. But he moves his fists back and forth as if he is sleep-fighting to save his daughter.

Metal screeches as a door on the opposite side of the space starts to open.

There's a growl.

As the door opens, light reflects from massive fangs of a snarling creature. Its jet-black hair sticks up on its back and giant claws protrude from its paws.

It leaps over the dirty water and onto the circular platform.

The crowd cheers.

In a metallic spider-chair, Lyra is face-to-face with a monster that towers above her head and gives a deep growl.

Lyra starts to unstrap the metal pieces on her arms.

"What is she doing?" I say. "I can't watch." I turn my eyes away and pull Minji closer.

Rhen leans in.

Gia fights to get her restraints off.

There are gasps in the crowd.

Still gripping Minji, I slowly turn to look.

The beast is lying down.

Lyra is out of the spider-chair, crawling to the creature. She strokes its side, then grips its fur to hoist herself onto its back.

"It is the heebo," says Rhen.

With Lyra on its back, the creature stands. It gives a howl that turns into a ferocious roar.

Standing on its hind legs, the creature roars again, then crashes its paws into a ledge. Onlookers scream and run away. The heebo reaches its head to the ledge and digs its teeth into someone's shoulder. The heebo yanks the person off the ledge, shaking its head back and forth and then slamming the person onto the ground.

Wailing, the person lands in front of us with blood gushing from the bite marks. Our guards yank open the metal door nearest to us. The wire fuser drops to the ground.

There's screeching as the heebo pounces on Lyra's metal chair. Sparks fly from exposed wires as the heebo rips off a metal leg and flings it at people escaping on a ledge.

"Let's go!" Gia yells as she reaches her arm around Ferris to pull her from the ground.

My shoulders droop as I look at the pile of torn metal. "Spider-chair," I whine.

"Help him up," Dad says to me as he pulls Arcturo upright.

Still hanging on to the monster, Lyra speeds through the open door near us.

Gia picks up the wire fuser as our group follows behind Lyra.

We hobble along in the wake created by the spider demoness and her heebo.


"Will he be okay?" Lyra sits near the heebo in the cavern.

The heebo sinks its teeth into what remains of the dead albharee, pulling the flesh off and chewing with tendons stringing from its jaw. The Trovantians had already cut away much of the albharee flesh to cook and, for some reason, had taken the teeth and claws. The heebo chews at what is left on the bones.

"He should be," Dad says as the two of us help Arcturo to the ground.

Arcturo flops down and lies on his stomach with his face on the ground. Dad and I try to turn him over.

Gia, Minji, and Rhen hoist up Ferris as they follow behind.

"We should be safe," Gia says as the group arrives near us. "We need to get these off." She holds the wire fuser as the group lays Ferris down and takes a seat.

Stench fills the collapsed cavern from the rotting albharee.

The heebo stops eating and howls.

Sparks fly as Gia starts to weaken the restraints around Minji.

"Are you okay?" Rhen says to Lyra.

"Yeah," Lyra says. "I just can't stand." She looks at her legs.

I turn to Gia. "Do you have an analysis?"

Gia pauses from removing the restraints. She looks up and down, examining Lyra's body. Lyra looks uncomfortable, but Gia doesn't seem to notice.

"I didn't see the force of the impact," says Gia. "So it's hard to say. If she can't walk after this long, there is definitely some injury. But nothing is apparently broken. She could have muscle injuries or minimally displaced fractures."

"Do you know the healing time?" I ask.

"Depends," says Gia. "It could be weeks. It could be longer. But we seem to heal faster in the Trovant— maybe because of the elevated oxygen levels."

"I'm sure I'll be fine," says Lyra.

"Of course you will," Rhen puts her hand on Lyra's shoulder and smiles. "You are the Arachna."

Lyra smiles, then looks at Ferris with the smile fading away. "Do you have an analysis for Ferris?"

With her eyes closed, Ferris trembles on the ground.

"It's not good," says Gia. "The sooner we get these restraints off, we can get her somewhere for medical attention." There's an electric grating sound from the wire fuser as Gia starts again to remove the restraints.

From the shadows, dark creatures lurk behind boulders and rocks. One steps into the open and looks at us. It's another heebo.

"Should we be worried?" I ask.

Lyra's eyes follow the heebo as it moves to the albharee. "I don't think so."

The new heebo takes a bite of the albharee. More heebos appear and join. Then, velsyrens pop up from rocks and climb the albharee. Creatures are littered around to feast on the rotting sea monster.

346

"I wondered if I would find you in here," Mica appears behind a boulder and walks over to us. She holds a bunch of sticks. Each stick has a cooked squid skewered on the end. In her other hand, she holds only one skewered squid. She takes a bite of the squid and sits next to Lyra. "Have you been here long?"

"We just arrived," says Rhen. "Our journey was slow." She looks at the chains that Gia cuts off and then at Arcturo and Ferris on the ground.

"So wait," I interrupt. "There was a raging monster and we were fleeing for our lives. And then you just stopped for a snack."

"You all seemed to be okay," says Mica. She takes another bite. "These are hard to get in the Trovant. I had to get them while I was in-between."

A velsyren leaps down next to Mica. It snaps at the squid sticks. Mica leans into Lyra and away from the small animal.

"Lyra," says Mica, "help."

"Why are you asking me?" Lyra asks. "What am I supposed to do?"

"You are brave," says Mica. "You must protect the squid."

"Go away," Lyra leans over Mica and shoos the velsyren away.

It still inches toward the squid sticks. Lyra picks up a small rock and tosses it near the velsyren. Startled, the animal jets away. It settles near others to continue eating the albharee remains.

"So," Mica says as she looks around the cavern, "this is all gone."

"I'm sorry," Lyra says, looking at the ground.

"You may have saved lives," says Rhen. "We could not know what the albharee would do. And people may still avoid these caverns." She looks at the scavenging creatures. "We may be able to stay here without being bothered."

"Lyra," Arcturo raises his hand from the ground and toward his daughter.

"Hi, Dad," Lyra scoots closer to him.

The last of the metal restraints clank on the ground. Gia pulls a tablet from the folds of her clothes.

Arcturo puts his hand on Lyra's cheek. "You're okay."

"I am okay," Lyra smiles. "Are you going to be okay?"

Arcturo grunts as he tries to move. "Not when your mother finds out about all this."

Lyra chuckles.

"Restraints are off," says Gia. "Now we need to plan our next step. I just sent a message to my dad's tablet for him to meet us here. While we wait for him, you can fill us in on the information sent to Eddi's tablet before we were separated."

"Gia," Dad says. He pauses.

"We don't know exactly what was on the tablet," I say. "It was in Trovantian."

"Well," says Gia. "We have translators. We can—"

"Gia," Dad interrupts. "That can wait."

Our fabric shoes thud on the metal floor of the Alaster ship.

"He's in here," Dad says softly as he shows Gia to a door on the ground level of the ship.

Gia has a strong stance as she opens the door and walks in. "Dad?"

The room isn't big enough for many people to fit.

"Dad?" Gia's voice trembles.

"Son." Dad looks at me and nods to the doorway.

I walk through the doorway, into the small room, and by Gia's side.

Garridon lies on a metal bed. His face is pale. He is motionless except that his chest moves slightly up and down.

Gia holds her stomach and stares at her father.

I put my arm over her shoulders.

"Is he going to be okay?" Gia asks. "Is he going to wake up?"

I hug her closer with one arm. "I don't know."

She leans her head on me with tears dripping from her cheeks and absorbing into my fabric sleeve.

I wrap my other arm around her. Then, I sing quietly over her sobs:

"Come what may, come what might

I'll be your friend through this night.

I can't promise things will be alright.

But I'm here to hold you tight."

I walk up the long path to the entrance of my living space. I want to see how Takara is doing, then I'll bring some food back to Gia, where she waits by Garridon.

My dad went to help get Arcturo and Lyra back to the Delphinos' living quarters. Minji stayed behind to work with the Trovantians to understand the information on the tablet.

I walk alone up to the intricate stone doors with silver handles. Pulling open one of the doors, I step inside.

"Mom?" I look around my living quarters.

There's a new object in my big community area. I step forward to see what it is.

"Ah!" I jump as I see a figure in the room.

It's Imeel, the person who sometimes translates for us.

"What are you doing in here?" I ask. "Where is my mom?"

"Your mother went to the market," says Imeel. "I want to show you this." He motions to the object and I start to realize what it is.

It's an albharee tooth.

"What—" I can't seem to find the right words. "Why?"

The tooth is on something that is held parallel to the ground.

"You are a champion," says Imeel. "We made you a table to showcase your prize."

I look at the short table. Then I turn around to look at the giant stone table in my eating area.

"You do not approve," says Imeel. "You would rather have a claw."

"No," I shake my head. I hope they don't put a claw where I can see it. "It's just that— why do I have two tables?"

"You did not have an entertainment table," says Imeel. "That big one is for meals. This one is for drinks or small treats when you are not eating a meal. You invite people over to sit on these cushions, then you use this small table for treats." He points to cushions on the floor next to the albharee tooth.

I look back at the big table again. I can drink things and eat small foods outside of a meal time?

"And this way," says Imeel, "you can show off your strength to all your guests."

"Strength?" I look down at my tiny bicep.

"Ha ha!" Imeel slaps my back. "Always so funny."

I'm pushed forward by the strength of his jesting slap.

"Now that I am here," Imeel says, "I should speak to you. Rasul Midian has been curious about the details of your triumphant battle against the albharee. Why exactly were you in that area?"

"Uhh—"

"Hello?" Mom walks through the door. She holds Takara in one arm and a bag of vegetables in the other. "Oh, good. You're home. Can you grab her, please?"

"Tak!" I smile and take my sister from Mom's arms.

Mom goes to the kitchen to put down the vegetables.

"I am interrupting," says Imeel. He must not want to speak in front of Mom. "I will go now. But I will come back to talk. Rasul would like to know what you have been doing." He motions to the albharee-tooth-table. "I will bring small treats when I come."

Mom steps into our community area as Imeel leaves and closes the stone doors.

"Good riddance," says Mom. "Those men just came up in here with that big ol' tooth. I did not like the looks of them. I don't trust that Imeel guy."

I bend down and sit in one of the cushions near the albharee tooth. Takara straddles my stomach and grabs at my hair. I wrap my hands around hers, then pretend to bite them.

Takara laughs and tries to pull her hands away.

"Son," says Mom. "What's happened? And where's your father?"

"We found the others," I say.

"Oh, thank goodness," Mom puts her hand on her heart.

"Dad is with the Delphinos."

Takara puts her hand on my face. "Buh buh."

"That's right, Tak," I say. "I am Bubba."

"Buh buh buh." Takara slaps my face with each time she says 'buh'.

"Okay," I set her on the ground. "I am Bubba, but that's enough of that."

Takara crawls over to the tooth and puts her tiny hand on the serrated edge.

I lean toward Takara and pull her hand from the tooth. "I hope they cleaned this." I sigh and lean back on the cushion. "Gia saw Garridon."

Mom leans her head to the side.

"I just wish there was something I could do." I rub my cheek. "And I don't know what we're going to do about everything else. Minji and the others are working to figure out what's on the tablet. Once we know what it says, I don't know what we're going to do next."

"You don't have to," Mom says. "You don't need to know everything that will happen tomorrow. Today, just be a good friend." She walks into the kitchen and shouts from there. "I made something." She comes back where Takara and I are. "It's like a bread, but it's sweet. Some of the other women showed me how to make it."

"Is it cake?" I ask.

"I don't know. They didn't tell me an English word. And I wouldn't know what cake is like anyway."

"From the footage of the surface," I say, "cake was coated in some edible paint and it would have a candle in it."

"Well, there's no paint or candle, but I'll pack some up for you to take to Gia."

"What did the others say?" Gia sits on the floor across from Garridon and leans her head on the metallic wall. She doesn't look up but stares at Garridon when I come into the room.

"About what?" I ask as I sit next to her.

"What was on the tablet?" Gia lifts her head from the wall but still looks at Garridon.

"Oh, I don't know. I haven't gone back to the caverns. I brought a treat." I lift up the sweet bread that Mom wrapped up.

Gia looks at the bread in my hands. "I'm not very hungry."

"It's a small food," I say as I unwrap it. "It's not for when you are hungry."

"What do you mean?"

"I'm not entirely sure." I break off a piece for her. "But you can eat small foods outside of meal times."

She stares at the treat in my hand.

"Just eat it so I can tell my mom you like it because you know she's going to ask."

Gia accepts the sweet bread and takes a bite. She chews, then pauses and looks at the rest of the bread. "That's amazing."

"See?" I say. "It wasn't that hard. Ahh!"

I shout as a velsyren leaps into the room and snatches the rest of the sweet bread. The creature gulps the rest of the treat.

Desman peeks his head through the doorway. "Sorry, Leal. I didn't think you'd be in here." He grips the door without coming in. The room might be too small for all of us.

The velsyren steps onto Gia's lap and rubs its face against her cheek.

"Hi Ari," Gia says as she wraps her arms around the animal.

Ari licks Gia's cheek and then nestles her head against Gia's chest.

Gia sniffles, holding Ari close and resting her head down by the fluffy animal. Then, tears start to stream down Gia's cheeks.

"Leal," says Desman. "Can I?" He starts stepping into the room.

"Sure," I stand up, squeezing past Desman as we switch places.

Desman lowers to the ground and sits next to Gia. He puts his arm around her, and she rests her head into him while still hugging the little creature.

I've rarely seen Gia touching someone other than to fight them. Now she's danced with Desman and cuddled with him. Desman's large biceps and muscular forearms wrap around Gia.

I'm feeling awkward standing here, hovering over them.

Desman kisses the top of Gia's head as she cries.

I inch my way out of the tight room.

"Phew," my sigh of relief echoes in the empty submersible.

I look at my thin biceps. I'm even flimsy for someone from the Trellis. I don't know what strength Imeel was talking about.

"How is Gia?" Minji asks as she sits in the cavern with Rhen.

Mica lies on the floor, wrapped tight in her cloak as she slumbers near a pile of sticks. The sticks have been picked clean of the squid. Ferris lies close by, squeezing a cloak around herself and shivering.

"She's uhh—" I think of how I awkwardly left— "with Desman."

Minji doesn't ask follow-up questions but stares at her tablet with Rhen looking over her shoulder.

Rhen stands. "If that is all, I need to get Ferris to some medics. After, I can tell the others about this information. How do you contact your friends?"

"Usually we start with Garridon," says Minji. "I've always told him or Gia everything first."

"What's going on?" I ask.

"I will explain," says Minji. She also stands. "But maybe we should get everyone together first."

"Will you—" Rhen starts to ask a question, but pauses. She looks at Mica, who snores. "Will you stay here?"

"Is everything okay?" Minji also looks at Mica.

"Everything is fine," says Rhen. "Mica will get scared if she wakes up alone in the cavern. Will you stay with her?"

"Oh-okay," Minji lowers back down.

I sit next to Minji, and we lean against a boulder.

Rhen lies on the ground near Ferris, then puts Ferris's arm around her own shoulder and rolls over so that Ferris is on her back. Rhen props herself up, then gets into a squatting position with Ferris on her back. She stands fully, carrying her friend on her back, then moves to the exit.

Minji starts to pull up information on the tablet to read through what they had translated. She has been through so much recently— getting stuck in the caves and getting captured in the in-between. But she hasn't rested after all that's happened. She's always the one trying to make me feel better.

I put my arm around her shoulder and try to pull her close.

"What are you doing?" she stops scrolling through the information.

"I'm," I stutter. "I'm being comforting."

"Your comfort is making it hard to move."

"Oh," I rub my head. "I was just— I wanted to—"

"It's fine," she grips the tablet. "I just— maybe it would be better if I could double-check these calculations."

"Yeah," I clasp my hands together. "That makes sense." I look down at the tablet and try not to look at Minji.

I skim through a chunk of code that includes the text:

```
def Frank (numbers):
```

"What is that?" I point to the line and try to read back to the rest of the code.

Minji moves the tablet away from me. "Nothing."

"Did you define a function and call it Frank?"

Holding the tablet, she looks at me. Then nods. "I can name functions whatever I want now that I'm not in the Trellis."

She seems embarrassed that I'm reading her code. But I'm enamored that I am in the presence of someone who wrote a complicated function and called it Frank. I smile a little.

"Don't laugh," she says, pulling the tablet to her chest.

"I'm not," I try not to smile. "What does Frank do?"

She looks at me as if deciding whether or not to show me. Then she leans toward me and scrolls through the lines of code. "Frank is taking the numbers interpreted by Rhen and calculating the force of pressure at the weakest point of the Trovant."

"Is the weakest point Winston?" I ask as I point to another function called 'Winston.'

"Yes," Minji leans against me to give me a better look at the tablet. "Winston is looking at all the measurements of the exterior walls and calculating which would be the weakest point."

"What is this one named 'Winston2?'"

"Winston2 is the calculation of the weakest point after adding the values of support beams that are throughout the facility."

I read through the code and find the calculations for the amount of force that the support beams should hold over the surface area in a given part of the Trovant— I see my name. I lean toward the tablet with Minji's head now resting on my chest.

"You named a function after me?"

She nods.

"I'm the values for the support beams?"

"Of course, you're the support beams. They're the hidden strength that keeps everything from caving in." She looks up at me. "Would you rather be something else?"

"I'm not—" I look at the intelligent and beautiful person leaning against my chest. "I'm not strong... or..."

"Yes, you are," she says.

She looks up at me. I don't know what to say.

Mica rolls over in her sleep and mumbles: "Please pass..." She rolls again. "The sauce."

"Umm," I look back at the tablet. "Why did Rhen want to get us all together now? Is the Trovant going to collapse and we'll all drown?"

"Not anytime soon," says Minji. "At least with the weight that the support beams could carry. But this area— calculated by Winston3— is getting thinner and weaker every week. It looks like someone is digging away at the Trovant wall."

"Why would someone do that?"

"That's what we need to find out. But if someone is digging, they could jeopardize the walls. And then maybe the Trovant won't last much longer."

"Or the other facility," I say, looking at Minji's formulas. "This Leal value is different from the others." I point to one of the values in the function named after me. "It's either very thick or connected to something else."

"That's in the same area that they are digging." The light from the tablet reflects from her black hair. "What do we do?"

"I normally ask Gia that question."

# Part III

# Chapter 17: Gia— The Reason We're Here

"Look," Leal kneels on the floor with his hands stretched toward Takara. "She's taking steps."

"That's sweet, Leal," I look up briefly from my tablet and then look back at Minji's lines of code. I lean against the stone table in Leal's eating area as he plays with his sister.

"You aren't looking," he says.

"I saw. She's standing up."

"Yeah, but you need to watch until she takes a step."

"She's taking too long."

"Gia!"

"What?" I look up from the tablet.

Takara chews on her fingers and steps into Leal's arms.

"Yay!" Leal cheers for his sister. "You did it, Tak."

"Very sweet." I look back at the tablet.

"Take a break," says Leal. "Staring at data isn't going to fix anything."

"This is serious, Leal."

"No, this is serious, Gia," he emphasizes my name. I look up at him as he holds Takara close.

"This is what we are working so hard for," he holds Takara's little hands so she can stay standing. "We couldn't get moments like these in the Trellis. And now we have a chance to spend time waiting for babies to take a step. Who knew we would have chances like this? In the Trellis, we couldn't buy this time if we tried. There's nothing else you can do until we start the plan, except hang out with me and my sister."

I set the tablet on the stone table and kneel next to Leal and Takara.

Leal situates Takara so she faces toward me. He releases her hands. Instinctively, I put my hands out in case she falls. She wobbles, picking up one foot and stepping toward me. Then, she topples over and falls into my arms.

Okay— Leal was right. This is cute.

Takara's dimpled smile hits some soft emotion inside me. But I don't want to feel it. Anything sweet or precious makes me think of a mother I lost and a father I might lose. Moments like these aren't worth it— they're too painful.

That's why Desman isn't here. I told him he should leave me alone.

"I remember when you all were that age," Eddi says as he comes into the room. "Except maybe you." He turns behind as Lyra limps through the doorway on makeshift crutches. "You might have been in the Sanctuary already by Tak's age. Of course, we all loved you before that." He pulls a chair from the table so that Lyra can sit down.

Mabel appears from the hallway as Lyra hobbles to the chair.

"What do you mean?" Lyra asks as she takes a seat.

"She wouldn't remember, honey," says Mabel.

"I thought maybe Arcturo would have told her," says Eddi.

"Told me what?" Lyra asks.

"The reason we're all here," says Mabel. "It started with you."

"How?" Lyra asks.

"Gee, Gee," Takara hits my face.

"Yes," I whisper and move Takara's hand. "I'm Gia."

"We weren't supposed to have multiple kids in the Trellis," says Mabel.

"You were an accident," says Eddi.

"Edison!" Mabel scolds.

"You were a product of love," Eddi corrects himself.

"Ew," says Lyra.

"When we found out," Eddi explains, "all of us got together to figure something out. We needed you to make it. Britannica and Vega were always getting into trouble before, but that's when Britannica really searched the Alaster ship for a way out. That's when Garridon first felt like he needed to break into the security systems. He and I worked it at both angles— I was more the structural guy working with the cameras and he was the software guy."

"What did Mom do?" Leal asks.

"I yelled at everyone," says Mabel.

"It's true, actually," Eddi smiles. "Which you wouldn't realize is such a valuable skill until every Facilitator in the entire Trellis is in one place trying to stop Mabel Fitzgerald."

"Why didn't they gas her?" I ask. I don't mean to sound so blunt— I guess I still have protocols ingrained in my mind.

"Garridon switched it off," says Eddi. "While Britannica and Vega went to the Alaster ship for the first time."

"I didn't know any of that," says Lyra.

"Yup," says Eddi. "You were causing trouble before you were even born. Looks like not much has changed."

"I'm not trying to cause trouble," Lyra says, looking down at her legs.

"I meant that as a compliment," says Eddi. "Trouble needed to be caused. As it does now." He looks at me. "Are you ready?"

"I was," I say, "until Leal distracted me."

"Well," Eddi slaps his thigh. "Let's go cause some trouble."


A rock pushes into my rib as I squeeze through a narrow passage. Water drips on my face as I get close to the spot where the Trovant walls should be at the weakest point.

Alone in the cavern, I pull the tablet from my bag and speak to it. "This won't cave in, right?"

Leal's voice speaks through the tablet: "Would I send you in there if the walls were going to break?"

After what had happened in the caverns, we decided to put a microphone on Leal's side as well as the one on the camera that I wear. We had to take apart some pieces from a communication beacon to reconstruct the microphone.

"That didn't answer my question," I say.

"You should be fine," Eddi's voice says through the tablet.

"Someone is coming," says Leal. "I'm going to mute you so I can't hear anything. Type if you need something."

I stay quiet, still inching through the narrow tunnel. We need to know if someone is digging at the Trovant walls. And then we need to know why.

A voice in Trovantian sounds through the tablet.

My grunts and sniffles bounce off the close walls and cover some of the noises from the tablet.

"It's okay," says Leal's voice to someone who apparently arrived near him. "I am just checking something in this area."

There are muffled voices and it sounds like someone else translates for Leal.

"There seems to be an issue in this area," says Leal. "It could be very dangerous. You should probably leave."

The person translates, then there's some shouting in Trovantian.

"Listen," says Eddi's voice, "we don't want to cause any trouble. We just need to make sure things are safe."

The crystal cracks in the tunnel let off a white light. The cave isn't entirely black or grey, but it has pockets of some green formation that looks like it could be from a different planet.

There is more arguing in Trovantian through the tablet.

Leal and Eddi both speak over one another. It sounds like they are trying to cause confusion.

I move forward and into a more open space. It's cold. I see my breath as I look around at what looks like bubbling swirls of green covering the walls or dripping from the ceiling like suspended waterfalls. I touch the wall. It's hard and grainy. It's definitely stone.

The shouting from the tablet gets louder.

"We need to find a solution!" Leal yells.

That's the code phrase to alert Lyra.

The shouting quiets.

"Heebo! Heebo!" the Trovantians bellow through the tablet.

"Watch out!" Leal shouts. His panic sounds entirely fake. "It's a heebo! Let's get out of here!"

It's a good thing our plan didn't hinge on Leal's acting skills.

There's some rustling around and shouting, then the tablet quiets.

"Gia," says Leal. "You're back on. Are you okay?"

"Yeah," I say. "Are you seeing this?" I circle slowly around the area to show the flowing green stone.

"It looks like malachite," says Leal. "It's beautiful."

"There's likely copper nearby," says Eddi.

"Are we looking for copper?" I ask.

"No," says Leal. "I don't think so. You're close, but you're not quite in the right spot. Can you go any further?"

"The cave continues to the left," I say as I scan the different parts of the green space.

"Try that way," says Leal.

The green stone is replaced with more plane-looking rock as I journey further into the cave. Instead of getting narrower, the cave gets larger as I walk forward. Soon, the walls on either side of me are far apart and the ceiling is high above. The cold air bites at my nose and I wrap my icy fingers around myself. My toes sting as a thin layer of water pools across the floor. I try to walk silently as my feet splash in the shallow water.

"Gia, stop," says Leal.

"What is it?" I ask.

"Can you look to the left?"

I turn to my left. Something streaks through the wall like a pale string.

"Can you see what that is?" Leal asks.

I walk up to the string. It doesn't look like crystal. I poke it. It's springy and flexible. Definitely not stone. I follow along the wall as the pale string gets large and spans into more strings.

"What is that?" Leal asks.

"It seems like a root," I say. "A really big one."

Following the tunnel, the root system grows more complex and expansive. In the distance, I start to hear muffled voices.

"Maybe you should turn around," Leal whispers.

"I'm turning you on mute," I say.

"Gia, you—"

I mute the volume on the tablet.

A message from Leal appears on the screen: "Turn around."

"I'm going to see if I can get any closer," I say quietly.

I follow the voice to a small opening in the tunnel wall. The opening is just above my head, so I grip the wall and get a foothold on a piece that protrudes along the side. Lifting myself up to the opening, there is a small crevice with light shining through. The voices are louder. They speak in Trovantian.

Still gripping the rock, I pin the tablet to the wall with my other hand. Pressing the tablet to the wall with my arm, I awkwardly move my finger to press record. Then I look again through the crack.

It's gold; the entire space is coated in shining gold. Luxurious cushions with multicolored patterns are dispersed throughout the area.

I don't understand the voices, but one of them is definitely Imeel. A figure steps into my view. It's Rasul Midian. I don't know what they are saying, but the tone sounds serious. Rasul looks up.

I duck down, looking away from the crack. I hope he didn't see me.

Quietly, I step down from the wall.

The two still speak, but it sounds like they step into a different room. Soon, I hear their voices coming from somewhere inside the cave.

Clenching the tablet, I rush back through the tunnel the way I came. I clamor through the malachite room and squeeze back into the narrow opening that leads to Leal and Eddi.

"Do you think they saw you?" Leal scoots the chair into the big stone table as he sits.

"I don't know," I sit with my elbows at the table and my hands clasped together.

"Now listen," says Eddi. "We were all here at the meal time like we were supposed to be. Gia, eat quickly in case someone comes."

I look down at the plate of food Mabel had made for me. For my survival, I shove food in my mouth and gulp without chewing.

"I told you to turn around," says Leal.

"I know," I say with my mouth full.

"Why didn't you turn around?" he asks in a panicked voice.

"We might have valuable intel," I say. "Whatever they were saying seemed important. Once we get it translate—"

"Well, isn't that just so nice?" Mabel says loudly as she comes in and puts new food on my plate. "It sounds like you have been working hard today and need some extra food."

There's a knock at the door.

"I'll get it," Mabel says.

Mabel must have been able to tell someone was coming. Some of the gaps in the wall are filled with translucent crystals. She might have seen someone walking up the path through the crystals.

"Imeel," Mabel smiles. "What a surprise."

"Yes," says Imeel as he walks through the door. "I am here to check on Leal and see how you are doing. I heard you ran into a heebo."

"Oh yes," says Leal. "It was very scary. I was warned about those."

"You must be careful," says Imeel. "I am also told there was an issue with your work today."

"Yes," I respond for Leal. "The methane readings were too high in that area. He needed to make sure that nothing was leaking from the waste piles."

"I hope it is okay," Imeel says.

Leal nods, but gives me a disapproving look. "It's fine now."

"This is good news," says Imeel. "You are doing such wonderful work. And we never got to talk about your battle with the albharee. Rasul Midian had kindly invited you to a meal with him. There, you can tell us about your successes in work and in battle."

Leal swallows. "That sounds exciting."

"Yes," says Imeel. "We will send you instructions and the correct clothes to wear. It is good to see you and I am happy you are safe from the heebo. I am sorry for such a short visit, but I will speak to you very soon." Imeel turns around and goes through the doorway.

Mabel closes the door behind him. We all watch through the translucent crystal as his figure moves down the pathway and out of sight.

"I think they saw you," Leal says to me.


There's not much left of the albharee except its skeleton. One of Lyra's Trovantian friends paces near a pile of boulders in the ruined cavern. She is tall and slender with long hair that sways with her pacing. "This is all because you disrupted the eternal flame."

"Vana," says Rhen, "We did not even reach the flame."

"You tried," says Vana. "And now our home is breaking, Lyra is hurt, and—"

"Now Lyra is the Arachna," Mica puts her hand on Lyra's shoulder.

Jarret now stands beside Lyra. He joined us to make sure Lyra got down the rock wall and through the jungle safely. We have been trying to rotate who is absent from duties in order to avoid suspicion, so Arcturo agreed to stay at the fields as long as others were with Lyra to help her get around.

"The Trovant is breaking because of people," says Rhen. "Not because of the eternal flame."

"So will you translate for us?" Leal pulls my tablet from the sling-bag made from a blanket.

Rhen nods.

Vana stops pacing and looks at the tablet.

Leal plays the recording. Rasul Midian's voice says something, but it's muffled. Then Imeel's voice responds with more clarity. The two have a short conversation.

"Will you play it again?" Rhen asks when the recording stops.

"Did they see me?" I ask.

Leal presses on the screen to rewind the footage.

Rhen shakes her head. "Rasul said he saw something, but he said he did not know what it was. He only saw black. Imeel said it may have been a black velsyren or small creature."

"Good thing you aren't blonde," says Leal.

"Or have purple hair," says Jarrett.

"How would I have purple hair?" I forgot Jarret is an idiot.

Lyra leans slightly away and turns her head to look at him.

"I don't know," says Jarrett. "I was just trying to think of a color that wouldn't appear on an animal."

I shake my head. "Play the footage again."

Rhen, Vana, and Mica listen intently to the voices conversing through the tablet.

Vana says something in Trovantian. Her tone sounds worried.

"What is it?" I ask.

"Rhen," Mica says. "Will my family be okay? What will happen?"

"I do not know," says Rhen, "but we will find out."

"What is it?" I ask again.

"The white string you saw," says Rhen. "You were right. It is a root to a plant."

"Is that bad?" Leal asks.

"It means we will have enough oxygen," says Rhen. "The Trovant will not need to trade oxygen with the plant people."

"That doesn't sound like a bad thing," says Lyra.

"Rasul says it is time to cut them off," says Rhen.

"Cut off sustenance supply?" I ask.

"No," says Rhen. "Cut the plant."

"My family is in the in-between," says Mica. "What will happen in-between?"

"And what about all the plant people?" Lyra asks. "Will they all die?"

"I don't know if the Trovant would survive either," says Leal. "The new plant roots are weakening the Trovant walls. It could crumble if the roots keep growing. And I don't see how they could disconnect the other facility without flooding the Trovant."

"Rhen?" Mica looks at her friend. She says something in Trovantian.

Leal looks at me. "What do we do?"

***

"We must say," Imeel says as he leans over a silver plate with different colored foods, "we were not quite expecting both of you."

"I thought it would be nice to bring a friend," says Leal.

The large table is covered in a multicolored cloth. Rasul Midian sits at the head of the table, across from me. Walls and ceilings are coated in gold. An albharee claw is strung from the ceiling and hangs over us across the length of the table.

Rasul says something as he takes a sip from a cup made of silver that has gemstones of all colors around the rim.

"This is not entirely proper," says Imeel. "But this is why Rasul is interested in you. You have a different way of living. Maybe thinking differently is what we need. Like with the albharee." Imeel motions above our heads at the claw.

Rasul looks up as he speaks. His dark beard hides some of his expressions.

"You have met a dangerous animal and have lived to tell the tale," Imeel translates for Rasul. "Twice, it seems. You also met a heebo. We are impressed and grateful to host such a warrior."

Leal gives an awkward smile.

"Now we would like to know," says Imeel. "You never did tell us what you were doing in that area near the albharee."

Leal looks at me.

"Same reason as Leal is in any place," I answer. "He was scoping out viable areas to store the waste."

Imeel translates back to Rasul.

Rasul looks directly into my eyes, asking Imeel a question and then taking a sip from his ornate cup.

"And where were you?" Imeel asks.

"Still sick," I say. "It seems my immune system isn't strong enough to work with Leal."

Rasul takes a bite of food and keeps eye contact with me as he chews.

"We are glad you are feeling better," says Imeel.

"Thank you," I say, taking a bite of food.

"It seems you are headstrong," says Imeel. "Where did you get such fire?"

I think of my father, now struggling to live as he lies in the Alaster ship.

The question Imeel asked would be categorized as a second-tier information-acquisition question. The first-tier is informational— *how did I become headstrong*? The second-tier is a deeper level— Imeel is wondering what kind of person I am. The way I answer the informational question will answer his underlying question.

"Can you say more?" I respond with the best way to get more information without revealing anything myself.

"Such fire!" Imeel exclaims. "Even before our great overseer. You must have no fear."

I am afraid. I'm afraid of losing my dad. I'm afraid my actions could ruin the life that Leal and his family now have.

At least one thing is sure— Imeel can't read me.

I smile. "You have provided such hospitality and made us little people comfortable. We have no reason to fear with you around."

Rasul still looks in my eyes as a woman walks to the table, takes his empty plate, and disappears into the corridors of the golden living space.

My mind flashes to training in the Trellis. My dad was showing me footage of a negotiation between Plangon and Vega. My dad said: "Strong-willed people would find it despicable and insulting that a negotiator would expect them to trade in their own values."

Someone leans past me and takes my plate.

"I was told about how you became the Trovant overseer," I say.

Imeel translates for me.

"You negotiated peace," I say. "You saved your people from suffocating. And now you've opened your facility to save people who have nowhere else to go."

Imeel translates as the servers come back with smaller plates. This time, the plates have tiny treats and cut fruit on them.

I'm about to ask a question, but Rasul begins to speak in Trovantian.

Imeel translates: "Have you ever seen war?"

I shake my head.

"Have you ever…" Imeel translates at the same time as Rasul's speech, "… believed in something that was worth your life? Have you known what is true, and you were willing to give what it might cost?"

I think of the Trellis. I didn't always know what was true or not, but I risked everything when I decided what was right. I didn't just risk death— I risked living a life that was uncertain.

I nod.

Imeel translates again: "Have you ever known what is right, to the point where it was worth taking someone else's life?"

I lock eyes with Rasul. His bearded face seems calm and his eyes are settled. He's like someone who has seen horrors, but has found meaning.

I haven't taken someone's life— not like him. I haven't been in a war or cut off a part of a facility to send it to sea— have I? I think of the screams blaring through the speakers when Ara's grandma faced the brine. I think of the door slamming shut with Plangon and Cloplin trapped in the flooding room. The water was so cold.

Did I push for what was 'right' at the risk of someone else's life? Did I kill them?

I look down at the small treats on my plate. Like a phantom, I feel like my dad's shadow could be creeping over my back. I'm not in control of the negotiation. Rasul is getting in my head.

"Lel mesde," says Rasul.

I look up.

He explains more in Trovantian.

"The Source," says Imeel. "It was generous to make our home, to make our soil fertile, to give us heat, to give us life. It gives life and takes it," Imeel translates as Rasul explains. "It is not for us to decide what is right or who is worthy of life."

"How does the Source decide who lives or dies?" I ask.

"We cannot know how, but it will decide," says Imeel. "In the end."


"You didn't ask him about the plant," Leal steps into the room.

Leal's living quarters has eight rooms with beds in them. Since I got back from the in-between, I sometimes stay in the Alaster ship near my dad and sometimes stay in one of Leal's quarters. The room in Leal's living quarters that I picked has stones that are such a deep blue that they hardly look real. There are pockets in the walls where the rough shades of blue weave in and out of ridges like blue cliffs. Leal says it's azurite.

"He wouldn't have answered," I say as I sit on the cushioned bed. I wear silky clothing that slips around my skin and on the woven blankets. The clothes were in the room when Leal first moved here. "I think it will be hard to get more information out of him." I try not to let on that

Rasul got in my head... He didn't get in my head— I am in control.

"You lied," says Leal.

"Lied?"

"Yeah," Leal rubs his arm. "You said you were still sick."

"Technically, I was still sick."

"You said I was in that area scouting for solutions for the waste heaps."

"Okay, I lied. What was I supposed to say?"

"Not a lie," Leal leans against the wall and looks down where I sit. "You aren't a liar."

"I'm a deceiver," I say. "I don't usually lie in negotiations but I don't tell the truth either."

"That wasn't a negotiation," says Leal.

"Then what was it?"

"A dinner party!" Leal tosses his hands in the air.

"With someone who is going to kill people," I try not to raise my voice. "We needed information from him without revealing our information to them. We don't know what they do to defectors here. It's too risky to let them find out what we've been doing."

"There aren't defectors here, Gia. We aren't in the Trellis anymore."

"But we're still somewhere where people stab each other, push each other off ledges, and send each other into the ocean."

"That doesn't mean you have to lie to keep us safe."

"Then tell me how to keep you safe," I say. "You, your parents, Takara— all of you. How are we supposed —"

"Maybe it's not about being safe. Maybe it's enough for now just to be alive. To be humans who care about other humans."

"Sure," my jaw clenches. I hold in my tears as I think of my dad lying in the Alaster ship. "That's easy to say for someone who gets to care about people and hasn't had to lose any."

"Gia," Leal takes a small step toward me.

"Don't come closer," I bite my bottom lip. Leal can afford to care about people and always tell the truth. I can't.

***

Ara's red hair pours over her microbial suit and her deep green eyes look down at the negotiation table.

"Ara," I say, "tell me what's going on, maybe I can help."

She sighs, "Maybe you can't."

"Then why did you ask me to come here?"

Her body stills. Her gaze locks onto mine. "I trust you."

I jolt awake. The room is dark and the silky fabric sticks to my sweaty skin. I yank the heavy blankets off and push myself up. Did I trick Ara into trusting me? Do people die because of me?

# Chapter 18: Lyra— A Healing Cove

Rhen grips her chin. Then, she rubs her cheek as she looks down at the rocky platform where Ferris shivers. Women have come in and out of the area that they call the 'healing cove'. Three women, to be exact. The same three have come in and out seven times since I've been here. They bandaged Ferris and gave her medicines.

Leal steps into the room with plants in his fist.

"What is that?" Rhen asks.

"It's a bouquet," says Leal. "I came to check in."

Minji steps in behind Leal and places her perfect hands around his arm.

"Bouquet cheea?" Rhen asks Minji.

Minji looks at the plants in Leal's hands and shrugs. "What are the plants for, Leal?"

"It's something they did on the surface," says Leal. "I saw it in some footage. They would bring plants to a sick person to cheer them up."

Rhen and Minji both look at him.

"But, in the footage, there was always a table or something to put the plants on," Leal looks around. "I'll just—" he bends down and puts the plants on the floor next to Ferris's bed.

"Is she doing any better?" Minji asks. She holds Leal's arm again as he stands back up.

Rhen shakes her head. "They said there is nothing more they can do."

Leal looks at me. "You know how to treat sick people, right?"

He makes me feel like I should know how to heal Ferris. I wish I did. "People didn't get injuries like this in the Sanctuary," I say.

My choice to explode the cavern is what put Ferris in the in-between in the first place. My solutions never work. It's always someone else, like Minji, who comes up with things that work. "Wouldn't a Facilitator be trained to deal with this kind of emergency?"

Leal shakes his head. "Not this serious. This would be the job of a specialized Cultivator."

"What about Gia?" I ask.

Leal looks at the ground.


"Will she get better?" Rhen asks as Gia examines Ferris.

Ferris's lips are pale and she no longer shivers. She doesn't open her eyes.

Gia bends down and looks at the skin around Ferris's bandage. She shakes her head. "This isn't good."

"What can we do?" Ferris asks.

"She needs intravenous fluids and antibiotics," says Gia.

Rhen looks at Minji.

Minji starts to say something in Trovantian. But she keeps pausing, thinking, and motioning with her hands.

Rhen shakes her head. "I do not think we have these things."

"Any chance you have antibiotics?" Gia looks at me.

"No," I say. "How would I have antibiotics?"

"I don't know," says Gia. "You've made bleach and cultivated bacteria. It seems like something you could have in your lab."

I shake my head. "What can we do without those things?"

Gia bites her lip and looks at Ferris.


Jarret holds my side as I hang on to him and limp into the room on the ground level of the Alaster ship. The room is next to the one where Garridon is. This space is bigger, but there is no bed.

Gia kneels on the ground that she had covered with microbial suits. She stands as Rhen comes in and lowers Ferris to the floor on top of the garments. Ferris hardly seems alive.

Jarret helps me lower to the ground. It's painful to sit, but it's more painful to try and stand. I bunch up microbial suits under me to try and get more comfortable.

"So, what am I looking for in your lab?" Jarret asks as he stands.

"Gia can go with you," I say. "She knows what we need."

Leal comes into the spacious room but Minji isn't there with him. He keeps his gaze on the ground.

"The sharp instruments are on the top shelf toward the very back wall," I start to explain where the supplies are in my lab, since I can't climb the ladders. "The container is probably somewhere in the middle shelf."

"I can start with those things," Leal keeps his head down as he leaves the room.

I explain where the remainder of the supplies are and then Gia and Jarret leave the room to retrieve them.

Outside the doorway, I see Jarret touch Gia's arm. She stops and turns toward him.

"What did you say to him?" Jarret speaks quietly, but I can still hear him.

"I don't know—"

"Don't act like nothing is wrong," says Jarret. "Leal won't even look at you."

Gia sighs and looks up to the ceiling.

"You're an idiot, Gia Hamiltoni."

Gia's gaze shoots toward Jarret.

"You try to protect what you love, but you're isolating everyone. And, what's worse," he motions to the room where Garridon is, "you even know what it's like to be on the other side of that."

Gia stares at him.

"You know I'm right."

She rubs her thumb and pinky finger together. "What do I do?"

"Just apologize," says Jarret. "And stop being a jerk."

Gia has a faint smile from his last demand.

When Gia comes back, she wears a grey microbial suit. I'm not used to seeing someone wear such tight clothing anymore. I can see what the Trovantians meant when they said we looked naked.

She kneels next to Ferris, with a row of supplies on the ground nearby. Gia dips each of the tools in a container of bleach, then places them to dry on a piece of fabric near her.

Leal comes in, also wearing a microbial suit. He kneels next to Ferris.

"Try not to knock the bleach," Gia says to everyone around the room. "I don't want it to kill the microbial suits."

Rhen sits near Ferris and grabs the hand that isn't infected. She stares intently at Ferris, who keeps her eyes shut.

"Lyra," says Gia, "You will need to hand me tools and take them when I'm done."

I maneuver myself toward the supplies to be ready.

"Leal," says Gia. "I will need you close and I will give you instructions about where to hold."

Leal nods and scoots toward the infected arm.

"Jarret," says Gia, "I already explained what you'll have to do. I want to ask again, do you think you will be okay?"

He nods, then squats near Leal.

"Hand me the piece of microbial fabric and the rope," Gia says to me.

Looking at the row of supplies, I hand Gia a rope and a piece of fabric that she had cut from one of the microbial suits.

Gia sits on her knees, tying a knot in the rope and making a loop. "The necrosis seems to end here," she points to a dark patch that crawls up Ferris's skin. "I will save as much as I can, but I think we need to cut off the circulation here. What do you think, Leal?"

He leans toward the arm. "The dark spot seems to end there. I don't know much more than that."

"Okay," Gia wraps the microbial fabric a bit above the darkened skin and then loops the rope over the fabric with a specialized knot. "Hand me the pipe," she says to me.

After I give her a metal pipe, Gia puts it through the knot in the rope. She then twists the pipe so that it tightens the rope.

Ferris winces, then gives out a wining sound. Her head starts to move back and forth.

Gia twists more.

Ferris screams. Her head jolts up.

Rhen puts her arms around Ferris and rocks her back and forth. Trembling, Rhen sings in Trovantian and strokes Ferris's hair. Ferris still screams over the singing.

Soon, Ferris starts to quiet. She goes completely limp.

"Is she okay?" I ask.

Leal checks Ferris's pulse as Rhen lowers her slightly. Leal nods.

We watch Ferris intently as Gia continues to tighten the rope. Gia occasionally pauses to check Ferris's pulse or push on the arm to examine the blood flow.

"Move that metal piece over here," Gia says after some time.

I shove a heavy piece of metal where Gia instructs. It moves the microbial suits on the floor, so I arrange the suits back in place as much as possible.

Gia positions Ferris's arm on top of the metal. She stands but bends as she holds the arm in place. Gia looks at the ceiling and her leg trembles.

"Are you going to be okay?" Leal asks.

"My dad made me practice this on pieces of equipment," says Gia. "It's a lot harder when it's a person."

"I never thought I would say something like this," says Leal. "Maybe pretend you are working on a piece of equipment."

Gia's gaze moves back to the arm. "This needs to be as quick as possible. Jarret, are you ready?"

"Yeah," says Jarret.

"Lyra," she says, "be ready with the blade."

I pick up the blade from the line-up of tools.

Gia raises her leg, then stomps on Ferris's arm. There's a loud pop as the arm snaps over the piece of metal.

Ferris convulses as Rhen tries to hold her friend.

Leal gags.

"Lyra," Gia reaches out her hand as she kneels back down.

I place the blade in Gia's palm. She slices the blade into Ferris's arm.

Spit froths from Ferris's mouth as Gia cuts.

"Turn her on her side," Gia lifts Ferris's bleeding arm and nods to guide the others on how to turn Ferris. "She could choke. We can't keep her on her back."

Some blood drips as Gia saws through the arm at the place where she had broken the bone.

"Jarret," says Gia, "take this." Gia hands Jarret the bloody blade. Then she hands Jarret the severed arm.

"Lyra, hand me the wire fuser," says Gia.

I give Gia the tool.

Jarret grunts as he struggles with his blade in the hand of the severed arm, cutting at a piece of skin that is normal-colored. His brows stitch together and his face turns red. He starts tearing up.

Sparks fly and the smell of burnt flesh fills the room as Gia cauterizes Ferris's wound.

Rhen rocks back and forth and she whispers to Ferris.

"Jarret," says Gia. "Are you close?"

Jarret sniffs, then lifts a piece of skin.

"Leal, take that," Gia commands to Leal as Jarret dangles the skin cut from the hand. "Lyra, I need the string and needle, and then give Leal the wire cutters."

Leal shakes as he holds the piece of skin.

I give him the wire cutters and hand a needle and string to Gia.

"I'll take this," Gia says to Leal as she takes the skin and puts it in place. "Cut this thread. Good, now hold this there. Not like that, pinch it here." Gia gives commands to Leal as she stitches a patch of skin over the place where Ferris is now missing the rest of her arm.

Jarret squeezes his knees to his chest and buries his head. He clenches his hair with his bloody hands.

I move closer to him and put my hand on his knee.

"One," I say in a quiet voice. "Two. Three."

"Four, five," he counts with me.

"Six. Seven." I lean on his leg. "Eight. Nine. Ten." I move closer and wrap my arm over him. "Eleven. Twelve." He's too big for me to reach around him. "Thirteen. Fourteen." I rub his back. "Fifteen. Sixteen." I put my head on his shoulder. "Seventeen. Eighteen. Nineteen." He uncurls from hugging his legs. "Twenty. Twenty-one." He leans over and puts his head on mine.

"Lyra," says Gia, "can you take this?"

I scoot back over to Gia as she hands me a bloody needle and the remaining string.

She binds a microbial suit over the wound. "Can you hand me that tablet?" Gia asks me as she leans over Ferris.

Gia accepts the tablet as she checks Ferris's pulse. She turns the brightness up on the tablet, then opens one of Ferris's eyes and shines the light quickly over her eye.

"Will she be okay now?" Rhen's nose drips and her cheeks are red as she holds her friend.

"I can't promise for sure," says Gia. "But this is her best chance."

Rhen still holds Ferris and strokes her hair. Gia had gotten up to check on Garridon and gather more supplies from my lab. Jarret and Leal both lean against a wall, staring at nothing and speaking to no one.

"Is it finished?" Mica takes a timid step through the doorway. "I can't look." She turns her head.

"Did you get what Gia said?" Rhen asks.

"I have it," Mica covers her eyes with one hand and extends the other in front of her. "What is it for?"

"I do not know," says Rhen.

"To give her fluids," Gia's voice says behind Mica.

Mica shuffles into the room to make space for Gia to come through the doorway.

Splotches of blood are being soaked up by microbial suits. Stained tools are piled to the side.

Gia kneels and with a new container of liquid and sets it to the side. She wraps the soiled tools in a microbial suit.

"Everyone, be careful over here," she says. "I'm going to let the suits clean off as much as possible and then I'll bleach the tools. But the needle and blade are covered, so don't step on this pile of fabric."

"Do you need this now?" Mica turns her head away from Ferris as she extends the object to Gia.

Mica holds a syringe.

"You could only get one?" Gia asks.

"Hey," says Mica. "It was very difficult to find someone who had one."

"Sorry," Gia accepts the syringe and picks up the container of liquid that she recently brought in. "I just can't use the same one for my dad."

"What did you have to trade for it?" Rhen asks.

"Nothing," says Mica.

Gia fills the syringe with the liquid.

"Nothing?" Rhen asks. "These are only produced for people connected to the chemist. How could someone give it to you for nothing?"

"It was an offering," says Mica. "The man gave it to me for a promise, as a friend of the Arachna. If Aracha Vishar comes back to the in-between to take vengeance, she will have to spare him and his family." Mica looks at me. "There's a man named Demar who has orange hair and only one eye. Do you promise to spare this man and his family?"

I smile. "I promise."

Gia has the syringe in Ferris's healthy arm to administer the liquid. Ferris is still limp in Rhen's arms.

"What is that?" Rhen asks.

"Saline," says Gia. "I made it from what Lyra already had in the lab. It could help."

"It could have helped your father, too?" Rhen asks.

Gia nods.

"Thank you," says Rhen.

Gia keeps her head down. A tear rolls off the tip of her nose.

It's cold and quiet. I look to the expansive wall from the circular platform in the Alaster ship. One of the chairs is missing from in front of the control panel. I use my metal crutch to limp to the remaining chair and sit. I stare at the wall in front of me. It had taken me a while, but I hoisted myself up ladders to try and get away from the other's at the bottom of the ship. It's the closest place to be alone. Or at least, semi-alone.

Words appear on the screen: "Hi, Lyra."

"Hi, Alaster," I look at the control panel. "A lot has happened."

"I know," say the words on the screen.

"I destroyed our cavern, I buried Garridon, and I sent my friends to the in-between." I try to keep my voice down. The others are still in the room below. "Would things have been easier if I had just stayed in here this whole time?" Tears start to well in my eyes.

"The purpose of life isn't ease," says Alaster. "Whether or not something is easier isn't a good reason to do it."

"Would it have been right to stay in here and not leave?"

"No," types Alaster. "People are out there."

"What difference does that make?" I ask.

"Lyra?" a voice says behind me.

I turn around.

Gia steps lightly toward me.

I look forward, trying to get the tears to go back in my eyes.

"This is kind of like when we met," says Gia as she moves beside me. "You showed me up here to talk to Alaster."

Still looking forward, I nod.

Gia looks at the screen and reads the words Alaster last typed.

"I guess there's no chance he's Gaines Cyro," says Gia. "There was a time we wondered if the Alaster-typing-thing was some trick of the Trellis heads."

"I didn't wonder that," I say.

"Right, I remember," says Gia. "What do you mean 'people are out there'?" She asks toward the screen now.

"It's normal to want to protect yourself or others from danger," says Alaster. "But the right thing isn't always the easy thing or the safe thing."

"How do we know what the right thing is?" Gia asks.

"That's what I'm here for," says Alaster.

Gia sighs and leans on the control panel. "I don't like that answer." She looks at me. "That sounds like what Rasul says about the Source deciding right and wrong— who should live or die."

"What do you think is right?" I ask.

Gia shakes her head. "I don't know."

I stare at the screen that is now blank. "What do we do?"

"Just wait," says Alaster.

"I also don't like that idea," says Gia.

"The time will come soon to depart," says Alaster. "But now is the time to rest."

"Depart?" Gia asks.

"Yes," says Alaster. "You've known since the beginning that you weren't meant to stay here. Only rest a little longer."

The words erase and the screen is blank.

# Chapter 19: Leal— Azurite

"Is Gia here?" Desman stomps up the pathway to catch up to me.

"I don't know," I step out of his way. "I'm looking for her too."

He marches up the path that leads to the door of my living quarters. Without waiting for me, he yanks open the doors and barges inside.

I hear Mom's voice yell.

He might be able to get past me, but not Mom.

"And another thing," Mom's scolding sounds through the door as I get closer. "Muscling your way into places isn't how you show care for people."

Desman's head hangs as I enter my living space and see Mom across from him.

"You'd better apologize to my son for disrespecting his living area," Mom says.

"Sorry, Leal," says Desman.

"Sorry for what?" Mom asks.

"Sorry for disrespecting your living quarters," says Desman.

"Now if Gia was here," says Mom, "and I'm not saying she is— you know she's in a sensitive place. You need to be a better man than to come up in here like some wild animal. This isn't about you, it's about her."

"Yes, Mabel," says Desman. "I'm sorry I barged in."

"Can I?" I look at Mom and then down the starry-looking tunnel that leads to the sleeping rooms.

"You can," says Mom. She looks at Desman. "I'm not finished with you."

I leave Desman behind and walk through the tunnel, turning toward Gia's room.

Crevices of dark blue azurite cover the space.

"Gia?" I peek my head into her room and look around.

There's a sniffle from the attached space where the robes are stored. I walk over to the small space and pull back the curtain.

"Gia?" I kneel down as I see my friend, curled in the corner of the clothes-storage space.

She hovers over a large marble bowl with tears on her cheeks and snot dripping from her nose.

"Leal?" She wipes her nose on her sleeve. She had changed out of the microbial suit and now wears the draping Trovantian clothes.

I don't want to ask if she's okay because she's obviously not. "You look— uhhh— worn out. When was the last time you slept?"

"I can't sleep," her cheeks become a deeper red and she grips the bowl. "I keep hearing the bone crack." She leans over. "There's blood everywhere." She gags into the bowl.

"Okay, okay," I lean in and put my arm on her shoulder. "Hey, that's okay. Let it out."

"What did you do to her?" Desman moves in front of me and squats down. "Gia, are you okay? What happened?"

"I'm fine," she says with a congested nose as she rocks back and forth over the bowl.

"You're not fine," says Desman. "Tell me what happened."

"Alaster said to rest," Gia's voice is breathy. "And I can't rest because everything starts coming to my head." She looks at me and more tears well in her azurite-blue eyes. "Leal, I'm so sorry."

"Gia," I say. "You don't need to keep apologizing to me. I told you we're fine."

"I hurt you," she says. "And then Ara asked me where her grandma was. I said I didn't know, but I could still hear the screams through the speakers." She covers her ears and squeezes her eyes closed. "Ara was standing in front of me when we went into the Sanctuary. The wave was so loud and then she was gone."

Desman wraps his arm around Gia. "It's okay," he says. "You don't have to apologize to us. I'm just worried about you."

"How about we get you some food?" I say. "I bet my mom would make some of that sweet bread you like."

She shakes her head.

"Do you know what will happen if my mom finds out you said no to her bread?" I ask.

She laughs and cries at the same time.

I think I broke her.

"What are we going to do?" Minji speaks in almost a whisper.

"I don't know," I also whisper.

Gia lies on the floor near the albharee tooth. Tears are dried on her cheeks. She just stares. She hasn't moved for hours.

"Should we try to get her to eat again?" Minji asks.

"No," I whisper and put my hands on Minji's shoulders. I pull her a bit further away from Gia so we can talk louder. "When she's out of this staring-trance-thing, she just sobs."

"Will she fall asleep if we put her in the bed?"

"That's even worse," I say. "If she closes her eyes, it's like she thinks she's in one of her memories or something. She jolts up and starts screaming." I rub both of my cheeks, thinking of the painful shrieks that have been coming from my friend's room. She had been screaming about Plangon— telling him to just come with us. "This staring thing is the best version right now."

"I wish she could get just a little sleep." Minji looks over at Gia. "Maybe then her head could be a little clearer. I bet her body is running on adrenaline and cortisol— that can't be helping the panic."

\*\*\*

"Gia," I say gently as I squat down. "We have something for you."

Her body doesn't move, but she breaks her stare and looks up at me.

"It's a drink," I say.

She shakes her head.

Minji and Lyra are now both in the room. Lyra sits on one of the cushions as she holds a small container.

"Mica was able to get something for you," says Lyra. "It will help you sleep."

"No," Gia squeezes her eyes closed. "No."

"Gia," I say, "listen."

She pushes herself up with her eyes still shut. She shakes her head ferociously to say 'no'.

"Gia," I say firmly. "It's Leal, your friend. And I know you're hurting, but I'm asking you to trust me."

It's like my words reach deep down and find the reasonable part of Gia. She stops shaking her head.

"Here," I take the container from Lyra and hold it near Gia.

Gia opens her eyes, then accepts the container. Putting it to her lips, she shoots it back and takes the whole container in one gulp. Slowly, she lowers the container and hands it back to me. Her gaze lowers. She crashes to the ground. With her eyes closed and mouth open, she finally sleeps on the floor near the albharee tooth.

"Maybe we should have put her in a bed first," says Minji.

I put my hands on my knees and catch my breath as we stand near Gia's bed. The three of us had to carry Gia down the hallway and into bed. Well, the two of us— Lyra came but she's on crutches.

"What can we do now?" Minji asks as she puts a blanket over Gia. "Without Garridon or Gia, how do we learn more about what the Trovant overseers are planning?"

Lyra shrugs, keeping her gaze down as Gia slumbers.

"Do we call a meeting or something?" I ask. "Is that what Garridon would do?"

"I feel like Garridon would gather intel," says Minji.

"But we aren't Garridon," Lyra sounds timid as she interjects.

"We are Facilitators," says Minji. "Technically, we're trained too."

"Not me," says Lyra.

"Yeah," I look at my little arms. I was an exception when it came to Facilitators. "Maybe we can go through the information that Gia and Garridon already have and then go from there."

Gia's eyes are closed and her face is finally peaceful. She is always the one who has to protect others. But she shouldn't have to be.

I try to stand a little taller. I can do this.

Alone in the jungle, I look down at Garridon's tablet and read information he had mapped about the Trovant. In my pocket, I have an incapacitator gun. I pat the gun to make sure it didn't fall out of my pocket. What if I can't use it properly if I see a big animal? I've never used one except in training, but Gia has used it on people before. I think she shot Jarret once.

Garridon had written a note about a drop or a cliff somewhere near the Source. His notes say that he put a communication beacon nearby and that the drop looked human-made. Garridon also wrote 16 possible scenarios as to why there would be a human-made cliff and how to plan and respond in the catastrophic scenarios.

My foot hits a root and I trip. I should watch where I'm going instead of reading the tablet. But how do I know where to go if I don't read the tablet?

Looking up, there's a sharp drop in the jungle. My heart races. I could have walked right off the edge if I hadn't looked up. I gulp— the important thing is that I didn't walk over the edge. I am a Facilitator and I am trained.

I look over the edge of the drop.

But I'm not trained to survive in a jungle. The drop reaches far down.

"Hello."

"Ah!" I jump back at the sound of someone behind me.

"Yes, hello," Imeel stands to my side.

I back up further from the edge.

"What are you doing here?" Imeel asks.

"I'm just," I look at the drop. "It's what I always do — I'm looking for places to put the waste."

"This is not a good place for that," says Imeel. "What are you holding? I often see your people with those."

"Oh, this?" I look at Garridon's tablet. "This is just how I make the calculations and stuff for my job."

"Interesting," says Imeel. "Rasul would love to see it. He is always curious about what you do."

"Actually—"

Imeel yanks the tablet out of my grip.

The tablet isn't mine— it's Garridon's. I can't tell Imeel it's not mine because he might wonder why I have Garridon's. I don't know what I can tell him that wouldn't raise suspicion.

How does Gia think so fast and come up with responses in the moment?

Is Garridon going to kill me for losing his tablet?

Imeel looks at the darkened screen. "You can teach us your calculations just as we teach your people how to grow food or swim."

I don't want to learn how to swim.

"Yes," I say. I think of how to turn his words back and get information from him like Gia could. "There are many things you could teach me. For example," I motion to the drop. "This drop seems to follow a path. Where does it go?"

"It goes to a cavern," says Imeel. "Just like many of the paths in the Trovant."

"Why is it here, though?" I ask. "It has been carved. Why was it made?"

"Ah, you have good observation," says Imeel. "There is a very good tale about this ravine. Rasul can tell you the story. He is just over here."

"What's a ravine?" I ask.

"All part of the story," says Imeel. He walks into the jungle, motioning for me to come.

I follow behind him. Why would Imeel and Rasul just be hanging out in the jungle?

We move along a narrow path in the dense jungle until there's a clearing with dark rock. After the clearing is the entrance to a cave. It's hot and it smells like sulfur. Sweat beads on my face as Imeel guides me through the cave opening.

Rasul Midian stands inside the dim cave near the edge of a hole in the ground. Heat presses all around and starts to feel like it's inside me.

Imeel greets Rasul and they speak to one another in their language. I hear them say my name in the conversation they have. Imeel hands Rasul the tablet.

"Are you going to tell me about the ravine?" I ask. The air feels thick and I start to get lightheaded. "Or tell me what's going on in here?"

"This is the Source," says Imeel. "The Source is here to guide us. It knows who is true and of good character."

The edges of my vision start to get dark. I can't leave. I need to find the information to know what to do next. I need to do it for Minji, for my family, and for Gia. I need to stay.

"Those who are worthy," says Imeel, "it will let live. Those who are not—"

I lose control of my body. I feel myself falling as my vision darkens completely.

# Chapter 20: Lyra— Deep Ravine, Deeper Questions

I hug my knees to my chest as I sit in the chair in front of my desk. With my fingers pressing on the cold metal of the control panel, I squeeze my fingers on the desk though my knees are still against my chest. It's somehow anchoring to hold onto something.

"I wondered if you would be in here," Jarret's voice speaks in the room, but I don't turn around. He walks over to my desk.

I still push the pads of my fingers against the cold metal.

"Your parents were wondering where you are," says Jarret.

"I'm here," I say.

"Maybe you could let them know where you're going before you go."

"Is that what you came here to say?"

"No," he says. "Leal's missing."

I look up and my eyes meet his.

"Minji hasn't heard from him," says Jarret. "Not since you were all at his place. And his parents don't know where he is. He left his tablet at his living quarters."

"Did you search for Garridon's tablet?" I ask.

"No," he says. "Why would we—"

"It's also missing," I say. I point to the disorganized shelf where other people have been storing their things.

Trovant

"We keep all extra tablets in my lab, but the one Garridon had been using isn't where we left it."

"Why would Leal take that?"

"I don't know," I lift up my tablet that was sitting on the desk. I pull up the information about each of the tablets. "It says Garridon's tablet is active."

"Can you tell where it is?" Jarret asks.

"It's closest to communication beacon 16."

"Where is that?"

I switch to the information that Garridon and Gia had been working on. They made a virtual map of the areas we knew about in the Trovant and where they set up the communications beacon. It looks like the in-between hasn't been added to the map yet. I can't tell when they last updated the information.

"It's here," I say, pointing to communication beacon 16 on the map.

"Which is where?"

"It's by the weakest part of the Trovant," I say. "Where Gia was almost seen by the overseers."

"Let's go," says Jarret.

"To find Leal?" I ask. "It will be hard to tell exactly where he is near the beacon."

"No, to tell your parents."


Eddi Fitzgerald is already at my parents' home when we get there. I hobble in on makeshift crushes with my blanket-bag hanging at my side.

"Oh, thank goodness," my mom stands from the circle of adults who sit on the floor in the eating area. She wraps her arms around me and kisses my head.

"I was just at the submarine," I say.

"Leal isn't around," says my dad, who sits next to Eddi. "We were just worried about you, too."

"He might have Garridon's tablet," says Jarret as he walks beside me to the eating area.

"Why would he take that?" Eddi asks.

"It would have Garridon's personal notes," I say.

"That's not like Leal," says Eddi. "Here, take a seat." He serves some food on a plate. "Mabel made this. She's watching babies for the afternoon meal but she said to take this."

Jarret helps me get to the ground and I try to sit in the least painful way possible.

Pictor yells from the rocky corridor: "Is it *sharaque*?"

"What is that?" I ask.

"The sweet bread," says my mom. She turns her head and yells down the corridor: "You need to eat something other than sweets."

Pictor stomps in the eating area and crashes next to my dad. He pouts at my mom as she hands him a plate of normal food.

"Are we going to look for Leal and Minji?" Pictor asks.

"Where's Minji?" Jarret asks.

"Looking for Leal," says Eddi. "Did you see where Garridon's tablet is?" Eddi turns toward me.

"Yes," I say. "It's near where Gia saw the plant roots."

"By Rasul Midian's living quarters," says Eddi. "Why would he be there?"

"Did you see where the tablet was before that?" my dad asks.

"I didn't," I take my tablet from the bag that I had made from a blanket.

Looking through the location history of Garridon's tablet, it left my lab and then went through the jungle. It was near the Source before turning and going toward Rasul Midian's area. I hand my tablet to my dad. Eddi and my mom lean over to also read the information.

"That's the ravine," says my dad, pointing to the screen. "I wasn't supposed to, but I followed it to that spot one time."

"What's the ravine?" Jarret asks.

"Something we just finished digging," says my dad. "They took a bunch of field workers and had us digging the rest of this massive trench. They had obviously been working on it for a long time, but it seemed like they needed it to be finished urgently. No one would tell me why we were making it. I followed the path to see how far it went and I got close to beacon 16."

"I think that's where I fell," I say as I take a bite of food.

"You fell down that?" my dad exclaims as both of my parents shoot their gazes at me.

"Oh," I rub my arm. "Well, yeah. It was when I first met the heebo." I never told them what happened. By the looks on their faces, I guess there was a good reason I didn't tell them.

"Oh, why?" Pictor dramatically swoons over my mom. "Why do we ever let her leave the house?"

"This is not a joke, Pictor," my mom seems annoyed as Pictor crushes her shoulder beneath his swoon.

"Dear me," Pictor gasps and puts his hand on his chest. "I would never joke about such things."

My mom rolls her eyes.

"Where did the other end of the ravine go?" I ask my dad.

"To a cavern," says my dad. "In the cavern was a massive pool. Everyone was scared to go into the cavern because they said the albharee could get in there."

"Hmm," Eddi rubs his chin. "Why would we need a ravine that leads to a massive pool of water?"

"Do we know where the water might connect?" My mom asks. "Maybe it leads to something else."

"Maybe they needed to dump things in the pool," says Pictor. "Just saying— my friends showed me where they had dug all these places where all the poop and stuff gets dumped. Maybe they need new poop-dumping grounds."

"Weirdly," says my dad, "that actually makes sense."

"Except that it's too far from where people live," says Eddi. "I'm not sure how waste would get to the ravine."

"What else is close to there?" Eddi asks.

"The jungle," Jarret answers.

I look up at my dad. "The Source."


Pictor kicks a rock and it hits my metal crutch.

"Why is he here again?" I whisper to my dad.

"Same reason as you," says my dad. "We don't want to be separated right now."

"It's not so bad," says Jarret. "Just think of it as sibling bonding."

I look behind as Pictor stomps on a plant that pokes from the bottom of the ravine.

My mom and Eddi had left to search for Leal and hopefully find Minji. The four of us went to see if we could find any more information about the ravine.

From the bottom of the dry path, there are scaling walls on either side. When I was down here before, I didn't notice that there were walls on both sides. To be fair, I was dazed from the fall.

Roots and rocks jut out from the natural walls— I don't know how Garridon figured out these were human-made. The walls really are massive. I can't believe I fell down that.

"Here it is," my dad says when we arrive at a wide cave entrance.

I can see the edge of the glowing pool from the big entrance. My crutches clink on the rock as I move forward.

"I'd rather you stay out here," says my dad, "if it truly is big enough for an albharee to get through."

"How can we figure out where it goes?" I lean toward the pool.

"You only need to ask," a voice sounds behind us.

"Ah!" Pictor jumps and runs behind my dad.

Rhen stands at the bottom of the ravine. A red microbial suit peeks from beneath her Trovantian cloak.

"Where did you come from?" Pictor asks.

Rhen laughs at Pictor's reaction. "You should really be quieter. I could hear you from the jungle. I was on my way back from my turn staying with Ferris. Now Vana will stay with her."

"Where does it go?" Jarret asks as he points to the pool in the rocky opening.

"It leads to an underwater tunnel," says Rhen. "The tunnel leads to the cavern."

"Which cavern?" Jarret asks.

"Ours," says Rhen. "Where an albharee now lies crushed beneath stone."

"Is that the only outlet?" I ask.

"Yes," Rhen nods. "But the cavern then leads many places. Including the in-between."

"Our cavern is now blocked," I say. "I wonder if the underwater tunnels are still connected."

"What are you thinking?" Jarrett asks. "If the tunnels are blocked, the albharee can't get in. Are you wondering if we can go to the pool now?"

"No," I say. "I'm wondering if my explosion ruined whatever plans the overseers were making for this ravine."

"What do you think the ravine might be for?" Jarret asks.

"Poop," says Pictor.

My dad scrunches his eyebrows and shakes his head at Pictor.

"I don't like the idea," I say. "But the closest thing is the Source. It was a hydrothermal vent before the Trovant was here. I guess now it would be considered a volcano."

"So what does that mean?" Jarret asks.

"The only thing that could flow through this ravine is magma," I say.

My dad looks down the ravine toward the direction of the Source. Then he turns toward to pool. "Do you think they might be making a backup plan in case it erupts or overflows?"

"I hope," I say.

"What's the other option?" Jarret asks.

I look down the ravine toward the Source. "They might be planning to break open the Source and let the lava destroy anything on the other side of this pool. If the underwater tunnels are still open, lava will go to the in-between. But, now that the caverns are blocked, lava will stay in the Trovant."

"Is there anything we can do?" Jarret asks.

I turn toward the pool. "Does anyone know how to divert lava?"

# Chapter 21: Leal— Fossil

A drip lands on my ice-cold nose. Sniffling, I sit up with chilled air biting at my face. With tiny roots hanging over my head, droplets of water run down the roots and patter on the dark, rocky ground. Shivering, I look around the empty space. I must be in the area where the Trovant walls are the thinnest. I stand, taking little steps away from the wall. If the wall caves in here, it wouldn't really matter how far I was from it, but I still don't want to be close.

Walking backward, I stumble over something in the ground. As I get my footing again, I look down to see what tripped me. Embedded into the floor is a massive fossil of a spiraling shell. The drips of water pool on the floor everywhere except on the fossil that is raised above the ground. I stand and examine the fossil. It's a giant ammonite. They were shelled creatures that looked like they could have been sea snails, but they were actually cephalopods and the fleshy arms were less likely to fossilize so it's hard to see that they had tentacles. Now that I think of it, some of the creatures in the pools kind of looked like—

There's a deep grating sound like heavy rock is scraping against the floor. I turn to see a piece of the wall slowly moving to the side. Imeel and Rasul Midian are in the doorway with some Trovantians who hold fiery poles. My attention goes to the moving rock piece. What sort of mechanism moves a giant piece of stone like that?

"We are glad you are awake," Imeel says as he steps into the cold space. "And we are sorry for the hospitality. You must understand, we have to stay true to our purpose."

"Which is what?" I ask as I rub my arms to keep warm.

As Imeel and Rasul come in, the other Trovantians follow with a smaller figure behind... It's Minji. Why would they take her here? She hobbles in, carrying a bag that clanks as she moves. It sounds like there are slabs of stone hitting each other in the bag.

"We need you to explain how to retrieve information from this," Imeel holds up Garridon's tablet. The screen is turned off. I guess they don't know how to turn it on.

"What is the information for?" I try to sound commanding. I don't think Gia would just give up information, but she would still somehow get information from them. They have Minji. I can't make a mistake.

"It is the burden of overseers to know such things," Imeel says. "And our patience is thinning."

Rasul motions to a guard.

The guard maneuvers and puts the fiery end of the pole to Minji's face.

Minji squeals and covers her eyes.

"Stop!" I yell before the guard hurts her. "I can turn on the screen."

Imeel hands me Garridon's tablet and I press a button to turn on the screen.

"We tried that," says Imeel. "How do we access the information?"

I type in the passcode for the tablet. Garridon had set his own code, but he told Gia in case anything happened to him. Then Gia told me... I'm not sure why.

The screen unlocks. Now they have access to Garridon's files.

Rasul takes the tablet back from me. He looks at me, then the tablet. Then he pushes on the screen— maybe he's mimicking how I typed in the passcode. I don't think he can read English, so I'm not sure what the tablet can tell him. He hands the tablet to Imeel and says something.

"Where is information about the explosion?" Imeel asks as he looks at the screen.

"What information?" I ask.

"Do not pretend," says Imeel. "You caused an explosion. How did you accomplish this and what areas have been blocked?"

"Uhh—"

Rasul motions and the guard moves the flaming pole closer to Minji.

"Stop! Stop!" I wave my hands toward them. "Just give me a chance to explain."

The fire crackles near Minji's eye, which she squeezes closed.

"Are you working with the chemist?" Imeel asks.

"What?" I ask. "No, I don't know a chemist."

"How did you cause an explosion?" Imeel asks. "We need to do this without breaking the Trovant walls. Just as you did. How did you accomplish this?"

"There's an outer wall and an inner wall," I explain as fast as I can. "And there's methane between them. And — I don't entirely know why— but there's a circuit in the wall and there must be some sort of insulator too or else the currents would jump to each other because the metals are close and the cave walls are probably somewhat conductive—"

"Stop," Imeel rubs his head. "Stop. You are not answering the question."

"I'm trying to," I say. "Why do you need to cause explosions?"

"If you are no use to us," Imeel says, "it seems you are a hindrance."

Rasul gives and command to the guards.

"No, no," I say. "I can be useful. Don't do whatever he just said."

Minji moves close to me as the guards back us up toward the fossil.

"Minji, now!" a voice yells from somewhere out of the room.

The Trovantians turn toward the door.

Minji pulls two marble plates from her bag and puts them on the fossil. She stands on one and yanks me onto the other. "Don't step off of this."

Gia's strong figure approaches the doorway.

"Where's the incapacitator?" Minji asks.

## Trovant

Carrying a bag with a large bulge, Gia steps into the room. She swings the bag and hits one of the guards in the head.

I reach into my pocket and pull out the incapacitator gun. "I don't want to accidentally shoot Gia."

"Hand it to me," Minji says. "Ready!" She yells to Gia.

Gia unwraps a white bowl from the blanket-bag, then swings it at someone's face when he lunges with the fiery pole. He splashes on the ground as Gia crouches low. She sets the bowl down and steps on it.

"Now!" she yells to Minji.

Minji points the incapacitator at the ground. Electric blue energy sparks from the gun and hits the water puddled on the floor. Blue currents spark across the surface of the water. Sparks climb up the Trovantians. A few lash around Gia, who is barely raised above the water.

The Trovantians tense, gripping their polls and then collapsing to the ground. The fire poles splash into the water and the flames go out.

"Did you kill them?" I ask.

The puddle gets still except for drips that fall from the ceiling.

Minji leans over the water to see the limp bodies in the water. "I hope not."

Rasul Midian moves his arm.

"Let's go," Gia steps off the white bowl and splashes into the puddled water.

# Chapter 22: Gia— The Dream

The Trellis walls reach high above my head. Bioluminescent panels on the ceiling give a purple glow— the lights must be changing from red to blue.

A woman stands above me and reaches down as her brown ponytail falls over her shoulder. She picks me up and holds me. I'm somehow small again.

"Gia, honey," she rubs my head and I bury my face in her shoulder. "I'm going away, but I will see you soon. I don't want you to worry."

"But you don't come back," I sob. Somehow, my grown-up thoughts are speaking through a child's body.

"Because you'll come to me," she says. "Until then, it's okay to be a little girl."

"What does that mean?"

"It isn't your fault that people are hurting," she holds me close. "I know you can't be apathetic when there is suffering, but it isn't your responsibility to save everyone."

"What do I do?" I ask. "I can't do something and also do nothing."

"Learn to live in between," she says.

"How?"

"Ask Alaster for the wisdom," she says. "He's been alive for a long time."

I cry, "I miss you, Mom."

"I miss you too," she holds me tighter.

My cheeks feel warm as I start to wake up and feel the heavy blankets hugging me. I keep my eyes closed, but my face feels tight with dried tears. My last memory was Leal handing me something to drink in the communal area. Where am I now?

As I open my eyes, Desman sits on a cushion in the corner of my azurite sleeping quarters. He moves a string that Ari tries to catch with her paw. I smile at the sight of him playing. I've never seen him playing before. Maybe Leal was right— these kinds of moments are the reason we're here.

"You're awake," Desman looks up from Ari.

I nod, squeezing the blanket around me.

He comes over to the side of the bed and kneels down. With his knees on the floor, he puts his arm on the bed and then rests his head close to mine.

"I was worried," he says.

"I'm fine," I say.

He puts his hand over my head and rubs my cheek. "I knew you'd say that."

"It's because I am," I say.

He moves his face closer to mine, then pauses, still rubbing my cheek.

My heart beats faster.

He puts his lips to mine.

"You always are," he says. Then he kisses me again.

***

Ari is curled in my lap as I sit on the cushion near the table made of an albharee tooth. My head still feels foggy, but my heartbeat is slower now as I stroke Ari's soft fur. Desman is in the kitchen. He insisted on finding me something to eat or drink. I don't know where the Fitzgeralds are, but I hope Mabel doesn't come back to find Desman looking through her kitchen things.

I think of the dream of my mom. Since being in the Trovant, I haven't let myself wonder if she really is still out there. Though I've been in the ship, I haven't spoken to Alaster much to get answers. I start to feel a weight on me again. My jaw clenches as I run my fingers through the soft ball of fur on my lap. It's easier to keep moving forward rather than think about the past. But how do I know I'm not repeating mistakes unless I think about what happened? How can I plan for the future without remembering the past?

Ara— I worry that I manipulated her into trusting me. I wanted to find the truth for her. I really did.

My mom— is she really out there? Or am I just wishing for dreams to come true?

Plangon— it's good he's gone. He never was my dad. He never actually cared about me. So why do I feel this stabbing pain when I think of leaving him behind in the flooding Trellis? I picture the lights flickering. The screen

strobing between Trellis heads and the word: "Run." I
shake my head and rub Ari's ears.

My dad— he was never there and somehow was
there the whole time. And now he lies alone in a metal
room. I should be there. He could be gone any moment.

The front door starts to open. Minji's thin frame
appears in the entrance.

"Gia," she sounds panicked. "I'm so glad you're
awake." She walks over to me and kneels by the small
table. "I don't know what to do." Tears well in her eyes.
"I'm so sorry to ask for help when you're not doing well,
but we've tried everything."

Desman steps into the room.

"What's going on?" I ask.

"Leal is missing," Minji says.

My head clears.

"Gia," Desman motions for me to stay sitting.
"You're in no condition to go out and—"

"When did you last see him?" I ask.

"He was here," says Minji. "We were deciding what
to do next and it was getting late so we decided to do
something in the morning. But I couldn't find him the next
day."

"Is that all the information you have?" I ask.

"No, there's more," says Minji. "Your father's tablet
is missing from Lyra's lab. We tracked it to the nearest
communication beacon. The tablet is somewhere near the
root system you found. But I can't work out the exact

location. Vega and Eddi are trying to find him now, but they keep running into dead ends."

"Is anything else missing from the lab?" I ask.

"An incapacitator gun."

"Where's the other one?"

"Jarret has it."

"Listen," Desman steps into the room. "I know you're worried about your friend. But let us handle it for once."

"What would your plan be?" I look up at Desman. I feel tense, despite cradling a fluffy creature in my lap.

"To find Leal," says Desman. "We can work out the details, just give us some time."

"He might not have time," I say.

\*\*\*

"You cut it a little close," Leal tries to whisper and somehow yell at the same time. "Why didn't you come in the room sooner? Why was Minji there at all?"

Minji walks ahead in the red-lit tunnel near Desman. I already messaged the others to meet in the Alaster ship. None of us should be in the Trovant now. I don't know what the overseers will do to us now that we've shocked them with an incapacitator gun.

"We didn't know exactly where you were," I say. "Minji had to be there so I could follow and see where they took you. Then I waited to come into the room to see if the overseers would give us more intel before we incapacitated them. And they did. We found out—"

"You used the love of my life as bait?"

I stop walking and look at him. "That seems a little dramatic."

"No," Leal turns toward me. "You were being dramatic. That fire pole was this close to her face." He holds his fingers close together. He actually seems mad. I'm not sure I've seen Leal truly mad.

Desman and Minji walk ahead. Either they don't notice that we've stopped walking or they don't want to intervene.

"Okay," I say. "I'm sorry. I just assumed I had it under control."

"Why wasn't Desman the bait?"

"He didn't want me to go," I say. "He said he wasn't going to be a part of any plan that took me out of the living quarters. I guess he thought that would stop me."

"He should have at least come," says Leal. "Even if you did think you had it under control." He loosens up a bit. "Did you have it under control?"

"To be honest, I didn't expect that much water," I say. I start to walk again. "I remembered the ground was wet when I was in that area, but I didn't expect such a puddle. That plan almost didn't work. I was barely above the water when Minji pulled the trigger."

"Did you get shocked?" He walks beside me.

"Yeah," I say. "It really hurt, too."

"I couldn't tell," says Leal. "You barely show it when you're hurting." He stops walking again.

I stop too.

"Okay, I still mean what I said about Minji." He looks at the ground and rubs his arm. "You shouldn't have put her in danger to find me. But I'm sorry you had to come find me. I wanted to..." he trails off, searching for the words. "Fix things like you do, I guess." His shoulders lower.

"Leal..."

"You were actually staying put for once," he starts walking again. "I mean, we drugged you. But you were actually sleeping."

I smile slightly, "I'm sorry I went crazy like that."

"And I'm sorry you don't get to go crazy like that."

Lyra sits with her back against the metal paneling in the Alaster ship. Jarret sits next to her with Vega, Eddi, and Arcturo across from them. Rhen has her arm draped around her knee while Vana and Mica sit with their legs crossed. Desman is close to me as Leal and Minji explain to the others what has recently happened. Mabel, Pictor, and Takara stand away from the group and play with Ari.

"So he asked you about explosions?" Lyra asks after Leal finishes his explanation.

"Exactly," says Leal. "Which could be connected to your thing." He motions toward Lyra, Arcturo, Rhen, and Jarret.

"They could be trying to seal off places so that lava doesn't flow into the Trovant," says Eddi.

"Or trying to divert lava away from people," says Vega.

"Or cause it to flow toward people," says Lyra.

"What do you mean?" Leal asks.

"If they blow up the side of the Source," says Lyra, "magma would start to flow through the ravine that they dug. They may have been trying to divert the magma flow and block off the other facility."

"What should we do?" Jarret asks.

"Without knowing what they are planning," says Eddi, "we're just acting on assumptions. There are too many variables. It's hard to know how we should respond."

"We could follow them," I say. "We know the most likely scenarios. We can send a group to scout each of the possibilities and see if they are creating more diversions, blocking paths to the in-between, or setting up explosives near the Source. My group can take the one with the highest stakes—"

"You won't be going anywhere," says Vega.

"I'm fine," I say. "I got some rest and my head is clearing up."

"We could just stay in here," says Leal. "And then we can go to the surface whenever Alaster is ready."

We all stare at him.

"Son," says Eddi.

"I know, I know," says Leal. "We have to think about others in the facilities and blah blah blah. Whatever. Let's just do what Gia said."

"I just don't get why it's always you," Desman says.

Wearing a grey microbial suit, I pick things from the shelves of Lyra's lab and put them in a bag.

Leal swivels in the chair and looks at the electronic pieces on Lyra's workstation.

"It's not," I say. "Leal got the intel from the Trovant overseers."

"Well," Leal says. "I got myself trapped. I guess I can't sneak around and get people to give up their information. But at least I answered the question."

"What question?" I rustle through the containers, wires, and everything else on the shelves. I find the wire fuser and put it in my bag.

"Why it's always you," says Leal. "Or your dad."

"I guess it takes a trained robot to do this kind of thing," I say.

"Half-robot," says Leal.

I smile and pick up a box that looks like it has dark skin covering large veins. Holding my thumb on the microbial lock, the veins creep back to unlock the box. I open the heavy lid and see my T-shirt.

"Finally," I take the shirt and put the box back on the shelf. I slip the T-shirt over my microbial suit. The veins on the box creep back into place.

"You two are acting like this is a game," says Desman as I smile at the kittens on my shirt that shoot lasers from their eyes.

Leal looks at the floor and doesn't say anything.

I look up at Desman. It reminds me of the time he broke into our workstation to try and find out what happened to Ara. He was just being a jerk because he was scared; he was trying to stop her from dying. Now he's just afraid for me. Am I going to die?

"What?" he asks as I continue to stare at him.

"Nothing," I say.

"Can you at least take that off?" Desman motions to my T-shirt.

"Why?"

"You'll blend into rock better without the shirt," he says. "It will be harder for anyone to spot you."


It's dark in the jungle as Leal and I creep through plants. I wear only a microbial suit; I did put back the shirt.

When we divided into groups, I needed Leal's help logging and interpreting any information. We needed as few people as possible in my group to avoid getting caught. Desman didn't seem happy about that. I understand if he's feeling protective, but I also need someone with me who can interpret readings about atmospheric conditions. Desman can't do that. So Leal is the only one beside me as we walk silently through the dark jungle.

"I don't like this," Leal says as we get closer to the rock wall.

"It's fine," I whisper. "The Trovantians said they don't hurt people."

"Then why does everyone stay away from this part of the wall?" Leal asks.

"Watch out!" I yank Leal backward as white goop crashes through the leaves. It spreads over the ground and settles into a white splotch. "That's why."

We both look through a clearing at walls that drip with dried bird poop. Birds flutter onto white nests attached to the wall.

"Nope," Leal turns around.

"Yup," I grab his shoulders and face him toward the wall.


I hang on the wall, trying to avoid patches of white; partly because it's disgusting and also because the dried bird poop could crumble from the wall and I might fall.

Leal mumble-sings something to himself.

"Leal," I whisper, "remember that we're trying to be silent?"

"I need a distraction," he says.

I keep climbing up the wall, avoiding the nests and white drips. I look into a nest where three tiny birds snuggle together. They're kind of cute.

"They rode these during the war," I whisper. Maybe I can convince Leal that they won't hurt him. "Rhen told me. And now they use some birds to send messages to the other facility because people don't want to go to the in-between. That's cool, right?"

"Not cool," says Leal. "People should not ride these. If we were meant to fly, we would have wings."

"People can swim," I say as I get near the top. "But we don't have fins."

"If people were meant to swim," says Leal, "we would have fins."

I pull myself over the edge and look around. My dad had been up here to test how far the communication beacons could reach. The signal reached here so he didn't place another beacon. But he did document a tunnel that let out near Rasul Midian's living quarters— that's where my dad's tablet is now. That means Rasul Midian might also be there.

I help Leal onto the ledge when he reaches the top. Silently, we move into the tunnel. It's almost pitch black. Our microbial suits make a padded thump with each step. Soon, it gets colder as we follow the winding path.

There are footsteps from the other side of the tunnel.

Leal looks at me, as if asking what to do. The footsteps are close, but maybe we can run out of here before they see us. I turn, but then stop. The people speak.

Leal grabs my arm and pulls me toward the exit.

I don't move, but listen to the voices.

The voices speak in English. They have accents, but it's not Trovantian.

I turn around to face the people as they turn the corner. When they see Leal and me, they freeze. There are three tall men, holding various containers with bags strapped to their backs, heads, and arms. One holds less in his hands and he pulls out a jagged blade. He has orange hair and one eye.

"Wait!" Leal says. "We're not trying to stop… whatever you're doing."

The man takes a step forward with the blade toward us.

"You don't want to do that," I say.

"Why?" says the man.

"Because Arachna Vishar told us to spare you," I say. "It would be terrible if we had to go back on our promise."

"Arachna?" The men look at each other.

"It was a misunderstanding," says the orange-haired man. He puts the blade away.

"Just a misunderstanding," says another man.

"We mean no harm," says a man.

"These supplies are for her, actually," says one of the men.

"Yes," the orange-haired man nods. "Exactly. We are only getting supplies to make more of the things she might ask for."

"You can go," I say. I motion for them to pass us.

"Thank you," says one of the men as he walks past. "Very kind."

The men pass us with thank-you's and various invitations to visit them in the in-between.

"He was lying, right?" Leal asks when the men are out of earshot. "Lyra doesn't need things for her part of the plan, right?"

"Yeah," I say. "It looks like they were stealing things from the Trovant. I guess we know why this tunnel is here."

"And why we were warned not to go out at night," says Leal.

We continue again in silence and follow the bending tunnel until there's an opening ahead. Before the opening, there's another tunnel to the right. I stop and look down the connecting tunnel.

"This is the way we want," says Leal as he motions to the opening. "This goes to Rasul's living quarters."

"Come look at this," I say as I look down the tunnel that has sporadic green shades. "What does this look like?"

"Malachite," says Leal. "Do you think this could connect to the area behind Rasul's place?"

"It might," I say. "That would be better than lurking around the front door."

The green tunnel does lead to the spot where I had first seen the root running through the walls. We had tracked my dad's tablet to this area and assumed Rasul would be in his living space. Leal and I were tasked with getting any information from Rasul. We will follow him to see if we can figure out exactly what he's planning.

We crouch near the opening, careful not to be seen.

There's a fire-lit glow through the opening to Rasul Midian's living quarters. Rasul's voice speaks, so he is awake. Imeel is there translating in English for some reason.

"This is the last warning you will receive," says Imeel. "You can turn from your ways now or the Source will destroy you."

"This is my last warning to you," it's a woman's voice that responds. "Destroying us will be a death sentence to you."

"We have provision," says Imeel. "We do not need anything from plant people. It is time for those who are worthy to be separated from those who are not."

"Finally," says the woman, "we agree on something." There are footsteps followed by the sounds of a door closing.

Rasul says something in Trovantian. I take the tablet from my bag and start to record.

Imeel's voice responds. They have a conversation in their language, so the woman must have left. Soon, there are footsteps again and the sound of a door opening and closing.

If Rasul goes to sleep, there won't be anywhere to follow him. So there's no sense in sticking around. But at least we recorded a conversation. Maybe there's something valuable there.

The fiery glow goes out.


"Did you find anything?" I ask as we approach the entrance to the Source.

Rhen and Vana sit on black rocks between the jungle and the Source. It's dark and the sounds of chirping and buzzing insects fill the air.

"Yes," says Rhen as she stands from her seat. "We found out how the overseers received information. The metal from the Sources gives a umm— *Presio*."

"What is that?" Leal asks.

"It communicates with us," says Vana. "The Source does."

"Alaster says he could communicate with you," says Leal.

"But it's coming from here," says Vana.

"From the metal part," says Leal. "How would magma communicate through metal?"

"How would a submarine?" Vana asks.

"Guys," I say, "focus. What are these messages?"

"It is like a secret writing system," says Rhen. "It was only used in the war to send messages. A certain number of presios and the length makes a certain letter."

"Oh, it's like Morse code," says Leal.

"I do not know this code," says Rhen.

"What do the messages say?" I ask.

"The end is near," says Rhen. "It is time to come to the surface."

"Does it say what the end is?" I ask.

"Is it a volcanic eruption?" Leal asks. "Are the walls caving in?"

"It does not say," says Rhen. "But the melted stone in the Source is higher than it used to be. And the smell was stronger. I felt like I could not be in the area long."

"That's not good," I say.

"That's very bad," says Leal.

"Can you translate this?" I ask as I get the tablet from my bag. "We recorded a conversation and need to know what Rasul and Imeel were discussing."

Rhen and Vana listen as I play the recording of the conversation.

"They say they need to fix the plan," says Rhen. "You were right that they planned to move the melted stone from the Source and block the in-between to cut off the plant people. The melted stone was meant to go through the ravine and into the pool and out through the cavern that Lyra blocked. Now they are worried it will back up into the Trovant. They want to seal the red lit tunnel before the Source flows freely."

"Did they plan to blow up the side of the Source?" I ask. "To pour the magma into the ravine?"

Rhen nods. "But the blocked cavern has delayed the plan."

"So Lyra bought us some time with that explosion," I say. "If they find another way to get the magma to the in-between, maybe they will go ahead with their plan."

"Either way," says Rhen, "the melted rock is rising. Our facilities are in danger."

# Chapter 23: Lyra— Jarret

Jarret carries my bag and my tablet as I crutch along the jungle path with him and Desman. I move slowly as I struggle to get my crutches untangled from plants and try not to place them on wobbly rocks. It's still dark, but the facility starts to brighten slightly. I think it's almost morning.

"Did Gia respond about the measurements?" I ask.

"Not yet," says Jarret.

Desman lurks ahead. He seems annoyed.

"Eddi sent a message," says Jarret.

"Did they find something?" I ask.

"He says there's information from Garridon's tablet. Something the overseers have looked at. He'll explain more when we get back to the Alaster ship."

"Can we just carry you?" Desman turns around and looks at me. "It would be faster. This whole mission has taken twice as long as it should have."

My heart sinks. I thought he was mad at Gia this whole time for choosing to pair up with Leal. I didn't know he was mad at me for being slow.

"Desman," says Jarret, "that was uncalled for. She's doing fine. And we wouldn't have any of this information without her. You're just the brawn here— same as me."

"Well, can we use our brawn to move this a little faster?"

I feel embarrassed that I slowed everyone down.

"You can," says Jarret. "You've been bad-tempered this whole time. Just go ahead, we'll see you at the ship."

"There's no point," says Desman. "It's not like they'll start any conversations without her there." He motions to me.

"Actually, I wasn't asking," says Jarret. "You've been making this whole mission hard, not Lyra. You can apologize to both of us, or you can leave."

"Apologize for what?"

"For being an oaf," says Jarret.

"Oh," says Desman, "Jarret Carpio is calling *me* an oaf. Jarret Carpio, who hardly passed the intelligence requirements to be a Facilitator."

"You're right," says Jarret, "it must be pretty bad if *I'm* calling you an oaf."

Desman turns around and stomps off.

"Don't listen to him," says Jarret. "He's always been a jerk." He starts walking forward.

"But he was with my sister?" I move slowly along with him.

"With her?"

"Yeah," I say. "Leal said they had a thing."

"Ah," says Jarret. "They were partners at work, definitely. Maybe they had a thing. Everyone liked Ara. I guess she was close to Desman, but she always seemed a little sad around him."

"Was she sad around you?"

"She wasn't really around me. After we got our roles, I only saw her in training and sustenance lines. And, of course, on security footage. That's when she seemed sad— when no one was watching."

"Sounds a little creepy," I say.

"It does," says Jarret. "I thought I was protecting people. But I guess my job was creepy."

"Leal said you liked her, too."

"I did," Jarret blushes. "Like I said, everyone liked her." A twig hits Jarret in the face. He rubs his eye and keeps walking.

I look at him, then look down at the dark path. "Sorry if this is not a good question," I say. I keep my eyes ahead and not on him. "What did Desman mean about the intelligence requirements?"

"Oh, that," Jarret still rubs his eye as we approach a clearing in the jungle. He walks toward the red-lit tunnel that goes to the ship. "We had to pass a lot of different tests to get our roles assigned. The most important tests were physical and intellectual. Desman's intelligence score was higher than mine, but I got the final slot as a Facilitator instead of him."

"Why?"

We walk into the red-lit tunnel.

"I am very strong," Jarret blushes again but it's harder to tell beneath the red light. "I'm kind of the opposite of Leal. He had the lowest physical score in Facilitator history, but they made an exception because of his intelligence score. I wasn't necessarily an exception, but I was picked over Desman because of my physical scores."

"What about Gia and Minji?" I ask.

"Minji is smart," says Jarret. "And she's agile. She doesn't look very fierce but her physical scores weren't low. And Gia— well, I guess she has a bit of everything. She had to have it all to survive Garridon's parenting. She would have been on her way to Head Facilitator if we were still back there."

"I think we might have starved if we were still back there."

"Right," says Jarret, "sorry. I forget what it was like in the Sanctuary."

"What it was like in the Sanctuary?" I ask. "I played games with my brother and sang songs with my parents. I could be sad in my lab and no one spied on me."

"Sorry," says Jarret as we get closer to the submarine. "I guess I don't really know what it was like growing up in the Sanctuary. Maybe you can tell me more sometime."


Gia stands near a wall with her arms crossed. My parents and Pictor are nearby— Pictor must be bored with hanging out with Mabel and Takara.

When Jarret and I approach, he places my bag down near the wall. Then he moves toward me, putting his hand on my crutch to help me to the ground.

"I'll stand," I say.

"You sure?" Jarret releases the crutch.

I nod. The metal digs into my arm and I'm tired of standing, but I don't want to sit on the ground and look up at everyone who stands.

"Leal!" Gia yells up toward the platforms. "We're ready."

Metal creaks through the massive submarine as Minji and Leal appear from a doorway. With Takara in his arms, Leal turns and gives his sister to Mabel. Leal kisses Takara's cheek and Mabel disappears back into the room.

Minji lowers down a ladder. Apparently, she's agile — I learned something new about her from Jarret. Leal follows to join on the submarine floor.

Rhen, Mica, and Vana appear from the room where Ferris is staying. Eddi comes from the doorway where Garridon lies. Desman moves to stand next to Eddi, now facing Gia with his arms crossed. I avoid making eye contact with him. He still seems mad.

"Lyra," says Gia, "can you start and tell us what your calculations said about the Trovant?"

Jarret leans down to get my tablet from the bag on the ground.

"Sure," I say, "we went through some of the caverns that Desman had explored when he was trying to find you guys in the in-between. He remembered that there was one place with a pool."

I think back to when Jarret, Desman and I were exploring a maze of rocky tunnels. Desman was in a bad mood the whole time as he showed Jarret and me the tunnels where he had been searching to rescue Gia and the others from the cave-in.

Jarret holds up my tablet so I can type in the security code. Squeezing my crutch with my arm, I type in the code. Then I open the file with the information. Jarret turns the tablet toward the group and Gia leans to read the screen.

"We mapped these caverns," I explain, "and I made approximate measurements of each section. Based on my measurements, we ended up on the other side of the wall from the place you were trapped after the blast. It's likely that the pool Desman found would be connected to that same pool."

Vana says something to Rhen in Trovantian. Rhen responds and sounds upset. Gia looks at them.

Rhen pauses, then switches to English. "Vana was just saying we could have made it out if we swam down other tunnels. But many people have drowned in the underwater tunnels. It's dangerous to explore underwater, especially without ropes to find your way back."

"What matters now," says Gia, "is that there might be a pool that connects the Trovant and the in-between. That will be the target if the overseers are going to block passages between the facilities. Eddi, tell us what your group found."

"Nothing, at first," says Eddi. "Vega and I wandered to the other known pools to see the likelihood they might connect the Trovant and the in-between. It was hard to say, until I remembered the sunken camera." He takes his tablet and taps on the screen. "We reviewed the footage from the camera's journey before it died." Eddi shows the screen toward the group. He points to footage of underwater passageways. "This isn't conclusive, but there didn't seem to be tunnels connecting in the direction of the Trovant." He pulls the tablet back toward himself and clicks off the screen. "However, there was an update to the metadata. It says Garridon's tablet had opened the file and watched the footage two hours before we did."

"So that means Rasul likely watched the video," says Gia.

"That would seem to be the case," says Eddi.

"If he has the same information from the sunken camera," says Gia, "he knows the passageways don't connect the in-between to the Trovant, so he won't need to block them. The other pools are less likely to be a target." She turns her head to look at my dad. "Arcturo and Minji, what did you find?"

Minji starts to take out her tablet.

"We scouted out the area around the ravine," says my dad. "I know the space well because I had been digging the ravine for my work, but I didn't see anything new. That's as far as I went with the mission, but Minji made some calculations about where to reasonably divert lava flow."

Gia looks at Minji. Her persona is as commanding as Garridon's.

"It's not ideal," says Minji as she looks at her tablet, "after my calculations, there's only one place that lava could go without killing people. It's the weakest part of the Trovant, where the roots are. That section is closest to the outside water and it seems unlikely the methane is flowing through the walls there. The pressure would expand outward, but the temperature there would quickly cool the lava."

"That's uphill from the Source," says Gia. "How would we divert the lava uphill?"

"It's like I said," Minji puts down the tablet, "it's not ideal. Maybe even impossible."

My mom looks away from the tablet and then at Minji. "Would diverting the lava there ensure the Trovant doesn't collapse?"

"Not necessarily," says Minji. "It just seems like the best chance."

"Leal," says Gia. "Based on the activity coming from the Source, how long until the Source starts to erupt naturally?"

"I'm not sure," says Leal. "All the information I could find about calculating eruptions was about volcanoes. I don't know if the same applies when we're in a hydrothermal vent field and one of the vents is inside a facility."

"Can you guess?" Gia asks.

"I don't know," Leal's shoulders inch toward his ears. "Maybe months, maybe weeks, or it could be at any point since we're seeing magma this close to the surface." Leal doesn't hold a tablet. Instead, his hand gestures move frantically. "That doesn't mean it will pour out uncontrollably. It might erupt slowly and the lava would slowly cool over the ravine. The only thing that would certainly be catastrophic is if the overseers blow up the side of the ravine and let the lava flow all at once from the Source."

"Rhen," says Gia, "you had said there were no explosives in the war, but the overseers asked Leal if he was working with the chemist. We keep hearing the name — who is the chemist?"

"We have not met," says Rhen. She shakes her head. She looks at the other trovantians, then back to Gia. "Not many personally know the chemist. He makes weapons, poisons, medicines— anything that can come from chemicals."

"We need to find out if the overseers have any way to get explosives from the chemist," says Gia. "If they do, we need to stop them. Mica," her sharp gaze moves to Mica, "what do you know? How have you obtained supplies from the chemist?"

"I have not," says Mica. She wrings her hands. "I asked my cousin and his cousin is one who gathers supplies for the chemist."

"What we do next," says Gia, "depends on whether or not the Trovant overseers have the capability to block the last connecting tunnel to the in-between or blow up the side of the Source that would release magma into the ravine. And there's one more obvious place that we haven't talked about."

"Where's that?" Jarret asks.

"Here," says Gia. "The red-lit tunnel that connects the Trovant to the Alaster ship continues toward the other facility. The tunnel is close enough to the ravine that they could divert lava through this tunnel since Lyra blocked the other way to the in-between."

My dad rubs his chin, "Creating that diversion would take months more of digging."

"Or one explosion," says Eddi.

"So it goes back to their access to explosives," says Gia. "We'll need a team to gather information from Mica's cousin and we'll need pairs stationed at every target location. Whoever is stationed at a target needs to be ready for a physical altercation. It will be dangerous; there could be explosives." She looks around at each member of the group.

"What can I do?" Pictor asks.

"Nothing," says my mom. "Both of you kids will stay here."

"I hate to say this," Gia says to my parents, "but I don't know how likely we are to get the information from the in-between without Lyra." She looks at me. "But only if you're willing."

"I want to do something," Pictor says.

"You can stay here," my dad says. "I don't want you near explosions or at the in-between."

"Aw," Pictor kicks the ground.

"Me and you could have the most important job of all," says Leal. "We need to keep Tak safe." He looks at

Gia. "Unless you need me. I heard 'physical altercation.' I can't imagine I'd be useful."

"That's fine," says Gia. "But I need you to be attentive to the tablet to interpret any information coming from the targets and the in-between. If and when we have information about explosives, I'll need you to calculate the likely outcomes based on the quantities so we know how to respond."

"I can help," says Minji. "I already have codes with the data from the Trovant infrastructure. I'll start now to set up ways to predict scenarios based on this data."

"We'll need tight communication," says Gia, "and for all teams to stick to their posts, no matter what. Does anyone want to stay back?"

No one responds.

"Here," Rhen holds a dead fish by its gills. I asked her to get a fish for me before we go into our collapsed cavern.

"Thanks," I say, but I cling to my crutches.

Desman stands next to Rhen with his arms crossed.

"I will stay out here," says Rhen.

"I can hold it," says Jarret. "I don't want you to go in there alone." He looks at me as he grabs the fish.

"No way I'm going in there," Mica stands by Rhen.

Desman takes a step forward.

"Maybe," I say, "we should start with as few people as possible." That's not entirely true. It wouldn't matter if Mica or Rhen came in. But Desman seems angry and maybe that would make the heebos aggressive.

I turn to face the entrance to the space where the albharee skeleton lies crushed beneath boulders.

"Here we go," says Jarret as he walks forward with the fish.

"I'll go in front of you," I say. "They trust me." I maneuver my crutches over staggering rocks with Jarret close behind. In my peripheral vision, I see his free arm out to the side, ready to catch me if my crutches slip on uneven rocks.

"Silver?" I speak through the boulders before I can see fully into the large space.

"You named it?" Jarret asks.

"Yeah," I say. "Silver!" I shout to the room as I turn around a boulder and see heebos scattered throughout their new den.

Some pups play in front of the dead albharee while full grown heebos sleep on ledges, lick pups, or gnaw on albharee bone. The adults perk their ears when I am visible in the room. One stands— looming tall even among the heebos— and steps toward me.

"Silver," I say, "It's me."

The giant paws stop in front of me. Then, Silver touches his snout to my head.

"Hi, buddy," I reach up and rub his face, then scratch behind his ears.

He licks my cheek.

"What the?" Jarret says.

Silver lowers and gives a growl.

"It's okay," I hold Silver's head. "Give him the fish," I say to Jarret.

Jarret trembles as he holds out the fish and lowers it to the ground.

Silver stares at Jarret, then leans down and gobbles the fish.

"Will you hold my crutches?" I ask.

"Sure," Jarret stares at the giant creature that consumes the fish offering.


Sitting on Silver's back, I rub his ears as we wait. The room has yellow cracks of light climbing the walls. I wonder if Silver can feel how uneasy I am that we are in a room flooded with yellow. I rub his ears 21 times and then start over. A man in tattered cloaks trembles in the corner and tries not to look at my heebo. There's a musty, sour smell in the air. Everywhere in the In-between has a very potent smell.

"Sorry to keep you waiting, Arachna," the man with a blue cloak comes into the room with a group following behind.

"You're the chemist?" Jarret asks.

"Me?" asks the man. "Of course not."

Other people in the group chuckle.

"The chemist lives above," says the man, "and is terrifying like a venomous snake. You must tread lightly. But not with me. I am friendly." He puts his arms out like he is welcoming us to the in-between. His blue cloak drapes from his arms. "And my friends are nothing but kind."

Men and women with crooked and missing teeth smile and nod their heads.

"How lovely to have a family connection," the blue-cloaked man motions to Mica, who stands in the corner with Rhen and Desman. "And we would love to facilitate business between you and the chemist. To start this relationship, we offer your request for this recent inventory receipt from the Trovant." He gingerly steps closer to Silver but hesitates as Silver growls.

"It's okay," I stroke Silver's head.

The man reaches up to hand me a piece of dried clay that has lists etched in Trovantian and English.

I accept the dried clay and read the English. It's a list of supplies followed by instructions about how to set up explosives and detonate them.

"Can you log this for Leal and Minji?" I reach the clay tablet down to Jarret and he pulls the normal tablet from the bag.

"If I can be so open to ask," says the man. "Where did you get such a device?" He points at the tablet. "Such fine metalwork. We have never manufactured something so delicate."

I don't know how to explain where we got the tablet or how it was made. "You may not ask," I say.

"Ah," says the man, "such discretion. This is why we look forward to working with you."

The tablet beeps. It's an alert.

People in the room lean toward the tablet.

"What is it?" I ask.

"A message from Eddi and Mabel," says Jarret. "There's been an explosion."

# Chapter 24: Gia— The Explosion

"Are you sure about this?" Leal asks as we stand at the bottom of the Alaster submersible. "Everyone else is in a team."

"This was the best option," I say. "We need as many people as possible around Lyra."

"What if there actually is an explosion?" he asks. "The target you picked would be the biggest."

"I know," I say.

Leal steps towards me and gives me a hug.

It feels awkward.

"Hug me back," says Leal.

I move my forearms to hug him. I give him a pat on the back.

He releases his hug. "When are you leaving?"

"As soon as I say goodbye to my dad," I look at the open door to the place where my dad lies, still unresponsive.

"I'll take care of him until you're back," says Leal. "And Vana is staying behind to watch over Ferris. Between me, her, Minji, and Pictor, we should be able to keep an eye on everyone as well as analyze data that comes in." He looks over as Takara pulls Ari's tail. "Don't do that!" Ari snaps at Takara, who falls over and starts to whine. Leal runs toward his sister to comfort her.

I turn and face my dad's door. There's a sense of heaviness as I walk forward. If he doesn't make it, we won't see each other again. If I don't make it, we won't see each other again.

When I get into the small room, my dad lies still on the metal bed. His breathing seems more normal now—that's a good sign. I bend down and kneel at the bedside.

"I'm going," I say with my head toward the floor. "But I'll be back as soon as the mission is finished."

"Gia," my dad's eyes are closed, but he says my name.

"Dad?" I look up. Is he waking up? Is he going to be okay?

His eyes open.

"You're awake," I say as tears come to my eyes. I can't believe he's awake.

"Don't," he struggles to speak, "go."

"I'll be back soon," a tear rolls down my cheek.

He shakes his head.

I nod. "I have to. But it will be over as soon as—"

"No," he shakes his head. "You don't... have to."

"I'll come back," I rub his hand as a tear drips off the tip of my nose. I wipe the tears on my microbial suit as I stand to leave.

I cling to a tree and look out to the ravine on one side and the red-lit tunnel on the other. My heart pounds as I squeeze the branches. My dad taught me how to climb; I used to practice on the equipment in the Trellis. But I never practiced climbing this high. I don't even think there was something this high up in the Trellis. I got used to the rock wall, but these tree branches feel so unstable.

In the clearing near the red-lit tunnel, Rasul Midian appears. Others appear after him; one holds a heavy bag. That could contain explosive devices.

I take the tablet from my bag while still gripping the tree with my other hand. There's a message from the Fitzgeralds: "Imeel is setting up explosives. Engage?"

I lean against the tree to try and feel stable while freeing up my other hand. I type back: "Engage."

Eddi and Mabel are stationed at the pool that the overseers would likely try to block. Once that is blocked, they would need to expand this ravine to let lava flow through the red-lit tunnel. Then, they could destroy the side of the Source, where Vega and Arcturo are stationed.

Rasul and his group get closer to the ravine. I have to stop them.

I descend the tree. When I get to the bottom, I can't see Rasul through the dense vegetation, but I know what direction he is headed. Pushing through plants, I move toward the edge of the jungle. I can just barely see Rasul and his group through the leaves as I stop.

A person pulls a device out of a bag. It's not what I expected— it has different glass containers that are filled with colored liquids. The containers are fused together with some sort of dried clay or dark metal. There's a string at the top— presumably, pulling that would let the liquids flow together and cause the explosion.

An alert sounds on the tablet.

Rasul and the others look into the jungle and spot me.

I pull the incapacitator gun and fire five quick shots — Rasul Midian and four others tense and drop to the ground. The only man standing is the one who holds the device— I don't know how fragile it is. I sprint from the jungle, elbowing the man in the side and grabbing the device. I turn and shoot the man with the incapacitator gun and speed away, holding the device and gripping the long string so it doesn't get caught on anything.

Looking behind, I don't see anyone following. I quickly set the device down and pick out a blade from my bag. Listening for signs of being followed, I cut the string. I can't risk it getting caught on something. My hand trembles slightly as I put the blade back in my bag and look at the alert on the tablet— there's been an explosion near Mabel and Eddi. No news from Arcturo and Vega. I need to get rid of this device as soon as I can and get to Mabel and Eddi.

I pick up the explosive and rise from the ground. We had already planned to bring any explosive devices to the collapsed cavern where the heebos and albharee skeleton are. That way, we can detonate the devices without the risk of hurting people or letting the overseers fulfill their plans.

I speed into the red-lit tunnel and try not to trip or drop the device. There are footsteps. Rasul and the others are behind me.

# Trovant

Going faster, I feel a sudden pinch in my shoulder. I keep running, then start to feel dizzy.

A figure appears in the tunnel.

"Dad?" I say as the room sways.

My dad is hunched over and limps toward me beneath the red lighting.

"It's an explosive." I lift the device toward him, trying not to fall. My body gets weak. I'm not sure I can make it. "We have to get this to the heebo den."

"I'll take it," says my dad.

He takes the device as I stumble into his shoulder. Then he pulls something from my back. It's a small object with a needle sticking out. They had shot something at me.

"Stay here," my dad helps me to the ground as my body gets too heavy to stand. He runs toward Rasul and the others.

"That's the wrong way!" I call after him, but he keeps running. I want to tell him to turn around, but words won't come out. My vision gets blurry and the glowing rocks swirl. I hear something loud and fire bellows. There's heat, but no noise. Then everything stops moving and fades away.


My eyes are closed, but I lie on something squishy. The texture reminds me of the microbial beds in the Trellis. Am I back home? As I open my eyes, the lighting is bright.

It can't be the Trellis. Desman stands in the room and speaks to someone I've never seen before.

"Gia," says Desman, "I'm so glad you're okay." He comes over and sits next to me on the platform. "I was so worried." He places his hand on my cheek.

Leal steps into the room with Ari prancing behind him. Ari leaps on the bed and rubs her face on me.

"Hey," Leal says quietly as he inches toward me. "How are you feeling?"

There is no urgent energy from Leal or Desman. There are no tunnels or explosives. Everything around feels quiet and still.

"What's going on?" I ask. "Where's my dad?"

"He blocked the red-lit tunnel," says Desman. "We managed to establish comms with the other side. Everyone is okay, including your dad. You need to rest now."

"Other side of what?" I ask. I look around the bright room. There are no rocks or crystal cracks. "Where are we?" Questions crash through my mind like waves bursting through a facility.

"We're safe now." Desman rubs my cheek with his thumb. "We're in the plant."

# Epilogue: Red Flames

Garridon's body was heavy as his friends leaned down to him. Arturo grabbed Garridon's right arm and Eddi grabbed his left. Flames raged over the jungle and singed the rock as the friends lifted Garridon from the ground and helped him limp. The Trovant overseers lay still, near the collapsed cave that Garridon had exploded.

"Where do we go?" Eddi yelled over roaring flames and squawking animals.

"There's a place just up here," Vega stepped into Garridon's view and motioned with her tablet. The light from flames reflected off her clothes.

The friends helped Garridon to a crevice in the giant rocky space. Squeezing through the crevice, there was a small room where Mabel knelt with cloths and a bowl of water. As the friends set Garridon on the ground, Mabel inspected everyone's injuries. She lifted a wet cloth to Eddi's eyebrow, where he had a bleeding wound.

"We need to get a hold of Gia." Garridon tried to sit up moments after his friends helped him down.

"We will." Arturo put his hand on Garridon's chest to try and keep him still. "Vega is starting now. You need to lie down. We don't know how bad your injuries are."

"But stay awake," Eddi said. "You were out cold. You probably have a bad concussion."

"What supplies do we have?" Garridon asked, looking at the bowl of water and cloths. "Does anyone have an incapacitator?"

"Garridon," Mabel said his name firmly with her eyebrows raised.

Garridon lay back down.

***

Sweat dripped down Garridon's neck as he walked through the jungle. He gripped a large knife, keeping his senses alert. He heard chirps and animal calls, but nothing dangerous. Arriving at the bottom of a large tree, he tugged twice on a vine that hung from a branch. Then, something cascaded down and hit the bottom of a tree— it was a ladder crafted from sticks and rope. Scaling the ladder, Garridon was careful to climb with his knife in one hand. When he reached the top, he pulled himself into a makeshift hut that his friends and he had built in the tree.

The Trovant overseers had survived the blast and found the original hiding spot in the rocky crevice. There could have been other places in the tunnels to hide, but Garridon had suggested stationing in the jungle. The Trovantians were less likely to wander in that area because of all the animals. He picked a place that was off the normal paths through the jungle.

"Comms are established," Garridon said as he sat on the floor of the small room.

"The kids?" Mabel looked up from a pot where she was stirring food.

"They answered," said Garridon.

"Are Lyra and Pictor okay?" Vega asked as she put down the tools she was making.

Garridon nodded. "So is Leal." He looked at Mabel and Eddi. "He's the one who answered the message. He also said Takara is doing fine."

"Maybe we should go tell Arcturo," Eddi said.

"He'll be back soon from getting sustenance," Garridon said. "We can wait until he's back."

"Is Gia okay?" Mabel asked.

"She's alive," said Garridon. "But she hasn't woken up yet."

"We should make a plan," Eddi said.

"We should wait for Arcturo," Garridon responded.

The lights had dimmed, but the animals still chirped outside the hut. Arcturo snored as Garridon stared at the ceiling, thinking they should try and make separate huts.

"So you talked to Britannica?" Eddi whispered and rolled toward Garridon.

"What?" Garridon asked.

"When you were in the Alaster ship," Eddi said. "I came to check on you one day and you mumbled something about seeing Britannica."

"It was nothing," Garridon said. "Just a dream."

"What did you dream?" Eddi asked.

Garridon sighed. "She spoke to me. It sounded like she came through the speakers on the ship."

"What did she say?"

"That she's okay," Garridon said.

"Anything else?"

"Doesn't matter," Garridon said. "It was just a dream." He thought back to hearing his wife's voice speak to him. She said she was okay and to go with the Alaster ship. It was the ship's fault she was gone. But he didn't even believe Alaster was something alive. So he didn't know why he was blaming an inanimate object.

He squeezed his eyes and then blinked rapidly. If the surface wasn't habitable, there was nowhere else to go. The facilities weren't going to last. How could he make sure Gia survived? It felt like there was no better option than the submersible.

www.ingramcontent.com/pod-product-compliance
Lightning Source LLC
Chambersburg PA
CBHW030543020726
47494CB00005B/1473